The Light Within

THE SOUL BOUND REALMS
BOOK ONE

CARLIANN JEAN

Copyright © 2024 by Carliann Jean

All rights reserved.

No part of this publication may be reproduced, distributed, or transmitted in any form or by any means, including information storage, retrieval systems, photocopying, recording, or other electronic or mechanical methods, without the prior written permission from the author, except for the use of brief quotations in a book review. For permission requests, contact Carliann Pentz.

This is a work of fiction. The story, including all names, characters, organizations, and incidents portrayed in this production are either products of the author's imagination or are used fictitiously. No identification with actual persons (living or deceased), places, buildings, and products is intended or should be inferred. Any similarities between characters, settings, and situations in this book and real people, places, or events is purely coincidental.

Cover Design by Melania Guarnieri from Miss Pink Coconut

Chapter Illustrations by Melania Guarnieri from Miss Pink Coconut

Maps by Selkkie Designs

Editing by Maddi Leatherman from EJL Editing

Final Proofreading by Daniel Esturain & Shelby Baker

First Edition: August 2024

Independently published.

Amazon Paperback ISBN: 9798329362985

Table of Contents

Playlist — xi
Mental Health Warning — xiii
Themes to Consider — xv
Prologue — xix

1. Eira — 1
2. Eira — 10
3. Del — 18
4. Eira — 23
5. Eira — 27
6. Eira — 33
7. Tryg — 42
8. Tryg — 50
9. Eira — 58
10. Nyx — 63
11. Eira — 70
12. Nyx — 78
13. Tryg — 87
14. Nyx — 92
15. Eira — 100
16. Eira — 105
17. Eira — 113
18. Nyx & Eira — 122
19. Tryg — 128
20. Eira — 134
21. Nyx — 143
22. Eira — 152
23. Tryg — 159
24. Nyx — 164
25. Eira — 173
26. Nyx — 189

27.	Eira	200
28.	Tryg	209
29.	Eira	216
30.	Nyx	227
31.	Tryg	232
32.	Nyx	241
33.	Eira	251
34.	Nyx & Eira	260
35.	Eira & Tryg	268
36.	Nyx	278
37.	Eira	291
38.	Tryg	300
39.	Eira	309
40.	Eira	319
41.	Nyx	334
42.	Eira	346
43.	Nyx	357
44.	Tryg	372
45.	Eira	376
46.	Tryg	384
47.	Nyx	388
48.	Eira	399
49.	Eira	410
50.	Tryg	419
51.	Eira	423
52.	Nyx	434
53.	Eira	444
54.	Nyx	453
55.	Eira	463
56.	Nyx	471
	Note from the Author	477
	Acknowledgments	479
	Special Kickstarter Acknowledgments	483

PART ONE
A GUIDE TO THE REGIONS ON FUTURE
EARTH & MAJIKAERO

Regions on Future Earth	489
New Africa Territories	491
New Antarctica Territories	495
New Asia Territories	497
New Europe Territories	499
New North America Territories	503
New Oceania Territories	507
New South America Territories	511
Regions on Majikaero	513

PART TWO
GODS & GODDESSES

| Gods and Goddesses Worshipped | 517 |

PART THREE
CHARACTER NAMES & PRONUNCIATIONS

| Main Character Names & Pronunciation Guide | 521 |
| Main Character Names & Pronunciation Guide | 523 |

PART FOUR
COMMON MAJIKAERO TERMS

| Common Majikaero Terms & Pronunciation Guide | 527 |

| *About the Author* | 529 |
| *Let's Connect!* | 531 |

Dedication

For those who feel trapped by their trauma and the monsters within. For those who've experienced significant pain. For those who question whether their soul can heal. This is for you. You do have the light within.

*And for my husband, Daniel.
Who never doubted me for a second.*

Special Dedication

For the best pup that we had to say goodbye to.
You lived such a short life, sweet Pierogi.
Yet you've made the rest of our years infinitely better.
Touching us with your magic.
Helping me see the light within myself as you sat with me on this writing journey.

Playlist for *The Light Within*

Listen to the complete playlist on Spotify.

Mental Health Warning

Special Note: It's important to me on a deeply personal level to share the darker mental health themes and trauma that my characters endure and grow through. Some of you will read these trigger warnings and be absolutely okay continuing through the story. Others might believe they'll be okay, yet a scene will trigger an emotion or memory within them.

As a therapist, I can't emphasize this enough: If you become triggered or upset, please seek the appropriate support. Whether it's a typical self-care plan or talking with a therapist or needing crisis support, please take care of your mental health.

For those needing suicide and crisis support in the United States: You can call 988 or go to www.988lifeline.org/chat. There are also local and international hotlines, depending on where you live.

Themes to Consider

Dark Themes
Mental Health Disorders
Impact of Trauma
Explicit Language
Suggestive Language
Violence
Gore
Manipulation
Suicide
Sexual Assault
Rape
Murder
Emotional and Physical Abuse
Torture
Mention of Kidnapping
Mention of War
Scenes of a Sexual Nature
Other Heavy Themes

Discretion is advised.

FUTURE EARTH
TORINARRY
KYAZSSIA
KYAZSSIA
TORINARRY
TORINARRY
KOPANIA
SWEAZN
GRICLIN
EDINALES
KYAZSSIA
TORINARRY
SWEAZN
HUNGATIA
BELAITY
KOSNIA
IDADA
CALANA
DAKOURIN
ZONICOMA
SAHLIOCCO
IRTUKISTAN
NIYA
TUNYPT
IEMANIA
ARABIA
GUAOAERA
GUIZEURAS
GUINEGALIA
TONHIANA
SUMALPIA
CONEA
NIGOON
NEW TASZEALIA
ZILBIA
PERADOR
N
W
E
S
BOCHENTUAY
ANTARCTICA

MAJIKAERO
DRAGEYRA
VIORFELLE
WYNDERA
REYKASHIN
REYKASHIN
LAGUNIT
SKUGVAYTIR
MYRELLDEN
SUNNADYN
RIOA
EIKENBIEN
SAYFTERS
SHYMEIRA
N
W
E
S
DRAGEYRA
VIORFELLE
WYNDERA
RIOA
SUNNADYN
EIKENBIEN
REYKASHIN
SKUGVAYTIR
LAND OF SHADOWS
MYRELLDEN
LAND OF DARKNESS
SAYFTERS
SHYMEIRA
LAND OF TROPICS
LAGUNIT

Prologue

It's a whisper of a chilled touch, puckering edges of skin before slinking down through the system, straight to the gut.

A sliver of pain barely scratching the surface. The caress of a lover squeezing hard enough to bruise, teeth grazing along plump lips, yet only skimming them without puncturing the flesh wholly.

A building of pressure unable to be seen—wholly felt— pushing against a film of skin until one ceases to exist.

As if they never existed at all.

They were scraps of flesh stitched together tightly enough to keep the organs and bones and muscles and tendons and fresh ruby blood from spilling onto the earth, bound together to keep the soil clean of a tortured soul.

It always finds you, tricking you into believing you've outsmarted it. Yet it comes back for you. Again and again and again and again.

You long for death, for a rebirth, for the chance to start again, the opportunity to be scattered into stardust, so fine and minuscule you'll be set free into the wind.

But it won't give you that.

You've struggled with unlearned lessons, unable to see through the fog of shadows blinding your withered eyes, unable to see through the dark.

Because it took your light. It took your desire to fight back. It took your ability to live.

And you're cascading down and down, falling where no one can reach you, with no knowledge of who or what you are.

You don't even know that your light is no longer yours.

Or that you even had it to begin with.

ONE
Eira

The soul is a window within a window
of endless possibilities.
-Dr. Morgan Lydahnia,
Advanced Human Exploration Course 530

My body is liquid fire, marred and bruised beyond repair. I reach out to anchor myself somehow, desperate for anything to hold on to. Before I can find anything, unbearable pain crashes into my shoulder once again, splintering my bones like wood. The realization that I'm trapped, and no one will come, settles in, and I squeeze my eyes shut, willing my captor to end it already. He's close—close enough that I smell his rancid breath fanning across my face. Pain in my shoulder ripples out through my arm and collarbone, and I'm—

Breathe in. Breathe out. Breathe in. Breathe out.

The shadows from my thoughts are slowly shaken out as I sense the sunlight dancing across my face. I focus on my breathing and how the light crackles under my skin, spreading warmth where moments ago, there were icy shivers.

Breathe in. Breathe out.

I focus as much attention as I can muster on the pace and feeling of my breath. It finally slows down, but only after cramping the space between my lungs and throwing me into a full-blown panic attack. My dreams have felt more and more real. A shudder skirts through me as I remember how I woke up with a tightness around my throat, aching from a residual, sharp pain. I hesitantly touch my neck and shoulders, convinced there will be markings littering my skin. A reminder of how I died in my nightmare, the man with darkened, glassy eyes staring into my soul as he pushed the nails into my bruising flesh.

It felt similar to a memory. He was inexplicably familiar, a voice whispers inside of me.

"Enough!" I cry out, untangling myself from the cotton bed sheets, noticing the dampness from my sweaty body.

Gross. I already experienced a panic attack and a heaping amount of self-pity; I don't need to bathe in my own sweat, too. I glance at my watch and heave a bigger sigh than I realize, considering Zaya, my headstrong and adorable cat, flies off the window and glares up at me in annoyance. *My apologies, my little heathen warrior.* I can't bring myself to chase after her to apologize when I have to scurry around, or I'll be late for work. Again. *Again!*

"Wake the fuck up, you beautiful mess," I sing out as I turn on the shower and pick through acceptable clothing articles scattered around my bathroom floor.

A year ago, I was horrifically organized, fitting the type A personality to a T. A year ago, I wouldn't have overslept this frequently and plucked wrinkled articles of clothing off my floor. I'm not sure what happened. *A year ago, the nightmares had started to plague my entire being.*

My heart wants to blame my disorganization on the onset of the nightmares, but I prefer to blame my borderline deranged roommates. *I'll wake you up in time for breakfast,* I mock as I recall our conversation from last night. Having watched as they gulped down their last glasses of wine—heathens, truly—I should have known they would be too hungover this morning to wipe their own asses, let alone make me breakfast or wake me up on time.

As the warm water cascades down my body, it chases away the last of the chilling remnants of the nightmare. I allow myself a whole minute to focus on the water, imagining it encasing me in a protective shell. The pain from last night is still too fresh in my mind. I opt for eucalyptus and lavender soap to help relax my body and heal any pain along my skin. *But why is there so much pain? Why does it feel real?* I don't allow myself to focus too much on these questions, instead fixating on the heat of the water and the smoothness left behind from the soap.

I still notice a heavy sense of fatigue, but it's nothing hot tea can't help, right? Realizing this isn't a spa, and I actually need to get to work, I regretfully turn off the shower. Still trying to bring myself comfort, I wrap the fluffy towel around my body. The sensation is enough to make me want to stay home, cuddled up on the couch.

Why are you daydreaming about cuddling up at home? Who are you going to cuddle up with? Your cat? A pillow? A guy you seduce in your wrinkled clothes on the way home from work? No, that would require you to give someone a chance.

Hastily pushing those thoughts from my mind, I scramble to get ready when I realize I spent ten minutes too long already. I'm finishing combing my hair when I hear what could only be described as a garbled, drowning animal. I hastily glance around my bedroom to ensure it isn't actually my beloved cat. The sounds of an alarmed yell and a body tripping on the stairs carry up to my space. I roll my eyes and take one more glance in the mirror. *What a beauty!* I bark out a laugh as my eyes scan along my reflection. When I return from work in the evenings, my skin is glowing and my laugh is so resounding that I feel its soft caress as it leaves my lips. After a nightmare, though? That's a whole other story.

My normally full, wavy hair is brittle—the white-blond strands comparable to broken straw. My eyes are sunken with a color unusually dull, can I really call them blue? My pale skin appears patchy and is stretched too thinly over my cheekbones, morphing me into a vampire overnight. Not the vampires people read in romance novels, oh no. I look starved and withered, not resembling my normal athletic self. The skin around my neck is particularly tender to the touch this morning, a reaction I haven't experienced after a nightmare before, and it's bruising. *Cool, so am I delusional now, too?*

As fast as I can, I pluck a pair of washed out black jeans, a passable undershirt, and a wrinkled rose sweater that swoops down my shoulder. The state of my clothes are unfortunate but not something I have time to fix right now. Muttering a number of colorful words, I manage to find my black leather boots and shove my feet in before hastily tying up the laces. I clip my favorite necklaces around my neck and run my hands over the many pierced backings on my ears. My teeth come down hard on my cut-up lips, gnawing on chapped skin, as I rummage around for my black leather jacket and wool scarf, hat, and gloves. Glancing back in the mirror, I typically brush off how I look each morning because, honestly, as long as I can still do my job, what do I care? I'm not getting ready for a beauty pageant. But even I can't be sure who I'm even peering at in the mirror this morning. *Is this truly me?*

I gingerly trace my throat again, my gut clenching as if in anticipation of another physical attack. *Or is that just my usual stomach pain? Gods, I hope no more cramps are coming.* I glance at my bathroom drawer, hesitant to apply makeup when I'm already running late. My boss probably keeps me around because I've helped heal most clients on the caseload and have a long waitlist asking for me. I bring in more than enough money to keep the business afloat, which is important during a time when war is on the horizon. Yet even she has her limits. No way can I keep showing up late. *You also can't show up like a ghoul from a horror film.* Sighing, I apply enough concealer under my eyes and cheeks to take away some of the gloom, I rush out of my room, hastily grabbing my bag and keys on my way downstairs.

My heart skitters in my chest as I see a person crawling up the stairs toward me. When Tryg glances up at me, I let out a quick breath and can barely contain the hysteric laugh that leaves me. Seeing a man come toward me in any way after that nightmare makes me feel uneasy. This sight especially almost gives me a panic attack—the man in my nightmare had the same exact eyes as Tryg. Those dark, rich brown eyes.

Yet when our eyes meet again now, and I see the unbridled despair as he struggles up the stairs, crushing a muffin in his fist, I can't help but laugh. *Okay, this might be worth being late to work.* His plaid shirt is inside out and the front buttons are off by a few. He clearly isn't awake yet, with his ruffled hair and partial drool still at the bottom of his jaw. Is he even wearing pants? And one sock? When my eyes sweep back to the muffin, I have to sit down from laughing so hard.

Straining to look up at me, Tryg gives me a lopsided grin, thrusting the crumbling muffin out toward me. "I scavenged you up some breakfast, lovely, just as promised!" He's terribly proud.

"Oh?" I ask. "Is that what was promised? I could have sworn you promised to wake me up on time *for* breakfast."

The emotions pass over his face in quick succession: pride, confusion, shame, exhaustion. "Do you still want this muffin? I found it myself," he states meekly, searching for my approval. I have to wonder what goes on inside that head of his, but on second thought, it's best if no one knows; perhaps it is best if only he is aware of that level of chaos and confusion.

"How sweet of you," I coo as I pluck the crumbs from his hand and promptly sprinkle them over his head. He goes to swat my hands away, scowling up at me as I lunge outside of his reach. "If you buy me lunch *and* dinner, I'll consider this a truce. I'm running late, you know, and not all of us can show up to work as we please, *my king*," I state as I give him a mocking bow.

Tryg rolls his eyes but manages to croak out, "I could be your king tonight if you'd have me."

"Ugh!" I yell as I continue down the stairs to the kitchen. He knows no bounds to infuriate me. If I hadn't known him for the last few decades, there is no way I would have agreed to live with him in the first place. Truth be told, he is closer to me than any of my brothers, and we've loved one another for years—platonically, of course. He has the grace of a pigeon and the maturity of a teenager, yet I'm sure he charms his way into others' beds more often than not.

"Okay, okay, calm down," he starts to say, until he sees me glowering at him. "Perhaps that was the wrong choice of words." He tries again. "But I'll swing by with lunch later today and pick up your favorite pasta this evening." He gives me a small smile, his eyes still straining against the sunlight filtering into the house.

"If that's the best you can do, then I suppose I have no other options." I sigh, but I secretly smile into my mug of tea, grateful for his friendship and, more importantly, the free food. I check my watch again. *Shit. Why does time move the way it does?* "I need to get to work. I'll see you around 1:00 p.m. for that lunch you promised!" I call out, turning to head out the door.

I feel a hand on my wrist, the grip hardening for a second. The tremors zip up my spine before I can stop them, and I freeze with my hand on the door handle.

Fear clutches my throat, but before I go into a full panic attack, Tryg turns me around to face him. Peering up into his eyes, I see his face change from good humor to wariness. "Eir, are you okay? You're painfully fatigued, and there was clear fear in your eyes a second ago," he says to me, his voice going softer.

I blink up at him, afraid to voice my concerns after last night. This last nightmare felt too real, and I'm not sure what to tell my friend. *I think someone meticulously put nails in my throat and shoulder and bled me out?* Yeah, that's the best thing to tell your housemate at 8:30 in the morning.

I breathe out a long exhale and plaster my best fake smile on my face. Tryg narrows his eyes for a second, his wavy, brown hair sweeping along his forehead as he tilts his head to the side. He knows I'm lying, but he also knows if he pushes me, I'll clam up even more. His hand comes down to graze my fingers, and he takes my wrist to his mouth, placing a faint kiss along my thin skin.

"You know you can tell me anything, I hope?" he whispers. "Or you can draw it out for me, like we used to do." He smiles down at me and lets go of my hand.

When either of us had trouble explaining our emotions when we were younger, we would draw pictures of our feelings. I haven't done that in years, and it sends a shudder along my whole body trying to imagine what I would draw for him now. He shouldn't have to see the same dream I had. *He shouldn't have to see his eyes reflected in the drawing.* I give him a chaste kiss on the cheek before nodding my head, smiling tightly as I walk out the door. I won't speak of the horrors from last night. I'm not sure I would be able to leave for work if I unwrapped all of that terror.

Breathing the crisp fall air in as deeply as humanly possible, I take a minute to soak in the nature around me. There are times when I wish we lived further south. Perhaps closer to more cities, no matter how small each of them is and how congested some might be, and a warmer climate. I've been a handful of times to the nearly tropical waters, remarkably different from the crisp lakes and rushing rivers surrounding the mountains in Northern Sweazn. But today, I'm grateful for the dense forests and rolling hills, for the winding roads that weave through the soaring mountains, taking me to our local markets and businesses.

Our city, Taolkin, is a mixture of buildings made out of slanted, wooden structures, stone, and metal—sleek and sturdy and charming. A fusion of colors and styles and folklore, similar to our people. And we're fortunate to have the wilderness all around us, forests full of creatures that can survive the piercing cold and have learned to adapt to even the harshest conditions.

Just like me.

I shake out my body, rolling my shoulders and neck. Regardless of this morning, I need to loosen up before work. It can be demanding, healing others, but I wouldn't trade it for anything. I feel it to the core that this is my life calling, and I'm honored to help those in pain find their peace. It's also not a possibility to cave into my emotions. My heart is deeply nestled inside a thick armor that extends outward, coating my skin. Shaken up from my nightmares or not, it doesn't matter. I'm as strong as a warrior when slammed with the force of my emotions and was taught at a young age that's what truly matters.

I stretch out before throwing my leg over my bike. It's one of the few antiques that's made a comeback, which I'm thankful for. Tryg and Ruse couldn't stop laughing the first time I brought up wanting a motorcycle, asking me if this was still the twenty-first century. Ruse is Tryg's co-investigator who was quickly adopted into our friend group and managed to squirm his way into being one of my housemates, and they're both equally infuriating. *Whatever, losers.*

Revving the engine, I go to take off when I notice a bird peering down at me. I thought it was a crow, but the more I stare at it, the more the feathers change enough to make me feel crazy. All of a sudden, I can't be sure of what colors I'm seeing. Or even the bird's shape. Or its size. I blink rapidly and look again, the bird still gazing down at me. Is that longing in its eyes? That wouldn't make sense. *It's a freaking bird, Eira. And even if it was looking at you, what would it long for?*

Annoyed at myself for taking more time than necessary to leave for work this morning, I start down the road, attempting to clear away thoughts of the bird and nightmare as I mentally prepare for a day of work. I glance back for one second, sensing the bird gazing after me, and almost as if by magic, it appears to shimmer out of existence. I rev the engine and find myself wondering if I imagined it all or if one day we'll meet one another again.

TWO

Eira

We have found there is no explicit end to trauma.
Only cycles that form like cyclones if not broken correctly.
-Dr. Antonio Piernt, Applied Therapeutic Ideologies
Course 472

"Again! Meeting just on time, same as always, huh?" Morgan says to me as I slip into my office.

Flinching, I reluctantly turn to face our lead therapist. Heat already stains my neck and face from the jog into the building, where I scanned my face at the side entrance, and narrowly snuck my way into the office unseen. Now sweat rolls down my back, soaking its way through my thin pullover. *The pits. It's always the pits that show my nervous sweating.*

"I'm a bit of a mess, aren't I?" I ask her, cringing at how out of breath I sound.

Morgan simply chuckles, shaking her head as she waltzes into my room. She's impeccable, as usual. Golden-blond hair is swept back into one of those messy knots on her head, but of course, it's cute and perfected. Mine would look as if a nest got stuck on my head from the ride over. Her lavender and blue woolen sweater brings out her near-violet eyes as her tight, dark skinny jeans frame her legs as a second skin. Click, clack go her heeled boots as she approaches my cozy den of an office. Not even an impending war could stop her from dressing her best.

"I'm teasing you, darling. You're my hardest worker, and you take on the trauma these folks bring in like the goddess you are," she says as she brushes a few loose strands from my face. *Ugh, even her nails are on point today.* Ice-blue color splashes against snow white with swirling designs. "I'll admit, though, I'm getting worried about you. You're not usually this flustered and so..." she trails off, motioning with her hand to my body.

"Crazed? Short-tempered? In the depths of losing my mind?"

Morgan snorts a laugh. "I was going to say defensive and down on yourself, but sure, we can go with those, too."

I roll my eyes, but a smile pulls at my lips as I turn to empty my bag. Morgan is our lead therapist at Heart and Mind Care, where we specialize in all levels of trauma. She might technically be my boss, but she has always been more of a mother figure to me. It's been, what? Fifteen years of knowing her through fundraisers, classes, and now work? The moment she spotted me checking out pamphlets about therapy programs, she plucked me from the crowd to talk about becoming a trauma therapist. It's one of the careers that will never die out. I gravitated toward her kind eyes and warmth that always envelopes me when she is near. I've always given her attitude about "mothering" me, but we both know I'm full of shit. I crave her love and support more than anything, especially after my family seemingly vanished.

I'm taking my last book out when Jace opens my door and steps inside with a cup of coffee. Oh, Jace. At our first training course, where my best friend Athena and I first met him, Jace promptly squeezed himself in between us and announced that we'd become best friends. I had rolled my eyes at his confidence and was even quicker than I am nowadays to put up a brick wall.

It wasn't worth my energy to get to know someone who'd toss my friendship aside at a moment's notice. Few friends have proven their good intentions over the years, even though Athena *insists* that there could be more if I'd only let them in without a fight.

Whatever. At least I let Jace in. All six-foot of him dripping in dark humor and sass. I'm grateful for his jokes, though. They kept me going as the three of us worked in different clinics in our early twenties, each facing vastly different populations with the common thread of trauma. I greatly underestimated the need for firm boundaries with my clients. A mixture of their pain and dealing with my own past caught up to me and nearly did me in. It's been a decade of leaping into new opportunities and trying not to fall off the cliff of my sanity—Jace being one of the people preventing me from falling.

Luckily, I've had Athena and Jace next to me each step of the way, and we all get to work in the same clinic now with Morgan. Even if it means enduring Jace being obnoxiously bright-eyed in the morning. Glancing at him now, I have to fight off a grimace. He's all smiles with way too much energy for such a cold morning. Gray eyes meet mine, and he winks before taking a bite out of his breakfast burrito. He's obsessed with those, and I swear he could eat them for every meal and never get tired of them.

"Thanks for the coffee, boss," he says with a mouthful of spiced rice, egg, and beans. His lip ring, the one Athena and I encouraged him to get for his birthday, is slathered in greasy sauce. Morgan laughs while shaking her head as he comes to join us. Rolling her eyes, she uses her thumb to wipe sour cream off his cheek. Jace scowls and bats away her hand before ripping another large chunk out of his meal.

She turns to face me again. "Here, before your first client of the day comes in. I brought everyone coffee today. The air is a little too chilly this morning, and we've all been drained," she says as she hands me the heated mug.

I let my eyes close while I breathe in the steam rising out of the top. My fingers are already warming up, tingles making their way from my fingertips to my wrists. There are moments when a cup of coffee is merely that—a cup with caffeinated liquid in it. Other times, like today, it feels akin to friendly encouragement, an extension of warmth from a loved one. A moment to simply be and breathe and taste the aroma; a second chance to wake up.

Roasted creaminess wafts up to me. Keeping my eyes closed, I ask, "Is there—"

"Yes, of course I put in a heaping amount of heated milk," Morgan chuckles.

"Only you prefer coffee with your milk around this clinic," Jace mutters.

My eyes flash open, ready to dish them both a healthy amount of sass. I might appreciate the coffee, but I'm still immersed in my experience from my last dream and rushing over here. One, perhaps Tryg, might say I'm rather irritable this morning. I prefer the term *feisty*.

A sharp knock interrupts whatever unruly comment was going to come out of my mouth.

Arching an eyebrow, Morgan says, "I think that's our cue. I didn't think you had a client scheduled right now, but with these waitlists stacking up? Who even knows anymore? We can chat more later, hun."

That makes two of us. My schedule is immensely cramped right now, I barely have enough time to breathe, let alone pee or eat. How is it possible to love what you do but desperately dread it?

"Message me if you need more coffee!" she tosses out with a wink before she opens my door.

"Or milk, in your case," Jace calls out with a grin and ducks in front of Morgan before I can throw something at him.

Before the door is even opened, a young woman loses her balance, stumbling into my office. It's as if she was clinging onto the door frame for support and strength. Wide brown eyes find mine as she shakily straightens up and blows out a quick breath. She licks her chapped lips, tucks her shoulder-length hair behind her ears, and tries to clear her throat. A sense of shame and embarrassment lingers around her as she fidgets, her weight shifting from foot to foot.

"I'm so sorry to barge in here, Ms. Karlson," she mumbles. "I know we had a session a few days ago. I haven't been able to sleep. I'm sick with worry. It's all coming down around me, you know? I can feel it all coming down. I don't know what to do. I didn't know where to go. This was the only place I knew was safe. But I'll leave if you need me to. I'm just—"

"Shh, it's okay, Mayra. You're doing fine," I quickly interject with a smile. "I just wasn't expecting you today. Thank you for trusting me and knowing this is a safe space for you. Even if I was with another client, we would have found a calming area for you to wait in."

Morgan quietly ushers Jace into the hallway while she gently closes the door with a muted click. Mayra's face immediately crumples now that we're alone. She doesn't make it to the cushioned chair, falling to the shaggy rug in a heap of a winter coat, ragged scarf, and scuffed tennis shoes. Her fire-red hair sweeps in front of her face, hiding her from everything but herself. Keeping her head tucked into her knees, she sobs uncontrollably, her dangling earrings swishing back and forth.

Crying is an action I encourage in my office. Always. It's an important release and communication from the body, and I never want my clients to fear this or experience shame, regardless of the reason. My heart aches to witness a person so sad, deeply shaken to the bone with emotion. I want nothing more than to ease Mayra's physical and emotional pain, and I'm extremely concerned that this is the third session this week. It's becoming a trend with a number of my clients. Violence and something darker, crueler, is seeping into our lives, and I sense there is nothing I can do to stop it.

Which I *hate*. If I can't fully use my gift of healing to help my clients manage their pain, then what am I even doing? Am I still enough?

Mayra was here a few days ago processing what has happened with her brother. She is convinced that he is no longer real and a demon has taken control of him.

We've talked about the ways war can change someone and the horrors he has been exposed to down in the south. Up here in Northern Sweazn, we've been oddly fortunate to be separated by the Narrow Sea. Often considered to be isolated from the southern and eastern parts of our country to the point of being criticized and almost becoming our own nation. It's now to our advantage. It's been more challenging and time-consuming for Hungatia to bring their conflict to the northern cities. Technology is making a swift comeback, but there are not enough resources to build enough artillery and vehicles for everyone.

But down in the south where Sweazn borders on Hungatia and backs into Belaity?

It's. A. Fucking. War. Zone. It's almost an entirely different world and separate country.

It's a requirement for most citizens to be trained in one of the main forms of combat. Not everyone traveled down to fight in physical combat and brave the smattering of bombs detonating across the borders, though. There are political strategists in each country that focus on psychological warfare and manipulation, which seems to be Hungatia's focus in the northern part of our home. And because of this, our senators and generals require those working in the fields of healing and health to be everywhere. They spread us as thin as they can get away with. Considering the government controls all its healthcare workers, we're like the last ounce of butter spread over a whole loaf of bread.

Sweazn has a national army, aviation corps, and navy, all built from the ground up after centuries of living underground. They're trained in a vast number of skills dating back to the tenth century up through the end of the twenty-first century, our generals searching for the most savage and effective tactics possible. Our people are trained in the ancient martial arts, close-combat weapons, ranged weapons, small arms, and from what I've heard, they're learning more about artillery and robotic technology.

I feel it's too much. All of it. Our leaders' fear of war has driven their countries to obsessively over-preparing. Just in the chance that it will happen on such a disastrous, nuclear level again. And now their nightmares are turning into a reality. While they hide behind their polished command centers, the rest of us fight in our own ways for survival and to cope.

Innocent civilians, such as Mayra, are impacted the most. There have been many discussions about what is within her control and ways to cope with this type of grief. We've also outlined ways to support her brother as he navigates through his PTSD. There are times when Mayra pushes herself to process these topics and can communicate with her brother. Sadly, there are many more hours, especially this past month, when she rushes to this clinic, terrified for him. Convinced the war didn't only traumatize him but that he's no longer there in his body. That she's talking to a ghost.

I take another sip of my aromatic coffee before placing it on my cedar desk. As much joy as I felt receiving it, this drink will be long forgotten by the afternoon. I slip my weathered leather jacket off and shuck off my boots, hat, and scarf. After I get my laptop plugged in, I turn on one of my soothing playlists and light a few candles, getting comfortable and into the right headspace before I start anything with Mayra.

Some of my abdominal muscles cramp slightly, never failing to make their painful appearance when I need them to chill the most. I grab a piece of chocolate and a few pain pills to hopefully soothe this oncoming pain enough. I used to jump and run to a client when I saw they were distressed, but I have a few tricks up my sleeve now. I want Mayra to ease into this space, and that certainly won't happen if I'm fumbling around like a fool. And I need a minute to breathe into my chronic muscle pain before I can truly focus on the woman in my office.

Music is playing, candles are lit, and I'm physically at ease after removing my thicker outerwear and taking my meds. The string lights and a few lamps are giving a soft glow. I breathe in slowly and exhale, allowing the anxiety I experienced earlier to leave my body for now. I know it'll have me in its tight grip later, but at least for now, while I'm with my clients, I'll find peace from it. I gather a basket with a few sensory items, lotion, and tissues with one hand and a fuzzy blanket with the other as I head toward where Mayra is sitting on the ground. She is still in the heat of her feelings. I place the basket to the side and slowly drape the blanket around her. Mayra burrows into it, still shaking with her tears.

"There is no pressure to do this, but if you'd like, you can hold my hand," I say to her. "I'll be right here with you. You are not alone. You are free to sit here for as long as you need this hour."

Sniffling slightly, Mayra inches her clenched fist toward me. I keep my hand open face-up, giving her the power to come to me when she is ready. Not every client wants physical touch, but after working for over a year with Mayra, we have established that this is extremely settling for her. Her shaky fist finds my palm and she uncurls it to lie flat against my own. Her hand trembles and is slick with moisture—as if she is shedding her tears this way now. I recline into the wall behind me and prepare to sit for a while.

We don't speak. There is no need to. I sit with her as she continues to release her cries, one breath at a time.

THREE
Del

*The Queen of Light shines too brightly on what should not be
seen. Good intentions don't always lead to preferred outcomes.
It'll be easiest if this solliqa remains hidden.*
-Correspondence from Zahara, High Manipulator

Time holds me in its clutches, and I don't dare to breathe. The seconds tick, tick, tick, going agonizingly slow, minute by minute. Heartbeat by heartbeat. This is torturous, but I'm already taking a big enough risk by being this close to her. Few of us can leave the barrier, and it's near impossible to keep out of their incessant radar even if we do. I managed to scrape through the near invisible wall by, what I believe, some divine intervention. We need confirmation that this woman exists and is alive. I'm honored that I was selected for such an important role, but damn, I'm losing feeling in my feet. Where is she? This mission is *everything*. I must get this confirmation if we are to have any hope.

In a flash, a woman rushes out the front door of a wood and brick two-story home, her white-blond hair swishing over her shoulder. She's younger than I expected, maybe early 30's, but beautiful and quick, with a subtle confidence in her gait. I focus on her face and nearly let out a squawk of disgust when I see how gaunt she appears, at least from this angle. I know that it's a miracle she's survived this long and remains hidden from the Sairn, but all the gods and goddesses, does she eat and sleep? What kind of survival skills does she possess? Being isolated in the forest is a smart move, yet she recklessly hops on that roaring bike. *Hm. Still. This is rather exciting.* I'm one of the first to land direct sight on her. And those *eyes*.

Shit, *those eyes*. She is looking right at me, straight into my heart. This should be impossible. There's no way she can see me in this realm. I notice my feathers changing colors so fast they're iridescent. *Fuck, fuck, fuck.* This happens rapidly when my emotions are out of control. I calm my breathing down and latch deeper into the rough branch below me, willing it to anchor me down into its stillness. I'm not sure what else is watching her, and it's certainly not a great thing if she can see me. This means that she could see other creatures. Something could steal her into an unknown world, ruining it all.

She squints in my direction for another minute before shaking her head. *Is she muttering to herself?* She certainly won't be alone. I talk to myself all day long, much to my cadre's chagrin. I'm no god, but perhaps we will get along as friends. With her helmet firmly in place, she starts up the motor and veers down the street at an accelerated pace. *Is she trying to get herself killed?* Maybe I'll convince her to kick that outrageously dangerous hobby of hers. *No, no, I can't get that far ahead yet.* She needs to safely travel to the other side before anything else can happen. She doesn't even know what she means to us. *Focus.*

Tick, tick, tick goes the sound of time. Again. Always obsessively counting those seconds. Its slender hand places unnecessary pressure on my chest—a sensation I'm all too familiar with. Time doesn't like when I'm outside the window of my current reality for too long. But I won't move, not when she could come back or other people could see me.

When I'm convinced she is gone and no one else is coming, I finally sigh in relief. I can't be sure how much she saw, but at least I'm alone and can relax. I fluff out my still multicolored feathers and stretch my talons against the jagged bark. Everything itches and my instinct is to collapse into a much-needed nap. But there'll be no delays; it's time to leave. *Now.*

I hardly have any *maji* left in me. I needed to get here as soon as possible in case she left earlier this morning. I muster what *maji* and physical strength I have left, launching myself into the chilled sky. Moisture lingers in the air and hugs against my wings like an icy coat, but I concentrate on pushing through. There's much to get done, and honestly, I'm terrified. I have knowledge no one else possesses, am presently in a world that is not my own, and my current form doesn't have the capability to adequately protect myself. It took me *months* to narrow down the point of entry, and with being here for too many hours, other aspects of time could change.

Change is beneficial—it's one of our top goals right now. But not all change would be for the better right here.

Swooping and gliding along the tops of the trees, I keep myself changing colors to camouflage against the leaves. I stay low enough to not draw any unwanted attention, so low that the leaves kiss my belly. There's a strong sense of life in this forest I'd normally want to explore. Yet, I worry. I *always* worry. As if I'm not aware enough about this problem of mine, Daru loves to remind me. *Whatever—someone has to worry, and it might as well be me.* Currently, I'm not exclusively concerned about the passing seconds but also what this particular life here in the forest includes. If something is here readying to lure me in, to take me down, this mission would be over. I refuse to let myself be seduced by the trickles of *maji* that exist in the realm of Earth. Not when my home desperately needs the information I bring.

The valleys quickly turn to larger mountains, standing boldly against the sky. They're a beacon of hope. More relief eddies through me as I clear the mass of trees. I'm still in danger of being seen, but that heavy presence of doom and fear has lifted. I glide along the rocky edges and soar down one of the cliffs. I'm an arrow breaching the air at the highest speed, and I will myself to fall into the veil of time and space I pinpointed earlier. Holding my breath, the tip of my beak dips into the barrier, the sensation chilled and refreshing, and before I know it, I'm swallowed up whole.

I'm here, I'm there, I'm everywhere at once. Until I'm greeted by the familiar tangled vines winding down my favorite species of tree.

Ropey vines and shaded colors surround me, almost clouding my vision as I readjust my senses. Radiant, yet deceptive, blues and purples and greens hide behind a layer of gray and white and engulf me. I blink repeatedly until I can see the outlines of other trees through the thick, glossy mist. The mist threatens to devour me whole. Other creatures cry out at the slight disturbance I made in the realm. They can't see me as I blend into the light gray air. Spotting a vermilion scaled back that briefly rises above the steaming water below, I consider this lucky. The sound of jaws snapping whips past my ears, and I tighten my wings even closer as I swerve in a loop out of the way.

I can't stop quite yet. I urge my wings to stay tight against me and bend to the power of the wind. I've never been as grateful for this family gift as I am now. If I keep my current speed and move with the flow of the current, I should remain undetected. Our kind doesn't usually travel through the barrier in such a round-about way, if at all, and I'm hoping this works in my favor today. One more minute of this tension. *Shit*, this is too much strain on one little body.

Finally, I land in Majikaero. What has been mere minutes has felt the same as hours, days, an eternity. My body craves to stretch, but I keep low behind the leathery shield of a blue leaf. The last of my *maji* goes to turning my feathers an azure blue with a few added light yellow streaks to match the leaves around me. The scent of dirt and moss smothers my racing heart and shaking body, calming my fraying nerves. I keep still. Any minute now, it'll happen. My cadre won't fail me, especially not at a moment such as this.

"Did you find her?" a hushed voice whispers to me. It's faint enough that it barely reaches my ears.

I breathe out the smallest chirp, enough to confirm that I did. I miraculously managed to find her. She is alive, even if rather ragged, and we now know how to locate her.

A louder bird call is made before his heavy presence vanishes from behind me. I detect the gust of Daru's wide wingspan as he launches through the trees, a mixture of gray and emerald flashing behind them. He looks *exactly* like the other birds perching in the nearby branches. Absolutely identical. *Show off.* What a talented, cocky bastard. It's amazing that even when under stress and pressure, he can find ways to frazzle my patience and make me want to wring his feathery neck. But he is already passing the answer to the rest of the cadre as his call gets quieter and quieter.

The code has been sent, delivery accomplished. I barely believe I survived this long. Even if they find me, the rest of the group knows that she lives and is *real*. It doesn't matter what the Sairn say. It doesn't matter that their loyalties are to entities from a different world entirely. That their gods needed Eira eliminated for their own nonsensical reasons.

It doesn't matter what they want. Because you can't hide a goddess from her own destiny. And they can't hide her from Majikaero.

FOUR
Eira

We're only as strong as our healed selves.
-Page 43, Guide to Intergenerational Trauma

I have to hide. Somewhere, anywhere, far away from home. I'm running through a field, the top of the willowy grass kissing my skin and tickling my nose. The way the wind moves them, they appear as feathers coasting through the air, rippling along the earth. Delicate scraps of silk cover my body. As the wind picks up, the cloth feels cool against my skin, which I'm grateful for; I'm running faster and faster and my body is growing warmer by the minute. The sound of my heartbeat in my eardrums drowns out everything except the rolling thunder in the distance. The faint sound of jewels jingle around my wrists, neck, and ankles, the colorful lights of them catching my eye for a moment.

I finally allow myself to slow down and throw myself to the ground, sinking my hands into the moist dirt. It pushes under my nails, and I sigh with relief at the sensation of connecting to the earth, my home. A mixture of rain and soil scents float around me *until they ease into my inner self. I take a deep breath, trying to calm my racing heart from galloping out of my chest.*

I move my hair until I find the hidden pin my aunt wove into my braids. It's a bird made of opals and amethysts, and I had felt immensely disconcerted when her hands trembled while placing it into my hair. Her eyes were distant yet mournful. When I asked what was wrong and why she was giving me this pin, she said, "My mother gave me this when I was your age, and now, it will be yours. It's a symbol of strength and a reminder that we are never alone."

Nervous laughter had bubbled out of me, and I stated, "Lydia, this is an engagement party. The only strength I'll need is to not burrow my way through all the chocolates and those orange cream puffs!"

She had smiled sadly at me before leaving me to finish getting ready. A servant stepped toward me to finish applying the crystal jewels lining my eyebrows. They especially stood out with my caramel tones and bright blue and silver eyes. I didn't need the servants and guests to tell me how enchanting I looked as I shimmered in the candle lights surrounding us.

My aunt must have known what fate awaited our family a mere few hours ago. The warmth and attachment I felt to the prince was real and strong, but his family had other plans for our party. All had been pleasant until, like the crack of a whip, shock battered me as I saw members of my family leaning over with blood trailing from their noses. Was it poison? Did others know this was a trap?

Pure chaos surrounded me, and my beloved's fury was nearly blinding; he was yelling for any guards he deemed still trustworthy and clutched my arms with his long, pale fingers as he pushed—dragged—me to the nearest darkened entrance.

"It seems fate was never going to be on our side, my love," he whispered frantically, his breath hot and full of the berry wine we had been drinking moments earlier. "I'm not sure what this

scheme is, and I'm terribly sorry about your family, but I'll protect you in whichever way I can. You know these tunnels extensively now, and when you escape, keep running through the fields. Don't stop until you are sure no one has followed you and the only sounds are animals and the earth itself. My spirit will always be with you."

Reality suddenly dawned on me, and I felt the vicious grip of fear strangle my throat. My gaze frantically swept through the dining hall until I saw my aunt. Oh, my aunt! Her eyes glazed over, showing me that her spirit had left this world. How did she know something would happen tonight? Why us? What did I do, or rather, what did I fail to do? Terror and grief convulsing in my heart, I brushed my mouth tenderly against my partner's lips before I realized the taste of blood smeared across my tongue.

A traitor had thrown a knife into his back. As much as it pained me, I couldn't fall with him as he swayed toward the ground, his eyes still full of sadness and confusion. I turned on my heel and quickly raced through the tunnels, knowing my speed would throw off anyone following my shadow. It didn't take long to find the exit, and I ran as fast as I could through the thick fields of grass. Run, run, run, run. Run! My breathing had been haggard, and I was woozy from the wine I had been drinking. Yet I had to keep running until all I heard was the earth itself.

Still on my hands and knees, I put down the pin from my aunt and continue to bury my hands into the mud, relishing in the sensation of the clay dirt. I breathe in the grasses and moist air, and I dare to close my eyes as the sweat beads down my head and neck. I have no idea where I'll go from here, but I know my aunt didn't simply give the pin to me as a family heirloom; she knew I would need it to buy my way away from these lands. But where will I go? And why was our family ambushed?

I don't have time to ponder this question when I hear rustling from behind me. Panicking, I hold my breath and become as still as the dirt. I pray my jewels won't jingle too loudly in the wind.

The rustling is picking up speed, and with fear thundering along my rib bones, I slowly turn my head to face behind me. Blue-gray eyes, as deep as the ocean floor, stare back at me through the grasses. No—they glare at me. My whole body shakes and I'm a trapped lamb, mere prey. The man before me is not a person I recognize, but he must have been a relative of my aunt's husband. Such beautiful, similar eyes that you could fall into. Yet these hold such hatred.

"Are you going to kill me?" I barely breathe out as he slowly crawls on his hands and knees toward me.

"Ah, I would have had that honor, but don't you know? You're already dead," he growls out.

Gasping, I reach for my aunt's ornate pin and, with a jolt of terror, realize I can't grab it. I glance down to see decayed flesh and parts of my bones sticking out through my hands. The earth swallows me whole, and the roots of the grasses and small stones in the soil are under my skin, weighing me down from the inside out. There are no breaths to take, solely the feeling of insects crawling where my organs used to be and roots tangling with my tendons and what was left of my muscles.

As I glance back up to the man, he gives me a wicked, terrifying smile and says, "He did tell you to run until all you could hear were the animals and the earth itself."

FIVE

Eira

During the season of war, a clinician without their team is a clinician lost at sea. With no life jacket.
Or food and water. So, we're basically fucked.
-Course note taken by Jace Nilhan, Trauma Therapist

Hearing the caw of a bird at my window, I jolt awake with a gasp and tumble off my desk chair. The dim lights in my office flicker, and I'm panting as if I finished a marathon. *What the hell was that?* I can still feel the insects scuttling under my skin and the weight of that man's eyes on me. Looking at the clock, it's 2:30 p.m. I must have fallen asleep after my last client left, but I have no recollection of dozing off. I have never done such a thing at work before. *Ugh, embarrassing. First, I'm running late. I didn't even have time to finish my coffee with the amount of work I've had this morning. Now this?*

Peeling back my undershirt, I sense my back is covered in a film of dampness. I feel achingly drained, and I can barely get up without my vision tunneling. The room is spinning slightly, and I stumble to my kettle and water. That cold, forgotten coffee won't do me any good right now—I need a drink that's fresh and hot. Something, anything, to break the chill crawling up my back. The hairs on my neck are still standing on edge, as if I'm being watched, which is absurd. I'm alone in my office. Utterly alone.

Before I fumble for a mug and tea, there is a light knocking at my door. *Oh, gods, can I not catch a break today?*

"Yeah, I'm coming—hold on a sec," I croak out while stumbling toward the door.

I take a few seconds to breathe and pull my long locks up into a high ponytail. Rolling up my sleeves, I try to wipe off my skin and fan out my pullover. *This is so gross; I'm literally soaked in sweat. Again. Fuck.* Breathless, I pull open the door and come face-to-face with my best friend, Athena. Forest-green eyes bore into me, keen and intense, already taking note of my physical state before I speak. They subside and ebb into concern when she realizes I'm still breathing hard and am clearly shaken up.

"My winter fox, what the hell happened to you?" she yells-whispers to me as she pushes her way into my office space.

I have no reason to fear the rest of the treatment clinic, but I hastily push the door closed and lock it. Twice. Leaning my sticky back against the door, I heave another breath as I close my eyes, taking a moment to get a grip. Athena clutches my shaking hands and brings them to her chest while I continue to settle my heart. She is sharp as a hawk and misses nothing, and she is extremely warm and kind—I can't keep anything hidden from her for long. Even now, my body melts as she pulls me into a hug, and I already know I'll be sharing these nightmares with her.

Gentle hands, rich and dark, stroke my ponytail and rub pacifying circles along my back, her many bracelets jangling with the motion. I feel more than hear her humming as we continue to stand together. One therapist folding into another, being cradled in the love I rarely give myself.

Slowly unwinding myself from my friend's embrace, I let out a breath of a laugh. Gratitude shines in my eyes and understanding radiates from hers. We've always had this kind of friendship where our bodies speak more than any words could. *Oh no, am I starting to cry?* A tissue is handed to me as she turns to make my tea. I'm convinced tea with rich, creamy honey can scare off most tension and anxieties, but who am I kidding? I'll need one hundred gallons of this to get back to my normal self.

Athena and I fall into two of the plush, *way-too-comfy* chairs in my office. It's truly a surprise I have never fallen asleep at work before with these in reach. Only my clients get that kind of luxury here. Athena lights a candle, plays a harmonic playlist we share on our team for when shit really hits the fan, and stretches her lithe body toward me with my mug of tea.

"So, we both know this is a losing battle for you. Go on, spill what happened. Is it a client? Your lady parts cramping up again? Tryg being an ass? Oh no... did you finally hear from your family?" she fires off these questions at me, each question laced with more concern than the last. As worry swirls in those green irises of hers, she distractedly plays with her intricate nose rings. The winding ends of her tattoos poke out from under her cardigan.

"No," I sigh. "I mean, Tryg is always dumb, and don't hold your breath waiting for my family to finally act like human beings." I untangle my hair from the makeshift ponytail it was in and thread a braid as I mull over how to even start this conversation. The mention of my family startles me even though they're a near constant thought in my mind, always simmering under the surface, waiting to remind me they're not here. It's different having someone else, even my best friend, bring them up.

I'll never forget the devastation that rained down around me like shards of glass sprinkling against my skin. I was barely ten years old. A mere child who went from playing in the woods with her siblings and searching for critters with her friends to having her innocence funneled through a vacuum of despair. I skipped up the stone path to our wooden house, already giddy for the freshly picked berries and snacks my parents would have ready for my siblings and I. Swooping around the towering spruce tree near the back door, I can remember stumbling to a complete stop as uncertainty and the beginnings of panic stirred around me.

If you grow up in a larger family, the house is *never* silent. Yet the air nearly suffocated me with how quiet it was. Especially as I peered into each room and none of my families' belongings were there. *Nothing*. No clothes, no shoes, no bags for work or school. Simply a building full of furniture and empty of love. If Tryg hadn't come over as he usually did and found me, voice hoarse and eyes puffy, I don't know what would have happened to me.

No one knows what happened to my family. The exact memories warp in my mind depending on the mood I'm in. Currently, I'm exhausted and alarmed, which means I'm on the defensive. It means my family, the ones who were supposed to love and protect me, weren't kidnapped. They purposely left me behind while they moved on to whichever adventure was next on their list.

Who needs them? A voice whispers inside me. *You're stronger without their love.*

"I'm still trying to wrap my head around what is going on. I doubt this will make very much sense to you," I say as I reweave my hair yet again and stuff down the lingering memories as far as they can go.

A small smile appears on Athena's full mouth, her knowing eyes darting toward my hair and back to the tea next to me. Rolling my eyes, I let go of my hair and take a sip from the tea. This one tastes smoky—one of my favorites. *I always love the taste of heat and smoke.* I expect Athena to respond, but she is still staring into me with incredible patience. She won't leave here until I give her the real answer. *I don't know how she always knows I'm burying the truth inside myself, but she knows.*

"Alright, this will sound completely bonkers, but I've been having strange dreams and, um, nightmares. They feel too real, as if I've been dragged into these experiences before. I don't know how else to say it..." I start to explain.

The last month of nightmares spill out of me, my tea long forgotten, but my hair now has four messy braids woven throughout it. My leg continuously bounces, and a rush of fear takes over my body. Disclosing what's been happening paints this as more real and problematic. I can taste the suggestions Athena will offer about all of this. Is this a nightmare disorder? Is this related to the gnarled scar tissue along my organs? Should I reconsider taking the medications my doctor told me about? Am I getting trapped in my head? I've heard it all in the past, which is why I'm hesitant to share any of this with someone now. All it takes is a few trusted professionals or loved ones to take you—no, *slam* you—down to the ground and make you feel ridiculous, for you to keep your experiences locked in a special place deep within yourself.

Athena, though. Athena always surprises me. I'm ready to add more bricks to the wall around me, and she finds a way to crash right through them. Her entire reaction to what I share is to kneel before me and pull me into a tight hug.

"I'm *so* sorry that you've been experiencing this, my friend. Tryg brought you lunch, which is why I was coming to your office in the first place. I'm grateful that you told me. Let's get out of here and see if you're up to sharing this with Jace and the others tonight," she says as she slowly rocks me. "But first, I think physical movement would benefit us all. You game for some yoga flow?" she asks.

"What about all of our clients?" I mumble, tracing the pattern of tattooed leaves going up her neck.

Athena snorts and gives me a no-nonsense look. "There were

a few cancellations for this afternoon with news of a winter storm coming. I may or may not have sternly told our assistant to *not* fill those openings with anyone on the waitlist. Not today, girl."

The logical part of me knows that she's right to do this and flowing movement would be good for me, but damn, I'm *exhausted*. This must show on my face because she says, "You know, scratch that idea. Let's head to that new café that opened up and get you water and coffee. Jace has been *begging* everyone to try it, but we've all been too exhausted to want to travel anywhere after work. We can decide where to go from there."

Before I'm able to respond, she pulls me up from the chair. I stare back at it longingly, willing myself to not take a nap. *Girl, what is wrong with you? If you take a nap again, you might have another nightmare. Dummy.* Shaking myself out, I nod to her that this plan is okay and flutter around my office to clean up before heading out. Loading my bag with my laptop, a healing workbook I need to finish reading, and a few supplies, I reach over my desk to turn the lights off and follow Athena out of my office.

"I can't believe you locked your door," she says as she watches me relocking it from the outside.

She's right. Locking a physical door won't keep the demons in my mind away.

SIX

Eira

The citizens of this country must still experience times of joy.
Without it, we have little hope of winning this war.
We are nothing without the courage of our people.
-Speech from President Chloe Li at the Committee of Sweazn

"She's far away from here. Eira, are you listening?"

I quickly blink toward my friends, the hum of the café jolting me back to reality. I'm still trying to follow the last thread of my thoughts, sensing I'm missing something important. Words were cluttering in my mind from the past few nightmares and that *damn bird* from this morning keeps poking around my thoughts. I don't know why it bothers me this much, it's only a bird. Maybe it was the way the colors and shapes kept changing, even though I *know* my eyes were playing tricks on me.

But *gods*, a moment ago I could have sworn I felt a feather drift against my shoulder and saw that bird staring right back at me from within my mind...

"Eira, seriously, are you okay? Where did you go?" Liv asks, worry evident in her normally lively tone. Her hazel eyes seek mine while she grinds her opal nails against her palms. At the tension in her sister's tone, Lyk snaps her focus to me, her colorful hair swishing with the movement and her equally colorful watch reflecting the nearest light. She doesn't go anywhere without being able to check the time, a rather unhealthy obsession she's had since I first met her.

I force myself to stare at a space between them, not quite making eye contact with either sister. I know the wall built around my emotions will come crashing down if I do.

Liv's energy often matches mine. She and her sister, Lyk, might as well be my own family. While I can't always verbalize what's racing through my mind, thoughts and images galloping like horses made of smoke and fire, Liv and Lyk *see* me. Each in their own brilliant way. They're both empaths and work with children from broken homes, inspired by their own upbringing. It's the same experience that allowed them to truly understand how it felt when I was left without a home or family.

Their parents had suffered from addictions that struck them down in unimaginable ways. The sisters were pre-teens when one of their parents overdosed, found face down on pieces of trash in the back of an alley, and the other parent willingly rejected them. Liv and Lyk had to fight through living with estranged, aloof family members or *worse*, strangers with wandering hands, until they were of legal age to manage on their own. This never stilled either sister's drive or desire to make other children's lives easier when swallowed by familial trauma.

Liv has the ability to remain logical and systematic during times of stress. She never misses a single snippet of detail when working with kids who are told they can't trust a therapist. Lyk has a talent of remaining both curious and grounded when interacting with someone frightened, a constant source of tranquility with a flair for creativity. They're a dream team in any clinic and roll off one another's energy in their own chaotic twin-like understanding of each other.

My love for them is a force to be reckoned with, and I'd do

anything for them. But that doesn't mean I can pry myself open when I'm too overstimulated in a new and loud environment. Looking away, I will them to accept that I won't be answering any questions right now. My friends are a few feet away and are already melting into the scene around us, adding to the sounds, colors, and human pressure within the café's walls.

Athena lightly squeezes my leg and leans in close enough to whisper, "Why don't we go get a coffee now that everyone's here?"

Eager for a chance to clear my head, I breathe out in a flurry, stumbling from how fast I scramble out of my chair. While the nightmares have been happening for months now, this past week has felt the most intense and is following me wherever I go. It's as if there is a substance under my skin itching to get out, waiting to eat me alive. I wipe my palms on my jeans and grab onto Athena's arm as she leads us through the maze of tables to the front counter. She knows movement helps me ground myself in the midst of anxiety, and while the sticky panic eases up a bit, the whirlwind of chaos is nowhere near settled inside of me.

"This place manages to have every flavor under the sun," Athena mutters before glancing my way. "What are you going with today?"

Ugh, I hate ordering in public when I'm this frazzled. How is it even possible to list 50+ flavor combinations? "I'll go with what they recommend. Something with chocolate. *Anything* with chocolate," I breathe out.

Smirking, Athena turns to the worker, who is entirely too cheerful with this many people packed into a room. He smiles brightly at Athena, his chestnut eyes lighting up, and the string-lighting in the café makes his golden-brown skin shimmer as he moves his head. My own face looks like a sullen swamp monster. Athena is a goddess, as usual, with her black hair woven around her bold, entrancing face. She is wearing enough eyeliner and color to pop those green eyes and has on a fitted dark green sweater dress. We are usually the same height and size, but her extra cardio training has her sporting an athletic build. Of course, she is wearing knee-high suede boots, making those legs appear even longer. I won't even entertain the idea of checking out my own physique and outfit, not with all of this fatigue weighing me down. *Sigh.*

"Hi! I'll have a winter mocha with two extra shots and a salmon with veggies croissant," she chirps. "And my friend here will have a latte with your number on it- she has a keen love for chocolate, you know," she says with a wink.

Eyes flying wide and heat already crawling up my neck and cheeks, I whip my head around to find her with bright eyes and a devious smile tugging at her lips. I open and close my mouth as if a flopping fish while the worker huffs out a laugh and leans forward toward me.

"I-I told her that I wanted a-anything with chocolate!" I stammer out like the mess I am.

"Oh really? Then it's certainly appropriate to include my number on your coffee. I myself fancy white chocolate and that strawberry mouth of yours," he purrs, tossing me a flirty wink.

Mortified and wishing I could sink into the floor of the café, I hastily shove Athena and cover my tomato-red face, spinning in any direction that is not facing the front counter. I hear giddy laughter behind me, but I'm too embarrassed to look back. "She's such a traitor," I humph out and immediately walk to the display of plants in the nearest corner.

There are a variety of ferns and palms blooming out of terracotta pots painted with warm and luscious designs. The smaller set of string lights with the faux fur rugs give a cozy sensation, inviting me to take a seat at the hidden two-seater wooden table. I run my chapped, shaking fingers down the pine wood, taking in the smooth surface and how cooling it feels against my hands. The howling wind barreling around outside is a sign that winter is dancing her way here. Living this far up north means my delicate hands and face are the first to notice. Snuggling into my wool scarf, I take out my chipped phone to add lavender and aloe lotion to my list...and maybe some better gloves.

I examine my old phone and its cracked screen for a second, tossing it back and forth between my hands. It's definitely time for an upgrade. I have no excuse; it's not as if I don't have the means to get one—simply my usual reasoning of being too busy with work. My mouth purses as I watch a couple walk past me with their eyes glued to their devices. *Maybe it'll be more trouble than it's worth to get a fancy new phone.*

These kinds of high-tech devices are still relatively new on Earth. Or rather, what everyone refers to as *Future* Earth. I roll my eyes at this almost every single time. Why make this distinction when we're pretty much living as if we're in the twenty-first century?

It wasn't always this way. We learned about this at school—*or what my friends prefer to call raging robotic lessons.* We'd be forced to sit in our cubbies with a personalized robot ready to "teach" us, a.k.a. not allow us to leave until we completed the lesson. Back in 2088, everything was relatively stable on Earth. The climate had been on the brink of collapsing, but people got their shit together. They were managing things like energy usage and water supply, and it appeared as if Earth might actually survive.

The joke was on the whole world when a handful of politicians got a little nuclear trigger happy. Completely unhinged, they started blasting the hell out of countries that didn't follow some commercial policy. It's taken centuries, *so many centuries*, for our environment to find a form of homeostasis, allowing humans to climb out from their underground communities to establish life on land again. It took even longer to dig up and preserve ancient cultures, languages, and spiritual practices, let alone recreate technology without a means for electricity originally.

Shaking myself out of these upsetting thoughts, I bring myself back to the café. The cozy environment is certainly helping me calm down, and I finally take in this new business. Even with the industrial theme, there is a sense of warmth and community already settling into place here. Stringed lights are layered throughout the café with local art placed along the walls. There is a mix of small and large wooden tables, each slightly different from the next, and plenty of faux fur rugs, plants, and candles. Tables have cards with questions to help connect to your partner or friends, and there's a back room for those wanting to focus on work. Lo-Fi music plays in the background, making a comeback yet again after many years, and I see a small area up ahead that could be used as a stage. My favorite part is the mouthwatering smells roaming throughout the café and how many creative flavor combinations are listed here. It's pretty cute, I'll admit, which is a real shame since Athena embarrassed me to the moon and back and there's no way I'll be able to show my face here again.

I'm also impressed that a new business is even able to flourish right now. It's jarring against the backdrop of trauma and war looming over our city. Definitely suspicious that the government allowed this coffee shop to be here, but it is a distraction I'll gladly take.

While a number of communities are certainly thriving on the continent and technology is making a serious comeback, apparently humans will never learn their lesson with war. It's always about control when we citizens aren't the ones fighting about this. The cities in Sweazn are on a tight leash financially, bracing themselves for the inevitable active fighting and stockpiling necessary resources. City taxes almost doubled this past year with many up top claiming it's needed to fund "even more powerful" weapons. Vague and secretive about brutal forces that will surely change the lives of many in our world.

My friends and I are already affected financially, but we're fortunate enough to be in high-demand jobs. I'm not sure I can say the same for everyone else in our city. It's curious, though, that the citizens vanishing are the same ones closely connected to our small businesses. Not those who are uniquely valued by the government, the ones willing to throw ourselves willingly into the mayhem of healthcare and trauma.

Perhaps we're all just pawns in the end game. Some of us need to disappear. Others of us are meant to be sacrificial lambs. Maybe history will repeat itself, and we'll live underground yet again?

My muscles are unwinding, and I breathe out the depressing thoughts I have about our country, savoring the restful energy around my little corner. I play with the edges of the nearest candle, daring to push my fingers closer to the flame. Fire has always fascinated me with the way it brings warmth and light, how it has the power to cook foods, yet it destroys as quickly as it heals and provides. My already rough hands barely notice the slight sting of pain, and I can't help wondering if I was engulfed in this flame, would I be harmed or repaired? Would I finally take in a full breath? Would I—

"Okay, I know that was a poor joke, but must you be so dramatic? I couldn't find you with this little corner swallowing you up, and when I do find you, you're seriously burning your fingertips?!" Athena rushes out as she places our drinks and food on the table.

Startled, I remove my fingers, now tinged with pink, and wrap myself in one of the chair blankets. Glaring at my friend, I say, "Excuse me for hiding. Not all of us want our friends to make crude jokes at the expense of mortifying us."

Rolling her eyes, she lets out a rather boisterous laugh and leans in conspiratorially. "The mortifying part was worth it if it broke you from the zombie daze you were in. You're finally awake again. And let's be real, that man was *fire,* and you haven't gotten laid in months now. Besides, you're cute when you turn bright red," she says, poking my nose.

Irked, I swat her hand away from me. "Oh, please! I wasn't that dazed. Even if I was, I doubt he wants to be objectified for the sake of 'waking me up,'" I mutter.

Taking my hand in hers, Athena says earnestly, "Winter fox, he thought it was hilarious and said it totally made his night. He also still wrote his number on your winter mocha—yes, I fixed the order for you—in case you are truly interested. And honestly, I would go to whichever lengths if it meant you weren't lost in your thoughts how you were. I'm really worried about you."

I sigh as I look back up at her, seeing the darker humor and playfulness slipping away and replaced by tension. She has always used humor and, to my dismay, compromising situations to shake me out of my anxieties or troubles. A piece of me is always tense and strangled by anxiety, but it especially rears its head when a man is interested in me. It's easier to cower behind my shield of fear than be intimate with someone who might never understand how deep my pain goes. What's the point in starting something I can't finish? Why bother if I know he'll leave when I can't deliver?

I gently squeeze her hand before releasing it for my mocha. My eyes light up when I realize she also bought me a buttery salmon croissant and a fresh cherry brownie.

"Does this mean you forgive me for my ill-timed and possibly objectifying jokes, my friend?" she asks.

With half the crumbling brownie stuffed in my mouth already, I adamantly nod my head as I savor the sweet bitterness popping along my tastebuds. My uterus contracts again, and I send it an inward scowl. *Lighten up, you unruly organ. I'm about to feed you chocolate.*

A small moan escapes me, and I go in for my next bite—

"Clearly, I wasn't invited to the party," Tryg says as his gaze narrows in on my mouth.

SEVEN
Tryq

We don't care how clever you think you are. The only thing we want to know is if you're brave enough to run into the heart of the fire, even if you save one kid and die yourself.
-Rike Tonish, Commander of Sweazn
Investigative Forces

Gravel crunches beneath my feet as I walk down the alley, my mouth clenched in a grimace. Layered buildings of stone and glass tower up around me, some smattered with vivid colors from the south, and others are a cool metal, as dark as my thoughts. My breath comes out in frozen huffs as I mull over the morning and try to get my head on straight. I had no business drinking that much last night, but fuck if I care about that now.

I'm not able to shake the feeling I had when Eira tensed up this morning. I know she has been off lately and appears way too fatigued—not that it diminishes her beauty and spunk—but I thought it had more to do with her increase in clients and winter coming. This is a rougher part of the year for all of us, but especially for her. The first chill in the air always reminds her of the day her family left. She did the work to heal, and she takes care of herself, but that doesn't mean the pain is gone. If anything, it's hidden in a bottomless pocket within her heart, and it grips her like a vise when she least expects it. It's been tiring enough for me over the years; I can hardly imagine how it impacts her.

I take out one of my cigs and the lighter Eira gave me years ago. *"I can't stop this nasty habit of yours, but maybe if you think of me when you smoke, you'll come to your senses eventually,"* she had told me.

I smile as I glance at the lighter—a white fox with smoky eyes and a tail of fire. That's been her nickname since we were kids—she's a white fox with that natural white-blond hair, ambitious nature, and knowing look she gives you. Even more so with how skittish she gets in social situations, and when people take an interest in her romantically. And they *do* take quite an interest. Eira has always been stellar at evaluating the room she walks into, aware of every possible escape and a person's movements. My little fox.

She always told me that I was her bear to protect her. I want to think it's because of my strength and loving heart. Eira enjoys pointing out that it has a lot more to do with my prickly personality. *Whatever.* I'm proud that she wears the bear bracelet I gave her for her last birthday. It's a reminder that I'm always there with her, since this stupid job takes up more time than I'd like.

Reluctantly, I jam the cig back in its box and keep walking, pushing through the sharp bite of this wind. Maybe she is finally rubbing off on me. But if these toxic cancer sticks have managed to survive war after war on this planet, maybe they're worth the risk. I pull my hat down snug around my ears and rewrap the scarf around my jaw and neck. This is the kind of cold that sears through you and pushes you to drink smooth liquor to warm up. *Fuck*, I hate living this far up north.

I quicken my pace, my boots stomping the ground even harder as I head out onto one of the city's main streets. A handful of small shops manage to still linger here, the kind the girls swoon over with all the artsy shit they sell. They haven't quite been touched by the threat of war further south in our country. Our city used to have mostly affluent areas, but that changed over time. It's now divided between those of us who can survive and those who are barely getting by. The government requires too much of each citizen to live up north. Citizens in professions not deemed "valuable," such as those who work directly for the government and anyone assisting during the war, are treated akin to trash—stuffed away and disregarded until they're entirely hidden from view, they're all but forgotten.

There's a line of buildings a few blocks down that almost *everyone* avoids at all costs. Even the homeless know to avoid that area. Those businesses had to close down due to money troubles with the government, but my team knows the truth: The owners were taken with their kids. What I *know* is kidnapping and now have to figure out a way to prove it.

Sometimes, I get called into the head office in the capital, located further south and swarming with hundreds of workers. I much prefer living up here, even if it's as cold as fuck. If I'm going to suffer through half a year of freezing my balls off, at least I live near the dense forest and can breathe in fresh air.

Four turns and a coffee stop later, I push the front office door open. I roll my eyes when I notice the fresh coat of teal blue paint and the polished doorknob. Good to know they can afford to tidy up this shithole but can't raise the assistants' wages. Alright, *fine*, it's not a shithole. The other management and the government as a whole causes it to feel like one, but this actual office and my team are the reason anything gets done around here. I'm the lead investigator here in our smaller region, Castburg, and am the luckiest man to work with these assholes.

"Eh, finally decided to show up this morning, boss?" Ruse says as he throws a stack of papers on my desk. He raises thick, dark eyebrows while peering at me with even darker eyes, swirling with sass and tinged with specks of honey and caramel.

Besides Eira, Ruse is my best friend, and I swear on my life, he should have been born as my brother. We even live together, and it was his idea to rope Eira into being a housemate. He's one of the few people who gets away with giving me attitude. Only because I give it right back to him. I can tell it's going to be one of those days where he messes with me nonstop. He calls me *boss* —even though we're co-leaders, and it's a name the rest of the team gave me that I *hate*—when he's in a mood.

"Oh, piss off. It's 10:00 a.m., and I had shit to do at home," I reply before taking a much needed gulp of my coffee. I savor the way the bitterness scalds my throat. "Besides, what's the point of having you on this team if you're not going to work once in a while?"

I hear grumbling from the other desks and know I hit a bullseye; none of these shits were working, and if they were, it was solely paperwork. A decent amount of friends or acquaintances work here, with the exception of a few older folks who come in part-time. Said friends were with me as we drowned ourselves with wine last night, trying to escape the misery of our current case. I also wanted to forget the fact that I'm going to have to let the part-timers go. Budget cuts upon budget cuts, slashing their way down the path to poverty.

Sliding into my seat and slinging back more of the coffee, I ruffle through some of the papers on my desk. I managed to organize most of it after Eira came by with lunch last week, her eyes nearly bugging out of her head when she saw the chaos of my files. I didn't have much of a choice when she came back the next day with too many paperclips, file organizers, pens loaded with ink, among other items. Sighing, I realize I'm already getting a headache from the new reports from the capital. We typically fight against what would be considered "normal crimes," such as drug trafficking, break-ins, family disputes, and murders. My team is known for being the quickest, even if the past few weeks have made us out to be the lazy slobs we probably are at heart. The reports in front of me? Disgustingly different from the "normal."

War crimes. Impossible and unheard-of human behaviors by enemy governments. Entire families are going missing. Children, in particular, are being targeted. And they want *me* to figure this out?

I rub my eyes and pray they'll push back into my skull, and I'll be done with this mess. *Alright, that's a bit much.* But I'm seriously done after barely beginning, and by the state of my teammates, this is going to be a long-ass work day.

It's at most been five hours, but we all agree that we need to call it a day soon. A few of them nearly jumped out of their seats when it was announced a winter storm was going to be rolling through already.

I called one of our close friends, Astira, during a quick coffee break this afternoon to ask how she would proceed when we're obviously plateauing here. Astira, Astira, Astira. She's a real-life savior with her quick wit and snark. There's a gentleness to her that I don't often get to see, which I'm sure has *nothing* to do with the fact that I'm horrible to her. I can't play *all* of my pranks on Eira and Athena, so Astira ends up getting the brunt of it. What can I say, I'm a real charmer. Astira works in a different line of therapy—*how am I friends with so many therapists?*—and when I'm at my wit's end, she's usually a good source of reason.

"I'm overloaded with people's PTSD over here. What do you want?" she snaps through the phone at me. My team and I aren't the only ones being handed war cases.

"If you worked yourself into a maze and are at least five coffees into the day, what would you do?" I ask her.

She heaves the biggest sigh, and I swear I feel her eyes roll. "Listen, your habits need to change, Tryg. Not just those cigs. What are you doing already having five coffees by this hour? And if I was in a maze, especially with the likes of you, I would need to completely remove myself and begin anew. All you do is complicate my life, and if I didn't get a chance to clear my head, I wouldn't be able to move forward. Now go back to work and leave me alone. I have clients who desperately need my attention," she grumbles before hanging up the phone.

Yeah, she's the best. And by complicating her life, she may or may not mean that I keep breaking off our friends-with-benefits arrangement. I never said I was Prince Charming over here.

Astira was right, though. We move to a new board in our work room and start fresh with the basics. No major details. We write out the main patterns we are seeing for each main war case coming our way. We are far from solving anything, but this looks a hell of a lot clearer than what we had before.

"Hey, man. Athena, Liv, Jace, Lyk, and Eira are at that new coffee place. I think it's called En Paz? Whatever it's called, they're there. You game?" Ruse asks.

I watch him shrug into his gray wool sweater. It does nothing to conceal his broad shoulders and hard muscles that line his lean body. When he lifts his arms up, exposing some of his chiseled abs and the landscape of mountains tattooed around his torso, I hear one of the workers suck in a breath. I remember the brief time when we were teenagers, and I couldn't fucking *stand* him. He had a huge growth spurt and went from a wiry kid with dangling limbs to a man sheathed in muscle and sex appeal. Eira and Athena went all gooey-eyed for him, going as far as to join us on our early morning runs. I knew I wasn't a dump, but that doesn't mean it didn't grind my nerves to see all the girls hovering around him, hoping for a taste of his dark skin.

That's all in the past. Not the girls, or even a number of guys, throwing themselves at him. But the immature rift between us. He's my right-hand man, and I wouldn't have it any other way.

"Tryg?" Ruse prompts. *How is he incredibly present with all this shit going on?*

Between the hangover this morning, Eira's tension and worry, these cases, and the never-ending guilt of wanting a cig, I want nothing more than to head home and knock the fuck out. Irrational annoyance laces through me when I consider it was probably Jace who encouraged everyone to go out. He's always wanting to try new food and drinks and shit. But I force that emotion away, wanting to see everyone, as always. I nod my head at Ruse while grabbing my coat, hat, and scarf. After bundling up, Ruse and I lock up and walk the quarter mile to the café. The wind is picking up, and I'm debating ditching them, when Ruse speaks up.

"Athena texted that she's worried about Eira again," he says.

The mention of Athena reminds me I need to ask Jace about that later. They've been denying it, but I'm convinced they're hooking up.

"Did she say anything else? More specific?" I ask him.

"Nah, man, you know how she is. Cryptic as fuck. She wanted to keep us in the loop about it all," he says.

So, it's not only me who's worried. *Huh. Interesting.*

"I can't believe we have over a hundred kids' names at this point," I mutter. A phantom hand urges me to inhale one hit of nicotine. Anything to take the edge off and distract me from how fucking tragic this case is.

"I know, man." Ruse blows out a breath and kicks a rock down an alley. "I know the game of war is brutal, but something isn't right about this. Most of the victims are kids, maybe whole families, and if the last report we read today is anything to go by, we aren't the sole country seeing this bullshit."

A piece of my brittle heart squeezes. And other countries aren't just having kids go missing—their broken and cut up bodies are being sent back to their families in wrapped boxes. *It's fucking disgusting to do this to these poor parents.*

We make our way to the meticulously painted café doors and hustle ourselves inside. I take a minute to bask in the rolling heat now enveloping us. The excited energy is palpable, and I search around for our group. Jace holds up a hand, and we head in their direction, not seeing Athena or Eira. Lyk walks past us with a steaming cup of tea as we do, still bundled up in her scarf with her amber eyes peeking out. Her eyebrow piercing twinkles in the glowing lights. I want to engage with them all, but Liv must sense who I'm searching for and points to a corner of the café. I see a wisp of blond hair move and Athena's face comes into view.

"I'll be right back, hold up," I tell our friends.

There's a part of me that knows I should leave Athena and Eira be for right now. If they separated themselves from the rest of our friends, they might need time to process whatever they're going through. But there's an invisible rope tied between Eira and me, and wherever she goes, I find myself following.

Making my way between the wooden tables and plants— *why are there so many fucking plants in here? Jesus*—I come up to Athena as Eira moans into a brownie. Huffing out a laugh, I say, "Clearly, I wasn't invited to the party."

EIGHT
Tryg

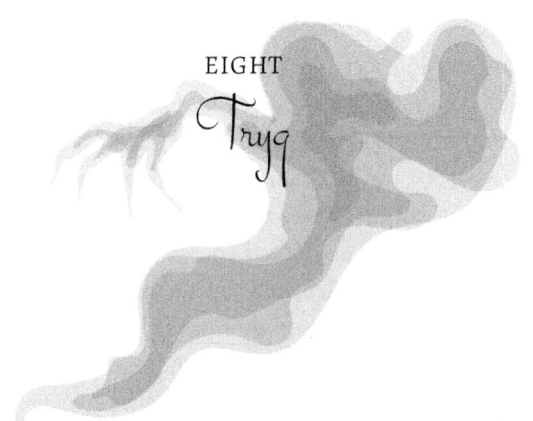

Humans have been practicing the ancient art of yoga for nearly 9,000 years. To practice, though, doesn't mean one has reached enlightenment.
-Shira Bonnalit, Medical Practitioner and Professional Yoga Instructor, 800+ Hours

I clearly, 100 percent, know that we are just friends—siblings more than anything at this point. I tell myself this weekly, no, daily. Eira is an extraordinarily beautiful friend. A talented and loving friend. An awkward and hilarious and resilient friend. I know where the boundary line is. But *damn*, when she makes that little moan and is licking the chocolate from her lips, it takes a moment for my hammering heart to quiet down. *Seriously, bro, calm the fuck down. Aren't you sleeping with Astira?*

"You absolutely weren't invited to this party. I'm very much into *chocolate*, Tryg, which clearly does not include you," she says and breaks into a fit of giggles when she turns to Athena. Athena joins her and they can't even stop to breathe as they sip on their drinks. This leads to more laughter as Athena snorts and coffee comes out of Eira's nose.

"Women..." I mutter as I start to back away.

"Men...chocolate men!" Athena croaks out, which leads to more laughter.

I arch a brow, wondering if either of them is going to clue me in on what's going on or if they're even aware of why they're laughing at this point. I'm waiting a little too eagerly for Eira to offer me a seat or to come stand up next to me. Positively ridiculous of me. Besides, I know how Eira gets in crowded spaces. She can turn into a different person if we're surrounded by people in crisis. But something social where people earnestly want to peel back her layers and get to know her? *Forget it.* She closes in on herself like a mountain collapsing, insisting it's "better that way." Eira needs to have space, even from her friends. *Even from me*, I think begrudgingly.

Instead, I watch as she giddily hiccups and devours her sandwich. As cheesy and horrible as it sounds, I can't tear my eyes away from her. There's a slight glow to her face that wasn't there before, and her body sits back with more ease. The candle and the stringed lights appear to light up as she shifts in her seat. Before I'm able to stop myself, I tuck a piece of hair that fell out of her braid behind her ear, the tips having dipped in her sandwich sauce.

Those silver-blue eyes meet my golden-brown ones, and I fight the urge to lick the little crumbs around her pouty bottom lip. She raises her eyebrows and asks, "What? Are you hungry?"

Smirking, I say, "You have no idea, little fox." She giggles and shifts her body to face me, leaving me unsettlingly upset that she moved away from my touch. Fortunately, for whom, I'm not sure, Astira comes bustling into the café. Athena and Eira both perk up and excitedly signal in her direction.

"Come with us, Tryg!" Eira calls back to me as they are already placing their empty plates by the other dirty dishes on top of the trash and recycling. Before I know it, Eira and Athena are linking arms with Astira as they walk toward our other friends. Where Eira and Athena have their thick hair woven around their heads, Astira's hair pours down her back in heaps of red, amber, and honey. The lighting in this place sets the mood because all three women are stunning while they walk. Graceful as cats, hair shining, ready to pounce on their next prey.

As I approach the table, Jace yells out to Astira, "Ira has arrived! Snag a coffee or a bite, you'll need the fuel for the yoga flow class later tonight. A little snow storm can't stop us from going."

"Ugh, not more coffee," Ruse groans into his hands.

"You know, not everyone has the same problem with coffee addiction as you," Liv teases as she breathes coffee breath into his face. Her newly cropped black hair has streaks of white through it, and it cascades across her face as she leans into Ruse. It matches the dark tattoo that swirls from her hand up to her neck, meant to represent different countries around the world.

"Yeah, especially when it tastes *so* divine," Lyk says as she crunches a chocolate-covered coffee bean in Ruse's ear. Unlike her sister, Lyk always goes the colorful route. Shades of dark and light purple weave around her head, blue, pink, and green cascading to her shoulders. She has it half pulled up, which means I get a quality view of her chomping away in his ear.

"*Ugh!* Get these barbarians away from me," he yells as he pushes away from the table, shooting a glare at Lyk and Liv.

A toothy smile stretches across my face while I watch them tease one another. I agree wholeheartedly with Ruse; I've had enough coffee in me to last a week. Liv and Lyk can be little spicy demon sisters, which I've learned the hard way. Shuddering at the memory of them changing labels on all the spices at home, I slide in between Jace and Athena while Ruse moves to show Eira a video on his phone. Her face lights up in delight when he wraps an arm around her shoulder in greeting. Jace smiles and gives me a quick side hug. He's always been more physically affectionate than most, and I'll admit, a hug from a friend can scare my darker cynical thoughts scuttling away.

I feel a scalding heat and look up to see Ira narrowing her eyes at me from the café counter. That tells me everything I need to know: I don't know what I did, but I know I did something.

"Don't mind Ira tonight. She's had a horrendous week at work," Athena mutters to me.

Sliding a hand down my face, I let out a sigh. "Yeah, that makes both of us. Or all of us, probably. Ruse said you've been worried?" I whisper back to her.

After a quick peek to assure Eira is fully invested in the video, Athena turns to face me and brings out her own phone. I think this is an excuse to talk to me, but she surprises me when she pulls up a list of times and dates. "I've been recording when our fox acts peculiarly. If you click on each of these, you'll see a list of what specifically I noticed. These range from staring off into space for entire hours, avoiding food, appearing exhausted, and bringing up names of people we've never remotely heard of before. She has no idea I'm doing this. If you even breathe a whiff of this, I'll tell Liv and Lyk, and we'll all destroy you," she says sweetly.

"What's got your panties in a twist?" Ira says as she appears out of thin air next to us.

"All the Saints! You're terrifying, you know that?" I grumble at her.

"Yeah? Your face is terrifying enough for the lot of us, so you'll have to do better than that," she snaps back at me. She sweeps her hair over her shoulder, causing her necklace to shimmer with the movement. The star pendant she always wears matches the sharp glint in her eyes.

Irritation rolls through me as she turns to Athena. "I need to talk to you now, as in, *right now*. Bathroom?" The way she is tugging on Athena's elbow tells me this conversation isn't an option. As they make their way from the table, Astira stops to call back, "Oh, and Tryg? I hope to see you at the flow class later. Don't use this storm as an excuse. Lord knows you need the flexibility skills."

Jace and Ruse both howl with laughter, and Athena bites back a smile. She mouths back to me, "Horrendous week," before following Astira to the other side of the café. Eira rolls her eyes while Lyk and Liv stare me down. Yup, I don't know what I did, but I most definitely did *something*.

"Fucking yoga, stupid stretching, bullshit flow..." I mutter as Jace, Ruse, and I walk down the sidewalk to the studio.

"Bro, if you hate it so much, you don't have to come. No one will get upset." Jace laughs.

Easy for him to say. He's as easygoing as they come and goes with the flow. *He* wouldn't get upset because he's patient and charming and all the good fucking traits that apparently missed their mark with me.

"Of fucking course I have to go. Ira has a problem with me that she obviously won't say. Athena will make a smartass comment about how I'm spending my time drinking instead of 'connecting with my body.' Don't get me started on Lyk and Liv. And Eira? She would without a doubt be understanding, but I want to see her in those pants she insists on wearing to these classes," I groan.

"Ha! You mean, the pants that are called *yoga* pants? The

THE LIGHT WITHIN

ones that are designed for this specific kind of class? How strange of her," Ruse says while laughing.

His laughter scratches like sandpaper against my senses. I'm not in the mood to laugh or be near others anymore. It's a sensation I can never describe, the sudden urge to isolate myself, as if I'm cowering in fear of others' presence.

"Whatever. Let's get in there and keep me as far away from Ira as possible tonight," I tell them. She was helpful for work issues before, but clearly I've fucked up enough that any interactions will be sour.

Ruse is still laughing as he pulls open the studio door, and we are instantly greeted by a sweet-smelling smoke and heat. We are quick to remove our coats, scarves, and hats, and we place our shoes and socks on the shoe rack near the front desk. No one is up front to check us in, which means the teacher is already getting set up in the next room over. *Get a fucking grip. You can't avoid this the whole night.*

We gather our yoga mats and other supplies—all items that I haven't used in ages because I hate going to these classes—and head into the open studio. Wooden floors are covered in the others' yoga mats, and there's a huge, intricate painting on one of the walls. It's a bundle of lilies made of different animals and designs. I'm not in the mood to ask what it means and instead, shift my focus to preparing my mat next to Eira's. *Yeah, I want to see that ass of hers.* But she is also my safe person, and I know when I fumble with these poses, she won't be mean. She is a healer, a helper, a safe person for many.

As I'm about to walk over to join the others, an older woman wrapped in a shawl silently crosses into the room. Her gray hair reminds me of one of the gray wolves we hear near home. She has deep wrinkles layered over her tawny skin, and when I glance up at her face, I immediately see the laugh lines around her vivid blue-gray eyes and the brightness coming from them. She carries a blanket of joy and ease in that shawl of hers, and it's borderline uncomfortable to detect myself relax this much around a stranger. Eira and the others? They already know this lady and run to hug her before the class begins.

I notice a few other people lurking along the opposite wall. The strain of the war and unrealistic work expectations have been too much lately. They're probably equally as antsy as I am, which is superb. I know that I'm shitty, but I don't want to be alone with these feelings in my body, and sometimes, you need to see others in your same situation.

"Tryg, this is Shira. She is our yoga instructor and often comes by the clinic to teach trauma-informed yoga classes. *And* this impressive woman practices medicine. She's basically our all-knowing mother at this point," Eira laughs and turns me in the direction of the teacher. Shira has a kind smile, but those eyes—they see way too damn much. She peers straight into my soul. No one needs that kind of negativity, not at a yoga class.

I manage a small smile, which I'm sure comes across as a grimace, and say, "It's nice to meet you, Shira. This is my first yoga flow class, but I'm sure Eira and the gang will drag me to more."

She pauses before responding to me. I get the sense that she is reading more about my body language than I care for, and she says, "You're welcome here anytime, Tryg. Let's begin, everyone. I invite you to take a seat on your mats and get into any position that is most comfortable for you this evening. If you want to grab a blanket, now is a good time to grab one from the far wall over there. If you would prefer to lie down for this first meditation..."

Shira continues with her introduction and directions, but I'm already laying on my mat and tuning her out. I have a bad habit of sinking down into my thoughts while others are trying to talk to me. My thoughts race like a rabbit around me, consuming me into their depths. They run from war cases to my friends to drinking to wanting a cig to Ira to this new woman...

Hm, I wonder if that's what Ira is all upset about. The fact that my mind goes nonstop. I mean, she could also bother to communicate that she doesn't think I'm listening, but *oh ho,* that would be too much, wouldn't it? For a woman that smart, she sure lacks—

"Eira! Are you okay?!" a voice yells out.

My eyes fly open as my head whips in Eira's direction. She's a mere few feet away from me, but I was wildly consumed by my thoughts that I didn't even realize something was wrong. She is laying on the mat with one of those fancy wool blankets tucked around her. I'm barely able to stand it because she appears too small and fragile this way. Eira's eyes are open without seeing, a look of absolute horror etched through them. Her mouth is open in a silent scream and her neck muscles are severely tense, her shoulders arching upward. Moisture is already dripping down her face. I go to nudge her arm to gently wake her up from whatever the hell this is. Suddenly, she roughly seizes my arm, yanking me a breath away from her face.

"You don't get to touch me anymore," she growls, hatred flowing from her core.

NINE

Eira

*Our spirits long for soul-level connections.
We're not always prepared for what this includes, which often
leads to pushing away the positive connections in order to
avoid anything negative.
-Dr. Antonio Piernt,
Founder of Seeds of the Lotus*

Flowing from stretches to core work in this studio brings me a strong sense of peace. Shira is the absolute best. Period. She brings me into an inner serenity I didn't even know I could get to. I leave her classes empowered and strong and believing I'm the badass bitch I want to be. Tonight is no exception. I'm already lighter after seeing my friends tonight. This afternoon is not entirely forgotten, but I can finally breathe and have settled back into my body. I didn't realize how much tension was rippling deep in my muscles. If anyone can help me work these out, it'll be Shira.

She has us start on our mats, and while I would usually prefer to sit in lotus or easy pose, I'm too exhausted to fight the urge to lie down. There is some kind of warning bell in the back of my mind telling me to stay upright, but when I'm this tired, I try to listen to my body. It wants rest. Athena thinks what I'm going through could be part of burnout, which is entirely possible. It could also be related to the cramping pain I keep having along my abdomen, back, and uterus.

I stretch my body along the padded mat even more. Covering myself with one of the snug yoga blankets, I burrow into the thick purple and green blanket wrapped around me. I tell myself that I'll absolutely *not* fall asleep to the sound of Shira's lulling voice. But I need to rest. I'm not quite ready to close my eyes and instead glance back at the intricate mural behind me that extends up onto the ceiling.

Each creature forms a different petal of the lilies and lotuses, and they look abnormally vivid, so *alive*. My eyes dart from the hummingbird's bright feathers to the mountain lion's vicious snarl. I gaze at the coral and teal snake slithering through a vine, and my eyes finally land on the dark blue whale toward the bottom of the wall. This one's majestic and has dashes of light purple and golden starlight along its belly and tail. I imagine myself gliding down the tail to the middle of its back, swimming to face one of its gorgeous eyes. This particular whale has glowing cerulean eyes, and I can't help myself; I want to be near it. Already I'm absorbed in this image, totally aware that I'm not following Shira's meditation and yet unable to stop myself.

Water engulfs me as I twirl around the whale. My mind doesn't let my body know that I'm submerged in the salty ocean with no other company than the whale drifting near me. All I focus on is the glow of its eye and the beauty of its form. The water feels smooth on my skin—not warm, not cold, simply a soothing liquid. We're dancing through the tides; the bold blue vastness is our stage. The vibrations of another whale's call sing through me until I'm another sea creature. There are no humans, no buildings, no concept of time. I just am. Breathing.

Swimming. Deep and blue. Blue and deep. A wave curling into itself as I spray myself into existence.

The ocean waves are my lullaby, keeping me suspended in sleep on this makeshift bed made of blankets. My toes dig into the warm, black sand as my legs stretch out and my ankles roll. I go to reach my arms above me when my right arm hits a rock. No, a body. There's someone dozing next to me. They smell like salt water and sand and fresh fruit. Their skin against me heats mine from the inside out.

Blinking against the midday sun, I slowly open my eyes and turn toward this person beside me. They cough a grunting sound as I move closer against them and finally turn their face toward mine. After a few heavy breaths, their eyes peel open, and my world stops.

It's him.

Eyes richly dark, they look black, with silver and gold crackling in the irises. They stare back at me, but I can't be sure what I'm doing. I'm deliriously stuck in this moment, frozen with joy and bewilderment. I'm not sure of his name, but I know that it's him *and that he belongs to* me. *A piece of my soul. A gift from the sea, perhaps. All for me.*

I'm saturated with excitement and can't take my eyes off him. His braided brown hair drapes over his right shoulder. Strands dangle across his forehead. He scrunches his eyebrows in concern and his thick, plump lips open slightly. There are no words for what I'm experiencing. Utter happiness that I'm truly with him once again, as if we have spent lifetimes apart from one another. Yet that's not possible because I'm remembering now that our village is nearby, and we saw one another yesterday. And the day before that. And the weeks before that. We're mates and the leaders of this tribe, and the elders agreed to watch our children, so that we could relax together.

Oh. Oh, no. We need to rest because there have been attacks on the nearby villages. We've been working day and night to gather enough resources to sustain our tribe and create enough weapons for all those who can fight. The fear must cross my face because his hand is suddenly cupping my cheek, his thumb drawing soothing circles near my mouth. I let myself lean into his hand, into the love that he is quietly sending me. I close my eyes as I breathe in and sit up on my elbows, making us level with one another. Leaning forward, I go to kiss him, until I notice his slight smile and the sad tint to his eyes. I'm becoming too distracted to notice what's happening. The sun has hit his eyes just right and there are swirls of golden tan, dark brown, and ebony peering back at me, the silver and gold popping even brighter. Wait, why is he terribly sad?

An inch away from his lips, I draw in a ragged breath, a scream unable to leave me. Those beautiful eyes. They're bleeding. Ruby tears fall from black, shadowy pits, dripping down his face. It's almost a physical snap of pain as I'm torn from his arms. The black sand is nothing but ash dusting my bruised body. The smell of smoke surrounds me, and I can't see past the fog. I'm choking from the fire, the ash, the scalding pain moving through me. I turn to search for my mate, my beloved, and all I see are thick shadows in his place squirming toward me.

I scream out a crazed sound, rolling down the hill of ash and bones. That is when I hear them. What I thought were ocean waves was merely an illusion, a dream from a few days ago. The whooshing roar of the ocean is the groans of prisoners followed by shrieks from women and children. Oh! Oh, oh. My children! Are they here?! Did they escape? I come to a halt a dozen feet away from where I was. Gingerly putting weight on my hands and knees, which are swelling twice their size at this point, I go to crawl. I'll go anywhere that's not here. But first I need to find my children, my beautiful son and daughter.

A child wails in a tent not too far from where I'm crawling. There's a gurgling sound, which causes a fresh stab of terror to tumble through me. A harsh, cruel laugh rings out, followed by swift silence. I'm shaking from panic and choking on a sob. What happened to that baby? That couldn't have been mine, right? Why don't I know if that was my child?

Before I move an inch toward the tent, something pulls me back, causing me to land harshly on my back. I wheeze out, a puff of smoke rising from my mouth, as a man places pressure on my hips, keeping me held down. Blinking away the sting of pain, I glare up at my captor and realize it's the Evil Man. The one everyone in the village has talked about and feared. White paint surrounds his golden-brown eyes. His face is formed into a deep scowl. This is the one who slaughtered my family. The Evil Man who binds my wrists and ankles, forces liquids down my throat that put me to sleep, beats me, starves me.

I hate him. He hasn't stopped torturing me in days. None of us have it easy, but he's taken a special interest in hurting me. It's a sick game that I'll never be allowed to win. I don't even know the rules. Another child cries out, taking my focus from my own fear and replacing it with raw flames. His calloused hand grabs my right arm, and I'm wildly angry, I'm nowhere near thinking straight. No! He will NOT harm me again! I'll take my own life before succumbing to him forcing himself on me again.

Finding strength I didn't realize I had, I take hold of his other arm, pulling him down to my face. His eyes widen in shock, not expecting me to still be functioning and alert.

"You don't get to touch me anymore," I growl in his scarred face. I swiftly pull the knife from his waist and—

"Eira!"

TEN
Nyx

*To blame others for the chains we shackle around our heart is
a disservice to not only our souls but those around us.*
-Cajsa, Goddess of Spirit

Like a knife to my heart, I'm startled awake as my heart flings up to my throat, beating as if it's a fluttering, trapped bird. The scent of smoke and piercing screams wrap around me in a haze. There are no words for how stunned I am. I battle with my mind, both needing to leave the dream but also wanting to stay. There are too many *feelings*. It's enough to make me dizzy, especially when I'm normally exclusively hyper-aware of my physical state and current environment.

My physical form is a hardened shell, littered with scars and reopened wounds. Perspiration glistens along my body, and my hair is knotted in layers around my face. Every muscle is still throbbing with a deep-rooted ache from what I had to endure this afternoon. I see a few small creatures crawl over the rusted chains scattered throughout my room. *More of a scummy dungeon than anything, really*.

None of that matters, though. I didn't realize I could still perceive anything beyond pain and torment, let alone what I just experienced. How could such raw feelings of love still exist in a monster such as myself? When I think of the woman from my dream, the sensation inside me becomes molten heat and muffled affection. It's dripping like honey from my chest down to my toes. Completely unexpected, yet so damn *intoxicating*. I'm waking up but not from the usual nightmare. And I can't stop thinking of those silver and blue eyes and how, when the sun hits them, they're the same as shimmering shards of crystal and ice.

My thoughts are surrounding me, suffocating me. *Who was she? How do I find her? Was she even real? How do I travel back to this dream? Was it solely a dream?*

I lay on the cool stone slab of my makeshift bed for what must be hours. Lost in the fog of my dream and spiraling into such gaping, forgotten emotions. It's unbearable to encounter anything positive after years of pain, suffering, and numbness. Rinse and repeat those three feelings. Every minute, every hour, every day of this miserable fucking life. I want to reach into my mind and throttle this woman, whoever she is, because who the fuck is she to shine light into my life when she isn't even real.

My arms instinctively wrap around myself as I turn to face the gated window. Moonlight glows into my room. It's soft and buttery and illuminates the thick moisture along the walls. It must have rained, bathing us all in humid air. Between the glow of the moon and the comfort of this rain, it's as if I'm a child again, staring out from the rooftop after a storm. My mother and I always did that together. It's been too long since I've felt this vulnerable, and honestly, it makes me sick with loathing. Vulnerabilities are nothing but weaknesses, and that's the last thing I need right now.

For this moment, though, I allow myself to feel held, even if I'm cradled against a slab of stone and blanketed in my chains. Eyes drooping closed and chasing the lingering hint of comfort I imagined, I let myself fall into the hallowed darkness within myself. But when I expect to see black, I'm greeted with silver and blue crystals staring right through me.

I've barely closed my eyes when there's a tug on my chains. My wounds still aren't fully healed—*lucky me*— and the metal glides right into the bloody wounds. Abrupt pain sluices its way through me. They're a reminder of what happens when I give in to the endless pool of anger, the need to attack a soul related to the Council too irresistible to ignore. The pain is worth it, though. Even if it awakens my inner demon, and I'm forced to chain myself down until the bloodlust passes.

The demon itself will never leave me. It's too ingrained in my soul at this point, ever since that fateful night when I lost control of my powers. These chains barely contain me as it is—at least I don't run wild in a mass of terror and shadows and smoke, feasting on any soul that comes my way. I won't further spread this fucked up plague of darkness unless I see a soul related to the Council members who did this to me.

Then my demon and I can't resist bathing in their tainted blood.

I'm unfortunately alert yet weighed down with the heaviness of a bruised and battered body. A second tug of my chains has me grumbling and twitching out of their reach. I'll never understand how hard it is to wake a soul up. They could try a simple greeting, maybe humming, or I don't know, maybe knocking on the fucking door and not waltzing in here. The third tug drives me to full on agitation. My blood boils, my eyes near popping out of my head from how irritated I feel.

I lunge outward and hear a stifled shriek, followed by something falling on the floor. Cracking my neck, I glance in the direction of the sound, ready to slap them out of their misery. As I raise my hand, I hear a whimper.

"Oh, no, no, no, no. Please Nyx. It's me!" Fraya whisper-yells at me.

Big hazel eyes peer at me full of mild terror and wariness. Her short hair frames her sharp chin and pouty mouth, and it falls in front of her face as she sits back on her knees. Fraya is already petite, but on her knees she comes across even tinier from this angle. My gaze traces the exposed tanned skin under her scraps of dark clothing. When I look back at her face, I see her biting down on her lower lip, the emotion in her eyes changing from fear to thrill. Fraya knows how enraged I get when I'm shackled down, which I've been doing more and more recently as a precaution more than anything. She knows my entire being screams to rip free of my flesh. I want nothing more than to revel in my strength and chase down creatures, *anything*, until I'm sinking my teeth into their blood. Just thinking about it stirs a low growl in my chest, my breath becoming more uneven by the second.

Fraya also knows that during these moments, it relieves me to drown myself in anything sexual and physical. Not that I don't normally enjoy a good fuck, but it's different during these surges of madness. I'm not quite myself and have given myself over to the beast within. I've told her a hundred times now that this will never be a true relationship, especially when she takes advantage of me. And the day I find my fated other half, what we call our *almaove*, none of this will continue. Fraya always annoyingly rolls her eyes with a smirk when I bring this up. She doesn't believe in *almaoves* and prides herself in choosing her own romantic path. She thinks the more we have sex, the stronger our physical connection will grow until I choose to stay with her.

The whole fucking reason I even manage to maintain a friendship with her is because I know part of this is her demon's doing. Any of us touched by the plague of darkness has to deal with a monstrous, demonic form that can take over at any point. It's initially a separate entity; it wedges itself into our souls as a disease and becomes a part of us. Until we can no longer tell the difference between our souls and the demons we become. Hers officially hatched in the depths of her soul when her soul father, one of the main family members she could trust, unknowingly caught the plague. In an uncontrollable act of lust, he forced himself on her. Over and over and over again.

By the time he realized what he'd done, it was too late for Fraya. She had been destined for the healer's path due to her ability to sense *everything* another soul experiences. When the plague spread into her, the demon sunk its grimy claws into her empathetic heart, and now the moment she senses another soul's negative feelings, she matches their energy. Fraya starts off wanting to show love and care, and then becomes completely unhinged, lost to every sensual feeling and negative emotion.

It puts me in a horrible position. I don't want her to be chained down at all times, but none of our group has been able to figure out a way for her to manage these crazed outbursts. And I can't fucking take being taking advantage of anymore. I *can't*. I've done terrible things since I met my own demon, but that doesn't mean I've given into it yet. I yearn to be healed, to be saved, to be understood.

And Fraya can only push her luck with a banished prince for so long until I fucking *snap*.

I manage to shake off the blood lust and am about to tell her that she needs to leave before we do anything I'll regret. It's best for everyone if I stay alone in this room until the suns rise and their light chases away some of my shadows. My beast does not always understand friend from foe, and *damn*, I hate taking these chances. *What if I rip Fraya into scattered pieces? What if I kill her and manage to escape the chains?* As I'm about to open my mouth to tell her these thoughts, Fraya crawls onto my lap and places a finger over my lips.

"Shh," Fraya whispers as she wraps one of the chains around my neck. "Let me ease some of the tension in your body. Let me give you my blood to take the edge off."

I instantly recoil. "No! We've talked about this before. I don't want a relationship with you and never want to take blood from my *friends*. And that's what we are, Fay. We're friends. And you're better than this. Please. *Please* don't do this to me."

Fraya manipulates me like it's an art. She's too clever and is always one step ahead of me. Or rather, my beast. She already made a cut on her finger and slowly traces the blood along my lips. *Fuck*, my beast can't resist the taste of this. My tongue darts out to get a lick. My control slips out of my grasp similar to rain drops dripping through my fingers.

Too quickly, my body morphs into what I hate most. The chains choke my expanding muscles as if corded rope, causing a pressure to build under my skin. I can't transform into a nightmare of claws and bloodied muscle and shadows when they're shackled to me. It's entirely too painful and smothering. I pray to the gods that will listen to put a stop to this, never eager to give in to this particular form of sin. A garbled scream is pulled from me, not entirely my own voice. A part of me is still trying to fight this, to resist.

Darkness gathers at the edges of my sight and slithers around my ankles and up through my body. My body grows larger, bones clack, and blood weeps down my grizzled cheeks.

Before I blink, one of my claws is ripping her tattered clothes, since Fraya stupidly unlocked one of the chains. Her look is too hungry, too desperate. A lust she'll never be able to hold on to in the end. Fuck, it's a swirl of blood and shadows and thrashing misery against my skull. It's always easier to just. Let. Go. A flicker inside of me tries to hold on to my soul. The part of me that wilts each time this happens and curls into itself, soaked in unshed tears. It pushes against Fraya's energy as her fingers trail down my arms. It's depressing that I'm not strong enough to fight this, and as this emotion settles downward, I'm sliding quickly to the darker parts of my mind and soul.

I close in on myself, letting the beast have full control.

Down, down, down I go. Into my own pocket of shame where I hide from what I've become. I twist and turn, tangled up in a torrent of despair and anger clinging to me. When I hit the bottom, there's a flicker of surprise.

I open my eyes to murkiness and am greeted again with silver and blue staring back at me, cutting through me to the center of who I am.

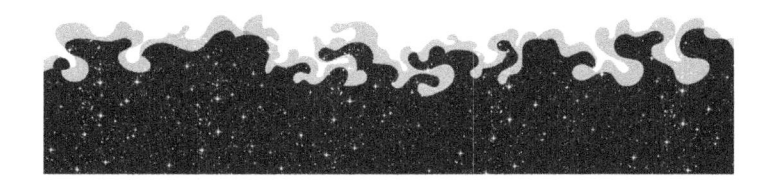

ELEVEN

Eira

Trust is a fickle thing in a nation founded on death.
-Recovered passage from Religion and War, Volume III

The center of my solar plexus trembles with the last of the emotions. In a flash, I'm back in the yoga studio. Any voices and sounds are muted, as if I'm stuck underwater, pinned by the weight of the whale. I sense movement scattering around the room and the weight of a body directly above me. Cold sweat coats my entire body as if a layer of frost, puckering my pale skin. I gasp for air, sucking it down greedily as my chest heaves from what must be a panic attack. The taste of ash still coats my swelling tongue, making it difficult to calm my breath and ease any lingering fear.

And anger. There is fresh anger hiding in the recesses of my dream, as if it doesn't control my very life. I squeeze my eyes shut —I'm too scared to open them and face what I experienced.

The sound of my name echoes around me, and I feel the worry settle in the air. This might not be the same dream. I might be back in reality, but I'd be kidding myself if I thought I had a hold on this concept. I barely know what is real and not anymore. Finally registering my name, my eyes fly open, bulging when I realize that I'm tightly holding onto Tryg's bulky arm. He is tense above me, eyes wide with terror as his gaze wanders along my body, appearing to check for any pain or injuries. *There's that golden brown again. Why do these eyes haunt me?*

I'm not sure what he'll find when I don't even know what's going on myself.

I shakily detach myself from Tryg's torso and fall back onto the mat with a grunt. Entrenched aches rage along my muscles, causing me to curl in on myself. An uncontrolled whine escapes me when the pain reaches from my toes to my head, like a domino effect. My calves ripple with cramps, as if I've been running for *days*. Total exhaustion consumes me similar to the smoke of a forest fire and clogs my veins with lethargy. I curl deeper into myself, willing my body to disappear into nothingness if it means the aches will subside. *I must look rather shrimpy right now, the same as cute little Zaya when she curls up in a ball. A perspiring, exhausted shrimp. Hmph.*

Before I wallow in self-pity, someone is draping a fuzzy blanket over me and picking me up. I try to tell them that I'm fine, to let the shrimp be, but I'm sure all that comes out is a mumbly mess of incoherent sounds. The blanket cocoons me like a freshly rolled burrito—*maybe I'm a little hungry*—and I'm cradled in the warmth of a broad chest and muscled arms. The scents of mint and lavender envelope me, and I sigh as I snuggle in closer to whoever is holding me.

"I have an inkling of what is going on with her, but we need to be careful with how we approach this," a voice rings out.

"I don't think she should go back to sleep right now. Based on what she shared with me today, this seems to trigger whatever is going on," a voice says.

"She isn't even coherent. Should we take her to the hospital?" someone offers.

"No. That would be a terrible idea. The last thing she needs is to be watched and monitored by a hoard of doctors and scientists. Let's take her to my private clinic," the first voice decides.

"We're all coming with you. Don't try to stop us," someone else says sharply.

"Tryg, she never said we couldn't come with. Stop being an ass," somebody cuts in.

"An ass?! You weren't the one she growled at. I'm making sure we're all there when she gets answers. I *need* answers!" the voice yells.

Voices loop back and forth, pinging between my ears. I want to tell them to stop and wrap another blanket around me. They can also bring me food because I'm *starving*. Shivering despite the warmth around me, I try to tell whoever is holding me that I don't feel so good. I'm not sure what kind of nonsense I mumble. The person cradling me whispers what sounds reassuring, and before I can blink, my vision tunnels and the world fades to black.

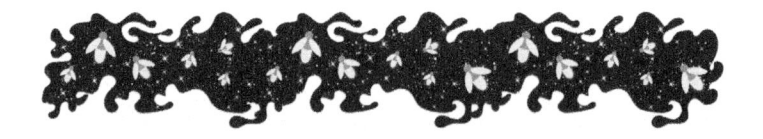

A damp cloth presses against my forehead. A drop of water rolls down my face like a tear. My body is loose and light, and I sense that I'm propped up on several comfortable pillows. It still feels as if my mind is sinking into a pit of mud, and it's nearly impossible to form actual words at this moment. This experience reminds me of the time, long ago, when Tryg dared me to stuff as many cotton balls as possible into my mouth in ten seconds. He boasted an idiotic record of fifty cotton balls, and naturally, I had to beat him. He had laughed unbelievably hard when the wad of cotton nearly choked me to death. Spit had dripped out of my mouth the more I tried to yell at him, and the whole situation ended with us throwing gross wads at one another. *Disgusting*.

Pushing the memory aside, I force myself to open my eyes and take in my current surroundings. I'm surprised to see medical equipment on both of my sides. A clear liquid is slowly dripping into my veins and the heart monitor beats at a steady rhythm. *Hey, at least I got that going for me.* This room doesn't appear or smell like a traditional hospital room, though. It's more of a cozy bedroom than anything. Gauzy pink and blue curtains frame the two windows, slightly blocking the view of dense forest and nightfall. Glowing candles and stacks of books sit on end tables beneath each window. Directly ahead of me, I see a huge framed art piece of a naked woman peering up at the night sky. Her rich, chocolate hair fans around her in a bed of wildflowers and prairie grass. At first, she appears as a woman, but I see her hands and feet are replaced with hooves, and there are antlers weaving out of her head. Her eyes are orchids with crescent moons as the pupils. *Trippy.*

I'm so invested in this artwork, I don't hear when Shira quietly opens the door.

"This was gifted to me almost fifty years ago," she says. Me being me, I nearly jump off the bed from fright. She gives me a small smile. "The creature's name is Theona, and she tends to have a calming effect on the patients who come to me for alternative medicinal care. I decided it was best to keep her close."

Shira pads over to my bed and places down a mug on the table to my left. She gives a cursory glance at the machines surrounding me before tucking the blankets closer under my feet and legs. She rubs a small circle on my feet before she tucks the rest of the blanket in under my hips and torso. I don't think I've ever seen her hair down before, and it hangs in a thick silver wave around her shoulders. Shira's eyebrows are drawn in concentration as she fluffs the sides of my pillows and examines my eyes and face.

"I brought you one of my healing green teas," she tells me, which in itself has me perking up. They're tremendously rare ever since Innmartana was destroyed. "Your vitals are alright so far, but you certainly gave us quite the scare tonight."

Shira's voice is tender and kind, a tone I'm too familiar with. I speak in this same way when one of my clients experiences a crisis. Parts of her face give her away, though. There's a glint of worry in her eyes and her lips are slightly pursed.

"I know that look. Please be honest—what's happening to me?" I ask her.

She bites down on the corner of her bottom lip as her head shakes slowly from side to side. Shira manages to be simultaneously present and lost deep in thought. "I have a theory of what's happening, but I'm not sure you will believe or understand it," Shira says. "You know my medical practice incorporates both the western and eastern medicines from long ago mixed with today's teachings. Some, well... *many*, disagree with my openness to different exercises and views on managing health, but it has never failed me. I'm able to bear witness to physical, emotional, mental, and spiritual illnesses and pain. Which means I'm now better prepared to help people heal and grow in all four parts of themselves. And I've seen your situation before. Years ago. But the signs are the same..." she trails off, engrossed in her train of thought.

"I'm confused. It's fine with me what you practice, but what do you call what is happening to me right now? Can you give me a name?" I ask her.

"That's the thing—there is no name for what you're experiencing," she replies while grasping my hand. Hers is incredibly warm, I didn't even realize how cold I felt. "This is common yet not discussed in our culture. You're having dreams and nightmares that feel vividly real, your body is literally experiencing the same sensations and physical impact that you dream about. Your body is immensely drained right now because it was this drained in your dream. You woke up starving because in your dream, you were being starved. And while your vitals are normal, your spiritual self continues to fade the more realistic these dreams become. I know deep in my bones that you're physically impacted, and in ways, also completely fine. You're mentally and emotionally changing the more you experience these dreams, or should I say, visions. I am positive that the most impacted aspect is your soul. I can't be sure where you're going, spiritually."

None of this makes any sense to me. Shira has a hard, severe look in her eyes as she gazes down at my body. She is serious about what she is telling me. It's akin to being told you have a rare diagnosis or stage IV cancer. Shira grips my hand tighter, stress evident from her fingers to the tips of her toes.

"I know this is a lot to take in right now, Eira. And this isn't what you signed up for. But I'm going to ask if you can rest in my care for a few days while I study more resources and consult with others in my field. I want to keep an eye on how you're doing and see if more of these dreams and nightmares come up. Is that okay with you?" Shira asks me.

I'm honestly bewildered, which says a lot because I've always been a bit of an overthinking basket case. It doesn't remotely make sense that I would physically experience what is happening in my dreams. I don't even want to know what Shira means by me going somewhere *spiritually*. There are gods people believe in here, but the borders of our countries change every few years; I never know which one is the god for me.

During the time humans lived underground, the traditional religions splintered into a hundred different pieces. No one knew what to believe in when half of the world was blasted into nothingness, and they were pushed to live in the unknown. New gods were born, some morphed from the original texts that people kept close to their hearts and others designed by new generations after centuries of living on their own. I can't be sure which ones are real or fabricated. The only thing that stayed constant was the belief of hell, except even that I'm skeptical of. I can't imagine another realm could be worse than our own. A planet full of blind fools willing to kill off their own species and cause irreparable damage to the world. A place where war is normalized and citizens are used.

Perhaps this is the hell everyone speaks of, and we've been in a different reality this whole time.

My brain immediately latches onto anything tangible, such as the idea of burnout or one of my many physical conditions, and my muscles relax. Shira can search for whatever she wants, but I'm sure this is physically explainable, and maybe I just need a few days off work to get actual rest.

"I trust you. You do whatever you need to do, Shira," I say. "Especially if any of it involves keeping me wrapped up in coziness and you bringing me food."

Shira snorts. "Yes, I'm aware of how much you love to eat, even when you're not hungry. Especially when you're not hungry! I'll go get you the soup I made, and then I'll let your friends in to see you. They were planning on barging through the door right when you woke up, but I distracted them with a dinner announcement. All of you, huh? All of you eat and eat and eat." She laughs.

"That's okay," Shira continues. "Food can be the pathway to the heart. I convinced them to grab the leftover dinner I had in the fridge, so they could better support you. I'll get you your own dinner now, and then you can see everyone. They are quite eager to speak with you, but I want to know that you are adequately fed and rested before being bombarded with a million questions."

Shira squeezes my hand before she stands up. She smooths down barely noticeable wrinkles in her shirt and pants. Giving me one more glance before she heads out, she walks back to the door and nearly trips as she opens it.

"Why are you all crowding the doorway, as if you're animals?! Go eat your soup at the table like humans, not on the floor as critters," she scolds as she steps into the hallway.

"But both critters and humans *are* animals, Shira," a voice snarks out. "They might as well be the same thing."

I hear a huff of annoyance as the door clicks closed. I can't help but laugh. I have no idea what's going on. The past, the present, and the future are horrifically overwhelming, but at least I'm not alone. If anyone can help me figure this out, it'll be Shira. And knowing the gaggle of friends slurping soup right outside my door, they will also be investigating this, bringing their raunchy humor along for the ride.

TWELVE

Nyx

It's rather interesting, isn't it?
Even those consumed by their demons tend to
flock together like a family of demonic birds.
-Council Member Enik,
Grand Commander of Waterfalls

What a fucked ride of a night, high on blood lust and brittle rage. My body craves actual rest, but apparently, the day has other plans for me. It's late into the morning, and rays of sunlight cascade through the window, roasting my skin as if for a feast. The usual icy wind is nonexistent and has been replaced by a humid breeze. I guzzle down the hydrating *lipva*, drops of it dripping down the grooves of my body and pooling in the cuts not yet scabbed. I push my tangled hair out of my face only to find crusted blood on my forehead. If the sweat and dried blood doesn't do it, the rancid smell emanating from me will surely kill me. All this wraps around my senses, causing my eyes to tear up in exhaustion. It doesn't feel as if I even slept.

THE LIGHT WITHIN

Fraya is draped against the corner of the room next to a pile of chains. She's naked. Of course she's fucking naked. Revulsion curls in my mouth as I scan her body. Tender purple and black bruises pepper her skin like someone used her body as a canvas. Grinding my teeth so hard I'm surprised nothing cracks, I push myself forward onto my feet and use the window ledges to keep my balance as I stand. Squinting, I gaze out at the lands surrounding this home we've created. Rolling hills of blooming flowers surround the half-destroyed building, giving way to a lake. Its turquoise waters shimmer the same as a jewel under the scorching sky and show the reflection of multicolored grasses and mountain peaks in the distance. A few *dayre* peacefully graze next to the lake, velvet antlers sprouting from their foreheads.

Breathtaking beauty swaddles our crumbling, stony home that houses those who've been abandoned and shunned—creatures of darkness. The irony is not lost on me.

There's a number of *solliqas*, the souls here in Majikaero, cooped up in this broken home in Reykashin. All banished from their homes when they were touched by the plague of darkness. The plague itself started centuries ago but has been uncontainable in recent years. It's the worst kind of disease a soul could catch. It fucking affects each *solliqa* uniquely and is as contagious as the dark itself, born from pain and sorrow and trauma specific to each soul. The disease eats away at the soul until the *solliqa* turns into a monstrous demon, typically a reflection of the pain and trauma it faced.

Misery attracts fellow swarms of misery, meaning all it takes is for the *solliqa* to face any form of anguish, and it's at risk of catching the plague. If a soul already has the sickness and forces more pain on another, they're absolutely fucked.

Seven of us banded together through this plague, though, and have formed an unbreakable bond. We each hail from a different region in our realm and had previously connected due to our positions or destined paths while visiting the capital, Rioa, for events and meetings with the Council.

I was mostly based on Drageyra, the Land of Fire, and am the prince who played with fire—a little too much, if the Council has anything to say about it. Hadwin comes from Eikenbien, the Land of Woods. His *maji* powers are of the earth, and he can shift into *anything* one finds in the woods and has the ability to communicate through the soil. I swear, he has other secret powers up his sleeve, but we'll never know for sure until he is eventually cleansed of the plague. Shymeira, the Land of Tropics, is where Fraya spent time as a young soul. The Council was eager to get their hands on such a talented healer, yet look how easily she was tossed aside.

The last of our group consists of Ivar, Ulf, Odin, and Erika. Ivar is from Wyndera, the Land of Wind, and he was set to lead the Archers and Forces of Wind after his father's soul was unexpectedly destroyed. Ulf comes from Myrellden, the Land of Darkness, which is no surprise to anyone. He might be struggling with the darkness of the plague, but he was born of the night. Ulf specializes in shifting, especially his infamous shadow wolf, and has a strong connection to the stars and the ability to find other realms. Extending way beyond Earth, where humans live. Even past the realm on the other side of Earth, Cudhellen, where demons originated and still torment souls. He might be the one I thought the Council would prioritize saving, since some of his gifts are especially rare.

Except one of his gifts is *too* rare. We're similar in that we can truly send a soul spiraling away from Majikaero to another world entirely, which the Council doesn't enjoy. Not at all. It doesn't matter that we've never willingly tried to harm any *solliqa* in such a severe way. At least, not until the plague spread through us like poison. It's almost funny how distressed the Council acted when they first learned about the other hidden elements of our *maji*. They had no idea what was coming for our realm and how many others would be able to cause such destruction as the plague continues to affect each *solliqa's* powers.

Odin and Erika are soul brother and sister and come from Lagunit, the Land of Many Waters. Odin was coveted for quite a while with his talent for manipulating time, and Erika was already commanding the Forces of Water. They can also shift into other forms, although they're different from Ulf. Ulf can manifest into *anything*, at least when he didn't have the plague. Odin can move between creatures of the air and water, and Erika can shift into and manipulate any creature of the sea. There are times when I swear she is the ocean itself.

We have yet to find any *solliqas* we know personally from Reykashin, Rioa, Sayfters, Skugvaytir, Sunnadyn, or Viorfelle. Souls are either being abolished or scattered to isolated parts of the realm, such as here in Reykashin, the Land of Smoke.

Similar to the other *solliqas* banished, we all grouped together based on our shared history. It's been us against the realm, going back and forth between trying to find a way out of this mess and giving into our savage urges. One of the main reasons none of us has fully transformed into an unrecognizable monstrous beast, even with all the trauma and continuous torture, is because we're holding on for our fucking lives. We have to.

Each of us was on a mission when the plague was still in its early stages, still controllable. And we *can't* let ourselves give in until we accomplish what we each set out to do. I know Ulf is the closest to giving in completely, but he won't. Not when he was so close to building a path to other worlds.

The worst part about it all is that it feels as if the Council and leaders have purposely given up on us, even when they knew most of us were trying to make changes for the better in Majikaero. It's certainly easier for them to send us to an isolated region full of uncontrollable creatures and smoke *maji* than it is to give the resources to try healing us. *Fuckers*.

The door creaks open, a subtle screech scratching at my eardrums. Hadwin's bulky form fills the whole doorway. His aureate eyes light up when they meet mine.

"Oh, terrific—you're awake. I was afraid I'd have to force you up again. Maybe I could've tossed Fraya back on you," Hadwin says as he waltzes into the room. He insists on walking around without a top covering, leaving his gilded black and green tattoos on full display. Each of them slowly getting eaten up by inky black markings, the unquestionable markers of the plague. They climb up his arms and torso in different patches, many in large spots and others similar to large veins or the roots of a tree.

I have my own markings on me, burned into me like a branded scar. Our whole group has been marked in fucked ways.

Tendrils of anger seep out of my neck and arms, ready to lash out at my command. I'm not the only one Fraya takes advantage of, and while everyone is bothered by it, most make some kind of joke in order to cope. Because we're all fucked up here. "Fuck both of you," I growl out. "Toss her into the lake for all I care. Get her away from me."

"Aw, come on, you know she loves you. This is how she shows affection, going through the same pain as you and making your beast happy, as nonsensical as it is," Hadwin tries to reason.

"It's fucking stupid. *Look* at her body. She's practically buried in bruises. Affection has nothing to do with it. She finds me when I'm at my most dangerous and vulnerable," I growl.

Hadwin shoots me a pitying glance. We all have our own demons, and there's hardly anything he or anyone else can do when the monsters all come out to play. Last night was even worse. I took the necessary precautions and chained myself to this room, as I often do. While I did this, Fraya, Hadwin, Ivar, Ulf, and the others were hit with a sudden urge to give into their shadowed monsters. It was a force so deadly sharp, it must have been riddled with curses. We don't usually lose ourselves on the same night, and I'm determined to figure out the reason behind this. Today. *Something* has been wringing us out, bleeding our sanity dry, causing us to go blind with madness. Last night was the final straw.

I sigh and rub my temple, already noticing a headache knocking at the entrance of my mind. "Take her back to her room and make sure she gets cleaned up. Send D'lia to check in on her and tend to any wounds," I tell Hadwin.

"What are you going to do?" he asks as he bends to scoop Fraya up in his arms, the glowing, tattooed leaves on his upper arms rippling with the movement.

"I look, feel, and smell like a week-old corpse. Don't give me that face, you know it's true. I'm horrendous right now. I'm going to bathe and take care of these reopened cuts. I'll meet you downstairs for food in a bit," I say. "I can't think clearly with this fucking stench."

"This is going to be one of those dramatic and moody kind of days, isn't it?" Hadwin mutters as he walks out the door.

With the flick of my wrist, a wisp of a shadow shoots out to flick his back. Hadwin yelps and sends me a heated glare before stomping toward Fraya's room. Grimacing, I turn back to watch the ripples of the lake. When you're brimming over the edge with fresh rage, it's indeed a moody kind of day. *Fuck*.

"You're honestly the most confusing being I've ever met," Ivar mumbles.

I snort, rolling my eyes, and snatch a hunk of meat and a handful of berries off the table. He's referring to the scalding bath I forced myself into. Sometimes when I'm achingly consumed by black flames inside, the way to bring me back is to burn even hotter on the outside. I crave to burn the night's sins away until I'm left with nothing but embers. I can handle those. They bite just enough to keep me focused on the task at hand while leaving me with a breath to maintain control.

Ivar couldn't possibly understand this. His demons run violently wild with the wind. He even sits at the table with such poise and lightness, as if he could be carried away on the breeze. Shadows and smoke don't strangle him. Fire doesn't ignite from a molten core. In many ways, Ivar is free. His issue is staying grounded enough and not withering away into nothingness, gone to the wind as if he never existed.

"Ignore him—if he wants to bathe in his sweat and more heat, who the fuck cares?" Ulf says around a mouthful of food. "Better him than us." Ulf's pitch-black markings travel up his arms and neck. They move as he swallows, giving the illusion they're choking him. *Maybe they are.*

"I'm saying he's confusing. And since we apparently need to investigate whatever shittery last night was, it might be easier if he's not stoking the flames at this point," Ivar counters.

"Oh, his flames are getting stoked. Or rather, *stroked*." Hadwin smirks as he plops down next to me.

"*Ugh*, fuck off," I mumble. "We've got to get her under control. This can't keep happening."

"That might be a good place to begin. We can come up with a new game plan and strategies for our demons in case last night continues to happen," Erika suggests. She and Odin bring decanters of various liquids and freshly baked pastries to the table. Steam sizzles from the top of the pastries and thick cheese oozes out the sides. These are the moments when I'm grateful to all the gods that our world is so close to the realm of Earth. Those souls long ago figured out how to take the most divine dishes from Earth and elevate them to another level in Majikaero.

"Yup, that'd be the smart thing to do. We'll be pretty useless if we continue to wake up essentially too hungover from a drunken night of pain to do anything. That even might be their plan," Odin says.

"*Their* plan?" Ulf asks. His thick eyebrows scrunch together, wrinkling the black intricate design tattooed across his face. "Who in Cudhellen is 'their?'"

"No clue." Erika shrugs, tossing her sleek black and blue hair behind her. "But it's a little too suspicious that *all* of us were out of control last night, at the exact same second."

A discomfited silence stretches over the length of the table. It settles into us and not even the heavenly taste of Vaira's cooking can chase it away. Last night was agony for this whole house, and we're all tense for our own reasons. I had the sense to chain myself before I involuntarily shifted, which happened because this *always* is the plan for my condition. The others have lapses in control but not nearly as often as I do. Especially when I encounter anyone even remotely related to the Council. *Lucky, joyous me.*

Hadwin was crawling in pain in a field nearby, trying to bury himself in the dirt. Ulf shifted into his wolf form and wreaked havoc through the woods and into the closest village, which is impressive considering how far away that is from us. Erika and Odin almost drowned in the turquoise lake, other lifeforms having risen to the surface, bloated with poison. Fraya could have fallen victim anywhere, but she has the strongest connection to me and that is the pain she was drawn to last night. Ivar was forced into his bird form and nearly died after being pushed by his own winds into a cliff. The few others that consistently live here had their own troubles, but they were nothing near to what our main group experienced.

What happened last night almost seems *too* intentional. As if someone or something wanted us gone.

I pour the crimson liquid from the black decanter into a

mug in front of me. Taking a long sip, I revel in its tangy, sharp notes. Vaira doesn't exclusively know her way around the kitchen—she also knows the best concoctions to wake us up, forcing us to feel alive again. It burns slightly as it travels down my body, but in a refreshing way. It's healing. Licking my lips, I roll my shoulders before grabbing the parchment at the end of the wavy, curved table.

Erika's right. We need to get a handle on anchoring ourselves before we can get too carried away with figuring out what even happened. Whoever or whatever is behind this, wants us at our weakest. They want us to be fragile. Well, *fuck them*. That's what makes us so damn powerful. When you're already shunned for something out of your control, your mask cracks until all you're left with is a fragile powder, a fine dust. And we used that dust to rebuild and mold ourselves into a fierce and unstoppable force. Unbeatable. And now, angrier.

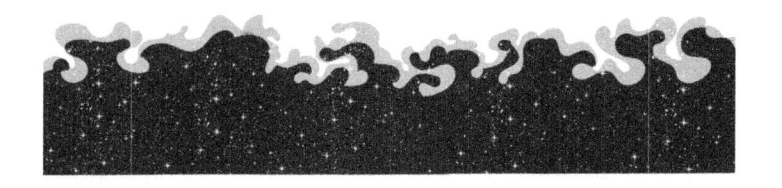

THIRTEEN
Tryq

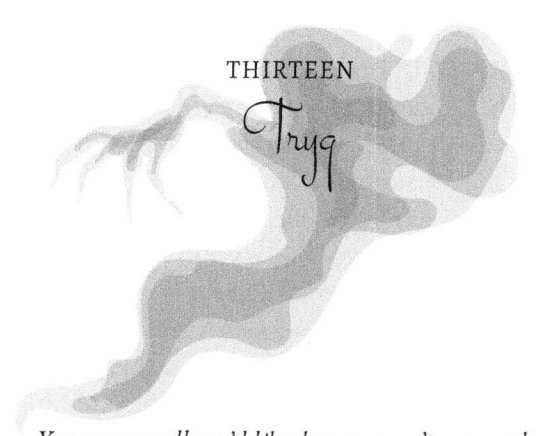

You can run all you'd like, but you won't outrun the
emotional turmoil your body throws at you.
-Anikita Longail,
Assistant Commander of Sweazn Investigative Forces

Anger barrels its way through me, enveloping me in its sweet sickness. I'm already stomping through Shira's living room when I hear my name being called from behind me. My shoulder knocks into a metal arc floor lamp, and I'm irritated that an object this sleek manages to take up the entire corner of the room. I pass the tan wraparound couch, nearly stubbing my toe on the stupid wooden end table next to it, when a hand lightly grips my arm. I snarl over my shoulder and let my feelings of betrayal and anger leap from my skin to the person who thinks it's a smart idea to touch me right now.

"Hun, I know that's not what you wanted to hear, but I need to consider what is best for Eira right now," Shira says. Her eyes show warmth and compassion, but her tone is stern and full of warning. No-nonsense. It doesn't matter that I'm a good two feet taller than her. She manages to show both love and concern and still look down her nose at me.

"Based on what Athena shared with me and Eira's reaction to you after waking up, I don't think it's an opportune time for you to be near her right now. After the next few days pass, and we can get a better idea of what's going on, she'll be free to come and go. There will be plenty of time to visit with her," Shira continues. "I understand that you of all people won't react kindly to this command, let alone being commanded, but please consider our Eira here. We don't want to unnecessarily trigger her again after significant physical distress."

"I don't give a *fuck*. She's *my* best friend. She's going to be safe with me around and as lead investigator, I'll be more help here than anywhere else right now," I snap at her.

"And she's *my* patient and is currently in my care. This isn't all about you, you know. You'll be more help checking your ego at the door next time you come through here," Shira whips back.

I recoil as if she slapped me and tossed a bucket of icy water on my head.

"I want to be with my friend. I'm terrified of what's happening to her, and you're kicking me out of your home," I mumble.

"I know," Shira responds, her tone shifting back to compassion. "But what Eira needs right now is space from everyone and to focus on what these dreams might mean. It'll be difficult for her to do this if she is crowded by others, no matter how much they love her. It'll be especially difficult if she gets triggered again without the appropriate amount of space to heal from it. *Please*, trust me. I'm a yoga instructor, but the work I'll be doing with her is my life's passion. Eira is safest here in my care, and you and her other friends will be better supports for her if you go home, clean up, and get some decent rest. I promise to send updates as soon as I know more."

My instincts urge me to argue with Shira, to insist that out of everyone in this building, I'm the one who has lived with Eira the longest and knows her inside and out. But one glance at Shira's sharp gaze has me taking a step back and blowing out a breath. This is both Shira's home and workspace. If she wants me to leave, legally, there is nothing I can do about it. Considering how much Eira and the others respect Shira, I know it won't lead me anywhere good if I keep forcing the issue.

Heaving another sigh, I say, "Alright. Fine. You have my number. I'm less than ten minutes away and will be here in a heartbeat the moment you have updates."

Shira nods her head and gives me a pitying look. I *hate* when people do that. "You'll be the first person I contact, Tryg. Go get some rest."

I manage to not roll my eyes when Shira doesn't budge a muscle while I put my shoes back on and slip on my coat and other gear. This bite-sized woman is standing with her arms crossed, as if she could truly block me from physically moving past her. Then again, I don't know if I want to find out if she could. It's always the tiny ones who appear weak that are, in fact, the strongest.

I stomp out into the night alone, momentarily relieved that the storm stopped as suddenly as it started. Shira closes the door behind me immediately. I'm sure she's relieved that I'm finally out of her space. I hear the others shuffling around and preparing to leave, but I'm not in the mood to talk to anyone. I tend to process my feelings best alone and in the woods. *Yeah, yeah*, it's not safe to wander around the woods at night with the likelihood of spies and with how many families are being captured left and right. I don't give a fuck. Let them fucking at me. The scent of the soil and pines cools me down, and it's either this or losing myself back in the bottles at home.

Tall, looming pines stand around me as I wander the runner's path through the woods. The darkness causes the chilled wind to sting harder against any exposed skin. A pack of coyotes howl in the distance, and an owl calls out to my right, an elegant shadow gliding from tree to tree. I long ago mastered how to silence my footsteps, how to merge with the ground and be an extension of the forest. A river bends on my left, its water crashing down the slope. I won't hear a single person for miles. This is my sanctuary.

As I continue to head uphill, I'm lost in thought. *How did I trigger my friend? Is she dreaming right now? What will Shira be doing with her?*

The thoughts swirl around me until I realize I made it to a clearing. Grasses cover the valley like a fleece blanket. Crows cry out before swooping above me into the open space. *Huh.* These birds usually sleep at night. I find myself following them, accepting their unknowing invitation and curious why so many are active this late at night. I'll admit, there's a small part of me that wonders if I should turn around and get some sleep as Shira suggested. But all it takes is for a crow to land on a lone tree in the clearing and tilt its head in my direction, like it's asking if I'm coming with on the ride. *Well, I don't want to disappoint.*

I break out into a slow jog down the valley, not taking my eyes off the crows. The waxing moon beams down around me. I soak in its light, another form of liquid courage. I have no idea where my legs or these birds are taking me, but my gut tells me to keep going. My body is warming up from the jog. I'm so lost in thought, I don't realize I'm at the end of the clearing until a low growl circles around me.

I nearly fall on my ass, my heart thundering in my chest. The dampness from jogging turns into a cold caress on my face and down my body. Glowing opal eyes follow my every breath, and my arms and legs start to tremble. Each eye is about the size of my head. *What the fuck is this shit?* I'm too jumpy to search around for those crows, but I shoot a nasty thought toward the one I saw on the tree back there. *Little fucker betrayed me if he led me to whatever the fuck this is. I hope he flies into a tree.*

I can't make out the shape of this *thing* in front of me, but those eyes creep another few feet toward me, staying hidden in the shadows of the trees. *I'm going to have a fucking heart attack tonight and will die in this clearing. I told Shira I should have stayed at her house. Maybe she can fly into a tree, too.*

A blink of an eye—that's all it takes for the creature to lunge at me. My brain can't even put together what my eyes see, what my body senses: terror and defeat. Razor-sharp teeth that match the brightness of its eyes extend around my body, saliva dripping from the front two fangs. A mixture of iridescent fur and black wings surrounds me and block out the milky light of the moon. There's no time to scream or yell out, and no one could hear me even if I did. The same earthy sanctuary from moments ago becomes a trap. The beast's mouth snaps closed, its warm breath rushing against my entire body, teeth piercing the first layer of skin—

And I wake up. Alone, disoriented, and shaking in my bed. For the first time since I was a child, I hug the nearest pillow against me and muffle my scream against it. *Alone*. I'm alone.

FOURTEEN

Nyx

*We often spend too long looking into the past instead of
realizing the present can offer us
the peace we seek and the future we long for.*
-Council Member Eliina, Grand Healer

Alone in the shifting shadows, I make my way along the stone bridge. Orange lights flicker from up high and cast a faint glow around the piddling village. It's on the border of Skugvaytir and Reykashin, finding a way to stay hidden in the vast realm of Majikaero. I leap from dark pocket to dark pocket, staying hidden—nothing but a whisper in the wind. Black armor covers every inch of my body and shields me from potential trouble. They won't come close, though. No one ever does.

The shadows rise around me and cloak me in smoky darkness. I *am* the darkness. Hadwin and Ulf are nearby, shielded in their own form of sinful shadows. We can turn into actual shadows, shapeless black clouds of mist, contouring from one form to another. A curse of the plague that feels *too* good not to embrace when we can. I sense their movements as strongly as I sense our connected souls. Hadwin ripples along dirt and garden paths mere feet away, slithering as fog made of snakes. Ulf lunges from my shadows toward Hadwin's, his wolf shimmering in and out, his paws like damp coals.

He turns his dark face toward mine, eager to move faster into the village itself. When I send my shadows and smoke to smother lit orbs above us, Ulf lets out a low growl, a wicked smile forming on his canine face. He's out for blood tonight. We all are. The very thought has my beast thrumming under my skin, excited that we're on the same page for once.

The others in our group don't always share the same thirst for revenge. Erika and Odin *scoffed* when we said we were leaving. Erika in particular relishes in pointing out when I'm being a hypocritical twit, insisting that by hunting down those who have harmed me only feeds my demon more. *Fucking weakens my chances of ever healing*. Ivar had similar sentiments and claimed that he'd be with Fraya, practicing more breathing exercises he's taught the other archers before. These kinds of comments wouldn't normally bother me, but now they're a sharp reminder of how I'm actively not trying to heal at this point.

That even though I'm the one who has taken command of our little group, somehow falling naturally into a leadership role, I might be the weakest of us all.

The three of us round the corner, chasing the scent of two souls. I'm in control enough that I won't cause unnecessary harm to those who are innocent. But these motherfuckers? They'll be gasping their last breaths tonight in a matter of minutes after we take them home with us and scare out any lingering secrets. Hadwin, Ulf, and I weave in and out of one another as I cast more shadows to the orbs. Tendrils of smoke drift up from where the burnt orange lights used to be, floating up, up, up and blending in with the night sky.

I gaze up at the speckle of starlight dusted above us. I have certainly no reason to think of her, but I immediately connect the silver of the stars to the silver in her eyes. There's no name, a mere dream that feels like a memory. Yet she wraps herself around me at another one of my darkest moments, a beacon on the horizon. Waiting for me, warning me. I can't be sure, but I know she is here somehow.

The snapping of jaws shakes me from my thoughts, and I see Ulf with his teeth around a guard's neck. Blood pools down his mouth as he tears the guard's neck right off his body. He has the disturbing power to become one with the darkness and can smother a soul's light, one few have in our realm. The head rolls down the dirt path, and he kicks the body to join it. Before I bark out a command to stop, Ulf is on the other guard in a flash. His sharp claws drag through coverings and flesh all the way to bone, splitting the human form into two. An enraptured laugh echoes against the towering gate ahead of me. It's Hadwin. His blanket of darkness covers the bodies and heads, or what's left of them, and sinks them into the ground, blood oozing into the trampled flowers.

"What the fuck, guys?" I hiss at them.

"We're here for revenge," Ulf's gravely voice whispers around my head. "And we'll take what we're owed."

"Yeah, revenge on the two fucks inside this house. You don't have to destroy others on your way inside, dumbass," I scold.

I feel more than see Ulf's eyeroll, as much as a wolf can roll its eyes, and turn my glare on Hadwin.

"And, you—leave those flowers alone! You said you ate earlier."

"I did," Hadwin whines. "What's up your ass? You're usually the one urging our primal ways."

I can't be sure what's wrong with me tonight. He's right—I'm the one who always wants to send a message to the rest of the village; let them know what happens when you fuck with us. When you pit yourselves against us time after time. Any species, any gender, any age. I don't care. Let them drown in their own river of blood for standing to the side and doing nothing while we were destroyed in pain. But tonight? There's a flicker of unease building inside me, and I'm eager to kill those two fuckers and be gone.

I crack my neck, trying to ease the coiled muscles lining my shoulders. "Let's get this over with," I bark out.

Hadwin throws me a bemused glance, but he slithers in a shadowed python form next to Ulf as he goes up the grassy hill toward the stone and clay house on top. Part of my vision sees red, and the other part tries to hang back and seek a release elsewhere. I get to the side of the house when Ulf jumps right through a child peering out the window. His shadows are death incarnate and lash through her little body. She falls over immediately, physically gone from this world, and her soul seeps up as gold mist until it fades into another realm. *Fuck*.

I'm lost looking at her small face, at her eyes flared open in fear and surprise. They're a silvery blue, so similar to what I was thinking about moments ago that my breath catches in my throat. *The fuck?* Hadwin and Ulf come barreling down from a destroyed bedroom with two sacks of forms on their shoulders, shards of the doorframe littering the hallway floor. I can't keep thinking about this. We need to slink back to our home with our new prisoners before anyone else is alerted to our presence. They shouldn't be for a while. All three of us are quieter than silence, and those who cross our path, we eliminate. No mercy, no chances, no opportunities except for ourselves.

I won't leave this child, though. She wasn't part of the plan. We targeted these two local leaders because of their influence over the other small villages in this region. Months ago, when Hadwin, Ulf, and I were still redeemable, they shut us down. Said we were *too much* and should be thrown out as outcasts until our dying days. I wanted to punch the sneer off their faces. They abandoned us as if we were nothing. Like we weren't worth saving. *The same as the fucking Council*.

As if they get to decide who has enough worth to live in this realm. All three of us vowed to return and destroy them and show them just how *too much* we are. Rip their judgy, beady eyes to shreds. With the stress from the past few days, we decided it was ideal to let our beasts have this revenge and torture them for answers. They might know who's behind this bullshit. And Hadwin has a surprise ready to show them.

But this girl. Something pulls me toward her, and I can't leave her here. *Alone.* I know that emotion intimately.

Scooping her up with ease, I fling her over my shoulders as I launch out the second-story window, willing my shadows to encompass both of us. We pass through the side of the house in a plume of smoke, and then I'm running, sprinting, leaping through the shadows. I'll decide what to do with her body when we get home, but a voice tells me not to leave her here. She belongs with me. Hadwin and Ulf are too busy concentrating on heading home to notice I brought the girl with me, which is convenient. I don't have the energy to argue with them about this right now, especially after I gave them a hard time for killing those guards.

The three—well, six—of us sneak through the paths and bridge unseen. I send my shadows to where the orbs used to be, willing them to burn brightly once again. The scarce evidence that we came to this village will be what is found in the prisoners' bedroom, the missing girl, and what's left of the two guards. We jog to the clearing before the woods when a crow calls out to me. Still running, I glance at the crow now flying next to me, its feathers gleaming in the moonlight.

"Nyx, you'll want to see what we found. Come, come quick!" it caws before moving with silky ease into the sky.

"Ulf! Hadwin!" I yell out.

Their shadows take more humanoid shapes, and they turn to face me.

"Take this child, and I'll meet you back at home. No, we're

not talking about this now. Jade sent a message for me that I must follow," I tell them.

They exchange wary glances with one another before Hadwin takes the child's body from me, balancing her with the other body. This whole week has been fucked, and tonight keeps getting better and better. Now I'll get to face their million questions about this and whatever the crows want when I see them later. So much for sleeping tonight.

"Anything we should do with her?" Hadwin asks.

"I mean, she's dead. Thanks to your doing. Be respectful and give her to Erika when you get back. She'll know what to do," I say.

Ulf doesn't say a word but nods with Hadwin before they run into the forest. Rubbing my tired eyes, I turn toward the clearing and shift into a crow. Other *solliqas* can transform into many different creatures. I wasn't able to explore much of my shifting abilities before the plague tainted my *maji*. My current form is different from the other crows, with smoke for feathers and opal-colored eyes. I stretch my wings and dive into the wind, letting it carry me to the murder of crows nearby. It's not uncommon for these specific crows to be out at night.

We're all part of the darkness and the darkness is part of us.

It's natural to see them, among other species, out in the middle of the night when they can be protected by the dark. Still, I don't like this. Jade doesn't usually come for me when she sees I'm in the middle of a mission, let alone carrying the dead body of a child in my arms. This must be important.

She's one of the few *solliqas* I'd trust the existence of my soul to. Jade was my main protector and closest friend back when we lived in Drageyra. She miraculously hasn't caught the plague, still free of its deathly grip. The moment the Council banished me and my family didn't do shit about it, Jade and my other protectors fled with me to the region of Reykashin. I'm not sure when any of them have shifted from their crow forms. Jade insists it makes it easier for them to hide from any of the Council members who suspect them as spies. They typically fly back and forth from where I stay in the outskirts of Reykashin to Skugvaytir and Myrellden. Anything to get closer to Rioa and stay aware of major events happening there with the Council, so they can report back to me and extend their protection to other *solliqas*.

I land in the highest branch of the tree, staring down at the rest of them. Jade peers up at me with light green eyes and looks tense. Flustered. Fidgety.

"What's going on?" I croak out.

"We found a human wandering into this realm. We don't think he realizes what he's doing, and normally we would guide him back to his body, but we caught his scent. You need to see this," Jade says, her tone tight with worry.

She's my strongest air fighter, next to Ivar, and seeing her this edgy is alarming.

"Alright, take me to this human."

It doesn't take the crows long to guide me into the forest next to us, using the human's scent as a guide. Something tightens in my gut when I sense it, but I'm not sure what it is. *This is a fucked night.* We fly another few miles when I'm hit with an overwhelming sensation of rage. It staggers me, causing me to nearly fly into a tree. I shake myself out and fly in for a closer look, landing directly on the ground near the opening of the forest.

"*See*, Nyx. I think it's *him*. He has the same eyes, and it's giving me the heebies," Jade whispers.

I glare at the man stalking toward the tree line. At first glance, I think he must be a warrior with how built and tall he is. He walks with a confidence I can admire. When I see his eyes, though—*dammit, what's with all of these fucking eyes lately?*—I suck in a harsh breath. He *does* have those eyes. Intense, angry, soul carving. Golden brown with an edge so sharp it can kill.

I don't even realize what's happening until I've already shifted again. This particular form I save for the ghastly and more gut-wrenching of nightmares. My fangs elongate, my eyes hyper-focused with the need to pierce into his very being. Fur and leather wings grow out from my shadows and claws sink into the soil beneath me. I don't know when I'll have another chance like this again to kill this motherfucker, since he can't seem to fucking die. He haunts me almost as much as I haunt myself. There are shreds of memories that are blurred to me, souls I swear were important to me, but I can't manage to remember. But him? I'll *never* forget his antagonizing aura and fucked existence.

He jolts in awareness and finally notices I'm here. This fucked soul comes to a standstill before falling to the ground, his body rigid and drenched in fear. Good. He *should* fear me.

In a flash, I lunge forward and have him trapped in my mouth. All it'll take is one bite and he'll finally be gone from existence. Yet as I crunch into bone and savor the taste of his spiteful blood, he disappears into nothing. Vaporizes into air. And I'm left with a rage even my beast can't reach, roaring dangerously loud that the trees shake around me.

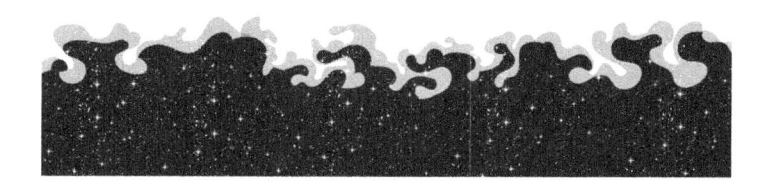

FIFTEEN

Eira

The fear that clamps our heart is stronger than any army.
-Dr. Morgan Lydahnia,
Founder of Heart and Mind Care

Shaking like a leaf, I wrap the shawl tighter around me as I stare out the window. Fresh snow falls quietly to the earth, layering the ground and trees as if puffy tinsel and feathers. A dense fog circles its way around the forest. It's quiet. The silence is thick and tangible, unlike the usual peace snow brings me. I lean forward to push the window closed. This weather typically sparks joy and something magical within me. I've always marveled at the change of seasons, fall to winter in particular, but today, I view everything as distant. Nothing special. Another snowflake, another frigid day.

Shira pokes her head through the doorway and is carrying a tray with various foods and what smells like coffee.

"I thought I heard you moving around before. I made you breakfast and coffee to warm you up this morning," she says with a small smile.

She pads over to the end table I'm sitting next to and carefully places the tray in front of me. The buttery scent of a hot croissant wafts my way. It doesn't quite hit my happy place, but it's enough to bring my attention to the rest of the food before me. Shira boiled eggs, apparently has baked ham in her kitchen, and brought what looks to be local yogurt with fresh fruit. She knows how much I love honey and has placed the whole jar next to the fruit, along with tiny bowls with a chocolate sauce and magenta-red jam. The coffee is steaming and, clearly, was freshly made. It has white foam at the top, thick cream having been poured already. I wasn't in the mood to eat, an idea quite strange for me, and thought I would nibble on crackers later in the day. Shira obviously thinks otherwise and pushes the tray closer to me.

"Your mind and heart might be closing off, but your body surely will appreciate homemade food after all that it's been through," Shira murmurs. She squeezes my shoulder lightly before taking a seat in the opposite chair.

"Are you not eating with me?" I ask her. Having anyone stare at me while I eat is the *worst*. Well, maybe it's no longer considered to be the worst, but it's still up there. I fight back a shudder.

Shira chuckles. "I didn't think that would bother you, but if I grab a plate and coffee to join you and that means you'll eat, fine by me." She saunters her way to the doorway and calls back, "At least take a few sips of your coffee. I added a little extra something special."

Rolling my eyes and muttering to myself about her pressuring me into eating, I take a small sip from my mug. Notes of peppermint and chocolate soak into my taste buds, and I hum in contentment. *Alright, Shira wins this round.* This coffee is pretty damn tasty.

Shira pops back into my room with her own plate and mug, and she glances at my face excitedly. "So," she asks, "What do you think?"

"I think someone told you the way to my mess of a heart,

but I won't complain too much," I say, covering my smile with another sip of coffee.

Shira laughs, the sound serene as a bell. She drinks from her own mug, painted with strokes of blue and purple. Mine has green and pink with splashes of light blue.

"You're admiring these?" she asks. "I got them from the same person who told me about your favorite drinks and foods."

I consider who it could be while I rip off a piece of the croissant and dip it into the jam. It's perfectly flaky and buttery and melts into my mouth. The jam must be a combination of fruits, but whatever it is, it's divine. *Oh!* This tastes like strawberries and cherries, my favorite. Turning the painted mug in a semicircle, my lips tilt up into a grin. "Morgan?" I ask.

Shira winks as she chuckles to herself. "She makes the best jams and is always experimenting with new art projects. I don't know how she does it between running that therapy clinic, helping her family, and teaming up with the investigators. Morgan is a magical woman."

I nod in agreement as I dig into the rest of the tray of food. "Tell me about it. I have a theory that she doesn't sleep. Maybe she's not even human," I mutter. "When did you last talk with her?"

"I called her right after I had you settled into your room a few nights ago and convinced your friends to head home to rest," Shira says. "I thought you might need a few days of rest yourself, and I wanted to give her a heads up that you'd be with me for a while."

Panic clenches my heart and I drop my fork, the metal ringing too loudly in our small space.

"*Fuck*, my clients!" I choke out. "I totally forgot to tell any of them. And it's been a few days already? What am I going to tell them? What did Morgan—"

"Eira, settle yourself," Shira says sharply, yet kindly. I'll never know how she's mastered the art of using those two emotions together. "This is precisely why you need a few days of rest, let alone everything else you've been going through. Morgan understands completely and gave me a list of your favorite foods, drinks, books, and surprisingly, a lengthy list of textures that soothe you. She will take care of your clients over these next few days, and she even insisted that you consider taking a whole week off."

"*Ugh*, this is so not cool," I mutter into my coffee. "I don't even know what's going on, but I hate having to miss work right now. This war is escalating, and my clients are in significant pain."

Shira's eyes soften. "I know, darling, but you won't be fit for healing others if you're exhausted and passing out from these nightmares or, rather, what I believe to be memories."

I slowly blink at her, not understanding. I mean, that's not a total surprise, considering the cogs in my brain get stuck daily. But what the actual what?

"Memories," I deadpan.

"Yes, memories. I was going to wait a little longer to discuss this with you, but this is as good of a day as any," Shira says. I don't miss the agitated look on her face. "I believe you are experiencing past life memories. These are memories from past lives you've experienced here on Earth. A lot of people have this experience, but I've met few individuals in my lifetime who have them as frequently and strongly as you do. The memories can be happy, upsetting, random, as a different gender, in a totally different part of the world. Based on your reaction to Tryg, I think it's possible that he's been in these past life memories for a while now and is following you from lifetime to lifetime, and…"

A small part of my brain, probably the part that doesn't have its cogs jammed daily, understands that Shira is still talking and has told me about this concept before. The rest of me, and I mean the entire rest of my brain, body, heart, and spirit, are rejecting what she is saying. I'm positive she's telling me that I'm a certified nutjob, and after our breakfast, a team from a different clinic is going to come take me to their facility for thorough medical support.

Shira sighs. "I know this might be a lot for you to handle right now. That's okay, Eira. We have some time to work through this and to piece together the puzzle. For right now, would you be okay with hearing my thoughts about your healing options?"

I nod my head because what else am I going to say? *You rescued me from a horrifically unexplainable experience, made sure I would be okay for work, and are now feeding me scrumptious food. But no, don't you dare tell me about these healing options?* Yeah, I'm nutty, but I'm not a dick.

"I'm thinking that we should begin with full body relaxation techniques," Shira says. "You're way too tense to do any past life regression work, and I want to ensure that you remain physically stable over the next few days. We'll do meditations, somatic work, and restorative yoga. Yes, all the nourishing techniques that you still learn about in school today. I'll loop your own therapist into what I'm doing with you, okay? We can check in again in a few days about these memories you're having and go from there. What do you think?"

"Yeah, let's go with that," I whisper. I'm still reeling that she thinks I'm having *memories* and detect my thoughts and feelings fluttering behind a wall in my head. They're trying to hide, and I want them to. They best get behind that numbing wall before they're locked out.

"And, shifting directions completely, I invited someone here who I thought you'd want to see," Shira says.

Sensing another presence in the room, I turn toward the doorway and see the one and only Athena smiling at me.

SIXTEEN

Eira

We grossly underestimate how easily humans will fall if they're constantly braced for impact.
-Gineva Blezk,
Director of Sweazn Human Recuperation Efforts

A smile breaks free, and I laugh with relief. I don't know how she managed to be here when her caseload is also overflowing, but I'll take any time with my friend that I can get.

"Little fox, your tail is kind of puffy today," Athena says with a smirk. She exchanges a glance with Shira as they switch places. Athena pulls out a book before dumping her bag on the floor with an unceremonious *plop*.

"Have no fear. I know the cure that'll smooth you out. Err, maybe. This one might get your blood pumping and make you feel rather, ah, excited," she says, laughing.

I roll my eyes and snatch the romance novel out of her hands, biting back my own laugh. One of the things we bond over is books, and we devour new romance novels like the treat they are. I lean over to set it on the edge of the bed, so I don't get distracted and start reading it now. Our governments might have obliterated actual countries, but the gods themselves will have to come down here to take away our books.

"I also brought a few other goodies," Athena continues. "I found a new passion fruit candle that smells tasty, a few bath bombs that claim to release muscle tension, and I might have gotten carried away with the chocolates. Half of these are from Jace, by the way. He *insisted* that I tell you that." She talks while taking items out of her bag, placing them in a neat pile on the windowsill. "There are a good thirty million things happening all at once right now. I figured you'd want some R&R tonight."

I'm already jiggling in a little dance, my body and mind excited to dive into everything Athena brought me. Between her, Shira, and Morgan, I'm feeling similar to a pampered queen. I look up to my friend, brimming with delight, and take her hand in my own.

"Thanks, truly," I say. "It means the world to me that you're here and even more that you were willing to miss work to spend the day with me. I know it's basically a chicken pen over there right now, everyone clucking and running around."

"Ha!" Athena laughs. "Yeah, that's an appropriate analogy. We're running around with our heads cut off, pecking at scraps of food, feathers are in the air, and you can't tell who is the client and who is the therapist right now. Maybe I should be thanking *you*. I finally could take a day off."

That certainly dampens my mood. What a depressing thought. We're terribly submerged in tragedy right now, we can't justify a break unless there's more trauma happening. *Cool*. So cool.

"On that note..." Athena mutters. "I'm glad I checked in with you. I know we saw one another a few days ago, but with everything that happened, it feels like a lifetime ago. Especially since you slept for two days straight, which is almost impressive if you weren't incredibly haggard. Shira insisted that you have space to rest and process what's been going on, and I convinced the others to listen because of how much I understand Shira's reasoning. Err, not quite everyone was convinced."

"Tryg was a pain, wasn't he?" I ask. Gods, I adore him, but he's a real ass sometimes. Okay, often.

"Yeah, that's one way to frame it," Athena says with a wince. "He exploded on all of us, especially Shira. I know he has a lot weighing him down with more war victims and kidnappings. Senator Niran made an announcement that too many families are going missing, and they suspect spies have infiltrated the higher levels at this point. There's also talk of a biological attack, but I noticed it wasn't mentioned *who* initiated this. It's getting wild, Eira. There will be another announcement tonight, and Morgan thinks troops are going to be deployed."

Fuck. Shit. Fuckity shit. "I know things have been rough for years now with Hungatia," I say bleakly. "I didn't think it would come to a full-on war. And a planned disease outbreak? They do realize it won't stay contained within our current borders, right?"

Athena's eyes appear heavy and pained. "That's the thing, friend. It *looks* like a full-on war when we get to the deployment and heavy violence stage. But there is no 'full-on.' There is war or there isn't. We've been at war since our first Sweazn citizen was captured, since the Hungatian senate had their first conversation about ways to harm us. We've been at war, and it's moving to the next stage. More visible, more concrete. A higher spread of death." She shakes her head and is incredibly drained in this moment, the opposite of her usually boisterous self. "But that is that and this is this. We are here right now, together. We won't be able to do anything to help our country if we can't take care of ourselves. I know it'll be hard, but try not to worry too much about the clinic or Tryg. Ruse is doing what he can to keep Tryg's lid on his temper locked down. Focus on decompressing your mind and body and working with Shira to figure out what is going on."

I glance out the window at the new flurries picking up speed. I know Athena is right about all of it. The reality of everything feels the same as rocks sewn under my skin, weighing me down from the inside. This topic is difficult enough to process—I don't have the strength, nor am I in the right headspace, to tell her what Shira thinks is happening. I hardly believe it myself and don't want to send Athena spiraling down with me, not when I sense her heavy heart.

And Tryg. *Oh, Tryg.* He can be the paper you use to wipe your ass with, but he also has such generosity and childlike playfulness in him. He must be going through so much as the lead investigator, having all that pressure on his shoulders. I'm sure much of it's self-inflicted, but that doesn't change what he's enduring. I chalked up his recent habits to simply wanting to party, to have fun. But if he can easily explode at his friends, our created family, and storm out of Shira's home like a petulant child, there must be more going on. I'll have a chat with Shira about it later on after I get the courage to ask her more about these "memories".

A whole week passes, with my sanity dangling by a thread. More snow graces us with her presence, bringing howling winds with her. Athena is alarmed at how early we're getting this weather. I'm alarmed by how much I'm a hypocrite. Shira keeps feeding me the hard truth that as much as I recommend these same therapeutic exercises to my own clients, I can barely bring myself to even try them. In no way, shape, or form do I want to experience how the nightmares are making me suffer. *Nope. No way.* Unfortunately for me, Shira doesn't care how moody I get. We hammer away at the issue until I can name even a basic feeling. *I'm pathetic.*

During one of the more profound meditation sessions, I finally experienced a so-called memory that was not a nightmare. I dare say it was pleasant and carefree, even if I was only in the experience for a few minutes.

A young boy held my hand, his grip tight and excited. He wore brown leather shoes, one which was untied, with dress pants and a button-down shirt tailored to his little body. A dark tan cap sat upon his head and tight black curls peeked out under it. His dapper outfit paled in comparison to his smile. In this dream, or memory, he was peeking up at me with such giddiness, his gray eyes bright. Shaking my hand, he giggled while he skipped in place, barely able to contain his happiness. I didn't see my own face, but I could see the creamy blue dress with sewn pearls fall to my ankles, layered over a white underskirt. Lacy white socks covered my slim feet and my shoes appeared to be black leather with buckles. This young boy and I were walking down a dirt road and with each step, we came closer to stunning horses. Their coats gleamed in the sunlight, and they had ribbons in their hair. The last sensation I encountered was pure joy and my own smile stretching across my face as I peered down at the child.

I'm still not sure I fully accept that I'm experiencing actual memories. It's a lot to chew all at once.

I do feel cautiously optimistic about the nightmares, though. For the nights I've stayed with Shira, I haven't had a single nightmare. None. Zero. I've managed to get some restful nights of sleep. I'm over the moon about this, but Shira perceives this differently. She is concerned and perplexed that I've been having them almost nightly at this point, and as soon as I stay with her, my body is able to slacken into sleep. If anything, being here is the one place I've had a positive dream, *or memory, ugh*. I count this as a win. Shira won't be satisfied until she can piece together what these nightmares mean and why I'm not having them now. I won't be satisfied until I'm free of all these "memories" and am cleared by her to return to my clients.

Going from working nonstop and having exhausting, terrifying nightmares, to doing absolutely nothing and having to be present is its own special kind of torture for me.

I'm starting to doze off in the plushy armchair. My muscles are still deliciously worked out from practicing yoga with Astira, Liv, and Lyk last night. And perhaps from laughing so hard when we caught up afterward with Athena, having a girl's night at Shira's home. I wouldn't have minded if Jace came along, but then I would have wanted to invite Ruse. Which means Tryg would have been there.

Guilt eats away around my heart. I love him with every broken strand of my heart, but Tryg's negative energy can swirl and twist around me like a hurricane. I haven't voiced this directly to Shira or the others, and I don't think I need to. Anyone who sees him when his temper is unleashed would understand.

I'm sinking under two blankets and my book, when Shira knocks on the door. I blink lazily up at her, not quite awake, yet not stuck in the realm of dreamworld. "Yes?"

Shira snickers, eyeing me lost in the bundle of materials. "I don't want to disturb your beauty sleep, but I come with some potentially exciting news for you," she says. "Morgan called from the clinic. She wants to come pick you up to assist her with a victim they brought in today, if you're up for it. He is a teen boy who was caught up in a brutal kidnapping and house fire, and he's unable to calm down enough to talk through what he saw. Medics are working on his physical injuries, but she thinks you'd be able to break through his panic. Do you want to try going? If you do, she'll be here in ten minutes to pick you up."

I'm so eager to work again, she might as well have poked me with a firecracker. I shoot up from my chair, only to get tangled in the blankets and fall flat on my face. I'm squirming like a dilapidated worm and all Shira does is laugh at me. Huffing my hair out of my face, I glare up at her with a pout.

"All you therapists are the same," she says in between laughs. "Your bodies beg you to take care of yourselves, yet here you are, frantic to get back to the environment that harms you in the first place. It's as if they've got you drugged over there."

"I want to be useful again," I grumble as I untangle myself from the blankets.

"Honey, you've been resting for a *week*. With this reaction, I'm scooping you up right after you're done today. And yes, Morgan already knows of my intentions. Save those puppy eyes for someone else," Shira tells me.

"Oooh, maybe for that guy from the coffee shop!" Athena chirps from around the corner.

"Guy from the coffee shop?" Shira asks, already leaving my room.

"Athena's here?!" I call out, now even more frantic to get a grip on myself.

"Yeah, girl. I took a late lunch today and figured I'd swing by to say hi. I texted Morgan that I'll take you back with me. We're heading to the MedClinic today," Athena says before thrusting a beverage into my hands. "This one's a strawberry matcha, and your friend asked why you haven't called him yet."

"I'll send him a message after I'm done helping Morgan," I mutter distractedly. I'm changing into semi-casual clothes, since I figure I can't show up at a hospital wearing a sports bra and my yoga leggings.

"Already got you covered," she says, wiggling her eyebrows. Athena types away at her phone before she glances back up at me, smirking. "He'll be expecting your message."

"You're unbelievable," I mumble. She should know by now

that I don't open up to guys. We'll both inevitably get hurt. His warm embrace will turn into a ghost of a memory. "Do you have any chocolate? I need a bite before we go."

"Sure thing, my girl. I'll send you a screenshot with his last comment about you."

Unbelievable.

SEVENTEEN

Eira

*Deceiving our loved ones can turn even the
sweetest flower into poison.
-Wiona Yoplen, Author of Family Relations:
Strengthening Connections*

This entire scene is fucking unbelievable. I know I don't usually spend my time at this center, isolated in the land of emotional trauma, but what am I even watching right now? I'm standing here gaping like a fish, the sounds muffled, while my vision zeroes in on medical workers darting back and forth around me. Some are carrying sterile tools and supplies. Others are hauling bloodied victims strapped down on stretchers. A woman runs past me with an IV bag, water, and container of medications. A man yells out as he is wheeled by, screaming about his wife. Half of his left arm is missing, and the other is puckering from a burn. In the far corner of the open room, a small pile of bodies is forming, draped in tattered blankets in an attempt to hide their faces from view. I was asked to support *here*? There's a chance Morgan might have underestimated my abilities to be of service today.

I'm still processing and trying to get my feet to wiggle free from shock when Athena and Morgan come to my sides.

"What, um, are you expecting *me* to do here?" I ask, my eyes widening when a little girl is carried past me, missing both of her hands.

"There was no real way to warn you," Athena whispers solemnly. "Hungatia made their move earlier than expected."

"Um, a *warning* would have been appreciated!" I scold. "Instead of *non-fucking-chalantly* handing me a matcha and joking about that guy. I thought the senators were still in conversation with one another." A nurse bumps past me and nearly drops her pile of bandages. I send her an apologetic look before turning my ire back on my teammates.

"Yeah, that was last week. A lot can change in even a minute, let alone seven days," Athena says, unnaturally stumbling over her words. "It's been all over the stations—everyone knows at this point."

"Obviously not me," I snap.

Morgan winces slightly. "That might be my fault," she says, not seeming entirely guilty. "Shira updated me on how you were doing a few days ago, and you finally had a pleasant memory. Your body was significantly more relaxed up until a few minutes ago, and I thought it would be best to give you a full week of rest. I only realized when I saw your face coming in here that no one updated you."

"Not fucking cool, guys," I say, rounding on both of them. "We're supposed to be a *team*. You honestly expected to keep the news hidden from me? For how long? And then seriously asked me to be here today without any form of communication?" I'm fuming, a fire burning under my skin as I turn away from my uncharacteristically stupid team members. *What the actual fuck?*

"Eira, we just—"

"You just *nothing*," I snarl behind me. "You call yourselves therapists and didn't think for a second what it would do to me to be left in the dark." I turn to face them again, crossing my arms and cocking out my hip. "And then to bring me here without any kind of warning or update about what's been going on in our city? A fucked up surprise party? Maybe I do need more space at Shira's. Time away from people who I'm supposed to trust."

Athena takes a step back, hurt clear on her face. She's fidgeting all over the place and bouncing back and forth on the balls of her feet. She is not one to get agitated, and the glance she throws Morgan almost makes me forgive her. *Almost*.

"This is all on me, Eira," Morgan sighs, pinching the space between her eyes. "I didn't want what you see here to cause even more nightmares and drain you physically. We're all scared of what you're going through, especially when Shira shared with me her idea about memories."

"Memories?" Athena asks, whipping her head between us like a bobble head. If I wasn't *out-of-my-mind* pissed at them, I would totally laugh.

"Later, Athena," Morgan mutters. "Look, I admit that I screwed up. I'll do whatever I can to make this right between us because you're right, Eira, we're a team. It wasn't my intention to cause you harm or put a wedge between us. We can talk about this more, today even, but I do need your help. You and Athena are my top therapists. Yeah, I know how that sounds, and yeah, I mean what I say. You're the ones clients request most frequently and people rave about. Do you think you can still help us out here today?"

I peer around the room again. Babies are wailing, blood is upsettingly marking all the surfaces, staff members are either frantically working or off to the side crying. This entire place is chaotic, and there's a sense of foreboding, as if it doesn't matter how advanced this center is; we are clearly not prepared.

Both Morgan and Athena are washed out, with purple circles under their eyes. Morgan typically looks borderline perfect, but I see the wrinkles and blemishes coating her face and neck.

Sighing, I pull my hair into a ponytail and roll up the sleeves of my sweater. "It's not these people's fault that you're both idiots. If you were so concerned about my well-being and stress levels, you shouldn't have even brought me here. A verbal update could have sufficed. But I'm here now. Take me to the guy having a panic attack. I'll see what I can do."

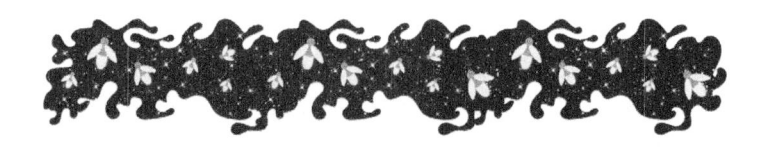

All three of us are now in periwinkle scrubs, and I'm grateful I chose my gym shoes today, not my winter boots. Athena trots down a different hallway to one of the elderly patients struggling with their oxygen mask. Morgan steps in closer to me as we round the corner, heading to a room on the opposite end of the center.

"I know you're upset with me and have every right to be," Morgan says. "But thank you for still sticking with us today."

"It doesn't make any sense. I understand wanting to shelter me from horrible news when I'm clearly losing my mind, but keeping a *war* attack from me? Not even prepping me for this medical center? Or better yet, insisting on sheltering me and, after a week, yanking me out of Shira's home?" I fire question after question at her, detecting sparks of annoyance skittering along my skin once again.

"These are desperate times, Eira. When Shira said you were making such wonderful progress, and our team was asked to support after the attack this morning, I went into crisis mode. That included pulling you in," Morgan responds.

We approach the door and before Morgan can turn the doorknob, I catch her wrist. She gives me a wary glance over her shoulder. As she should—I'm not one to get physical or grabby.

"Alright, well, let me be clear," I say, still fuming. "Don't pull this bullshit on me again. If you want my help, regardless of my health, you better tell me what the hell is going on. I don't appreciate being kept in the dark."

Morgan smiles slightly, but it doesn't reach her eyes. "Alright, little fox, you've got it."

I don't respond and Morgan opens up the door, leading me inside the dim space. A young man, maybe in his midtwenties or so, is crouched down in the corner of the room with a frenzied look on his face. A hurt animal surveying his predator. His dark brown hair is wild and sticking to his face, matted with dried blood. He isn't wearing a shirt, and cuts and bruises litter his torso. A massive cut is slashed from his collarbone down to his elbow on his left side. I can't get a good read about his legs and feet, but they're probably somewhat okay if he is putting his weight on them. Four med team members are facing him, and one of them is trying to convince him to get hooked up to the machine for his vitals.

I shouldn't be this insensitive, but these workers are dumber than rocks.

"Way to make this guy feel cornered and scared. There are way too many people in this room," I say. "Let's remove three of you, for starters."

"But we need to—"

"Did I ask you?" I retort. "You called for support, and lucky you, here I am. If you can do this on your own, feel free to keep going. I won't stop you."

The four workers exchange puzzled glances before the one furthest away steps forward. She tucks a brown lock behind her pierced ears, her earrings a startling bright amethyst, and rolls back her shoulders. "I'll stay to complete any medical work, but I'll be here in the corner."

"What's your name?" I ask.

"Sheila," she responds.

"Greetings on this fine day, Sheila. Now the rest of you can be on your merry way," I bark out.

The three of them grumble while they gather their supplies and hurry out one after the other, similar to agitated ducklings in a row.

"You're responding rather harshly to them," Morgan murmurs.

"I wonder whose fault that is," I reply.

"You know what we practice, Eira. We're ultimately the ones in control of our behaviors—"

"Save the lecture," I rush out in a breath. "I'm in no mood or space to hear it right now."

Without another word, I square my shoulders and cautiously take a step forward to the patient in front of me. I close my eyes and take a deep breath in, holding it for a few seconds before exhaling out. I repeat this a few more times until my galloping heart slows to an easy trot and my shoulder muscles loosen. My stomach and pelvic floor unclench, and my fingers and toes slightly shake out my tension. After my next exhale, I open my eyes, and it's as if a mask has been placed upon my face. Gone is irritated Eira, replaced by a serene and composed therapist ready to tackle a trauma response.

The patient is still peering around but has visibly relaxed his feet and torso. I move my body to the floor inch by inch until I'm sitting with my legs crossed, about five feet in front of him. I keep my hands loose and exposed on my lap while continuing to slow my breathing, mirroring my calm body to him.

"Hi," I begin. "My name is Eira. I'm here to help you today. There is no pressure for you to do anything. You are here. You are alive. You are safe."

The patient turns his razor-sharp focus on me. His eyes are still wide, and his breaths come out in quick pants. This is going to take the whole afternoon.

"Morgan?" I call lowly behind my shoulder. "Can you bring me water and a snack?"

I hear her shoes clacking away on the floor as she leaves on this mini quest. Within minutes, she wordlessly sets these items down next to me and backs away toward the door.

Looking in the patient's direction, I slowly pick up the water and the bag of crackers and place them a few feet in front of me.

"You don't have to drink or eat this," I say. "But here is water and some food if you'd like to try them. Water can help our bodies alleviate tension, and I imagine you're quite hungry after what you've gone through today. Take your time. These will be here for you."

The patient eyes me warily. *Yep, this is definitely going to take forever.*

I'm not sure how much time passes, but enough has gone by that I'm losing all sensation in my legs and my lower back is throbbing. *Awesome.* At least Sheila isn't getting impatient. Morgan left a few minutes ago to help elsewhere, which is by far better. This patient only has to deal with the two of us now. Suddenly, in a blink, he reaches forward so quickly for the water and the crackers that I'm convinced I imagined it.

I continue to sit. He scarfs down the snack as if he hasn't eaten in days and noisily guzzles down the water. It dribbles out of his mouth and down his chin, splashing onto his chest. And still, I sit.

There's a large part of me screaming in the depths of my mind, especially with my tailbone hurting, when he finally speaks to me.

"I'm Jason," he rasps. "I don't want to be here. I need to get to my sister."

"Hi, Jason," I breathe. "Thank you for sharing this with me.

I understand that this situation is challenging and horrible right now. *Of course,* you don't want to be here. Do you know where your sister is?"

"*They* left her," he spits out with venom, glaring at Sheila behind me. "I told them that she could still be alive under the bricks, but they took me into the ambulance and *left her.*" His voice cracks at the end, thick with emotion.

Oh, dear. "I can go get information about your sister," I offer. "If you give me your information, I can go right now while the woman behind me checks your vitals. We can then get you out of here."

Jason grunts an unintelligible sound, which I interpret as potentially an "okay."

"You get my vitals," he demands. "You do it. Not that witch."

This is totally my jam. I'm really loving today. "A-alright," I say. "She'll, uh, talk me through what to do. I'll need to move closer to you, though. Is that okay?"

Jason nods his head now, much to my relief. I'm not 100 percent sure what I'm about to do is professional or ethical, but hey, some of this shit doesn't come in a rulebook.

I scoot along the floor until I'm directly in front of him. Sheila slowly approaches us, and I'll give her credit—she's as cool as an ice cube. Only her shaky hands are betraying her. *Damn, what was this guy doing that has her this freaked out?*

She's a step away when Jason grapples my arms and yanks me closer, an inch from his battered face. *Shit, shit, shit.* I smell smoke and dirt and blood wafting from him. His mouth is set in a snarl; his fingers dig into my flesh like claws. A mountain lion preparing to tear apart the doe.

It all happens so fast. One inhale, I see his dark brown eyes dilate; one exhale, I hear Sheila call for support.

The next inhale, his eyes turn a wicked black; the next exhale, that smoky, dirty, bloody mixture is on me, is in me.

Inhale, a worker yells out behind me. Exhale, he says words that send a chill down my spine.

"We've been waiting for you, Eira. It's time to come home."

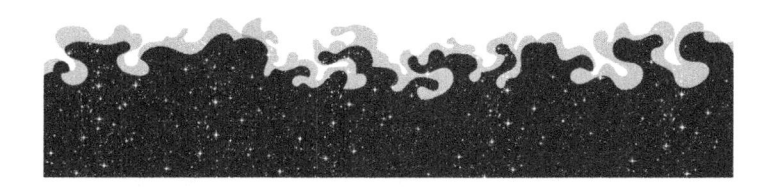

EIGHTEEN
Nyx & Eira

*True love can span across universes if we're
not too scared to grasp it.
-Lydia Karlson, Mother of Eira Karlson*

Nyx

Home is on the horizon, which is a relief considering the night I had. When that soul disappeared into nothing, my beast ravaged across the forest for hours. I didn't bother to stop it. It's rare, but we were on the same page, undergoing both rage and agony. I was *really fucking close* to destroying that pathetic excuse of a soul. It took hunting three different creatures for my beast to calm down, to lose the scent of him. And now? I'm tired as fuck and want to collapse in a bed. Any bed. Even the vexing Fraya can be there.

As I stomp down the dusty path leading to Erika's workstation, it dawns on me that I haven't slept in two days at this point. This adds fuel to the fire, and I'm huffing in irritation by the time I slam open Erika's door.

She's stooped over a thick book with her hands in a bowl,

mixing fresh herbs into a chalky paste. While her magic is primarily water-based, she's taken an interest in the power of different herbs and earth life here in Majikaero. After her soul was tainted by the plague, she and Odin threw themselves into discovering other ways to cure the disease. They're convinced there must be magic in the earth of our realm that could help. When Erika gets lost in experimenting with fresh ingredients, not much can sway her attention. Such as right now. She isn't even phased by my visibly agitated mood. I'm not sure how I feel about that.

"Not even a flinch," I grumble, my voice raspy from roaring and screaming throughout the night. "What, were you expecting me?"

"You sound as if you'd *prefer* for me to be scared," Erika responds, not looking up from her passage.

"Maybe," I say. "Or wanting you to notice that something's up."

Erika snorts. "Something's always up with you nowadays. You're coiled up so tight, I'm surprised you can walk straight."

I choose to ignore her.

"I can't keep that body preserved forever, by the way," she says, finally standing to face me. Her cerulean-blue eyes, framed by dark markings of the plague, take in my face and posture, falling over me like a wave. I'm too exposed, which furthers my foul mood.

I scowl at her. "And I didn't ask you to."

"Why did you want me to protect it, anyway? The soul has already passed. Her body needs to be given over to the healers for the next stage," she says.

"I don't know," I murmur. "A piece of her called out to me. I couldn't leave her."

Erika arches a delicate eyebrow. "I know Fraya can be a lot, but a dead child? That's—"

I throw one of the pieces of fruit at her before she can finish speaking. Why am I connected to such a morbid, disgusting creature? *Blegh.*

Erika snickers to herself as she turns back to her book and takes a handful of another herb. I don't have the energy to keep speaking to her. I go to leave, hoping I find a few hours to sleep. Before I move even a step, a movement catches my eye. It's the child. *What the fuck?* I move a little closer, convinced I'm seeing things. Her arms quiver, yet her eyes are closed. Still dead to this realm. Her body twitches.

"Uh, Erika?" I ask.

"Yeah, Nyx?" she responds, thick with sarcasm.

"It might be my eyes from not sleeping, but this child is moving. She's fucking moving," I growl.

Erika's looking at me as if I sprouted a second head, but she comes to stand next to me. Of course, as soon as she walks over, the child's arms stop twitching.

"Nyx," she says. "Maybe you should get some rest for a few hours. You can use my room if you want to avoid the others for a bit. Although, it'd be great if you washed up first. You kind of stink." She wrinkles her slight nose while eyeing the dried blood on my shirt.

"I'm *telling* you, she was moving!" I insist.

"Okay, okay, but you can still wash up and rest. Maybe she'll do it again by the time you're done," she says.

I'm becoming increasingly frustrated and am close to wringing Erika's neck. I angrily stab at my wild hair. Both to my relief and dismay, the girl's arms start to twitch again. *Thank fuck I'm not going crazy.*

Erika and I exchange glances, and she's clearly freaked out. Which is saying a lot. Erika is the gross, weird one of our group. She and her brother are like that. You've got to show them something extra strange to get them riled up. I nod in the direction of the girl, and we both tiptoe toward her, bracing ourselves for an attack. Or whatever kind of attack a dead little girl can give us.

I'm a few inches closer to the child than Erika is and go to grab one of the arms. Erika slaps my arm. "What, are you nuts?! Don't touch her yet. You don't know what's happening," she scolds.

Rolling my eyes, I say, "What do you think is going to happen? She's already dead."

"That's *exactly* my point. She's already dead, and she's moving. Dead equals not moving. Don't move her until we get everyone else," she demands.

I bark out a laugh. "Yeah, right. The last thing I need is for the whole group squeezed around this little thing right now. I'm barely containing my beast as it is. I'm going in."

Before she can stop me, *as if she could*, I gently prod the girl's bicep. Hissing, my head flies back. A shock of energy sizzles up my arm. A luring sensation winds through me like a snake, and I stagger closer, my head a few inches from the girl's face. I don't even feel in control of my body. I should be used to that sensation, but this is different. Instead of a quelling sense of dread, I sense excitement and a sensation I can't explain bubbling under the surface.

I lean in closer, hoping the girl will wake up and tell me what the fuck is going on. And time slows. Her tiny body seizes up, her back ramrod straight. Her hair, hanging limply down her shoulders, lifts up on a phantom wind. She opens her eyes wide, and I suck in a breath. *Alright, maybe I am going crazy, and this is sleep deprivation.* Her eyes. Crystals. Blue and silver and electricity. Light hums through her body and she gasps, her eyes flaring even wider in terror.

I don't know how I know, but I do. This is her. The woman from my dream. And she's fucking peering at me through the eyes of this child.

Eira

What?! What, what, what?! Maybe this is death. If that's the case, it's entirely possible I'm not as honorable of a human as I thought I was. Because what the fuck is staring at me? Where am I? Why does that woman have pointed teeth? Why is this man covered in blood and oh gods, are those shadows coming out of him? No way. Get a grip, Eira. Those are probably just snakes. Wait, snakes?! Shadowy snakes?! This is so crazy. Why don't I know where I am? Is this another dream? Oh shit, a memory? I can't breathe. I seriously can't breathe. How do I—

I hesitantly inhale a jagged breath, but it feels wrong. Cold. Pieces of ice sticking to my lungs.

My eyes dart around the room. It might be a work room full of plants and glass containers of liquids. Purple, blue, silver, cream. Some of the liquids are as smooth as glass and others are sizzling. Huge windows are to my right, facing a turquoise lake. *Okay, that can't be a bad sign. I love plants and pretty lakes.* I glance down at my body and let out a jumble of sounds. *Am I a child? Is this reincarnation?* My whole body tenses, and I'm choking for air.

I look back at the two creatures above me and can barely repress my fear. They have human features, yet there's no way they're from Earth. What I think is a female has a sleek, jet-black and raven-blue bob and slanted, breathtaking blue eyes. She appears human. Her mouth is parted in shock, which would comfort me that I'm not alone in my stupor, but that exposes her teeth. Very pointy teeth. Potentially stabby teeth. *Eeek.* A herby paste is sliding off her hand, but I don't think she's aware of what's happening.

The male creature standing closest to me is... uncomfortably handsome. I'm extremely troubled by this. He has more blood on him than exposed skin. His tattered shirt reveals deep scratches. He's pretty bulky, and I'll admit I'm swooning over those muscles, but something innately scares me about him. The scent of smoke gathers around the two of us, and I detect the weight of darkness on my body. Inside my head. I gather as much courage as I can muster to meet his eyes, and I'm *stunned*.

Entrancing black and brown eyes with silver and gold crackling the same as lightning.

Oh. Shit.

The floor might as well have disappeared beneath me. I'm being swallowed in a vortex of insanity, staring into his eyes.

He looks equally astonished, his mouth slack and what little skin I see is getting more pale by the second. I can't speak, I can't breathe, I can't process any thoughts. We're completely stuck in this trance, neither one of us knowing what to do. Until this body I'm in decides for us. It twitches and shakes uncontrollably, and the male creature goes to lunge at me, frantic desperation in his eyes. My body seizes up, and in a poof of air, I'm being lifted from the child's body until I'm spread out into a glittery nothingness.

I'm thrown back into my own body with the force of a storm, fumbling for a rational answer to what just happened.

NINETEEN

Tryg

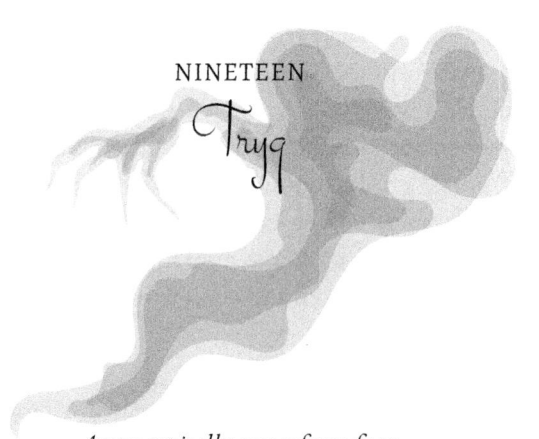

Anger typically comes from fear.
Unless, of course, love is involved.
-Dr. Korula Rewlo, Ancient Civilizations and Human
Emotions Researcher

"What the hell happened?!" I scream. My chest is heaving, and my fists are clenched, ready to punch another hole in the wall.

"Tryg, you need to calm down," Athena says sharply, yet not unkindly. "You've already put two holes in Shira's wall and shattered one of her lamps. Seriously, control yourself or you're gonna have to go."

I pace the length of Shira's living room, stabbing a hand into my hair and pulling a fistful of strands. I relish in the burn tickling my scalp. Shira told me that she would contact me first with any updates, yet I'm somehow the last one in our group to learn what happened to Eira. She was supposedly improving throughout the week, so I focused my energy on my work. Yeah, Shira updated me about the positives, but today? This? This is

THE LIGHT WITHIN

what I wanted to know about. I want to be there as the emergency unfolds. I *deserve* to be there.

"I don't understand why I'm the one being kept in the dark here," I bite out. I'm barely keeping the lid closed on my rage. I know I'm the one in our group who is quickest to feel... anything, really. Quick to anger, quick to laugh. Big emotions that lash out and terrorize others. But that doesn't make it okay to be the last person to know when my best friend is in danger.

Astira appears as if a summoned ghost in front of me, nearly sending me flying out of my own skin. One second, she's glaring up at me, and I'm already bristling. In the next second, I'm slapped hard enough that my head cracks all the way to the left, and I'm at a loss for words. She crosses her arms and not an ounce of mercy can be found on her face.

"Get. A. Fucking. Grip," she grits between clenched teeth. "You're not the only one who loves Eira. Jace was already helping Athena at the medical center, and he first called Liv. She called Lyk, who immediately messaged Ruse. All in the time span of thirty seconds. Jace probably called Liv before you because you've been a snarly asshole *demanding* to be seen. Liv has been acting like, you know, a normal, decent human. You might be the lead investigator in this city, but you're *not* in command of your friends, Tryg. So, chill the fuck out and stop whining like a baby."

She pivots away, flipping her hair over her shoulder and strutting toward Athena, Liv, and Lyk, who are sitting on the tan suede couch. I'm still reeling from getting slapped that hard from someone as pint-sized as Astira, of all people. Liv and Lyk are huddled together and are clearly avoiding eye contact with me. Athena darts a quick glance my way, full of apprehension laced with disappointment. I scrub a hand down my face. I'm fucking exhausted, my bones are essentially weights dragging me down.

I head to the kitchen, pretending the girls don't flinch as I walk past them, and see Jace and Ruse sitting at the wooden dining table with a few glasses of wine. I instinctively pull out one of my cigs and hesitate, remembering Eira calling them *cancer sticks* a few weeks ago. This pisses me off even more, and I crush the box of them as my hand squeezes into a fist again.

"Hey man," Jace mumbles, glancing warily at my shaking, clenched hands. "I know Eira would scold us for going right for the booze, but today is all sorts of fucked up. Want a glass?"

"Of course *he* wants one," Ruse mutters. "He destroyed Shira's living room like an animal."

"Maybe it'll sedate him?" Jace offers while he pours a glass of red wine.

"I'm right here, assholes," I grumble. I don't correct them, though. I'm apparently the raging alcoholic prick of our group. Might as well own it at this point. Eira would tell me to *own up to it* or *take accountability*, but I'm not in the mood for that bullshit right now.

We sit in silence for a while, all lost in our own thoughts. A pressure is building from the inside and pushing against my skull, trying to break free. Soft fur brushes against my leg, and I look down, seeing a black and brown striped tail slink behind Jace's chair.

"Zaya's here?" I ask.

"Yeah, Athena asked me to grab her before coming over here," he says. "She thinks it'll cheer Eira up to have her cat around. You know how she gets about her pet."

Zaya peers up at me with a light blue and a dark green eye. Little tufts sprout from the tops of her ears and her black and brown fur coats her large body. I'm not trying to be mean about a cat—she's in no way fat. She's literally a large cat, terrifyingly so. I remember when Eira came home with her some years back, a teeny kitten bundled in her scarf. She had said Zaya followed her around during her walk in the woods, and she took this as a sign that it was "meant to be". *Whatever.* The cat's alright. When she feels like it.

As if she can sense my thoughts about her, Zaya slinks around the edge of the table and hisses at me. *Yeah, you and everyone else.*

"So, uh, how're you doing now?" Ruse asks me before he takes another swig of his drink. He's unnaturally awkward around me right now, which disturbs me more than I'm willing to admit. He's spent the past week embarrassingly acting as my shadow. Making sure I consume "normal" food and not surviving off of liquor. Upping our runs and weight sessions. Forcing me to watch an old movie with him when I said I couldn't sleep.

He's fucking semi-mothering me, and it's infuriating.

I press the palms of my hands into my eyes, sighing deeply. "I don't even know how to answer that. I'm pretty numb at the moment."

"Yeah, we all are," Jace says. "But you've been snapping at everyone and everything this past week. We know work is rough right now and seeing Eira that messed up is bothering all of us. Today didn't help. Fucking Hungatians."

"Is something else going on? You can talk to us, Tryg," Ruse asks, turning to face me.

My friends' stares burn into my neck. I don't know what to fucking tell them. Is it the crushing weight of my new responsibilities? The senators contacted me today to have my team join their military base. Is it seeing Eira upsettingly fragile and hurt? It's starting to click that she might have more of my heart than I realized. Is it that wack-ass dream I had last week? I could have sworn it was real, though, that I was physically in those woods and following the crows. But *what* was that creature? I shudder, remembering the grip of its teeth clamping around me. Is it my lack of sleep? It seems whenever I close my eyes, I'm hit with some form of a nightmare or freaky shit.

I settle with, "It feels like I'm juggling iron weights. That are covered in flammable cloth. That are now on fire. And I can't keep up with it all. I can't keep up."

"Hey, man," Ruse says, clapping my shoulder with his hand. "We're all juggling a bit too much right now, and the missile attack isn't helping. Everything was dead silent until those buildings were raging with flames. Today has been fucked. But you're not alone in doing this, alright?"

I glance up at my friend, my closest team member. Technically, my co-investigator. My brother. His honey-glazed dark eyes shine with such kindness, it's hard not to believe him.

"Yeah, we're in this together," Jace adds. His gray eyes are a shade darker than usual, and his bronze skin has a greenish tint, as if he's going to be sick but is trying to hold it together. "We're all going to process everything in different ways. Although, it might be in your best interest to not, uh, destroy Shira's home. I'm not sure she'll be too happy when she sees what you did out there. Did you have to rip up the pillows?"

"I don't even remember doing that part," I huff out a forced laugh. "I saw red. I was told that creep caused Eira to pass out and left bruises on her arms, and when I got here, I couldn't even see her. Who does that? Who prevents friends from seeing one another?"

"I don't think that's what Shira's doing, Tryg," Jace says. "She is working with her own team to help Eira. I'm more concerned with who that guy was and how he left actual black bruises and burns on her skin. Not even purple. It looked and smelled like cooked meat. Athena barely made it to the toilet to throw up—it smelled revolting. And the worst part? The guy was unquestionably horrified. Genuine fear. He let her go like she'd hurt *him* and was sobbing in the corner."

Huh. None of this is making any sense. "Did someone take him in for questioning?" I ask.

Jace and Ruse share a strained look. "Uh, no," Ruse says. "No, they couldn't take him."

"And why the fuck not? Do I need to do it myself?" I sense my anger surging to the surface again.

"He killed himself, Tryg," Jace rasps. "He lunged for the worker's mug of coffee and shattered it. Before she could stop him, he used an edged piece to slit his throat. Blood splattered over Eira because he couldn't get a clean cut. That sent Athena running to the bathroom again. It was... disturbing. By the time I rushed to him and moved Eira out of the way, he was dead."

Dead? He was in a panic, inexplicably harmed Eira, acted terrified, and then killed himself.

I blow out a sharp breath, swirling the last of my wine in the glass.

I don't know what the hell is going on, but I have a feeling it's only the beginning.

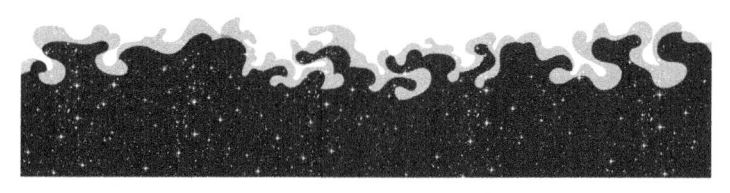

TWENTY

Eira

Death is only terrifying to those not at peace with it.
Peace is only obtainable by embracing the terror of death.
-Mural quote at the Seeds of the Lotus

Beginnings and endings of too many things swish past my blurred vision. I'm nothing and everything. I'm emptiness and fullness. I exist, yet I don't. Around and around and around it all goes in my head. Parts of me are scattered to the wind, lost and forgotten forever. Other parts are nestled in the soil, cradled with love and care as a mere seedling. I'm the crashing waves and the fire that licks the bark of a tree. I can't be contained in one thought or sensation or place or moment in time. It's too much and pushes and expands me to my limits, beyond my limits.

Yet I don't feel enough. This sensation of power and awareness is but a small taste. Will it ever be enough?

A small hand grasps my own, a little girl with bright blond hair appearing in front of me. The barely clear part of my vision. Dizziness threatens to overtake me, and she pulls me closer to her, forcing me to stare into eyes eerily similar to my own.

"You must be brave, sweet Eira," she whispers, her voice as soft as satin. It curls around me in ribbons, blocking everything else from my view. "There's more to this war than you know. It's been building for centuries—the Sairn biding their time until the perfect, most awful moment. They wanted you so trapped under your traumatic death that you'd never resurface."

She holds my face. Her hands are as soft as velvet. "Listen to me, Eira. Remember what I tell you. You *must* find the other pieces of your soul. Go to Nyx. Trust your soul mates, all of them that you find. Remember who you were created to be in these realms, caught up in a frenzied upheaval."

As quickly as she comes, she disappears. Yet another scrap of nonsense. Names I don't understand or know. An urgency that scares me, but I can't bring myself to move from where I'm floating in this unknown space.

A blissful sweetness invades my senses and glides subtly within me like cotton. I let out a breathy laugh as it tickles and skims against my sensitive skin. *Skin*. I have skin. It's too thin to contain all that I'm now connected to.

Have I always been this fragile and weak? Immensely powerless to the unseen forces billowing around me?

That sweetness lies on me as a cloud, a blanket for my inner self. I'm relearning the feeling of skin and bones, all rooting me down while this smell lifts me up to the sky. Something flicks my neck and shoulders and runs down my arms, down my torso, down my legs. *Ah, I have muscles*. Trembling muscles and connective tissues.

Cool liquid is rubbed into my forearms. It's alleviating and quiets my mind. I notice that I'm lying on a comfortable surface and that withered hands are massaging different muscles. They're waking them up. But not me. I don't want to fall back into existence again. My body is here, and it's simply a body, an instrument for my soul to use. I don't need it to function, to fly free into the world and explore what lies beyond what the eye can see. There's that cool liquid again, now being rubbed into my hands. A sharp prick hurts my palms and extends out to my fingertips.

I don't want to experience this pain again. My body can keep it, I don't need it.

Pressure moves up my neck into my face. My jaw feels too tight—that sweetness can't help it. More muscles are waking up. *What's that sound?* A hum in the background, hidden from view. No, no, it's not my muscles that are waking up. It's something else. There's now a pressure in between my eyebrows. It's my true mind. *I have a mind.*

My mind hears, "Wake up, Eira."

Gasping and coughing, I force my eyes open. A sweet-scented haze wisps in front of my face. Shira and a few unknown faces come into view, all with various levels of concern. Shira is continuing to shake an item over my body and chanting in a low tone. Breathing life back into me, into my physical form. I'm covered in oils and am trying to fully process where I'm at and what's going on now. It's like waking up from a fever dream.

"Welcome back, hun," Shira murmurs, pushing strands of hair out of my face. "I wasn't sure we'd get you back there for a second."

I blink up at her, not quite processing all her words. The other people are kind of freaking me out. They're watching me, and the weight of their stares is building an uncomfortable pressure under my skin. It's too difficult to get a full breath in, and I just—

"Thank you for your support today. We can discuss more after dinner," Shira says quietly to the others. She's blocking their view of me while she continues to speak with them in hushed voices. They silently leave the room, and I can finally take a breath.

"They're rather kind," she says to me. "And curious about what you're going through. Maybe different from others. But kind, nonetheless. They dropped everything they were doing to come assist me today."

"That's, uh, nice of them," I mutter, unsure what to even say. My throat feels caked with chalk and sand, and my voice sounds like a lizard. *Gross.*

"I'm sure you have many questions," Shira says with a small smile. "One of the doctors at the center thought you were having a seizure, and another thought you were hallucinating. I have tremendously different thoughts. But don't worry, we'll have plenty of time for that later. Before, I kept your friends from you so that you could get actual rest and have space to process everything. I fear Tryg is at his wit's end out there. If you're up to it, I'll let them in now?"

My friends. I close my eyes, trying to visualize each person's face. "This will sound crazy, but can you list their names for me?" I ask.

"Nothing sounds crazy around here, dear. Athena, Astira, Liv, Lyk, Jace, Ruse, and Tryg are waiting in the living room," she says.

Their faces pop up in my head as she goes through their names. Yes, these are my *friends*. I perceive them as far away and disconnected right now. I want to ask for space to rest and reorient myself, but I remember a conversation about Tryg acting unusual and upset. I have enough going on and certainly don't want that on my hands right now.

"Um, yeah. I want to see them," I mumble. "Can I have some water, please?"

"Already done," she says and moves a large glass of water closer to me on the wooden end table. "There are also crackers, dried fruit, and chocolates on this plate for you. You might want to eat a few of those now. I know how those boys can get around food." She winks before walking out the door.

The water soothes a layer of the dryness in my throat. It's as if I've been wandering a desert, which let's be real, I would never be caught doing. I can't understand why I'm responding this way and what the hell happened to me. I'm munching away on a few chocolates when my friends crowd through the doorway. They're pushing at one another to get in here first, and I can't help but smile at their juvenile ways. I rasp out a laugh when Liv pushes her hand into Jace's face and Lyk ducks in between his legs.

Before they can reach my bed, a furball flies across the room and jumps on top of me. I'm not sure who thought to bring her, but my heart is bubbling with delight.

"Zaya! My baby," I cry into her fur, already smothering her against me. Most cats would struggle to flee. *My* cat purrs and licks my chin like the little pampered and tolerant queen that she is.

"You were right; it was a good call to bring Zaya over," Jace says with a smirk, glancing at Athena. *Of course* it was her. I shoot her a grateful look, and she smiles down at me, appearing exhausted but relieved.

"So, uh, welcome, everyone," I say, suddenly self-conscious and awkward. I know they're my friends, but I still regard them as too far away from me. And there are seven pairs of eyes watching me. Tryg is studying me intensely, effectively burning holes through my skin. *Ugh, I want to sleep.*

"We came for the party," Ruse says. He's already reaching for my bowl of snacks when Astira knocks his hand out of the way.

"Those are for her, asswipe," she snarks. She shoots him, Jace, and Tryg pointed glares before turning to me, her eyes softening. "We're *really* glad you're okay, friend."

"Yeah, you gave us a scare," Jace adds, moving a step away from Astira.

"But you're alive and awake now!" Lyk chirps. "And we brought you flowers."

Liv had jogged out of the room a second ago and is now returning with bundles of different bouquets. "We weren't sure what to get, so we picked one of everything," she says excitedly. "They can keep you company while you sleep tonight." I don't miss Lyk's devilish grin and the little baggie of stick-on googly eyes in her hand. I know the immediate creepy direction her thoughts are taking. Both sisters are into the most harrowing, weirdest shit. If I didn't know they're trying to pull a laugh out of me, I'd be terrified of how many flowers are now surrounding me.

Athena snorts. "Yeah, that's exactly what she wants. Flowers guarding her bedside. With tiny eyes. You weirdos." She turns to face me and plays with the ends of my hair. "The only thing Eira wants right now is to eat and sleep, but she's too nice to tell us to fuck off."

Scowling, I say, "*Maybe*, but maybe I also want to see you freaks."

"Hmm, we can help with the food part," Ruse offers. "I placed an order for pickup about fifteen minutes ago. It's your favorite pasta, and I know how you feel about those breadsticks." He wags his eyebrows suggestively.

I giggle and nod enthusiastically. Yes, *please*. I'll always accept breadsticks. Well, anything to do with bread.

"Alright, we'll go pick it up while you take a power nap, and we can talk more. For however long Shira allows us to hang out with you," Ruse says before messing with my hair. He and the others pile out the door, eager to grab the food and head back here. Athena and Tryg stay by my bedside.

"Do you want some company while the others get the food? Or would you prefer to rest before eating?" Athena asks.

"I normally would ask you to stay, but my eyes are burning. I think it would be best if I close them for a few minutes," I say, scratching behind Zaya's ears. My eyes droop and I sense they're aching to close.

Nodding her head, she squeezes my hand and glances at Tryg, motioning for him to follow her out.

Tryg continues to stare at me, his usual rich eyes a shade darker tonight. I can't quite read the expression on his face. There's exhaustion and sadness and what could be despair. He quietly walks to my side and leans close to me, keeping eye contact the whole time. A beat later, he kisses my cheek and stands up, walking swiftly out the door. Athena raises her eyebrows and gives me her classic *that's-some-wild-shit-right-there* look, and I have to suppress a laugh.

She follows Tryg out, and I fall back on my pillow, heaving a resigned sigh. My heavy eyelids are already closed, and I feel myself getting pulled under the veil of sleep. Zaya curls on top of my stomach, her fluffy tail swishing along my forearm while she kneads her little claws into my abdomen. Seconds tick by, and it's all going in slow motion. Slower tick by even slower tick. I recognize the disconnection from my body again and have the briefest thought that the doctors might be right: I could be dissociating. But that thought is gone in a flash as I experience a tugging sensation, and I'm ripped out of my physical body.

I'm floating above myself and wonder if I've died. If this is what happens when you take your last breath. *Am I a ghost? Am I a spirit? Oh, shit, I better not be a demon. Surely, I wasn't that horrible.*

I don't get to ponder my existence and journey into death. That tugging sensation returns, and I'm not even sure how to describe it other than traveling. I'm drifting through time and space. I leave through the walls of this house, through the surrounding trees until I'm in the forest, and I continue hovering above and through creatures out in the early evening. I can't detect the cold or what I pass through, and suddenly I'm jerked up high, high, high into the sky, gliding with the chilly breeze. I'm taken all the way to the mountains, which are painted pink and purple by the dusky sunset.

There's no warning before I'm free falling down the side of a cliff, and if I was in my body, I would absolutely be screaming my lungs out. I was confused before, but now I'm terrified. *Where am I going? What is pulling me? Could I bargain with it for death at this point?* Mistakenly, I look down and realize I'm about to crash.

Well, shit. Death it is, then.

Except I don't crash. Not even close.

I continue to fall through the ground into a vacuumed space hidden in the air. It's the size of a pin, and then I'm once again nowhere and everywhere all at once. I get the sensation that time is both happening yet stopped. There's no concept of anything here, and it squeezes in around my essence. There's no way to scream, but it builds up in my very being anyway, begging for a release. I can't take this, I need help, I need to stop somehow, what do I—

I land with a groan onto moist soil and a bedding of thick, wavy leaves. It takes a few minutes to realize that I'm in a physical body again, and after what I went through, there's no way I'm opening my eyes. *Nope*. Not a chance. This might be one of those dreams or memories, or I might be losing my mind. Either way, I don't need to see which body I'm in now. Once was enough for me, thanks.

A rough hand gently shakes me, and I can't stop the scowl on my face. *This has been the longest day of my life, and I'm over it.* I decide that between being touched again and opening my eyes to assess what's going on, I'd rather open my eyes. Maybe they won't keep prodding me. I hate being touched when I've had an exhausting day, and I don't care where I'm currently at. They better keep their paws off me. Unless those paws belong to Zaya, obviously.

I cautiously open my eyes, squinting into the bright light. It's overwhelmingly sunny and warm here. The humidity is already coating my skin in a fresh layer of sweat, and my hair is sticking to my face. *Lovely*. The leaves beneath me feel like cushions, but the edges tickle my back. Glittery vines curve around me, framing around my body and keeping it safe. The oddest sensation overcomes me, and I realize that I'm miraculously *not* enduring the weight of my usual fatigue and constant pain that withers away at me. Before I get a proper read of my surroundings or investigate these pain-free feelings further, a violet and cobalt-blue bird pokes its face in front of me.

"Welcome home, Eira. You finally made it."

TWENTY-ONE

Nyx

Drekstri are the leaders of the twisted mountain ranges, allies solely to those who've been equally as misunderstood as their kin.
-Correspondence from Cania, High Shapeshifter

Erika and I finally make it back to the main living area. We're plopped down on two worn cushions against the wall, not able to stumble to the chairs across the room.

"So, to make sure I'm understanding you," Erika whispers. "The woman that you dreamed about, who you think you're connected to, made an appearance through the dead child's body in my workroom? And you're convinced that you loved her at some point. But you don't know what she looks like except for her eyes. And she poofed into the air as a magical, golden dust."

I'm chewing the crunchy bean snack that Vaira made while Erika talks this out. I nod my head, staring at the floor in front of me. "Yeah, that about sums it up."

"Huh," Erika mutters, reaching over for a handful of the

spiced beans. "And you haven't told anyone about this mystery woman?"

"I told you, I *just* had that dream a few nights ago," I hurl at her.

"Yeah, I know. But if you're convinced she is the love of your life or whatever, you'd think you would've said something. Not dove into bed with Fraya," she responds.

Scowling, I pluck a dried bean and flick it at her. "I also already told you that Fraya came to me when my beast was salivating for blood. And I felt that woman inside me the whole time."

Erika side-eyes me and says, "I didn't realize you were into that sorta thing."

I grab a handful of the beans and am about to throw the whole thing at her when Hadwin waltzes through the archway, humming a raunchy song. He takes in the scattered beans, Erika laughing, and my demeanor before dragging another floor cushion our way. He looks like he'd rather be anywhere else, but here we are.

"Are you, um, good?" he asks, eyes flicking between Erika and me.

"I don't know, why don't you ask Nyx about his girlfriend who uses dead children's bodies to contact him," she says before cackling and rolling out of the way as I fling bean after bean at her.

"The first thing I'm going to ask the healers today is what hurt you in the other realm to turn you into such a morbid and screwed up animal," I say. I try to roll the irritation out of my shoulders before turning to Hadwin. His eyes are slightly bulging, and he looks beyond dumbfounded. "What did Odin say before? That human expression? Oh, 'it's probably a defense mechanism and how you respond to fear.'"

Erika lets out a frustrated growl at me before rolling into a standing position. She brushes off her pants and sends me a vulgar gesture. "I'm going to get more food and work on my *defense mechanisms*. Just because I make a joke after watching a dead child awaken doesn't mean I'm a screwed up animal. It means some part of my soul is still *human*, Nyx, even if it's a little fucked up. If that bothers you that fucking much, maybe you should take a gander in the mirror to figure out why," she huffs before stalking off.

I flinch, not expecting such a sting to my conscience. I didn't realize I would hit such a nerve.

I didn't realize that I would *care* that I did.

"You know not to call her or Odin animals," he says, shaking his head. "You know how they were treated before their souls crossed over to our land."

I don't respond. What's there to say? That I'm sorry? *I'm not.* I don't know who that woman is, but she isn't simply a girl-friend, and she definitely isn't trying to use dead children to contact me. This whole situation is beyond me, beyond any of us, and I'm not in the mood for dark, sickening comments. Erika is fierce and loyal, but she also doesn't know when to stop with the morbid and twisted comments. *I'm so tired.*

"Care to clue me in on what's going on?" Hadwin asks. "One minute, you're behind us with that child slung over your shoulders. The next, you're handing her off and following Jade into the woods without another word. And I'm afraid to ask what Erika meant by girlfriend and an awakened dead child, so if it's not necessary, feel free to leave that part out. Really."

I knock my head back against the chilled wall, breathing deeply through my nose. I didn't want everyone knowing about this woman. Not, at least, until I made more sense of it. But I *do* have to tell them about what Jade showed me last night. And while magic is the very air we breathe here, that doesn't mean children die easily, even by Ulf, and then awaken with someone else's soul inside them. I don't know what's going on and already decided to speak with the healers about it. They work with pain and suffering but also with death. And they're the few *solliqas* who won't turn us away because of uncontrollable sins.

"Alright, get comfortable. But I don't want to tell it again to the others. Either get them now or be okay with sharing this with them after," I tell him.

Hadwin doesn't respond. He narrows his eyes at me and gives a quick nod of his head. I tell him about the dream I had and what happened when Fraya came into my room. I explain what I felt when we went to the village and who Jade led me to, and I finish with what Erika and I saw in her workroom, leaving out as many details as possible.

Hadwin is one of my closest friends, more of a brother than anything. He has seen some scary shit over the years, especially with me. For most of the story, he can take it without much of a reaction, soaking it all in and organizing the information around in his mind for later. But even *he* is visibly nervous when I go through the part about Jade and who we saw.

Swallowing, Hadwin breaks his steel mask and notably pales. "You... you're sure you saw *him*? We destroyed him, obliterated his soul, and sent any broken shards of it to another world entirely."

"I know what we did," I snap, growing agitated and worried with raw fear. "I'm the one who opened the portal of shadows and kicked any of his remains to a place so far from here, there's not even a chance his slimy carcass would be able to slither its way back. I also know what I felt and saw."

A moment passes by, and we don't say anything. We sit in strained silence. The gears in my brain are slowly churning, searching for puzzle pieces from the last few days of events.

Hadwin breathes in sharply and squares his shoulders. His golden eyes harden into stone. There's the warrior I know, ready to strategize and take down the threat. "None of this makes sense to me, but if what you're saying is true, we need to get to the healers *now*. Go get whatever you need, and for all our sake, apologize to Erika. Unless you enjoy waking up to a flooded bedroom and decaying fish. I'll brief the others and we can head out."

I strap the last knife to my thigh and sheathe my favorite dagger, a gift from Eliina, a magnificent healer, back in Rioa. The sapphire jewel in the hilt creates a star shape when light hits it a certain way. She had said it would provide the direction I need when the time is right. I snort, pulling my unruly hair back into a bun. It's been a decade now. I highly doubt that it will ever be *right,* and the only direction I seem to go in is spiraling downward.

I'm rather fond of pointy objects I can stab *solliqas* with, though, so I carry it with me whenever I can. Even if my powers are more than sufficient to destroy others.

Unexpectedly, Erika knocks on my opened door and leans against it. She crosses her arms and gets in her *don't-fuck-with-me* stance, but her eyes betray her. They're a little puffy, as if she's been crying. *Shit*. On instinct, I hold my arms out, willing her to come over. She hesitates, but walks somberly toward me and burrows her head into my shoulder. My arms fold around her, pulling her to my chest, and she sniffles.

"I didn't mean what I said," I murmur into her silky hair. "I felt frustrated that you made a joke about what happened, and I fell into my own usual defense mechanism—lashing out. I'm sorry for being a shithead."

She gives me a watery smile. "Don't worry too much about

being a shithead. You'll end up having to apologize daily for that."

I arch an eyebrow down at her. She continues with a shaky voice, "I'm sorry for how that came out before and hurting you. You're like my big brother, and it scared me to my core to see that child staring back at us. Even more so when you said you saw those eyes before. I'm scared, Nyx. If I don't try to laugh, I'm not gonna survive any of this."

I tug Erika back into me and stroke her hair, rocking us. She feels vulnerable right now, even though I know her other forms are immensely terror-inducing, frightfully destructive, that she was banned with the rest of us. She's lethal with any amount of water, even one drop, and I suspect her soul was always this powerful if the humans kept her locked down as a slave. No one does that unless they're scared they'll be overpowered. And Erika? She could drown all of this realm's regions if she wanted to.

She pulls back and glances up at me, appearing more like her normal plucky self. An unspoken understanding settles between us, and she nods, turning to walk out the door. I follow behind her as we head down the winding stairs. Bracing myself for the others' reactions, we reach the tunnel that leads to the *drekstri*.

"Hey, Nyx?" Erika asks.

"Yeah?"

"Something's changing in you. I—I think it might potentially be wonderful."

I don't respond. Mostly because she's right. I actually communicated my *feelings* to her. These are indeed dark times.

Ulf and Odin are already loaded up and ready to go, leading their *drekstri* outside. Each creature is a work of art, albeit stubborn and wild. With powerful legs that end with hooves and hidden talons and large, leathery wings covered with colored feathers, they're unique and deadly. Thick scales coat their necks, backs, and chests, as well as weave in patterns along their faces and legs, making it *extremely* challenging to kill them. They have big, pointed ears and a flowing mane, yet their faces are reptilian, with large fangs and jagged teeth. Coming across one can mean certain death if you don't know what you're doing. It takes months, not to tame them, but to convince them you're worthy of their loyalty and care. The bastards in Rioa don't have the patience it takes to bond with them, but we sure as fuck do.

They throw us out to Reykashin, and we rise up stronger than ever with the other abandoned beasts they've deemed unworthy.

We have a full corral of *drekstri* now, but we're only taking a few to see the healers. Ulf's is a dark gray with white markers on its face and back. Odin's is a mixture of blues, matching his affinity to water perfectly. And mine? Mine is black and gold with streaks of silver in her mane. She flies through the clouds like smoke, and we're so in tune with one another, it at times feels as if we share the same mind. I named her Ambra, and while I can't be sure what she thinks about it, she responds and has accepted this name.

"Who are you riding with today?" I ask Erika while I strap a few supplies to Ambra's back.

She scrunches up her nose and glances out at the others. Ivar is humming while dragging a crabby-looking Fraya out the gate. He's the peacemaker of our group, convinced there's something worth saving in each of us. Or maybe that's the tragic story he tells himself. I can't see how he can act this content with Fraya acting the way she does.

Erika's eyes harden when they settle on Fraya's grumbling form. It's not entirely her fault that we all have such complex feelings toward her. She can be selfless and caring and in tune with the emotions of each creature around her, even the *drekstri*. Yet the image of Fraya slinking her way into my room where I'm purposefully chained washes out any good that's visible. It's been getting harder and harder for her to control her darkness.

And *maybe*, a voice in my head whispers, *maybe it's easier for Fraya to be the scapegoat when her faults are much more visible.*

Yet does that excuse her actions?

"Can I hitch a ride with you?" Erika asks. "I'm always with Odin, and Ulf gets a little too flip-crazy in the air. I'm meant for the water, Nyx. Not rolling around in the sky."

Biting back a smile, I nod my head. The last journey she rode with Ulf, he steered them down so unexpectedly swiftly, she toppled off, and I had to catch her shrieking form.

"Alright, hop on," I say. "Quickly, before Fraya sees and throws a fit."

Erika chuckles and launches herself up. As I guessed, when we meet the others outside, Fraya is already bristling. I pull myself up in front of Erika and shake my head. "Don't even start," I cut Fraya off before she can speak. "It's a mere few hours' journey. You'll be fine with Odin."

"What if she wanted to ride with me?" Ulf asks, wiggling his eyebrows.

"I'm sure she does," I say with a smirk. "But you'll also use this as an opportunity to finally get rid of her. We don't have time for that kind of drama today."

As if sensing his rider's desire, Ulf's *drekstri* bares his teeth at Fraya, causing her to yelp and stumble back a few steps into Odin.

Smirking, I clasp onto the mane in front of me and squeeze my thighs, letting Ambra know we're taking off. "Let's ride."

"Aye," Hadwin yells out from behind us.

He trails out of the tunnel, strapped with weapons, and is in the process of plaiting his hair back out of his face. "Typical Nyx fashion—leaving me behind without a kiss goodbye."

Rolling my eyes, I turn Ambra to face him and urge her a few steps closer. She swings her head back and forth, edgy to get into the sky. "I thought we agreed that's exclusively for your bedroom," I say, smirking. I love him like a brother and am in no way interested in anything more. But I do love how much it makes Fraya squirm.

She wants to be with me so badly that she's willing to cave to her illness. Even if it means she'll be consumed by the dark. Even if it means she forces herself upon me when I don't want it.

So, I *love* watching her get worked up in the worst way possible. It serves her right.

Hadwin pats Ambra's side and lifts his gaze to mine. "When I finish up here, I'll head to the base. I should be there by tomorrow night. Don't have too much fun without me." He winks before stalking off toward our crumbling home.

"What does he mean?" Erika whispers behind me.

"He wasn't talking to you. Don't worry about it," I reply quickly. I don't give her a chance to respond before I'm kicking Ambra's side and she's taking off at a gallop. The only sounds I hear are my own pounding heartbeat and Erika's high-pitched scream.

TWENTY-TWO
Eira

A new world is only new to those who haven't been there.
-Page 893, Introductory Lessons in Realms and Worlds,
Volume I

A scream lodges in my throat and a small squeak comes out. I push my body as hard as I can into the ground, desperately trying to put any amount of distance between me and this bird. *The bird that speaks. What the actual fuck? Therapist has officially turned client. Someone help me.* It twitches its head and hops a step closer to me, and I instantly recoil while hovering my hands above my face. This is all the protection that I've got right now.

A slender hand pulls the bird back and tosses it at the thick, winding tree to the right. The bird changes from violet and blue to a deep shade of red and fluffs out its feathers.

"Rude," it comments. "Rude, but totally expected from the likes of you."

A man, or at least I think it's a man, appears above me. His body is lithe, and he's wearing what appears to be a normal T-shirt and jogging pants. Wait, no. The materials are shimmery and gauzy. *Interesting*. He has dark blond hair pulled back in a bun, a slightly curved nose, and mossy green eyes in the shape of almonds.

"Hi there," he breathes and clears his throat. "I'm sorry about Del over there. He's an idiot and doesn't quite grasp the art of social interactions." He takes a step toward me, and I scuttle my way back a few feet, the vines traveling with me as if they're protective snakes. "My name's Daru. I imagine that you're a bit, uh, stunned and overwhelmed right now."

He sits back on his knees, peering down at me with a gentleness that puts me at ease, which surprises me. I don't know where I'm at, what I'm doing, or who these creatures are, yet one of them can lull me with a look. I'm emotionally terrified and physically at ease. It's entirely unsettling.

I muster up what confidence I have left. "Who-o, wh-at are you?" My stupid shaking voice betrays how scared I am. Tears prickle at my eyes, and I'm hoping the faster I blink, the longer I can keep them at bay. Whatever these things are, they sure as hell aren't seeing me have a breakdown. Yet.

"This poor girl. You rip her away from her reality and bring her right to this swampy forest, of all places, with zero explanation. It's a wonder either of you can still function with the few brain cells you have," a woman mutters as she walks closer to us. She has cropped, wavy auburn hair and hazel eyes framed with swoon-worthy lashes. Her skin is unrealistically smooth and kissed by the sun. I see a slender body, but muscles ripple along her arms and abdomen as she walks. The scowl she sends at this Daru guy gives me hope she could be a potential ally.

"The name's Daya," she says with a smoky voice, smirking. "Daru is marginally better than Delano, but don't hold your breath. They're both trouble."

"I was doing fine before I was *thrown* at a tree," Delano grumbles, and the color-changing bird is now a man. Yeah, *a man*. Because that's normal. At least, I think he's a man. I still have no idea who or what they are. When he walks over to Daya, I immediately see that they're related. The same shade of hair and hazel eyes, even the same height. Delano is packing more muscle than Daya, though. He's also quite fidgety, kind of anxious looking. Daya appears laid back and relaxed, the total opposite.

It must be obvious that I'm connecting them together. "Yuppp, we're twins," Daya says, rolling her eyes. "It's as annoying as it sounds."

Delano huffs in vexation and pushes her. "Hey! I'm not that bad. I'm the one who figured out how to bring her here."

"Uh, yeah, and you didn't bother to give her any warning or heads up. Or *me* a heads up. You're a real genius," Daya snarks back, crossing her arms.

I'm watching their conversation, eyes darting back and forth between all three of them. A coppery taste fills my mouth as I continue to gnaw at the inside of my cheek, debating what I should do. The twins are bickering with one another a good five feet away, but Daru is still kneeling near me.

This place *feels* similar to a humid, swampy forest, but it looks like something out of a fairy story. Not all the colors are lining up, which is already giving me a headache. Leaves are shades of blue, purple, and yellow streaks. The trees are not the usual brown bark, but rather a dark green, the same as Daru's eyes. I can't tell what color the water is, and the grass, or what I presume to be grass, is fluffy and bright white, as if it was sprinkled with snow. There's a sun above me that's mostly blocked by the huge leaves, yet it's still scorching. *Ugh, I hate sweating like this. I'm already a wreck and don't even have deodorant with me. Yikes for them.*

Daru meets my gaze, and I notice that calmness wash over me again. Startled, my eyes rove over my body, confused where this sensation is coming from. My mind's racing, chasing its own tail in circles. This is my body, yet it isn't. There's more muscle packed along my arms and legs, and my skin is uncharacteristically clear and smooth as marble. I didn't realize how much the imperfections mattered to me until I can't find them. Maybe because they are *mine*. I need a sense of normalcy.

"Would you stop that?" Daya snaps at Daru.

"I'm trying to help her feel better," he says, wincing. "She's projecting all sorts of tension and negativity right now."

"She doesn't need, or I'm sure *want*, you to do anything to her right now," Daya continues. Her eyes flare with light, but it's gone so quickly I wonder if I imagined it. "What she needs is fluid, food, and answers. In a comfortable location. Not in the middle of the swamp. If you would have waited even a few more minutes before bringing her here, we could have had everything set up and ready to go."

"But she was dozing off and connecting to this realm already," Delano starts. "It was the perfect—"

"Oh, calm your beak, featherbrain," she mutters. "You're even worse than Daru, talking to her in your fucking bird form. *Ridiculous.*"

My breathing becomes uneven again and my nervous system rushes into sensory and information overload. My hands tremble as I push myself up into a sitting position and I clumsily scoot backward another few feet from this trio of creatures. All three stop to watch me, and Daya shoots both men a warning glare. Daru slowly moves back a few feet and Delano joins him on the ground, not making sudden movements. Part of my brain can recognize that they're trying to show me they aren't a threat and are treating me how I would treat one of my clients with a trauma response.

The majority of my brain is saying *fuck this* and urging me to hide under one of these massive roots until I can figure out what to do next.

Daya approaches me with careful movements and removes

an item from a blue sack. "Can I come closer to sit near you?" she asks in a low tone.

I'm incapable of speech right now, but I manage to dip my chin in a shallow nod. Daya walks extra slowly, maintaining eye contact. Both of her hands are at her sides. Her right hand holds a type of jar with liquid sloshing around and her left hand is open and facing me. When she's a foot away, she carefully lowers herself to the ground and crosses her legs, sitting across from me and blocking my view of the two men. I let out a long breath I didn't realize I was holding, blowing a few strands that were sticking to my face.

"This is going to be a lot to take in," Daya says. "I can either start talking or you can ask me specific questions. Please know that you're safe. Those morons mean well, but they took you from your actual home," she cuts Daru a seething glare over her shoulder, "a little sooner than expected. That doesn't mean you're not safe, though. We will not harm you or will ever have any intention of doing that to you."

I nod, taking in everything that she says one word at a time.

"Before talking, though," she continues, "I think you might need some *lipva*, similar to water in your native language. And yes, I'll clarify how we're communicating right now, but first, water." She takes the lid off the jar and hands it to me. I look at it suspiciously, as if it'll squirt up and attack me. "It's safe to drink," she says. "Here, I'll show you."

Daya takes the jar back from me and takes a sip before handing it back. Nothing happens, and she gives me an encouraging smile. I hesitate because this could be the perfect way to trap me in this unknown place. My throat has that chalky feeling again, though, and I'm dying for refreshing water or even spiced tea. I bring the jar to my chapped lips. *Here goes Stage One Kidnapping.*

The liquid spills down my throat, and I experience cooling, immediate relief. There's no way this is water. This *lipva* is water on steroids, leveling my whole immune system up. It's as if I left the spa, yet I'm extra hydrated, rejuvenated, and, as the old saying goes, ready to rock and roll. Daya lets out a small giggle, and I realize she must be reading these thoughts on my face.

"It's nice, isn't it?" she asks. "Water reacts differently here. It's already healing where you come from, but this stuff... It can awaken the soul. Even a few sips can heal internal injuries and soul damage. A bigger jug of it can connect you with your higher self. Wait until you bathe in it!"

My eyebrows are inching higher and higher to the top of my head, and I swear they are going to disappear.

"So," Daya chirps, setting the jar next to her hip and settling further into the fluffy grass. "Where would you like to begin?"

I probably should ask where I'm at, why they took me, who they are, what they are, and a million other questions. Anything to stifle the rising panic when I think about Shira *not* getting the chance to explain what's happening to me. But for some dumb reason, the first question that pops out is, "All of your names start with D. Are you part of a club or something?"

Daya looks perplexed before she bursts out laughing. "*That's* your first question? You're more interesting than I originally thought." She shakes her head. "No, we're not part of a club. We are part of the same group of shifters, though, and come from a region in between Lagunit and Eikenbien. It's a coincidence that we all have names starting with D. Delano and I are named after elders in our family. Daru's family comes from the pine forest."

Shifters. What the fuck. *If this is still a dream, brain, feel free to wake up now. You made your point. I'm a basket case. The wires aren't connected. I get it.*

"Oookay," I say. "Shifters. Huh. Um, so, where are we?"

Daya smiles broadly. "You're in Majikaero. The realm known for its magic and spirit work and is where souls dwell. Our world is closely connected to Earth, yet entirely different, as you can already see. It's the land your soul craves, and we're so excited that you made it, Eira."

Magic? Spirit work? My soul craves? Shifters?

My body is one step ahead of me. Before I can blink, I'm having tunnel vision and I free-fall back toward the ground, hoping I wake up from this madness.

TWENTY-THREE

Tryq

*The eyes. It's always the eyes. If you have the courage to look
your victims in the eyes, you'll often have all the clues you need
to know who they are and what happened.*
-Rike Tonish, Commander of Sweazn Investigative Forces

Madness, that's what I'm witnessing. Half of our group are licking fingers full of oil and cheese. Jace, Ruse, and Lyk already snarfed down the breadsticks that we had to double back to order more. I can't judge them. This place does have the best bread and pasta in the city, and if I wasn't stricken with nausea, I'd be joining them right now.

"Have we entered the brooding stage?" Athena asks, nudging my shoulder with her own. While Astira is explosive fire, full of venom when it comes to me, Athena is quick-witted and focused but wraps you up in a heated blanket. Her eyes remind me of the forest, able to shift from a bird of prey to peaceful earthiness, the kind that grounds you.

"More like the *trying-to-loosen-fear's-tight-grip-on-me* stage," I mutter. It hit me brutally hard when we went to see Eira.

Embers were still smoldering in the pit of my stomach, ready to ignite into a raging flame. As soon as I saw her, though, a frigid fear pierced through me. What's worse is I can't even describe why I'm reacting this way. It goes beyond feeling keyed up for my friend. It's as if death's warped hand has clutched my heart, warning me that something is coming.

That it was already *there* in that room with Eira.

Athena glances at me, her eyes lined with genuine concern. "We're all afraid, friend," she whispers. "It's what we do with that fear that matters."

She grabs my hand and squeezes lightly. It's the same hand that punched a hole through Shira's wall an hour ago. But Athena pushes past that act of rage and laces her fingers with mine, not letting how I acted stop her from giving love. As if sensing my thoughts, she squeezes a second time, a knowing look on her face. *I don't deserve her friendship.*

"Let's get some food in us," she continues. "All that caffeine and lack of sleep need to be balanced out. And *not* with wine." She arches an eyebrow at me with that last comment. "We'll have water, carbs, and scavenge up more treats at Shira's. Then we can talk about what to do next. As *friends*." She offers me a tentative smile and pulls me along as we pile into Shira's home.

I blatantly ignore the entire living room, going as far as looking the opposite way as we walk past it. Astira coughs obnoxiously in front of me, and if it wasn't for Athena, I'm sure I'd be acting wildly inappropriate.

"We have returned!" Ruse yells out as we march down the hallway to Eira's room. "Prepare yourself for a feast."

"It's a wonder you can still eat," Liv mutters. "You already ate like ten breadsticks."

"Those were ten breadsticks too few," he replies, smiling widely as he opens the bedroom door.

Ruse's smile fades a bit, though, and the rest of us rush forward to see what's going on. Athena squeezes my hand even tighter and whispers, "I don't know what we'll see, but knowing how this day has gone, it won't be anything pleasing. Stay with me, Tryg. Eira won't be able to handle seeing you lose yourself again."

I wince, but nod my head. My breath snagging my lungs, I ready myself for a bloody and chaotic scene, and peer into the room. Everyone is standing there, gaping at Eira and her cat. *Silence.* The kind that withers your body down into nothing with how loud and imposing it feels. The kind that can't possibly happen when there's life. The kind that tugged at my heart earlier and whispered what I already knew but wanted to deny.

Eira and Zaya are physically in front of us. But I already know in my heart that they're dead.

There's no room for rage or fear. Only the wave of sadness filling me up, readying to wash me out to sea. The silence is too overpowering, drowning me, pulling me—

"Something's happened, I can feel it," Shira says, pushing us to the side like she's a river roaring into the mountain pass. She moves to Eira's bed and checks her neck for a pulse. After a few seconds, she does the same to Zaya. Shira brings her head down, her ear facing Eira's mouth and chest. Humming to herself, she squeezes along Eira's arms, torso, and legs, stopping at her feet.

"They're both alive," she tells us, and a cautious relief splits through me. "But something jarring has happened. To both of them."

"What do you mean?" Liv asks, taking a step toward Eira. Astira, Athena, and Lyk quickly follow, and then we're all standing around her in a half circle, subconsciously leaning on one another. Unable to take our eyes off our friend, who might be breathing, but she is clearly gone.

"I'm not entirely sure," Shira mutters. "They're breathing, but their energies feel off. Not the same as before. It's not necessarily bad, but I also don't detect Eira." She continues to talk under her breath and bustles around the room, gathering a few items I'm unfamiliar with.

Fucking gods. I can't take much more of this shit. What should I do? Think, Tryg. Think.

I follow my instincts and take Eira's hand in my own. My other hand plays with the bear bracelet dangling off her dainty wrist. Not entirely knowing what I'm doing, I take the bracelet off and put it against my heart, speaking to Eira mentally. *If you're in there and can hear me, please come back, my fox. We're so worried. We need you. I need you.* I close my eyes and take a shuddering breath. *Please. This bracelet is the thing on you that connects us. If you can hear me, please wake up and come back to us.*

Nothing happens. Which makes sense because this was a fucking dumb idea. I had the urge to place her bracelet against my chest, and now feel like an idiot for thinking that would do anything. I place the bracelet in my pocket, not wanting it to get lost if they take Eira elsewhere after this.

Athena and Liv lean into my sides, resting their heads on my shoulders. Jace asks, "So, what do we do, Shira? How can we help?"

Shira opens her mouth to respond, but Eira's body spasms and tenses before she can. We're all hovering over her and the cat, eager for a reaction, for *anything* at this point. Fuck, I'd give one of my arms to have Eira come back to us.

We collectively hold our breath as Eira calms down and flutters her eyes open. Zaya gives a slight twitch before doing the same, stretching her long body on Eira's chest. My entire body locks in place as she glances in my direction. They're still a silvery blue, those unique eyes that I've only ever seen on Eira, but they're also not. There's too much blue, they're too dark, there's something critically wrong. I want to call them *dull*, which pains me, considering nothing about Eira comes anywhere close to that word.

"Eira?" Astira asks, sounding docile and timid for, I'm sure, the first time in her life.

"Are you with us?" Athena croaks out and comes around to the other side of the bed, trying to get a better look at her.

"Hi, guys," Eira rasps. "Why's everyone all rattled and upset?"

That's not her. That's not my friend. That might be her voice, but the pitch is off. This is *wrong*.

"Who are you?" I snarl, narrowing my eyes as I glare down at her.

"Tryg!" Lyk scolds. "Don't mind him, he's being an overtired dick," she says to Eira. Except *not* Eira. I don't know who the fuck this is, but it's not her. I'll go to my grave believing this.

Shira taps my arm, and I whirl on her, my body going into fight mode. She silently shakes her head, her eyes flared with alarm and telling me that I need to be quiet.

I push her hand off me. "You know, don't you?" I step into her space, chest heaving, my neck straining. "Who is that, and where did Eira go?"

"Tryg, she's struggling to wake up. Why don't we unpack the food?" Ruse offers. Jace appears near my back, putting enough pressure on my shoulder to tell me he's bracing himself for me to explode.

"No!" I yell. "I'm this city's expert in solving cases and now in finding missing people. This is my fucking life. I know when someone's gone. And I'm *telling* you, Eira's missing. Her body might be here, but she's not *our* Eira. You might be too blind to see it, but I know this is wrong. And I'm going to figure it out, even if I have to do it alone."

I get in Shira's face, barely restraining myself from ripping out her throat. She has the good sense to look nervous.

"But I won't have to, will I?" I growl. "Because you're going to help me."

TWENTY-FOUR

Nyx

Give yourself over to the winds. They'll carry you to where you need to be, not to where you think you should go.
-Aapeli, Goddess of Air

"Help me, Goddess Derya, I beg of you," Erika whimpers, squeezing my chest to the point of constricting air flow.

"If you don't behave back there, I'm going to drop you onto Ulf and Ivar," I threaten, urging Ambra into a sudden steep dive for emphasis.

"Don't!" she screams. The high pitch pierces the space between my ears, making me regret taking her with me.

"Then I need you to loosen up," I call back to her, making sure she can hear me above the wind. "If I can't breathe, I won't be able to steer us, and then what are you gonna do? Close your eyes and lean your face into me. We're almost there."

Erika nestles into my back, her short hair shielding her view of the wispy clouds and vast sky. Two suns inch toward the horizon, one a yellow and orange fireball and the other a bright blue, the hottest flame. It's as if we're heading directly into them, ready to be engulfed in their smothering heat.

We're soaring exceedingly higher. I want to reach my hand out to skim against the stars beginning to appear. To soak their brightness into me, a weapon to be used against my darkened being.

Movement below catches my attention, and I see Ivar morph into one of his other forms. I blink, wondering if I'm imagining things. Where Ivar was free falling is now another *drekstri*, a purple so deep it looks black. I chuckle under my breath and give him a nod as he flaps his wings, dotted in what might be actual opals and amethysts. He drifts up next to me.

"I see you've been practicing," I shout, laughing in amazement at his abilities. Even Erika moves her head to the side and gasps. I don't know many shifters of his breed who can take on this many new forms, yet he somehow manages to do it. It's *incredible*.

Ivar glides to the side, brushing his shadow-covered wing against Ambra's, and dives in front of us. He does a flip and within seconds, he's bolting back up to us, elation dancing in his now lavender eyes.

"Show off!" Odin yells before moving out of the way, Ivar charging toward him. His laugh sounds carefree, so at odds with our situation and the reason for flying in the first place. Being up here does that to you, though. We're as free as the wind weaving around us, except for Erika. She's a frightened sea creature, barely scraping by up here. I suspect Odin encounters a similar panic, but he's always desired both the winds and the water. It's the land and fire that has him acting skittish.

"Nyx," Ulf shouts from beneath me. "We're approaching the valley. Where do you want to land?"

I steer Ambra down, flying closer along the edges of the cliff before the mountains open up into the valley. This is where these specific healers base themselves, as it's in the middle of the

Myrellden villages. Even though we're banished to a territory between Reykashin and Skugvaytir, the healers have made it clear they're neutral territory for anyone who's been tainted by the plague. As long as we can get to them. We can arrive quickly if we fly instead of ride, and I'm grateful for the *drekstri* that trust us.

I see a few healers working at the far end, and others are walking back and forth between their tented structures.

"Let's land down that way," I yell back, pointing to an area half a mile outside of their base. "I don't want to startle them. We're here for help, not to attack."

Ulf smirks up at me, a demon in humanoid form. "If you say so."

Ambra swerves on the current, bringing us closer and closer to tall, willowy grasses. Erika finally straightens up to take in the valley, already appearing more like herself. She's searching for something and squeezes my arm.

"Look! There's a river," she says with a sigh. "Can we land near there? I need to recharge for a sec before we walk over to the healers."

I want to tell her no, there's no time to recharge. But I forget how different her magic is from mine. There are shadows and smoke everywhere I go. They find me naturally. Ivar is always breathing air—he's charged up before he even wakes up in the morning. Her brother takes to the wind and to the sea, and as long as he has access to at least one of these elements, he's fine. The same idea applies to everyone else. Erika is the one who currently needs physical contact with water.

Without answering, I nudge Ambra closer to the river, which is another half mile away from where we were going to go. As we land, Ambra gradually slows from a gallop to a walk, and Erika scrambles off her back and runs straight for the river. Odin sends me a grateful nod before he jogs to meet up with her.

Ulf and I wrangle the three *drekstri* and lead them toward

the water, so they can get a drink. Fraya is sulking after tangling with the different energy in the sky, which I'm sure I'll be hearing about shortly, but luckily Ivar saves me. He lands right in front of her and, in a flash, is back in his humanoid body. She cuts me a glare, and Ivar puts an arm around her shoulder. He leads her up a few paces to a patch of shorter grass and drags her with him when he sits down. She looks grumpy enough that I stay clear on the other side of the *drekstri*. I'm hoping to avoid her a little longer while I calm my own emotions down and figure out what the fuck I'm going to do about her recent surges in evil behaviors.

"She didn't respond kindly to the news about this mystery woman," Ulf grunts, pulling out a parcel of food Vaira made for us.

"She's acting like a brat," I respond, rubbing Ambra's back as she gulps down water. "We're here to find answers. If she's not going to help, she should have stayed back home. Bothered another soul with her twisted kinks."

Ulf laughs while unwrapping some of the food we brought with us. He offers me a piece of smoked meat and a handful of bread. "We can only hope, Nyx. Let her ride with me on the way back. I'll take good care of her." He winks, eyes glowing black.

"Nuh uh. You'd be terrible for each other," I grumble, waving a finger at him. "As Odin says, just because we can turn into monsters doesn't mean we have to *act* like them. The last thing this realm needs is for you two sick fucks to get together and reproduce. It's challenging enough to bring a new *solliqa* into existence, but I'm positive you'd make one the first time she pounces on you."

Ulf cackles while he walks away. "I need to let off some energy before we get started. I'll be back," he calls over his shoulder. Alarm flares within me, but I get distracted when Odin and Erika pass him, appearing refreshed with dewy skin and shining eyes.

"Thanks, Nyx," Erika breathes. "I really needed that."

I nod toward her, happy that she's no longer cowering in fear. I'm also glad that she's jacked with power. The healers shouldn't harm us, but I lost all trust in anyone from Rioa, and honestly, the rest of the regions, long ago. I absently touch my weapons, reassuring myself that we're all ready for whatever the night brings us. *Maji* or not, a weapon is always good to have.

"Don't worry," Odin says quietly as they near. "We have weapons hidden under our clothes, too. They won't stand a chance if they try anything. And what are they gonna do? Send us to Reykashin again?" He barks out a laugh. "They can't do shit when we're now the rulers of such a scary place," Odin says in a mocking voice.

Erika hooks her arm in mine. "Yeah, they shunned what they feared, and now we're stronger than ever. We've got this."

I smirk, playing with the hilt of my dagger. In all honesty, we probably don't need any of our weapons. We *are* the weapons. But there's something comforting about honed steel decorating my body like a second skin.

The three of us slowly walk toward Ivar and Fraya. I'm silently praying to whichever god that listens that Ulf calms his wolf down before we walk over to the healers, wherever the fuck he went off to. The last thing we need is for him to go all *I'm-a-shadow-alpha-look-how-mighty-and-powerful-I-am* on them. I personally never need or want to deal with that shit, but he tends to act on it more when we're around others.

We all linger by the river while I make sure the rest of them get something to eat.

"Alright, is everyone ready to go?" I ask. Ivar nudges Fraya's arm, and she sighs dramatically but glances at me with a neutral expression and nods her head. I don't want to give her more ammo, so I choose not to respond and focus on everyone else. Ivar helps Fraya up and Odin cracks his neck, whispering into Erika's ear.

THE LIGHT WITHIN

"What will we do with the *drekstri*?" Fraya asks, sounding entirely too whiny. *Maybe I should stick her with Ulf.*

"You can stay with them," Odin suggests. "But no one is going to do anything to them. Anyone else living here is afraid of them and the *drekstri* have made it clear they're loyal to us."

Fraya considers this before shrugging and turns to face the base. Odin and I exchange looks and I sigh, hoping she'll figure out her shit. I want to avoid any form of conversation with her.

"Let's head over," I say. "Be on the lookout for Ulf."

We start walking when the tall grasses suddenly bend and flutter. A robed figure pushes the fucking demon himself out in front of them, his hands tied with thorny vines. Ulf grunts as he's pushed to his knees, sending a glare behind him that would make most souls cower in fear. But this is no ordinary *solliqa*. Cream and shades of green swirl along the robe that billows in the gentle breeze next to the river. While Ulf is struggling to move his hands and legs, vines continue to wrap tightly around him, pulling him to the ground. He glowers at me, obviously in pain, which is surprising. His pain tolerance is unnaturally high, even for us abandoned freaks, which means...

"Eliina," I whisper, taking a step toward her. I refuse to kneel to anyone, but I bow my head and shoulders as low as I can to show respect.

She steps around Ulf, not even casting him a glance, and comes to stand less than a foot in front of me. Delicate hands, adorned with stone rings and glittery bracelets that funnel her magic, lower her hood until her head is fully exposed. White-blond hair is pulled back in an intricate braid, and her green and black eyes assess me from my head to my toes. Her usually care-free smile is gone, replaced with pursed lips and shadows under her eyes, like she's also struggling with sleep.

The others take a giant step back, and despite what Odin and Erika said a few minutes ago, they *should* be afraid. Standing before me is the top healer in our realm. She has such a strong bond with the soil and rocks and plants that it takes half a thought to send her *maji* careening into you. If she was a different creature, she could use this for such evil and harm. But she's Eliina. A heart of fucking gold, so nauseatingly loving it could alone coerce Ulf to writhe on the ground.

I'm so captivated by Eliina's presence that it takes me a moment to see the robed healer standing behind her. Their head is bowed, humble yet skittish energy rolling off them in little gusts of wind. The left sleeve is ripped wide open, exposing three slashes of bright red on the healer's smooth skin. I can smell the taint of blood from here. Erika must see the bruises when I do because she gasps loudly, covering her mouth in horror. Nasty black handprints litter their arms and neck. Tendrils of smoke climb into the air, reeking of Ulf's scent.

I shoot him a lethal gaze and the fucker merely smirks at me and barres his teeth in a wolfish grin. As if attempted assault is a tantalizing game we should all be enjoying. *And how the fuck did he hunt down a poor* solliqa *this quickly?*

Fortunately, Eliina's vines tug him closer to the ground and he cries out in pain. She turns to murmur quietly to the healer behind her, and they vanish into the tall grasses back toward the base. Gone in such a hurry, as if they vaporized into thin air.

"I know you're shocked to see me here," her resounding, serene voice resonates with the parts of me that are still pure, still *good*. "The earth spoke to me and shared what you've experienced these past days, Nyx." She raises a hand to my chest, and I can't stop the tremble. Breathing in wholly, she pushes into me, and a spark of light blooms around my heart. "I see *you*, Nyx. I've come to meet you here and escort you back to the base. We've much to discuss. Come, all of you."

I peer back at the *drekstri* and as if reading my mind, Eliina says, "A few of my dearest healers are on their way to walk them back. You might remember them. Daglo and Rada. They've been warned about your animals' fierce and protective nature. Fear not, all will be well."

"What about Ulf?" Ivar asks, carefully avoiding his eyes.

Eliina looks momentarily annoyed. "Argh, *him*," she shoots him an irritated glare. "I caught him prowling toward one of my new healers in his wolf form on my way over here. Paloma is strong, but she's also new and hasn't worked with the likes of Ulf yet. I know the darkness overtakes him, and he can't always help himself when his shifter form gets anxious, but I won't tolerate any form of assault on my healers. I should leave him trapped here overnight as punishment and warning on how to behave around others. But he'll play an important part in what's to come, so I suppose I'll release him. And his self-sabotaging behaviors might be punishment enough."

The vines loosen enough for him to stand, and he lets out a startled yelp.

"Yes," Eliina says with a knowing smile, a bit mischievous. "The vines will stay on your feet and the earth will move you. You lost free will of your body the moment you tried to force your will on the body of another tonight. Let that be a warning for the rest of the time we'll be together."

Ulf glances at me expectantly. I shoot a dagger-shaped shadow at his legs, forcing him to fall to his knees. He's gotten too out of control lately and has to learn his fucking place.

"Rest of the time?" Erika squeaks, her tone laced in confusion.

Eliina's expression grows wary. "Yes, child. We'll be together for quite a while. Nyx knows I would have preferred our meeting to go differently. I never wanted any of you *shunned*. It's despicable. But the Council has need of you, and I—I have a different need that must remain a secret among us." She pauses, considering her words. "Something unexplainable is happening in this realm, and it's going beyond the plague of darkness with an attack in Rioa. Hundreds are wounded, homes have been destroyed. It's—it's devastating."

"Ah, so now that the Council requires our services, we're to bow down to you and do as you say?" Odin bites out, not nearly as reserved as he should be right now.

Eliina shakes her head. "No. While the Council is being rather demanding about using your, ah, talents, no. I would never allow for you to be abandoned in such a shameful way and then forced back into service. I'm here for a different reason under the guise of bringing you back to help the Council." She glances around the valley, eyes flaring with her power. "I'd rather say more when we're in the protection of my own tent and wards."

"You said you've seen what I've experienced these past days?" I whisper.

Solemnly, Eliina says, "Yes, my dear. And you're who I need to speak with the most. She's coming back. Not only to this realm, but to you."

TWENTY-FIVE

Eira

*When you feel too overwhelmed to even speak,
start with the breath. Calming your
breath will lead the way to clarity.
-Shira Bonnalit, Medical Practitioner and Professional Yoga
Instructor, 800+ Hours*

"You need to work on your posture, little girl," Mama clucks. Her calloused hands, so worn from working outside without gloves, pulls another piece of my hair tighter into its braid.

I straighten up without a word. Mama doesn't want a response, not even a positive one. She wants to see a physical change. One of her favorite sayings from when she studied history in school was that actions speak louder than words. She reminds us about this almost every day. I figure it must be pretty important.

Thoren races past the big open window in front of us. He squeals with laughter after Tomas shoves a toad down the back of his shirt. I have to stop the giggle from escaping my body. Mama won't like it if I move while she braids my hair.

"Your older brothers are quite the role models for you," she *mutters. She squeezes gently as she finishes twisting the braids together to form a crown on top of my head, the roots getting pulled in the process. I don't mind, though. This is my favorite hairstyle, and I beg Mama to do it each week for me. Her warm hands frame the top of my neck as she turns my head to watch my brothers play in the garden outside.*

"Look at them, Eira," Mama whispers. She turns my head the other direction, my body pliant and trusting her, and I see Jora, Kota, and Jorgan. Jora is the eldest of us, older than me by nine years. Then it's Thoren and Tomas, seven years older and playful twins. Mama then had Kota and Jorgan before she stopped with me. I eagerly watch as Jora twists flowers into Kota's golden hair while Jorgan lays peacefully in the grass, watching the clouds above them with fascination. I kick my legs excitedly and try to jump off the rickety chair Mama had me sit in. We all enjoy playing together, and I want to join them outside.

But Mama's hands tighten their grip around my neck, and she holds me in place, almost choking me. "I said to look at them," she hisses. "Take a really good gander at your brothers and sisters, my sweet child."

I try to obey her, but it's hard to think about my siblings when her hands are hurting me. Thoren and Tomas run near the window and wave at us, both kissed by the sun with dark blond hair swaying by their shoulders. I love my whole family, but I'm closest to Thoren and Kota. We have the most similar eyes and skin, adore being in nature, and can all be found in our huge library. I'm the one with uniquely bright white hair, though. Mama and Papa say it's because the sun and the moon had so much light, they were going to explode and cause another problem on Earth. They say I need to keep the light safe for them and use it to help others.

As long as Mama keeps braiding my hair, I don't care what color it is.

Mama's hands start to choke me with her strength. "Did you get a nice, long look at them, Eira darling?" I try to swallow and nod my head. "Good. Now you must remember what I'm about to tell you. You're surrounded by all of their love right now. But you need to be strong. You need to be so strong you won't even think about needing your siblings or us. Because none of us will be there with you. Do you know what is thicker than the blood of your family?"

I realize she's waiting for a response, but I can't open my mouth.

Mama leans down to whisper in my ear. Her breath tickles the few strands of wavy hair that have escaped the braids. "The only thing thicker than the blood of your family is the blood that flows in your own veins."

I don't have time to react to Mama's scary words. When her hands move from my neck, I peer up and dark red and black blood pours from her eyes and mouth. It splashes onto my face, and I shrink back from her in horror. When I glance outside to get my siblings' help, they're all staring at me with the same swirling blood dripping onto the ground below them.

"You see, sweetheart? We don't have the same thick, sweet blood as you most certainly do."

Mama smiles widely down at me, her teeth stained red and black, globs of it still gushing out of her like a waterfall. I flinch back and realize I'm soaked in her blood, and all I can see is red and black and emptiness where all their eyes once were and I can't breathe, I can't—

I lurch upward in panic. Blinking rapidly, the wet, soaking blood fades away and the sounds of the swamp carry back around me.

"You shouldn't have told her that much at once," Delano snips in the background.

"I *didn't*," Daya lashes back. "I told her three things: what our water does, which is pretty damn important if she's going to survive here; that we're all part of the same group of shifters, not a *club* as she suggested, and I didn't even go into detail about that topic; and the name of our realm."

I force myself up into a sitting position. Someone propped me up against the tree, a pack serving as my pillow. Delano is fishing for an item in his bag and bickering with Daya, who's scowling at him in annoyance.

"Good morning," Daru says from where he's sitting under a nearby tree. He flashes me a toothy smile, but I don't experience that sense of ease anymore. Worry etches the corners of his eyes. "How was your little power nap?"

I crack my neck and stretch my arms up above me, still adjusting to the feel of my new skin. That nightmare has stoked the flames of fear, and I have to get myself together if I'm going to have any kind of conversation with this Daru. There's no way he can't sense what happened to me while sleeping. I peer down again at my body and take in my blemish-free arms. If I was shaken by the first answers, I can only imagine how I'll react when I'm told about this new body I have. I shudder. *One step at a time, Eira.*

"I can't believe I passed out," I whisper. "That's not like me. I'm pretty freaked out right now."

"Here," he says. "Why don't you try more *lipva*?" Daru gently rolls a jar toward me, obviously not wanting to make any sudden movements. I must narrow my eyes at him because he laughs and says, "I don't want to startle you anymore than I did already. I promise it's safe to drink that. It's the same *lipva* you drank a little while ago."

Inhaling abruptly, I snatch the jar off the ground and take a few sips. It slides down my throat similar to a gentle waterfall, and I'm taken aback by how soothed and rejuvenated I now am. Even my eyesight becomes sharper, the colors more vibrant. I didn't realize how foggy my brain felt until I could recognize my physical sensations and quell the frantic emotional part of myself down.

I glance over at Daru, taking in his features now that the overpowering panic is simmering down. His hair has natural highlights in it, maybe from this *hot-as-fuck* sun, and he has incredible eyes. I thought they were a mossy green, but I also see flecks of ginger and violet. He's not incredibly tall, and I wonder if that has anything to do with the animal he can shift into.

Shifters. That's going to take some getting used to.

I try to shake off fragments of the fear still coursing through my blood. My mind isn't entirely accepting what I'm seeing yet, and at the same time, my instincts are telling me that these people—err, *shifters*—won't harm me. But I also have told myself that same idea countless times with *normal* people, and none of those relationships work out. Except for the freak shows who I call my friends.

"So…" I mumble. "You're a, uh, shifter? That helps people feel relaxed?"

Daru looks like he wants to tease me, but quickly reels that back in. Smiling, he says, "You'll find that those who live in Majikaero have various talents or magical powers. We call this *maji*. Certain *solliqas* can shift into many forms, and some can shift into one form, if that. Others can connect with different elements or can manipulate the body. The talents individuals have here can range from positive and healing to negative and destructive." He pauses, letting this information sink in. "Not all shifters have the ability to connect with other types of magic. I'm fortunate that I do. I help others feel calm in tense situations, can manipulate the wind, and am able to shift into many different birds. I've been pushing my *maji* more and more lately, and I'm close to being able to shift into other animals from the forests." Smirking, he asks, "Want to see?"

"No!" I yelp, pushing back into the tree. "No. N-not yet, *please*. Words are enough for now." I force a smile that I'm sure comes across as a grimace.

Daru laughs, the sound similar to a wooden chime dangling in the wind.

"How can we talk to one another?" I ask, wary of his answer.

He's about to respond when Daya comes over and lies on her stomach near him. Her feet swing back and forth like a windshield wiper and kick Daru's jaw. He gives her an irritated glare and pushes her feet further away before backing up half a foot. I can't help but giggle at their interaction. It reminds me of how Astira would act around the guys.

"It's one of the reasons you're so exhausted," Daya says, picking at the fluffy grass in front of her. Hazel eyes meet my own, the colors swirling back and forth as if paint drops. *Interesting*. "When you cross over from Earth, your soul absorbs the main language used here. Think of it this way: Our realm is one of many worlds separated by veils of time and space, where time moves differently in each realm or world. Some of the veils are thinner than others. Majikaero is the world closest to Earth and is known as the realm of souls. That makes it easier for those on Earth because they actually have souls and are able to cross over after they've learned their life lessons. We have a special connection between our worlds. It's quite challenging for even *solliqas* here to cross into other worlds—you have to have the right *maji* and powers to do so. Since our worlds are so close to one another, the transition is easy. And the Council made sure any soul coming here would be welcomed by their soul family and be able to communicate. The Council is an all-encompassing source of magic that has dreadfully few limitations. Personally, I think if the *maji* is capable of teaching you our language, I don't see why it can't inform you about nourishment, the forms of magic, the Council, and everything else."

Questions tumble right through me. "Time moves differently? You have one main language? There are *other* worlds? If I died on Earth, does this mean I'm in the afterlife? What do you mean by a soul family?" I ask in one breath, cautiously enthralled by what I'm learning.

"You curious thing," she giggles, not at all phased by me firing questions. "Time moves incredibly differently in each world. It's a construct created on Earth meant to control you and keep you in line. Here, it moves *a lot* slower than in your home realm—think of it like your year being one of our weeks. Each *solliqa's maji* can also influence how slow or fast a moment is perceived, with there even being *solliqas* that specialize in manipulating time. The closer you are to a thinner veil here, the easier it is to get lost in what time and reality even is. All in all, Eira, time is constant here. And at the same time, your perspective of it can change. It can be extremely fun and also unsettling, depending on who you are. And let's see... there's one main language that connects all the regions together. The Council uses their *maji* to give everyone, no matter the *solliqa,* knowledge of the language. Each region and village has their own dialects that you can learn or have a *solliqa* use their magic to teach you. There's a number of ways to learn how to communicate with others here." Daya shrugs. "Some souls communicate entirely via mind, which can get *real* trippy real fast."

I feel my eyebrows raising again, disappearing under my hair. "Can any of you do that?"

She shakes her head. "Nah, that's not what we can do. The three of us have talents with both shifting and other forms of *maji,* but nothing with the mind. I play with fire, which Daru *loves.*" She smirks.

Daru's cheeks tinge with rosy pink, and he looks away, getting flustered.

"What about Delano?" I ask, peering across the trees to where he's still rummaging around in his bag. Daru sends me a grateful smile. *Don't think you're safe yet, buddy. If the girls have taught me anything back home, it's how to rile a guy like you up. Daya will spill the tea later.*

"My brother is special," she says quietly. "Daru can manipulate mood and wind. I use fire. Delano? He can send messages through other types of nature, such as trees or insects. It can be incredibly useful, but he isn't the only one who can do this. There are souls who are, um, against us, you could say, that have this talent and are now constantly monitoring for any signals sent from him. That's a bit more complicated to describe. I promise I'll tell you more—it might be easier when we have more of our cadre and supplies with us."

I nod, taking in what she's shared. I don't want anything complicated yet. I can barely digest *this*.

"To answer your other questions, yes, there are other worlds," Daya continues. "The few *solliqas* I've read about being able to travel outside of our realm or Earth describe the worlds as almost being layered on top of one another. They're almost touchable, a thin border away. It's frustrating to many, *especially* the Council members, that almost no *solliqa* can travel between worlds right now. The few who could were destroyed. I don't think the Council wanted them gone, solely contained, so their special world-traveling *maji* could be used and manipulated."

She pauses, getting a faraway look in her eyes for a minute. "Often I wonder if it's intentional that our souls can't travel to other worlds. If something is blocking us out and for good reason." Daya shakes her head and turns back to face me. "And Majikaero isn't an afterlife for you. If I recall from my studies, any form of living after death on Earth is considered to be a type of afterlife. But that's not how others view it here or what the world-traveling *solliqas* understood from other realms. We're all simply existing in one world or place in time or another. There's no *before* or *after*. When your soul is trapped in a human body on Earth, it can often forget that. Forget its purpose, where else it could travel to, what type of life lesson the gods deemed necessary for it to learn among other souls before it could have the opportunity to truly wake up and be *free*. You're not dead, Eira.

You never were. You're living in a new world and, who knows? Maybe you'll get to live in another."

I absently weave the ends of my hair while Daya talks. It never occurred to me that there could be other realities happening at the same time as my own. Or at other times.

"And," Daya huffs, "we do indeed have soul families. Your soul often finds them on Earth. We're constantly reaching out for one another and sometimes get lucky to be born in the same city or within the same family. You'll either find each other on Earth and then again in Majikaero, or you'll cross over without ever meeting them and will see them for the first time here. It depends on the soul. Souls can also be created here, although it's typically rare, and won't have to exist on Earth."

"Were you on Earth?" I ask.

"I was," she nods. "I was there for quite a while and fortunately, Delano was always in my life. The moment we crossed into Majikaero, our soul parents welcomed us with open arms and taught us everything we knew. Our human forms you see here were our last forms back on Earth when we were fraternal twins there."

I nod in agreement, like I comprehend and accept everything she's telling me. It makes me wonder who my soul family is, and if I'll get to find them. If Daya, Delano, and Daru are part of them, since they're the ones greeting me here.

My mind is still swirling with questions about who these gods are and what they get to decide about souls on Earth, but I have a more pressing question for her. "I'm not sure if you can tell me, but why... why *me*?" I ask, peering between them with an uneasy feeling. "What did you mean by 'Welcome home'? Why am I here?"

Daya and Daru exchange glances so quickly, I swear I imagine it. Their bodies tense, enough to tell me this is a bigger, more complicated topic than I might be ready for.

"Please," I whisper. "I *beg* you. I need this answer. I've been going through hell and am now separated from the people I-I love." I blink back tears, my eyes burning at the mention of my friends.

"Hell? As in Cudhellen?" Daru asks sharply.

"Does that matter right now?" Daya hisses at him. She sighs, scooting closer to me and takes my hands in hers. All playfulness and snark are gone, replaced with a serious look that pierces right through me. "What I'm about to tell you might come as a shock. I'm hesitant to share anything, but I also think it's unfair to leave you in the dark. I'll start with the basics. Forgive me, but I can't go into more detail until we're with the others and you've met with our leader. *She* should be the one to tell you everything. But I imagine not telling you anything won't work in anyone's favor."

Taking a deep breath, she continues. "I'm comfortable telling you this: Your soul has a strong connection to our realm, and you've been here before. *Something* destroyed you, which rarely happens here. We're not exactly immortal, and there are certainly ways to kill us, but it's not common. You were a prominent figure, a light to us all. It feels strange to even be talking to you like this, having to explain how our realm works when your *maji* was so strong, so powerful, so mighty. I can't be sure what kinds of powers you have now. I know that after you left, darkness festered in the corners and crevices, hidden by shadows. It's a *disease*. We have all been told that there's nothing to fear, that it was a tragedy that you were mysteriously shattered and killed from this realm. Yet when those of us pushed back and demanded answers, we were met with resistance. Violence. Torture. Banning us from our homes. It wasn't intentional, but those of us who are awake and see clearly that something is going on, that we're being manipulated, started to group together. While there are a lot of details that can't be shared right now, what I'll say is that *you* are what is most important. If a soul full of love and grace was killed with no explanations, we knew you were needed to combat whatever is happening. And whatever is coming our way."

My mind is spinning out of control, reminding me of the night Athena made us chocolate martinis, and I couldn't even walk to the bathroom without falling flat on my face.

"But, why *me*?" I whisper. "I was powerful?"

Daru crawls over to where we're sitting, putting his hand on top of ours. I don't miss how his fingers are trembling. "Yes, you were," he says, not breaking eye contact. The light flecks flare brighter in his eyes, his eagerness growing a little too quickly.

"We have various forms of rulers and royalty here, similar to what you have on Earth. They are in charge of the different regions: Drageyra, Viorfelle, Reykashin, Wyndera, Skugvaytir, Myrellden, Sunnadyn, Rioa, Sayfters, Shymeira, Lagunit, and Eikenbien. They each are known for different types of *maji* and powers, and there's a ton of history recorded about each region's relationship with areas on your Earth realm. Of all the worlds that exist, Majikaero is closest to Earth. We also have the Council in Rioa and smaller committees in the different regions. The smaller committees take what has been decided by each region's rulers, such as changes to their laws or concerns they have about *solliqas* and events there, and will send that information to the Council. The rulers might go themselves to Rioa to meet with them. The Council is technically supposed to have all the power here, but you'll find that the different rulers can be *quite* influential and are starting to break the mold they were squeezed into." Daru takes a deep breath. "But within these structures, you weren't technically a ruler. You were still called our Queen of Light, dazzling with your flames and ability to heal the most broken and tortured of souls. Your magic expanded beyond shifting and the elements. It—"

"Oh, my *gods*, Daru, *stop*," Daya scolds him. "Give her a moment to breathe. You're past giving her a crash course in our world and are officially crushing her lungs to a pulp. You're talking as fast as a bird sings. Can't you detect her panic?"

Daru flushes with embarrassment and bows his head slightly. "Sorry," he murmurs. "I feel immensely excited and amazed that she's here with us now. We don't know what she can do yet, but she still has the same name. *Eira.*"

I'm doing the exact opposite of what I tell my clients. I'm breathing in and out, in and out, sensing the incoming attack of doom and blustering dizziness. *Queen?* Absolutely not.

My laugh comes out breathy and unhinged. "Alright. I still don't understand the fucked-up nightmares and dreams I've been having. I can get behind being drawn to this realm, I *think*. I definitely sense a connection to this place. But a *queen*? Yeah, no." I let out another manic laugh. "Totally not me. I'm a walking mess, spilling all over the place. You've got the wrong girl."

"He's not lying," Daya insists. "It's okay if this is hard to take in right now. You weren't exactly a traditional queen."

I blow out a quick breath. "I wasn't ruling over a country with a crown on my head?"

Daya laughs, the sound putting me slightly at ease. "Not at all. You were a 'queen' in name only and didn't rule over anywhere specific. You went where people were in pain to heal them. It's what the souls here called you because of how many you were able to heal and your caring nature. You couldn't connect with all the elements, but you were able to shift in between species and the earth itself—wherever light or fire could be found, you could go. And unlike some of the others, such as the Elders, with powers beyond our comprehension, you didn't cause *any* intentional harm. It was unheard of. You'll find that the creatures in our realm can be mischievous and use magic to manipulate, well, *everything*. You didn't want a role of power and refused a position on the Council, which, personally? I think that's what made *someone* angry enough to go after you."

Daya sighs, her head falling against Daru's shoulder. Her fingers are still laced with mine, but her hands have gone icy cold and rigid. She feels... stressed.

"There's much to say," she mutters. "We've been desperate to find your soul because the full force of the plague of darkness started soon after you left our realm. It's not clear if you can be the salvation we seek, but we knew if we could find you, then we'd at least have a chance at beating this. We were *convinced* you weren't destroyed. You're too powerful to be fully obliterated. Look... we can't get into everything else right now. It'd be better to take you to our leader and the others on our squad. Can we do that?"

She's brimming over with sincerity, and Daru is pulsating with tension. I don't believe a single word about me being a previous queen, even if it was an informal title given to me, but I'm not going to keep arguing. *Jokes. So many of them.* "This is... alright. Yeah, okay. Let's go meet this leader of yours. I do have other questions, though."

Daya perks up and says, "Yes?"

"Where did I live before? Was it *here*?" I glance around the swamp surrounding me and try to hide my wariness. It might appear pretty here, but if I've learned anything from working with people, the most beautiful creatures and images can be the most dangerous.

Daru shakes his head adamantly, his eyes wide. "Oh, no. You apparently weren't a fan of this area when you were here, either." He barks a laugh. "You had a few homes you liked to frequent. One was on the coast in the region we call Sunnadyn. It's known as the Land of Sunlight and for those who are passionate, loyal, fiery, and loving. You also stayed on the island of Drageyra, known as the Land of Fire and where souls are bold, ambitious, competitive, and direct. There were a few other places you preferred to visit that connected to other soul connections you had."

Daya hums in agreement. "Now that you say this, I think it makes a lot of sense that our queeny *fim* here lived in those regions. I can already sense all those traits in her, especially that fieriness." She shoots me a grin and winks.

I find myself fighting a smile. "Yeah, you could say that about me." I filter through the information overload. "Wait, what's a *fim*?"

"Oh, it's a way we describe souls here. Everything is based on *maji* and energies and the spirit. We traditionally have *fim* and *misn* energies, similar to your feminine and masculine terms on Earth. Each soul falls on a spectrum of these energies, and many have both types inside of them. There are a lot of names that I think would overwhelm you right now. Let's just say you're giving me a lot of *fim* energy," Daya elaborates.

"I'm scared to even ask this, but what exactly is my energy telling you?" I ask.

Daya laughs. "It can tell me a lot of things. You're passionate and intuitive. Emotional and perceptive. *So* much more. Try not to get too caught up in this kind of label. As you meet *solliqas* here, it'll become easier to feel out what kind of energies they're giving off. And it won't simply be *fim* or *misn*—there are dozens of terms you'll learn. Some are clear warnings that something is wrong and others are an obvious soul bond. This will come naturally to you as a healer."

I highly doubt that any of this will come naturally.

"Oookay... So, will this *fim* go to this Sunnadyn and Drageyra? Or are we stuck here?"

"We're in this soggy pile of mud of a region because a *certain* solliqa has a special affection for this corner of our realm." Daya full-on glares at her brother. She turns back to me with an evil glint in her eyes. "Del *totally* has misn and obnoxious energy."

He makes a face at his sister, and I burst out laughing. Except it comes out more like a sob.

THE LIGHT WITHIN

Daru frowns at me. "Why? Are you already yearning to explore?"

I find myself shaking my head, suddenly overcome with emotion so thick, it feels tangible in my body. "No, I—I don't know how to orient myself now or take any of this in. I have no one from home with me. *No one*. Now that I'm here, is everything from home gone? Will I ever be able to see my friends again? Or my pet?" I blow out a breath and remove my hands from Daya's, cradling my head in my hands. "I didn't ask to be here. I *need* my friends." It's staggering how I don't experience the urge to return to my home world, only that I need my friends. My people. I once heard that people make places, and I couldn't agree more now that I'm gods know how far away from them.

There's a rustling sound near Delano and he calls out. Whipping our heads in his direction, we see his leg poking out from behind one of the thick trees. He appears to be squirming around on the ground with something. *Gods, he's really weird*.

"Del! Are you okay?" Daru calls out, jumping up in a fluid motion and jogging over toward him.

As he gets to Delano's foot, Daru rocks back in surprise, nearly losing his balance in the process. "Oh ho! What do we have here?" he asks, laughing.

Daya squints at me before getting to her own feet and walking over, hands on her hips. *Back to her sass, I see*. She peers around the tree and jumps behind Daru, pushing him in front of her. "Del?" she asks. "Did you seriously bring back *two* souls?"

Delano manages to stand up and clears off his pants, muttering to himself. "*No*," he says brusquely. "I'd think I'd know how many souls I brought back, considering it's hard enough to bring even one here." He looks over at me. "You must have quite the connection with that pet of yours. She snuck along for the ride."

He gingerly lifts up a squirming feline from behind the tree and holds it above him as he walks over to me. It has similar coloring to Zaya, but this cat is even larger, and her eyes are liquid gold. She shimmies out of his hold and is bounding toward me, her tail puffed up in agitation. Three seconds go by and after fully processing what I'm seeing, I shriek with joy and run toward her. It's as if we're in one of those sappy romance movies Liv makes me watch. Zaya launches into my arms, heavy enough that I fall on my back from her weight. She gets alarmingly bigger for half a second before shrinking back down to her normal size from back home. Her eyes turn from gold to blue and green again, and she's marking every inch of my face. Not caring what she'll think, I wrap my arms around my fluffball and burrow my face into her fur, breathing in her scent.

This might not be one of my friends, and there's a high chance that I'm stuck here, but Zaya followed me. *I'm no longer alone.*

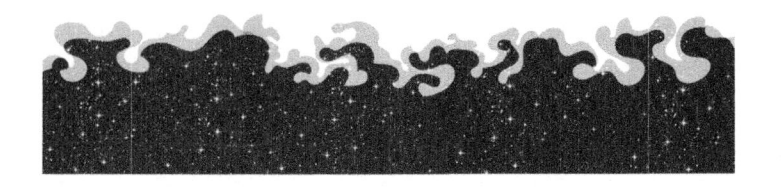

TWENTY-SIX

Nyx

Being a solliqa doesn't necessarily mean you're awake.
It just means your soul exists in Majikaero.
-Page 3670, Understandings of the Soul, Volume II

I'm alone with my thoughts in the back corner of Eliina's tent, tucked behind a makeshift room divider. There are suspended spherical purple lights above me, little replicas of one of our moons, *Hyspair*. They're dusted with green and gold flakes, and judging by the scent, I'm guessing I'm supposed to feel untroubled back here. *A lot of good that'll do. The Goddess Cajsa could shit her magical love all over me, and I'd still be tense and bitter with my darkness slithering around me like the nuisance it is.*

Eliina walks into the tent and closes the door, muttering a protection spell to strengthen the already powerful wards. *She must want to share some highly secretive shit with me. Interesting.* She clears her throat and walks back toward where I'm sitting. I don't miss how the lights pulse as she walks by, impacted by her presence. Eliina swipes an intricately woven blanket and wraps it around her body, her shoulders caving in slightly. For a moment, she's just a weary and tired soul, her face going slack as she dips her head to her chest and takes a ragged breath. She turns and approaches where I'm seated, and she gracefully lowers herself to sit in front of me, not once lifting her head.

After what must be an hour, she lifts her gaze to mine, and, *fuck*, I *feel* her sorrow and worry. Not much can surprise me anymore, but this? This is terrifying. This woman is a pillar of strength and has the confidence you could only dream of having. Eliina is one of the few virtuous leaders on the Council and does everything she can to honor, heal, and care for others. Even the likes of me. When the rest of them wanted me gutted in front of the world, using one of their Soul Readers to shred apart my soul, Eliina firmly rejected this motion. If it weren't for her, who knows where I'd be right now? She managed to single-handedly persuade the rest of the Council to ban me from the life I had. They shunned me from my birthright, my family, my home. All because no one could figure out what was going on with me and what caused such horrid darkness to warp my mind. My *heart*.

We don't speak. I might be angry with the Council, and this rage can extend to Eliina, but I also owe her my life. She's empathetic enough that she understands the complexity of what I'm going through, how I suffer. I don't want to do anything to disrespect her or interrupt her thoughts. But after an actual hour passes by, I can't help myself.

"You wanted to meet with the Prince of Darkness and Ruin himself? I'm honored." I force myself to smirk.

"Don't call yourself that," Eliina whispers. "We both know that's not who you are."

Her words grate against my skin, pulling it tight around me. Flashes of who I was trained to be flicker behind my eyes. I was *not* the Prince of Darkness and Ruin. I was bold yet disciplined. My family and their private council had me in lessons for everything from war strategies to history to the art of language. My mother taught me how to empathize with souls, especially those

THE LIGHT WITHIN

new and wandering a magical world, and ways I could care for them as a leader.

I was so much more than anyone gives me credit for. Except for the damaged souls I've bonded with. They're the ones who can narrowly look past the mood changes and violent urges.

"You're right," I say, my voice tight. I stare down at my hands, the marking that winds itself up my arms and neck in diseased vines. "It's the prince the Council forced me to become." I grunt, feeling entirely too uncomfortable with the emotions rising up right now. They take me back to a time before I was banished.

Everything changed one evening in the time it took my soul to expand and breathe. Those of us who grow up in Majikaero experience different stages of our *maji* powers. My soul parents came from Drageyra and Myrellden, basking me in their fire and darkness. They were always proud of my siblings and me, but they watched in elation as I learned to wield *both* types of *maji*.

The moment my powers combined together in a moment of unexpected lethal anger is when everything changed. It's when I learned I could do something quite rare in our world at the time—to not heal a soul, but *destroy* it. The ability to erase the sense of peace our realm so proudly boasts. And it wasn't any random soul that I sent hurtling into the empty space between worlds; it was the soul most important to me in my family. Now gone, all because of *my* fucked powers that I hadn't even known existed.

It wasn't long before the Council learned what happened. The rest of my family insisted that it was out of my control. That didn't stop the accusations hurled my way. *That I was secretly working for the Sairn, a twisted group, set on striking any soul down that doesn't align with their beliefs. That my soul was deformed. That I had plans to accelerate the plague in the outskirts of Reykashin and should be sent there with the rest of the tortured souls. That I was a soul of darkness and ruin and would destroy any form of love sent my way. That I'm the one who should have been disintegrated into nothing.*

The Council holds all the final power and decisions. They isolated me from my family, allowing them to continue their rule in Drageyra, deciding that even with practice, I couldn't be controlled. *Like I'm a ravenous beast.* Guilt and grief and a dark despair I didn't know could be felt twisted in each part of me. The Council first kept me in the dungeons of Rioa, held down with chains of starlight that could combat the darkness stewing inside me. Until my thoughts and emotions poisoned me so thoroughly, not even starlight could hold me down, and it was too late to try Eliina's healing sessions with my broken self.

I don't even know how my family is doing. The last soul to try to reach out to me was imprisoned in the dungeons. It was my first clue that I wasn't being irrational from my blinding misery. This was planned, for *all* of us, and I hope this will be my chance to figure out what's going on.

The memories feel as fresh as they did years ago. *Fuck.* I peer up at Eliina. I might still be in pain, but I'm not proud that this is how I began our conversation.

"I'm sorry," I say quickly before Eliina has a chance to respond. "I didn't mean to throw that in your face. I know that you've done everything you could without raising suspicions from the rest of the Council. And I know that it was you who sent us Vaira and the others. We'd be lost without their love and care."

Eliina smiles, but it doesn't reach her eyes. They vacillate between a hazy sorrow and hardened determination. "It's fine, Nyx," she says. "You have every right to be as angry as you are. The fact that you haven't gone completely mad says much about your strength and training before this all started. But never apologize for enduring such rage, even toward me."

She has no idea how much rage is ready to be unleashed. The Council holds too much power, and I don't give a *fuck* if it kills my soul in the end—I won't let them get away with this. I know they're connected to this plague somehow. I know they're the reason the regions' leaders have such little power now. I know this all the way to my deranged core and won't let the Council members harm other *solliqas* just because they have the fucking nerve to call them out on their bullshit.

Eliina shakes her head, strands of hair falling to frame her oval face. She lays part of the blanket on my lap, fixing it unnecessarily around my knees, and she pulls the rest tighter around her arms. A somber emotion cracks a piece of the shield around my heart. I did *not* ask for all of these feelings tonight.

"There's a lot that I want to share with you, but I don't think I can tonight," Eliina continues. "I'm glad that you made it here, even in the company of a soul like Ulf." She scrunches up her face, dripping in disdain. "That'll be a different conversation. The first thing I wanted to tell you is I think I figured out how to help this..." she motions the length of my body and out toward the shadows dancing next to me, "darkness you're dealing with. I was amazed that I couldn't pinpoint the source of this before, and it's driven me crazy trying to figure it out. My poor lead healers. When they're not working, they're helping me research anything and everything in our library that's related to what you're going through. I realized recently what I think will finally help you."

"Help me?" I rasp. "After all this time, you've made that a priority? And you mean *save* me, right? I need this destroyed. Cut it out of me. Anything to get it out."

"I don't think that's how it's going to work," Eliina replies, a shred of pity lining her eyes. "You've always been inclined toward powers of the night. Remember, Nyx, the dark isn't always bad. It's what we do in the shadows and smoke and influence of the night that can lead us down a path of destruction and pain. There are plenty of *solliqas* in our realm who practice magic tied to the dark that don't respond the way you do. Some can even release a soul from their pain and set them free."

I focus on controlling my breathing, keeping it slow and steady. My instinct is to argue with her, but that's not going to get me anywhere good tonight.

"I believe the pathway to your redemption will be through this woman you've encountered," Eliina says, watching me carefully. "My powers connect me not only to our realm but also to the ones closest to us, such as Earth. Each world has the potential for magic, but depending on their development and ability to truly see it, not everyone can access it. Magic is all around us, begging to be seen and felt. But the people on Earth? They're as blind to it as they are to their own emotions and spiritual awakenings." She shakes her head again.

"For a while now, there has been a decrease in souls from Earth traveling through the veil between our realms, finally able to seek enlightenment. Not everyone on the Council is worried about this. Most believe it's for the better, so that we can focus on everyone who is already here and the souls able to be born in our own realm. Me, though? It's been a knife to the heart, twisting more and more as the years pass and so few souls trickle through. Too many sink back into another human's body to repeat yet another life in the hope they'll eventually learn their life lessons and awaken enough to come here. A soul is not meant to be bound to one physical form and one realm. It's a magical entity and should be free to roam whichever world it pleases. That's the restrictive way of life on Earth, though. A soul can't break free of its chains there until it learns its lessons and then is free to pass on to our realm... or to another. And when those sad, burdened souls do cross over, finally free to explore other realms and not remain tied down to Earth, it takes quite a lot of work to even start the healing process."

My eyebrows crease, my mind swirling with information.

"What does all of this have to do with the woman I met in my dream?"

"She's different from the others," Eliina says, her eyes finally lighting up again. "Her soul was trapped in bodies on Earth for an excruciatingly long time. It was broken and shattered, lifetime after lifetime. I'm not sure what changed, but she has finally woken up. It might have to do with the violence spreading here or perhaps with the war in her home world. I can't be sure yet. What I do know is that when you first had a dream about her, my connections to Earth vibrated with an awareness of her existence. I was able to get a sense of this soul's appearance, what she was doing for work, who she interacted with, how she felt. It was *incredible*, as if finally pushing the right key into a difficult lock. Based on the dreams she herself was experiencing, or what I know now to be memories of her past lives, I knew her soul was piecing itself back together and would soon awaken enough to come here."

Eliina sucks in a breath. She's speaking so quickly in her excitement, there's no way I'd pick up on this if I didn't grow up interacting with her. My legs are twitching back and forth. Fucking restless. I'm eager to learn what this all means for me but don't want to interrupt her. Yet.

"I had one of my most loyal shifters take action, especially when I saw how her soul was growing out of her physical self. It was aggressively expanding before her body was ready. I didn't want her to overexert herself and not make it here this time around. And what a fright I had when she connected with that poor child, Agilika."

The surprise must be clear on my face. Eliina gives me a pointed look. "Yes, Nyx, I know all about your little acts of revenge throughout these years. I was already in tune with Agilika's tiny soul. More and more innocent young souls have wanted to join my team, wanting to do what they can to help fight against the plague and find our Queen of Light again. Agilika was tremendously talented. She reminded me of you, actually." Eliina sighs sadly. "Her little soul has already been corrupted, though, and scattered in the wind to an unsuspecting body on Earth. Such a tragedy there that we'll need to discuss with everyone here."

"What kind of tragedy is—"

Eliina hushes me. "Not now. Not without everyone else present to hear what's happening on Earth. What you need to know right now is that Agilika could sense the connection between you and this woman from your dream, and she had the ability of a seer. She *knew* you were coming to that village and took advantage of any way to get you to speak with that woman. Although, I imagine she thought she'd still have her soul intact when that happened. Not carelessly destroyed by Ulf's demon and sent spiraling back to Earth. Yet another reason that he's infuriating."

A minute passes and Eliina manages to wipe the scowl clean from her face, excitement returning once again, and she prattles on, not stopping to breathe.

"But this woman was able to survive being drawn into Majikaero. By this time, my shifter and his cadre had found a way into Earth, and he swiftly found her. When he confirmed with me what I had felt about her appearance, I thought I would burst like a star from anticipation. You might have noticed the warmer weather lately?" She chuckles to herself. "I've barely been able to contain myself and desperately hope the Council hasn't noticed. Do you know who this woman is? Which soul she is?"

I'm about to respond when Eliina cuts me off, shaking with emotion.

"We found her, Nyx. We found *Eira*."

I gape at her, the information not entirely clicking in my brain. "Wh-what?" I whisper. "The lost queen?"

Eliina flicks her hand in impatience. "Yes, that's what

everyone calls her. But she's so much more than that. Her soul was not fully crushed into nothingness as we thought, shattered into pain, scattered to a different world. It's taken her *lifetimes* on Earth to remember who she is. Their lifetimes are mere months in our realm, Nyx, and it's been some years in Majikaero at that." She sits up on her knees and takes both of my hands. "My dear child, this woman, with her eyes of silver and blue and electric light, is the *same woman* that you saw in your dream and in that child's body. Her soul is trying to find yours. She's trying to reach you again and to remind you. Do you remember?"

My thoughts are pinning like sparks of lightning throughout my head. Remember *what*? Why would Eira, a lost queen known for her healing light, be trying to find *me*?

I must look as stumped as I feel because Eliina lightly taps the side of my cheek, bringing my attention back to her.

"Do you remember what had made Eira hide deep in the Viorfelle mountains? Before she was killed?" she urgently asks me.

I wish Eliina would just tell me what's going on instead of making me think this hard when I'm this fucking worn out. I'm starting to remember why I hated sitting in training so much. "Didn't she lose a soul she loved? She went missing right before my soul was created here. I remember my mother teaching me about her missions of light. The plague messes with my memory sometimes, though, making it hard to remember everything."

Eliina beams at me. "Yes, you're exactly right. Eira, radiant in her healing light, became nothing more than a flicker of a flame when she lost her strongest soul mate, her lover, her partner, her *almaove*. She traveled into the mountains of Viorfelle, a place a soul can delve into the depths of the universe inside the mind, to learn how to find you again. Do you remember who he was, this soul mate?"

I snort. "I'm surprised that I remembered she lost a *solliqa* she loved when most of my energy goes toward keeping my beast under control. I have no idea who this *solliqa* was or how he looked."

Eliina stares at me, her eyes wide. I suppress a shiver, not enjoying all her power and attention directed at me. "His own eyes had the same electric gold and silver light, but they were as dark as night's shadows, the polar opposite of her own brightness. Where Eira shone light and fire, he countered her powers and smothered the brightness when it became too much, when it bordered on the edge of healing and teetered into pain. She mastered how to help others with light, and he learned how to use his darkness to do the same in his own way. On the surface, they were opposites, but in their souls, they fit perfectly."

I slowly blink, understanding what she's saying but not accepting it. Not yet. There's no way. Maybe I'm a descendant of this guy. But even that'd be a stretch. *The others will get a laugh out of this*.

"Nyx," she whispers. "This is important. I need you here with me, mentally, emotionally, physically, and spiritually. I need you to hear what I'm saying and truly listen. Why do you think Eira is trying to find you?"

I shake my head so fast, my neck cracks sharply. I'm scared out of my mind. Even if I wasn't a monster, this idea is unquestionably ludicrous. I'm still an exiled prince. I wouldn't call myself ordinary, but there are other princes in our realm, other extremely talented creatures that live outside of royalty. There's no way.

"Tell me what you already know inside your heart, Nyx," Eliina demands, the leader in her making an appearance, forcing me to respond.

"What you're saying is impossible," I breathe. "Eira is finally coming back to this realm and is searching for me. She's finding me because I'm... I'm her *almaove*. You weren't able to heal me because even though you're powerful and strong, you're not full of the same light and abilities as Eira." I pause, overcome with confusion. "How do I not remember what I had with her?"

Eliina's eyes shutter. "As you both work on your healing, I believe that answer will become clearer. Her soul was nearly obliterated. Yours was fractured, perhaps from trying to protect her when she was attacked. I'm not sure where you went in the beginning, but I do know that you spent a handful of lifetimes together before your soul crossed back over to Majikaero. Reborn into a tiny form and reunited with your soul parents. Eira wasn't that lucky, but at least she can finally heal and reunite with you now."

"Right... she's going to come here, come back home, to find me. She'll be the one who can heal me," I rush out.

Eliina smiles widely, and she squeezes my hands. "She isn't coming here, Nyx," she says, leaning forward so that she's an inch from my face. "She *is* here. She's home. And she's going to arrive here before the Council can sniff her out and connect all this themselves."

TWENTY-SEVEN

Eira

When people fail to help, try holding an animal.
They're much better healers than most give them credit for.
-Journal notes from Dr. Morgan Lydahnia,
Founder of Heart and Mind Care

I first made a connection with Zaya about eight years ago. She was a precious kitten, mewing for milk and stumbling after me on the forest path, tripping over broken sticks. When I peered into her tiny eyes, I felt a zap of electricity. I *knew* she was meant to live with me and wouldn't take no for an answer from Tryg or his family. Before she showed up, I was wandering the woods alone. It wasn't the first time I sought solace in solitude and nature. Especially after my family abandoned me, it became one of the few places where I was truly at peace. That was the first day I felt drawn toward a place in the forest, walking in a trance. I still remember the urgency coiling around me, festering like an infected wound. I *had* to keep walking. There was somewhere else that I needed to be if I could only learn the way.

I brush Zaya's fur with my fingertips, thinking back to the

THE LIGHT WITHIN

day she found me. The cracking of a twig snapped me out of my daze, and I had felt so alone out there. Zaya cried out, and it didn't even phase me that a kitten was this deep in the woods. I remember thinking of my housemates and Tryg's parents and the likelihood of them saying *hell no* to a lost cat from the forest. I decided to give the kitty a chance, and if it followed me, we were destined for one another. *I mean, there are worse things to happen in life. The cat wasn't Prince Charming, but at least* one creature *was meant for me.*

Still lost in thoughts from the past, I don't realize something's wrong until Zaya hisses and sinks her murder claws into my abdomen. She springs off me, her fur standing on edge. She's growling at my arm, and a choked scream leaves me when I glance down at it.

Where I normally wear the bracelet Tryg gave me is a bear burning into my skin. *It's the same fucking bear. Why can't I have even one normal minute here?* As if this wasn't freaky enough, I hear Tryg's voice echo in the back of my mind, as if a forgotten memory that you can't quite hold on to. He's saying, his voice distant and ghost-like, "*If you're in there and can hear me, please come back, my fox. We're so worried. We need you. I need you. Please. This bracelet is the thing on you that connects us. If you can hear me, please wake up and come back to us.*"

Fortunately, Zaya's antics and commotion get Daya's attention, and she sprints over, sliding on her knees by my side. I'm not sure where to focus: part of a bracelet being burned into my wrist, that I'm seriously hearing voices now, or Daya's frightened behaviors. Oh, wait, I know where to place my attention. Zaya is now burrowing into Delano's bag and, consequently, his items are being pushed out all over the ground. Delano is as red as an angry tomato with how irritated he's getting, and he's poking my cat's swishing tail with a broken branch.

"Eira!" Daya gasps. "Your skin!"

I mentally roll over into a ditch and would rather do absolutely anything else than look at my skin. There aren't enough words in the dictionary to express how badly I *don't* want to know what else is going on with my body right now. These people, *who legit shift into animals*, are already insisting that I'm a queen and previously had magical powers. That's more than enough to digest without bringing my skin into all of this.

My body doesn't leave me much of a choice, though. It's searing me from the inside out, and liquid flame is bubbling under the surface. I instinctively glance at my body and go rigid in panic from what I see. My skin, all of it, is *lighting up*. It's blazing in heat and blinding me with how bright it's glowing.

Okay, okay, new idea. Maybe this has all been a dream, and I'm getting abducted by aliens. That's a thing people have experienced, right?

As I'm starting to accept that aliens might be involved, the heat banks to a low simmer and the brightness dies down to a dim light, mere embers. My eyes meet Daya's, and we're too shocked to form words, looking from my body back to one another. I'm breaking out into crazy amounts of sweat. I might be turning into a puddle.

New option: Hot flashes. I knew entering my thirties would be trouble.

I go back to that mental image of a ditch and wonder if I lay there long enough, maybe I'll wake up and realize this was all a wacky nightmare. Or if I stay this warm, will I become fried Eira? *Tasty.* As quickly as it came, the heat and bright light go away. If I wasn't still drowning in my gross, sticky moisture, I'd think I imagined the whole thing.

Daya is instantly examining the marking on my arm, muttering colorful profanities under her breath. She rips off a few pieces of her shirt and ties them around my hand and the rest of my forearm, covering the areas surrounding the bear still sizzling into my skin. I dare to glance down at it and immediately wish I didn't. The bear itself is gorgeous and identical to the one on my bracelet—each body part is made of a piece of nature. Leaves, branches, water, and stones. A symbol I don't understand and is definitely not on the bracelet from Tryg curves down the bear's spine. The skin around the bear is puckering into a scar and splashes of black and dark purple outline the bear itself. The pain is sharp and unbearable, branding me like an animal.

Daru peers down at me with glee and lets out a low whistle. "This day is getting more and more thrilling."

"You know what would make it even more exciting? Shoving my bird-brained brother down your throat and chucking you into the water." Daya glowers back at him.

Daru tsks. "Violence, cannibalism, and unnerving amounts of kinkiness. You're in a special mood today, Daya. I'd have thought you'd be overcome with excitement about what happened."

"Are they this way on Earth, too?" she asks me, acting bewildered. "Yeah, it's great that Eira is showing some of her powers. What's *not* great, if you'd bother to look further than the length of your dick, is that this started while *the* bear sign was burned into her skin. You know, the same sign that was marked where she died by her killer? And, I know this part will be hard to grasp, but she's clearly in pain and overheating, and, I don't know, *not* an experiment to observe?! Instead of standing there like a goon, you could do something to help?"

A number of expressions cross Daru's face, and it's hard to keep up with them all. Surprise, fear, worry, shame, among others. "Sorry, Eira," he mumbles before dashing to his bag and fumbling with a few bottles of shimmery liquids. He runs back over and helps Daya pull me up into a sitting position. I lean against his body and immediately rub my face against his arm. *I'm turning into a cat.*

"You're *so* cold," I moan into his skin. "I want to cover myself with all of you."

"That's the heat talking." Daru laughs nervously. "Souls say creepy things when they're experiencing their powers for the first time and this soon after entering this realm."

"Not creepy, just nice and cold," I insist, rolling my head back and forth.

Daya pulls my head back gently and plaits my hair down the middle of my head while Daru uncorks one of the small bottles full of amber liquid.

"Is that whiskey?" I ask, feeling a little too hopeful.

Daru arches an eyebrow. "I'm not sure what that is, but I can assure you that it's not. A few drops of this will cool you down. Now open your mouth for me."

Daya snorts, finishing the last of the braid. "And you said I have unnerving amounts of kinkiness. Tell us what you really want to do with our newly found queen."

A blush crawls up Daru's neck, and I don't miss how he cautiously avoids my eyes. I open my mouth to ask what else he wants to do, feeling dazed and feisty, and he quickly pours a few drops into my mouth. He grips my arms tightly, and before I ask why, I'm exploding with sensations. Chills and a freshness similar to the first winter snow meet the blistering heat of my body. Combating temperatures rise within me, both frigid and humid steam, until my skin wants to crack from the pressure. I'm vaguely aware that my body is convulsing, and I'm slipping into a state of shock, but all I focus on is the lick of fire and taste of snow on my tongue, chasing one another.

My body seizes and with a final stab of pressure, release finally washes through my muscles. I sigh, leaning back into Daya, content to feel normal once again. Clammy and unnerved, but normal. I lean to the side, having the urge to cough, and nearly collapse when a black tarry substance oozes out of my mouth.

Third idea: I have the plague and am practicing magic. Time to burn me at the stake.

I'm heaving this viscous fluid out of me, my abdomen clenching in pain. All three of my new friends are next to me at this point, and Zaya, in normal cat fashion, is behind my legs, licking the beads of sweat. When the last of this shit comes out, and I'm lying on Daya's lap, a drooling heap of skin and bones, Daru approaches with a damp cloth. He gently wipes around my mouth and holds a tiny vile full of clear liquid to my cracked lips.

"You need one drop of this," he says. "It'll clean out your mouth and ease any rawness in your throat."

I want to resist because I officially have developed trust issues with these mystery liquids, but Daya whispers in my ear, "You can trust this one, Eira. You shouldn't have thrown up. This will help you feel better. We'll get you more *lipva*, and then we're going to a healer."

Oh great. More magical beings putting things into my body. I let Daru pour the drop in my mouth, and this part is remarkably better than what just happened to me. All in a few seconds. My mouth is rinsed, even better than going to the dentist, and the aches in my throat and torso are gone. I curl into Daya and one of the worst things that could happen, happens. A sob works its way up my throat, and I'm absolutely powerless to it.

I'm not sure if it's my normally delayed emotional reaction to stress or whatever came out of my body, but I'm now fully experiencing *everything*.

Daya rocks me back and forth, easy and slow, gliding her hand along my back in circles. I start to cry harder, shaking with distress, as I think of Athena also comforting me a day ago. One day. That's how quickly my life turned upside down. My tears soak into Daya's pants, and the embarrassment kicks into overdrive. Which is awesome for me because that means even *more* crying. Spilling each feeling through a teardrop onto this shifter, this person I don't even know. I move half an inch, and the bear mark scratches on the grass, igniting my wrist with more pain. My hands move on their own to my hair, pulling hard on the strands to ignite anything to take my mind off what I'm currently experiencing.

Hands tangle with my own and uncurl my fingers from my knotted hair, thrusting Zaya into them instead. She spats a little hiss at whoever did this, and I eagerly pull her into my chest, silently begging her to comfort me. She purrs, the sound vibrating against my heart, and marks my collar bone in response. I don't know how many minutes go by, but by the time my sobs die down to tragic-sounding hiccups, Daya is still holding me. Zaya is sleeping against my chest, and Daru is now sitting next to me with a jar of *lipva*. Silent and waiting and ready to help me. *Me*. Someone they might have heard about but also only met today. They might be as overwhelmed as I am or more so.

Delano is across from us and has his hands against the roots of the nearest tree. His eyes are closed, brows bent down in concentration, whispering against the bark. He puffs out quick breaths with each word, his chest moving faster and faster. When his eyes open, they're intimidatingly black with no irises. Nothing but satiny, painted darkness. It takes him a few moments to slow his breathing, and, after a blink, his hazel eyes return and pin straight on me.

"The message has been sent," he says, nodding his head at Daya and Daru. "I took a chance and hope no one will intercept it at Rioa, but even if they do, I made sure the message was heavily coded."

A few blue winged creatures fly swiftly above us, their wings a blur.

"I'm also sending the coded message through a few of my birds," he motions toward them, weaving through the trees in the distance now. "I'm hoping Eliina receives the message in a few moments, but I'm sending the birds as backup in case anything goes wrong." Delano's gaze darts back to me and stays fixated on my wrist.

THE LIGHT WITHIN

"Regardless, there's not enough time to wait for a reply," he mutters. "We need to leave immediately for the healers. I don't think we should take any more chances today, and if something changes, the others will find us."

Wordlessly, Daya leans me up against Daru and repacks any items into her bag. There weren't too many supplies out, only a few jars scattered next to us on the ground. Delano already has the other two bags packed up and uses his hands to make a bird call into the swamp, his eyes narrowed and searching.

"This was not part of the plan," Daru mumbles, carefully cradling me against his chest as he stands up. Zaya swipes a paw at one of his legs, growling that he disrupted her sleeping session. "We thought we would have more time to describe this world to you, Eira, but we don't want to wait to leave. Your wrist and chest need to be healed immediately. I hope that you can trust us."

My body is beyond spent, and he might as well be carrying a sack of potatoes. I manage to nod and mumble, "Okay. Where are you carrying me? Don't forget Zaya."

He breathes sharply through his nose and peers back down at me, his green eyes wary. "We just met, but I don't think Zaya would *let* me forget her. Especially if it involves anything with you. And I'm not sure how you'll respond to this, but we'll be riding on the *alklen*. I believe you have similar creatures on Earth, but these are, ah, um, a bit different."

The vagueness of what he's saying is too staggering for me. I don't have to wait long, though, to see what he's talking about. Three black and shadowy deer-like creatures approach the clearing, their fur sleek with streaks of maroon and starlight. White, crystal eyes peer at us, catching the light of the sun, and velvety black antlers rise in a cluster above their skulls. The ends of the antlers appear as fingers of death, curled into lethal points.

My face must show *exactly* what I'm thinking because Daru tightens his hold on me before saying, "Yes, we will be riding those. No, you don't have a choice unless you want to stay here in agony. Yes, you'll be riding with me. No, I won't drop you. Yes, they look scary at first. No, they won't harm you. They can sense a soul's intentions, so unless you plan on attacking them, you'll be fine. And *yes*, Zaya is coming with us."

I gape up at him, scared out of my mind to get that close to their antlers. Daya and Delano are already mounted on their *alklen*, and before I can utter a single protest, Daru has thrown us both on top of this creature. Zaya digs her claws into my leggings, swishing her tail, and we're galloping off into the trees.

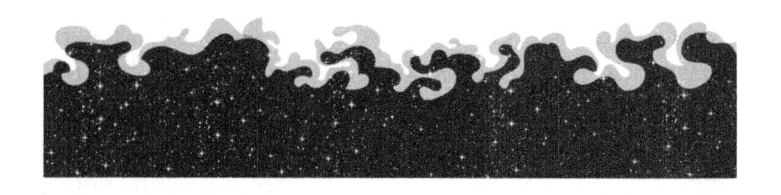

TWENTY-EIGHT

Tryq

Illusions come in all shapes and sizes.
Most can be found in your own reflection.
-Healing Documentary Film, Version 421.96

The trees blur around me as I race through them, running from my own jilted emotions. Cold air chips away at my lungs like broken glass. My feet push my body to break into a hard sprint. Blinding anger has thoroughly taken control of my emotions, and I'm barely holding on, weakened by my confusion and fear. The snow crunches under my shoes, and considering how low the temperature gets up here, I'm surprised I don't slide on a patch of ice. Even if that were to happen, it doesn't matter.

I rushed out of the house when I realized how close I was to bashing Shira's face into the doorframe. Frustration poisoned my mind until all I could see was blood red. *How can the others not see Eira is gone? I know people only see what they want to see, but* damn*. How can they stay by Shira's side when she clearly knows something she's not telling us?* A small part of me, maybe the part that still has a conscience, forced me to leave the house and head into nature before I did anything I'd truly regret. Yet now here I am, still angry and surrounded by entirely too much snow. *Fuck.*

A large buck leaps across the path I'm on, and I skid to a stop, snapping out of the haze clouding my senses. Leaning forward, I brace my arms on my quads and heave ragged breaths. I turn my head to the left to see where the deer went and instantly go taut. *What the hell is that?*

The buck is peering over its shoulder at me, smoky tendrils drifting out of its flared, leathery nostrils. From its black coat to the tips of its dark antlers, I'd think a demon was watching me if it weren't for the orbs of light shining out of its eyes.

It turns to face me head on, and I instinctively go into a defensive position, keeping low with bent knees and putting my hands up in front of me. I have no idea what the fuck is going on, but I *swear* this animal is looking right into me. A pounding ache throbs beneath the surface of my head, a deep pressure I haven't felt before. I stare back into the deer's eyes, and it's hypnotizing how they pulsate and sneak their way closer. There's a nagging sensation in the back of my mind, as if this creature is nudging me, trying to get my attention, communicating in its own way. The pressure grows unbearable. My hands fly to my hair, fingers digging into my scalp, trying to fight the burn rippling beneath my skin.

If I didn't already think I was losing it, I unquestionably do now.

A whisper slithers into my mind. "*It's time*," it says.

All the trees, the snow, the glacial temperature, my body—it all fades away into the distance. I'm falling down a rabbit hole, a tunnel leading me straight to this creature that's right in front of me, yet I *know* it's not truly here. *Am I hallucinating? Did Jace put something in my drink before?* I resist at first, but then I let go, letting my surroundings consume me, diving fully into myself. Right into the black hole where my heart should be. None of this makes sense. I can't—

"Tryg?" someone says frantically, shaking my body.

I blink. Once. Twice. I'm detached from my body, yet I feel the muscles of my neck move until I'm peering into Athena's green eyes. No, not simply green. The colors of the forest—dark green, brown, tan, and splashes of colors I can't identify. I'm aware of each eyelash and the pink blossoming on her cheeks. Has her face always been this detailed? I'm so transfixed by the details of her face, I barely notice that she's talking to me.

"Tryg? Tryg!" she yells at me. "Are you there? What's going on?"

It takes an insane amount of energy to force myself to pay attention. *Jace, you bastard. What did you do? You're the one who's into this shit.* I manage to blink multiple times and clear my throat before pointing to the buck still in front of me. It's glaring down at me, agitated, its eyes flaring even brighter.

"What is *that*?" I ask Athena, still pointing to the buck.

"Huh?" she asks, searching the area all around us in a frenzy.

"*That*," I say, more harshly. "With the crazy, twisted black antlers. A demon deer. Don't you see it?"

Athena's eyebrows furrow in concern, and she doesn't say anything. It's starting to click that she's kneeling in front of me, the snow soaking into her light jeans. I know she works out, but she's as fast as me? She doesn't even look like she broke a sweat.

"I found him," she calls out behind her. The ground is shifting under me, and the edges of Athena's body blur into a fuzzy line.

Jace, Ruse, and Shira stumble to a stop next to Athena, almost crashing into us. A gut feeling tells me that I'm upset with them, yet I can't remember why. Their presence is a balm to the burning sensation in my head, and I don't want them to leave.

"Do-o you see i-it?" I ask them, my words sputtering out of

me. I flail my hands out next to me, gesturing at the deer growing larger and larger in the shape of a flame. *Oh, gods, it's turning into black fire, its antlers are nothing but smoke.*

Shira stares directly at it, her eyes piercing with fierce awareness. She doesn't respond. Instead, she clutches one of her stone necklaces and mutters unidentifiable words under her breath. Jace and Ruse are staring at me as if I've grown a second head and am in nothing but a speedo, which, honestly, wouldn't even surprise me at this point.

"I know things are wildly confusing right now, Tryg," Athena says quietly. "But let's get you back inside, okay? Burying yourself in the snow isn't going to help anyone."

I begrudgingly drag my eyes in a circle around me and can't believe what I'm seeing. Snow covers my feet and calves, and when I look up, I see the outline of the smoky antlers and flashes of light where the buck's eyes used to be. Jace and Ruse come around to my sides, lifting an arm around their shoulders before helping me stand up. I lean my body weight into them and the ground shifts again. Before Athena comes back into focus, I clearly see the outline of Shira's home.

"Let's get him inside," Shira barks out. Her voice is rougher than usual. "Take him to the spare room next to where Eira is staying. I'll handle it from there."

I glance at Shira, ready to ask her what the hell is going on with me. Her eyes are no longer pleading with me. They're *commanding*, thick with warning that this is not the place to talk. She isn't as terrifying as the animal I saw, but she's a close second. Her silver hair billows around her in the winter wind, and her eyes, so similar to the sea, shine like polished agate. Her skin is pulled tighter, emphasizing her cheekbones, and the snow dances around her bare feet. For the briefest moment, she doesn't appear to be human, but rather a snow witch, preparing for a tumultuous storm.

One second, I'm taking in Shira as I think she truly is,

hidden behind an illusion. The next second, the world turns black.

Warm fingers sweep through my hair, replacing the tangled tension I was experiencing with an ease that cascades down my head and trickles through my neck and back. I go to stretch out my arms and flinch, taken aback by how sore and exhausted I feel.

"Don't worry about getting up yet," Athena says, her voice hushed. "Allow yourself to rest a little."

My eyes crack open, and I see her sitting next to me, her head resting on one hand and the other sitting next to my face on the pillow. Her face has that calming ease she gets as a therapist, but her fingers are twitching all over the place, making it clear she's on edge. The room I'm in is different, yet similar, to the one Eira's in. *Was* in. This one is a nest of fur rugs—what you'd see in a magazine about fancy winter cabins. I'm surrounded by wooden furniture, rugs, throw blankets, and carved statues of forest creatures.

She's definitely a witch. I'm royally fucked.

"What are you doing here?" I croak, clearing my throat. Athena hands me a mug of piping hot tea, something I'm sure costs more than I'll ever appreciate or enjoy. But I take it from her shaking hands, grateful that at least *one* friend is here and is trying to take care of me.

Athena doesn't say anything for a few minutes. She goes back and forth between smoothing the blanket edge and ruffling it up, lost in her thoughts and far, far away from here. *Welcome to the fucking club.*

She lets out a sigh. "I wiggled my way past Shira, ignoring her suggestion to leave you alone for a while," she says, still in her own world. "I didn't see whatever fucked up shit you were looking at outside, but I—I believe you. About Eira, I mean."

My eyebrows fly to my hairline. "Yeah?"

Athena chews on her lip before glancing at me. "Yeah," she whispers. "The Eira I know wouldn't have lazily watched you lose your shit on Shira and fly out the door without another word. She tends to want to keep the peace, but we both know her. There's no way in hell she'd let you talk that way to *anyone* she loves. She also wouldn't lay there while you're clearly frantic and upset. Even if she couldn't get up herself, she would have nudged one of us to follow you to see what's up. But she didn't, Tryg. She didn't even bat an eye and kept her focus on Liv and Lyk. I can't find all the words for what I'm feeling right now, but I know in my heart that whoever is in the other room, it's not our friend."

Blowing out a breath, I say, "At least I'm not the only one. I felt pretty alone back there."

"Oh, you're still alone," she quips, shooting me a sharp look down her nose. "While I don't know what's going on, you don't see me pinning Shira to the wall and lashing out at our friends. I'm here with you now because I don't want you to think you're crazy. I sense it, too, that Eira isn't here with us anymore. I also get the idea that Shira knows more than she's letting on, and I'm not planning on leaving this room until I find out what that is. And... honestly, you're kind of acting how Eira was over the past few weeks, Tryg."

I narrow my eyes, flushing with both embarrassment and irritation. "As much as I appreciate you telling me this, I'm not acting how Eira was. Do you see me waking up from a psycho nightmare?"

"Not all nightmares are found in the world of sleep. With the work that you do, I'd think you'd know that," Athena says before standing up.

"Where are you going?" I ask, already regretting my stupid comments. *Always on the defense.*

"I'm going to get Shira," she says firmly. "I want to know what's going on, and just because I'm not bursting with anger doesn't mean I'm not as shaken and anxious about this as you are. I trust that Shira, as anyone else, will respond better when met with respect." She sends me another pointed glare before going to the door and calling down the hallway for Shira.

I blow out another breath, readying myself for some truth, even though I already know it'll be a tough pill to swallow.

TWENTY-NINE

Eira

A soul belongs to no one but itself,
no matter the form it takes for others.
-Nicola, Goddess of the Soul

I swallow the last of the *lipva* before Daru can snatch the jar away from me again.

"Would you *stop* that?" he asks, annoyingly breathing down my neck. The whole top of my body is already itchy from the worn sports bra I'm still wearing, since there apparently wasn't time to find new clothes. But *this* is better than that heavy sweater I arrived in. "This might be a magical realm, but we can't snap our fingers and have more of this appear when we run out."

"Speak for yourself," Daya says next to us. "Plenty of other shifters can manifest elements. It's not Eira's fault that you lack the necessary skills."

She's full of such sass, I swear her *alklen* sways its hips when she talks.

Scowling, Daru says to her, "Oh, shut it. I'm not listening to someone whose name rhymes with Eira's cat."

Not missing a beat, Daya retorts, "And your name sounds like something I coughed up after breakfast."

Delano snorts and cuts off Daru before he can respond. "Everyone calm down. We'll be there in a few hours. And if Eira wants to finish the *lipva*, let her, Daru. She was knocked out cold for most of the journey, and her arm keeps glowing on and off."

I'm not sure I would say I was *knocked out*. Each time I drifted off, I woke to another scene. The details felt flimsy, each out of reach in my memory, but that stranger's eyes drew me in each time. Those swirling, dark, and electric eyes. I could tell they wanted to ravage me in vicious and unspeakable, yet the most delicious, ways. A sliver of contempt and grief hidden within their depths that I didn't understand, and each time I woke up, I wasn't sure I wanted to.

"I'm well aware of that," Daru hisses back. "I'm the one carrying her and this furball. I want to ensure she has enough supplies today when we were wildly unprepared for this kind of journey and situation." Zaya sends a loud meow Daru's way in response.

Daya flicks her hand. "It'll be fine. You think the healers won't have enough food and *lipva* for us?"

"I can't be sure of anything or anyone," Daru mutters behind me. Zaya stretches her paws out in front of her. She gives a brief scathing meow at Daru again, and moves to sit on top of the *alklen's* head, sheltered in between the pointed antlers. I shudder, still not comfortable sitting this close to them. Daru tenses behind me, as if he's about to start another argument with the others or worse, with my cat, so I shift my body to better face him.

"Can I ask more questions before we arrive?" I ask, hoping this will distract him enough.

His gaze shifts to mine for a second before staring ahead of us. *I'll take that as a moody, but firm, yes.*

"So, what's up with this bear marking?" I ask, plucking up some courage from gods know where. This is such a rough topic to bring up, but I want to get more answers before we arrive at these mysterious healers.

Daru unbelievably tenses even more, his body a metal armor around me. Daya exchanges a glance with her brother and rolls her shoulders before responding. "I can only say what I've noticed. Eliina will be able to give a better understanding to all of us when we arrive. She's our leader. When we stopped earlier, you said that the bear marking is similar to the bracelet that guy friend of yours gave you. Your description of him is eerily familiar, and the situation is rather unfortunate. I believe that bracelet was keeping you trapped in your body on Earth. It wasn't the piece of jewelry itself, but rather his intentions when he gave it to you. I know, *I know*. You're not going to believe any of this. But I sincerely do believe that he's connected to you in a negative way, no matter what, and the bear symbol tied you to him and the earth realm."

I shake my head quickly, stamping this idea out of my mind. "That doesn't make any sense. He gave me that bracelet because I've always called him a bear as a nickname, like he called me a fox." All three of them look at one another but don't say anything. *Weird*. "Even if Tryg did have power and wanted to keep us connected, it wouldn't be negative. He's one of my closest friends. I love him."

"What did you call him?" Delano asks, whipping his head to me.

"Uh... Tryg?" I say, suddenly uneasy with how alarmed all three of them are acting.

"That's rather disturbing," Daru mutters.

Daya shoots him a warning glare. "Whatever the reason is, you were always meant to be in this realm, Eira. Your friend delayed this, perhaps unintentionally, because of *what* he is."

"I hate talking about other men, especially ones I haven't

even met. Or seen. What if he's prettier than me?" Daru says, clearly trying to distract me. My lips tug into a smile, and it's annoying that he can do that so easily to me.

"You don't have to state the obvious. Literally *everyone* is prettier than you," Daya snarks. Zaya perks her head up and gives an adorable chirping meow in agreement. "See? Even kitty agrees."

Delano laughs again. "I've been thinking about your pet," he says to me. "I still can't pinpoint how she came with you, but I'm thinking it has to do with your soul connection to one another. We all have different soul connections and mates, some stronger than others. While you obviously don't have a romantic relationship and what you probably view as a 'soul mate', I guarantee that you're closer than you realize at the soul level. Zaya already showed that she can transform into a larger version of herself, which means she could have other magical talents. I'm hoping Eliina can shed more light on this topic."

"That's fucking crazy," I mumble, scratching Zaya's back. I'm not quite refusing to think about soul connections, but there's a large part of me that's blocking this topic for right now. "What happened to my body? How did you figure out how to get me here?" I wonder out loud. I'm not even expecting an answer, more wanting to change the topic away from *soul connections*.

"Now *that* is a long story," Delano says. "It took me *many* months to figure out a way to Earth. There are creatures here that have the ability to shift back and forth between the veils in time and space with Earth, but I'm not one of them. I am, though, *big surprise*, persistent and stubborn. When Eliina asked if I could find a way to get in and bring you back, I couldn't say no. Not because of who Eliina is, but because I don't back down from a challenge that tests my intelligence."

Daya drops her head back and heaves an exaggerated sigh. "He's going to take way too long and end up cramming your head with information overload—*What?*—That's what you *do*, and she's not asking for a detailed speech. She wants to know what generally happened before she can process more details. Get with it, Del. Basically, he went to an area in our realm that has the thinnest veil between us and Earth. He spent weeks practicing the kind of magic that these other creatures were born with, which allowed him to create the tiniest of holes in the veil. This meant he could easily go back and forth between Earth and Majikaero while he spent *months* searching for you," Daya side-eyes Delano. "For someone who values his intelligence so much, it took a long time to find you and, consequently, put him in the foulest mood of his life. I didn't realize he could achieve that level of outrage, which, mind you, irritated the fuck out of *me*." Delano is now fuming, and a gust of wind cycles around us. I'm getting worried that his *alklen* is going to take off from all the jittery energy.

"When he finally found you, and I won't bore you with all the details of this right now, his soul was able to call out to yours. Imagine a line of connection being established between you two. Even though humans on Earth rarely see creatures from our realm, it's possible to notice us if you're either close to passing into our realm or you have a strong soul connection. Maybe you recognized him on a subconscious level?" Daya shrugs. I think back to the last few weeks and remember seeing a strange bird one morning before rushing off to work. *That could have been him!*

"Del was also able to recognize other souls' energies there that felt familiar," Daya continues. "But he didn't spend the energy it would take to really *see* them and build a connection. He wasn't there for them—he was there for you. Now thinking about it, though, I wouldn't be surprised if those that you felt closest to show up in this realm soon. Especially since your closest protectors and friends also disappeared when you did. Those are your soul connections. They can be your fated soul

THE LIGHT WITHIN

family, friends and platonic relationships, and romantic soul mates. You won't always know right when you meet a *solliqa* if they are your soul connection, but at some point, it becomes extremely clear that you can't live without them. You'd rather die than watch them be in pain or find yourself always gravitating toward them. When your souls finally recognize one another, you'll each receive a tattooed marking on your skin connecting you. It appears in a whirl of *maji* on your body and can always be found, no matter your form. Our *maji* will formalize our bond, and we always find a way back to one another."

My mind is reeling with this information. I'm still not grasping what this veil means or looks like, and the gears in my brain keep stopping when I think too hard about the differences in time between Earth and here. It's too much. But I'm also cautiously hopeful. Does this mean my friends will cross over, too? *All* of them? Are any of them my true soul family?

"You're making it sound unnaturally easy," Delano snarls at Daya. "It took me *months* because we also didn't want to alert the Council to what was going on, and they keep a tight leash on the shifters and elementals under the Sairn. Those *damn imbeciles* somehow convinced the Council that certain *solliqas* are either too evil or will eventually corrupt our realm."

Daya rolls her eyes before peering back at me. "Yeah, yeah. *Details*. As for your body, that's, um, going to be a little challenging for you to wrap your mind around."

"Oh, yeah, compared to everything else she's learning, this will be the tough one," Daru grumbles.

Daya sends a spark of fire at Daru's face. "As I was *saying*, I'll be as general as I can, but don't try to process it all right now, alright? You're even paler than you were before, and I don't want you to pass out from this." She takes a deep breath and cocks her head to the side, mulling over how she wants to phrase everything. I brace myself because I'm sure it won't be pleasant and will serve as another reminder of how *over* everything I am.

"Think of your physical body as separate from your spirit or soul. It's incredibly important, but its job is to hold who you truly are at your core. Your soul can pass on to other bodies as your physical form dies, whether from an accident or murder or natural death. When your soul comes *here*, the land kind of, ah, creates a physical form for you, depending on your soul and abilities. I know it sounds ridiculous. But even here, the physical form doesn't matter as much and you can learn to manipulate it, which also depends on your magical talents. Take us, for example. We can stay in our bird forms for *years* and still switch back to these bodies as if nothing happened. Others can learn to change their physical humanoid forms. It's all about the soul here," Daya pauses, watching me.

"Souls are typically pure, or at least not overly corrupted. Lessons are fully learned by the time they cross over to Majikaero, or they are created and developed here and not on Earth. But something strange has been happening here. A pain and darkness that's too vile." She trembles. "But that about sums it up. Oh, and there are no *people* here, Eira. We're called *solliqas*."

I feel my eyebrows furrow and my eyes narrow in concentration. "Okay. *That's* a lot. I'll need time to, um, process that. If you can stay in another form, why would you choose to be human?"

Daya shrugs. "It's the easiest form when we first arrive here. Especially since we have the same kinds of bodily functions and urges here. Each *solliqa* eats, drinks, shits, fucks, and bleeds. Remember, we're extremely close to Earth. One of the biggest differences here is that the soul can change how its skin appears on the outside. It doesn't necessarily matter how we appear in general, but we cross over in our most recent human skin. And as we explore our powers, it gets easier to make changes to our bodies—skin color, hair, body type, and all that. Besides, it's not as if the humanoid forms you'll see here look *bad*."

THE LIGHT WITHIN

Delano flashes me a devilish smile. "Yeah, don't you think Daru and I are rather attractive?"

I pause, not sure how to respond. Daya snorts at my silence. "I think that's a good enough answer. Let me rephrase what I said: *Most* humanoid forms you'll see here don't look bad."

Laughing at how both Delano and Daru are turning to chew her out, I bring their attention back to my questions. Because I'm confused as hell and need all the information I can get from them. "So, to make sure I'm understanding this, I'm here in this created physical form, but my soul hasn't changed. It's the same as it was on Earth. My body held my soul. And now that I'm here, that means my body has died over there?"

"Err, sometimes," Daya says. "It might have died. Another soul could be in your body if it didn't die for some reason."

Horrified, I gasp, "*What?!* So, my friends could be interacting with me, and it's *not me*?"

Daya nods, still watching me carefully. I'm entirely too close to a full mental breakdown and have no idea how I'm keeping my shit together. Daru tightens his grip on my hip, obviously feeling wave after wave of panic welling up inside me.

"Yeah, that's a possibility. So crazy, right?" Daya laughs neurotically. "It's also complicated because souls here don't always appear similar to their physical forms from Earth. There can be certain characteristics that don't change, such as eyes or general build or even hair, but you are the spitting image of how you looked on Earth. Except with more muscle and not as fatigued and like you don't need makeup—"

"Yeah, thanks. I get it," I say dryly.

"So, there's a lot of unknown factors at play here," Daya continues, unfazed by how I responded. "We'll also see if Tryg will be coming here or not. I mean, in theory, he will at some point. But I'd really rather that he didn't," she mutters.

Hope blooms in my chest. I would give everything to see *any* of my friends right now, but especially Tryg or Athena.

"I know you're getting all gooey-eyed over the possibility of him coming here, but trust me, that's going to be trouble," Daya says. "Between his name and the way you describe him and the bear symbol, it's too much to be a coincidence. I'll see what Eliina has to say about it before I spiral down that path."

"Besides, you should focus on finding any strong soul mate connections in this realm," Daru says, switching out his hands on my hip bone. "They might be in your friend group back on Earth, but you might also find other mates, such as your *almaove*. That's one of the strongest soul bonds you can have and is typically romantic and physical. You did have—"

"Daru," Daya says sharply. "Now's not the moment to dive into that. It might never be. Let's focus on the task at hand and let Eliina take the reins for that conversation."

I want to ask Daru to keep going and twist around to tell him so, when a huge orange and purple bird swoops down in front of us. I desperately claw at Daru's chest, the sky swaying as we fall to the right. He grunts and is forced to swing our *alklen* in a rapid turn to hold us steady. The poor demon creature shrieks in alarm.

Good thing Daru is holding onto me because if I was alone, I'd definitely be on the ground right now with a broken back. *Absolute heart attack. How did I not see a creature so blindingly colorful? Like BAM, bright-colors-uncomfortably-in-your-face-on-a-huge-ass-raptor, colorful.*

My staccato heart rate beats harder when the raptor transforms into a man. *I'm never going to get used to this shifter shit. And what's with all the birds?* He has purple and black hair tousled in different directions, as if he's spent hours shoving his hands through it. His skin has been kissed with sunlight, a tawny bronze. I suck in a breath when his eyes meet mine, entranced with his swirling orange and yellow eyes. *Woah.* He smiles broadly, lighting up his face.

"Hauke has a way with the ladies," Daru mutters in my ear.

"He'll never cause you serious harm, but keep your wits about you. His magic is similar to Del's, yet he's more of a predator. And as hot as he looks, you don't want to be his prey."

Hmm, *debatable*. I'm not sure I agree with him. My normal jitteriness fades away, and my eyes wander his exposed, ripped chest greedily. *He can sink his talons into me.*

"Aye! Focus," Daya barks. My jaw drops when she snaps her fingers at this shifter whose beak was the size of my head. "Attention over here, buddy. What's the word?"

Hauke peruses my body, causing a hot flush to rise up my neck, before turning to Daya. "Eliina received your message and is ready for you," he says, voice rough and gravely. I fight the urge to fan myself. Athena would be drooling right about now, yet she would be pouncing on him. Where I'm more timid with physical touch, Athena dives right in. "She sent me to escort you to the healers, since they changed course unexpectedly."

"Changed course? What happened?" Delano barks.

Hauke simply smiles widely, reminding me of an unhinged cat. "You'll have to wait and see." He turns to face me and purrs, "I'll carry you over, if you'd like, my queen."

Daru tightens his hold on me imperceptibly but doesn't say anything, giving me the freedom to explore this option. That, mixed with his earlier warning, has me leaning back into him before croaking, "I'll stick with my ride, thanks." I cringe at how weak my voice sounds.

Arching an eyebrow, he says, "Suit yourself. I'll come around later to play, that is, if you don't seek me out first." He winks before transforming into his gigantic bird form in the blink of an eye. Purple feathers are tipped in orange and yellow, matching his heated eyes. Hauke soars above us and dives back down in between Delano and Daya, rattling both Delano and his *alklen's* nerves, and veers ahead of us.

"That was a savvy decision, Eira," Daru mumbles behind me. He pulls me a little closer and blows out a breath in relief.

His hot breath fans across my neck, causing a shiver to roll down my spine. "Take things slow here. If he's an actual soul connection, he'll understand and go at your pace. If he's not, then he can get fucked, and you've got us to help you out."

Smiling, I squeeze Daru's hand as we follow Hauke into a valley. Zaya is now, disturbingly, dead asleep on our *alklen's* head, even with the commotion of Hauke landing in front of us. I reach forward to pet the space between her ears. She curls up into her little shrimp form and presses her head into my hands. *Cutie. Even if she's communing with a demon deer right now.*

Glancing over at Daya and Delano, they're both watching Hauke with a predatory focus. I just met them, and they're already in full protection mode around me. *Maybe they are some of these strong soul connections—ready to guard and protect me, even from their own kind.* It's mind-blowing to consider that I tentatively trust them, knowing they could leave me at any point.

THIRTY
Nyx

How can one lead when they're too overtaken by sorrow?
-Correspondence from Quinn, High Intellect

"Point being, we're *seriously* teaming up with the healers?" Ulf bites out.

"No, we're camping out here for fun," Erika snips from the hot spring. She's been bathing in the healing thermal water for an hour now and has a blurry light blue hue around her. Turquoise scales layer along her wrists as glimmering bracelets.

"Cut the sass, you reeking fish," Ulf snarls.

Erika chuckles under her breath. "You know how to get me all riled up, Ulfy." She winks before submerging herself in the steaming water, completely unaffected by the scorching heat. Or, apparently, the combative wolf pacing the rocky corner in our impressively large tent.

Ulf stalks toward the hot spring but doesn't make it further than three steps before Odin throws out a stream of water, lashing out at Ulf's feet like a whip. Steam sizzles upon impact, making Ulf howl in agony. His legs are still cut up from Eliina's thorny vines. Odin cocks his head to the side, looking more animal than human. "Practice good pup behaviors," he says with a smirk. He flashes razor-edged teeth, his pupils forming into slits, the white gone from his eyes.

Fraya's head darts back and forth between them, her body frazzled and strained with the building aggression. I smell her arousal from here, and I want to slam my head through the boulders lining our tent. She's arguably the hardest one of our group to snap out of her monstrous form, especially since she still appears deceptively *normal*. Fraya becomes a creature from our worst nightmares when she's already got you hooked and latched under her skin. This part right now? It's the arousal that wraps around your senses, the sensual movements of her body, the way she becomes pliant in your arms. And it starts with the beginning of an argument or simmering rage. You don't choke on her venom until you're so far gone in blinding pleasure, you don't even feel the sting of her bite.

Ivar acts busy sharpening his arrows but meets my gaze and nods subtly, ready to jump into action. At this point in the night, the *last* thing we need is our demons to rear their ugly and destructive heads. I'm barely containing my own emotions after Eliina spoke with me earlier. I can handle working with her and her squad—I know deep down that she was never the problem and not even my shadows can smother that truth. But the idea of meeting this woman? In the flesh? I'm beside myself with the impulsive need to find her on my own and the torment of what this will mean for all of us now that she's here. If she's even who Eliina says she is.

Erika pokes her head out of the water, and while she doesn't say anything, I can tell from the glint in her eyes that she's the reason mist is gathering around Ulf now.

"Nyx?" a meek voice calls out from the entrance of our tent.

A breath whooshes out of me, and I quickly respond, "Yeah, Isa?" I send a warning glare to the others, and Ivar crouches down next to Fraya. He seems to be one of the few souls completely unaffected by her, which has implications I'd rather not explore. I cut my gaze to Ulf and say sharply, "Don't be stupid. Take a breather."

Ulf huffs out in annoyance and continues to pace the corner in agitation. A lone wolf trapped by his own darkness and now dangerously cornered and smothered in mist.

I pull back the tent entrance and am greeted with dark brown eyes peeking out from under a teal silk hood. The robe drapes around her body and cinches at the waist, emphasizing her curves. The pattern fades from the teal blue to golden dragonflies, bringing out the ocher flecks in her eyes.

"Eliina is requesting a meeting with all of you and her core squad," Isa says lowly. "Immediately."

"Of course," I murmur. I turn to alert the others, but she stops me with her hand.

"It's normal for them to be this worked up," she whispers, barely loud enough for me to hear. "While you live in a building together, even that was abandoned long ago. They're used to freedom and acting on their wills at any given moment. We understand. You'll find no judgment from us tonight."

I smile, and my heart constricts again. It's uncomfortable to feel such gratitude when I'm used to spite and suffering. "Thanks, Isa," I respond.

Her hand squeezes my arm before she walks toward Eliina's tent. I don't let myself think of who else will be at this meeting. The anticipation is enough to send me hurtling toward the cliff wall.

"Alright," I begin. "Gather any important belongings. We're to meet with Eliina and her team right now. *Yes*, we all have to go. *No*, I don't care if you don't want to. Odin and Erika, I don't want to see one drop of water on Ulf. Ivar, help Ulf gather any weapons and keep him distracted for the next few minutes. Ulf, lighten up or do us all a favor and go home. And Fraya, *would you get a fucking grip?*"

She's lounging against a cushioned chair, half of her top undone. Fraya pouts and bats her eyes at me, as if I seriously ruined her night.

"But you know how *antsy* I get," she says, her voice low. In a flash, she's giving me a sultry look and dipping her fingers into her pants. She gives a whine, and my shadows lash out, shaped in the form of daggers. For a beat, no one dares to breathe. Fraya *finally* acts genuinely scared, as if all this time together, I've given empty threats. She wholly succeeds when my monster is breaching the surface, and I've, fortunately, got it firmly buried inside. Here and now? She sure as the bullshit she speaks better be afraid of me.

"What the fuck did I say?" I ask, seething, smoke curling around my feet.

"I-I need t-to get a f-fucking grip," she rambles, stuttering all over the place.

"Odin," I command.

One minute, Fraya is cowering on the ground, my armed shadows pointing at her neck.

The next minute, Odin has her encased in a sphere of water. Her eyes are bulging, her face stunned with terror. If he keeps her here too long, she'll drown. Fraya arches her back and stretches her hands to the edges of the sphere, desperately trying to claw her way out. My shadows strike out, switching into a vine-like rope, squeezing her neck until she's suffocating.

I walk toward her slowly, my breathing ragged, my body rigid with gleeful fury. The smoke swirls around my entire body, hiding my face except for my hardened eyes, letting her see that this is *me*, not my monster. That I'm not always going to be kind and do not give a fuck what that means for her.

"When I tell you to get it *fucking* together," I snarl. "It means you'll do what I say or face the consequences. We might be shunned from Rioa, but I'm still your fucking *prince*. A prince of nightmares and shadowed terrors beyond your wildest imagination. And if you continue to disobey me, I'll make sure you remember who's in charge, who the fuck *matters* here. I won't bother asking if I'm clear. You'll spew more lies, pretending to understand a simple question." I pause, letting the rope tighten.

"Let this be a warning for what you do next while we're with Eliina and these healers. With anyone else on her squad. I'll rip your soul to shreds in the time it takes you to inhale a single breath without a drop of remorse. Because honestly? What have you done except bring chaos and humiliation to your own created family, let alone everyone else? You don't need to respond. *Because I don't care.*"

I snap my fingers and the shadows disappear. She breathes in water for a second before Odin releases the water, letting it drench her on the ground. Fraya lets out a sob and glares at me, a mixture of fear and anger battling with one another.

"I *hate* you!" she cries. "I hate that I love you."

"And may that hate eat you alive for what you've done to each of us, especially me," I say. "Now, clean yourself up. We don't have any more time for your bullshit."

THIRTY-ONE

Tryq

Evil is infrequently black and white.
Take all of you, for example. You're training to take down
leaders and innocent citizens in another country.
Are you not as dishonorable as them?
-Rike Tonish, Commander of Sweazn
Investigative Forces

Bullshit. That's what my current life situation is. Athena's foot taps restlessly on the floor, rocking steadily on the cushioned rocking chair in the corner of the room. She's staring at a tree outside the window while chewing on her bottom lip. She called for Shira an hour ago and was told she'd be with us in "just a minute", yet here we are, waiting in strained silence.

My stomach curdles and squeezes with each passing minute, consumed with anticipation and nervous energy. It's the same sensation I used to get before marathons. The sensation before races would build and build in my body, scraping at the surface and heightening all my senses, putting me on edge. As if something life-changing was coming but was still unknown. It's the same sensation now. My heart is rattling around in my ribs, barely caged in, and I'm about ready to explode.

The ping of Athena's phone rings like a siren in the quiet room. I glance over at her and feel a twinge of guilt. Her face is obviously drained, her eyes sullen. She must be terrified by what's going on, especially if she hasn't even *seen* anything yet. Her fingers fly over her phone before sending out a message.

Sighing, Athena rubs her hand down her face before glancing at me. "That was Morgan," she says, her tone dripping with exhaustion. "I put in a request for temporary leave after what happened with Eira at the hospital. I need time to process everything and want to be here to support her, although now I'm not even sure who I'm supporting."

Oh, shit. *Athena* is feeling bad enough to ask for leave from work? This is seriously impacting her even more than I thought. *No shit, Tryg. They're best friends, and there's a war. At least try to stop being so stupid.*

I want to comfort her, but I don't know what to say or where to begin. Athena and Eira are the most empathetic of our friends, followed closely by Jace, Astira, Liv, and Lyk. Ruse is up there, better than me by far. But me? An insect could help her more than I could, and she's one of those girls who squeals when a minuscule ant crawls over her legs in the woods. I used to be better than this, relatively carefree with Eira and my brothers while growing up, cracking jokes with everyone. I don't know what happened and when, but I've felt especially worn out this past year. It's been months since I last spoke with my family—only my friends have forced me to remain social and communicate with them.

I'm a shell of my past self, and I've disintegrated more and more under the hardened shield I've been hiding behind.

Shaking my head, I urge myself to snap out of it and focus on Athena. "I'm, uh, I'm sorry to hear you've been so, um, stressed." I cringe, willing the bed to swallow me whole.

Athena barks out a laugh. "Thanks, Tryg. I forgot how awkward you get with emotions." She smiles sadly before peering out the window again, pulling a blue woven blanket over her arms.

God, if you're even there, please cut me a break. I get it; you probably can't change the dumbass that I am. But at least help Athena out. I'm hallucinating, our friend is gone somehow, and Athena's suffering from all this shit and the war.

The door opens with a loud *bang,* and I nearly climb out of my skin in shock. Athena is standing and whirls toward the door, face as fear stricken as mine. Shira marches in with a bundle of supplies and a stern expression, heading toward the table.

Alright, here must be the break. I'm ready. Sorta. Alright, I'm not. Whatever.

"I apologize for the delay," Shira says with a sigh. "Another situation took my attention for a while. There are a number of upsetting circumstances happening right now." She takes out each item and carefully places it on a magenta towel. A tattered old book, a few jars with prismatic liquids sloshing inside them, and smaller items that I can't see from where I'm sitting.

"Thank you for coming here," Athena responds. Her face and body appear remarkably relaxed, but her voice is strained. I move my stiff body up higher against the pillows behind me.

"Yeah, we appreciate any information you can share or anything you recommend that we should do," I grind out. My throat feels like sandpaper, and I fumble for the tea again.

Shira turns toward us, her face set in a grimace. "There's much to discuss, but I'm afraid we don't have enough time for it all." She uncorks one of the jars on the towel and downs it in one go. I think her eyes flare brighter for a second, but after what I saw outside, I'm not sure what to believe anymore. It's probably my fucked-up head.

"Come, my child," she says to Athena, opening her arms.

Athena runs to her, and they stand in a locked embrace for a minute. Shira gently pats her back and then turns her around, motioning her toward the bed. "What I'm about to share is going to be a lot to take in. I recommend you get comfortable."

Athena hesitates, her eyes narrowing ever so slightly. She twists her mouth to the side and, after a second, gives a quick nod of her head and walks over to where I'm lying. She crawls in next to me, and I scooch over to give her more room. We're extremely close friends, but things have only ever been platonic between us. After hooking up with Astira, I'm mindful to put a good few inches between our bodies, even though we have clothes on and are trembling with nerves. Athena must notice because she snorts before inching closer and patting my hand, giving me a heaping dose of side-eye before turning her focus back on Shira.

Shira situates herself on the rocking chair and moves it closer to the bed. She's mindlessly messing with that necklace again, and I can't fight back a blow of nausea. *This is it.*

"Where to start?" Shira mutters to herself. "Let's go with the basics. You're both aware of the work I do, correct?"

Athena nods her head *yes*, but I'm gaping at her, wondering if she remembers that I became aware of Shira's existence hardly a few weeks ago.

"Ah, yes, that's right," she says. "We recently met one another, Tryg. In simplest terms, I work therapeutically and physiologically with clients, but I continued down a different path after getting my degree. I work with clients' energies and help them connect with past lives they've experienced with the purpose of healing individual and generational trauma."

"Oh?" I ask. "*Energies.*"

"Yes," she continues. "I also incorporate other areas of study and resources into my work. This ranges from natural remedies to shamanic work to holistic medicine."

"Oh, *great*," I mumble. "So, as I thought. You're a witch."

Athena slaps my arm and scowls at me, but Shira chuckles to herself. "I wouldn't use that term to describe what I do and who I am, but if that's what you want to call me, that's fine."

I was wrong. My current situation is worse than bullshit. It's cat shit. I'm in Zaya's fucking litter box.

"I'm often called in for support after modern medicine doesn't work for clients. Because of what I know. What I can do. Who I can call on for additional support and knowledge." She peers at the wooden animal statues in the room. Her eyes, deep as the ocean floor, bore into mine as she continues. "It's not an easy life calling, but this is what I do. And it's effective in helping people heal and find their true selves under all those layers of life lessons and trauma and pain. It's why I took Eira in immediately. Although, I'm afraid I was too late with her."

"Too late?" Athena asks, worry shining in her big eyes. "What do you mean? What's going on, Shira?" Her voice catches, and I thread my fingers with hers, letting her know that I'm here with her. That my heart is also confused and slowly breaking into too many pieces.

"Yes, too late," Shira says. "Her soul was already being pulled from this world to the next. I was meant to keep her here a while longer until after the war. There was no denying that she rebuilt herself enough to transition back to the other realm, but it wasn't supposed to happen yet. She's felt suffering but not the trauma necessary to truly break her in this lifetime."

"*The fuck?*" I ask, looking at Shira incredulously.

She simply nods and hums. Athena has gone stiff next to me, and I squeeze her hand again, needing her to be with me on this.

"There isn't enough time to explain what this all means to either of you," she continues. She holds up a picture of a bear made up of different pieces of nature. *Eira's bracelet.* "Do you recognize this, Tryg?"

Swallowing, I nod once.

THE LIGHT WITHIN

Shira nods to herself and says, "I thought you would. What does this picture feel like to you?"

Narrowing my eyes, I study the different parts of the bear. Originally, I thought of Eira and the bracelet I had gifted her a while ago. Now, I'm filled with a sense of *rightness*. A calling to this image. *Home.*

"It's familiar, isn't it?" she asks. "More than a bracelet?"

Without giving me a chance to answer, she glances at Athena and her eyes turn a different shade. Darker, full of regret. "And you weren't supposed to be here at all. I'm afraid that I've grown rather fond of you and your friends over these past years. I wasn't supposed to, you know. There must be enough of my Earth self in me to have influenced such a love for you. No matter, though. My soul uniquely serves a few true purposes, and connecting with your group is one of them. And now, we are here."

Athena slowly shakes her head, trying to understand what Shira is saying. "I—I don't understand, Shira. Any of what you've said. But mostly why you're staring at me with such sadness. What's going on?" Tears line Athena's eyes. Her lips wobble, and she clenches her jaw, clearly trying to stay strong and focused.

Shira breathes harshly through her nose and squares her shoulders. "I've traveled many lifetimes in search of your souls. Wretched years spread out for longer than a soul my age enjoys. It's been centuries in this world, longer than even my leaders anticipated. After each human death I've experienced, they encouraged me to stay focused on the task they gave me, that I would find Eira and her soul connections, eventually. So *confident* that you'd somehow survived and would be on Earth with it being close to Majikaero. My soul has been reborn in enough bodies that I was ready to give up, but this year, I was lucky enough to have each of you given to me on a silver platter. A gift, perhaps from our gods."

She licks her lips and takes another step toward Athena. "Having to live life after life through the nuclear attacks to living underground with the rest of civilization like a grimy worm to settling into civilizations as they cultivated new cities... it's all been worth it. I can *finally* fulfill what the Sairn have sent me here to do and make sure you're all sent *back* to our realm, marked and ready to truly die this time, in this current lifetime. My Earth self hopes you'll find Eira, and she'll be able to answer your questions. Since she went before completely breaking in on herself, I have no doubt that she'll be with souls who can help you. But my true soul can't stand for her to fight against our gods and wishes for her to fail miserably."

I'm regretting that Athena is sitting frighteningly close to Shira. I have no way to push her behind me, and I'm officially in full defense mode now. Shira looks back at me and says, "You're much farther along than I anticipated. You shouldn't have been able to see an *alklen*, and not that particular one, especially. They're loyal to Eira, and that one was trying to give you a warning. Don't fret, Tryg. You couldn't have communicated with them, and even if you could, it's too late for any messages."

"Too late for *what*?" I spit, fully sitting up and laying my arm in front of Athena. She's clutching to me and trembling, shaking her head back and forth slowly. I'm realizing too late that we're too lost in what Shira's saying to try to leave the room. We're trapped, like her wooden animals.

"Too late for Eliina to heal you, too," she says softly. "The Sairn await your arrival, and any *maji* left in your veins will be depleted soon enough. You'll be back home and destined to be found by them. It'll start with you and end when the last of your friends have been sent over, ready for the Sairn to devour them whole. Even *you*, Tryg. You were meant to be one of us, but your traitorous heart had other plans. Stopping before you could finish the job, your soul growing a conscience we didn't know you had. I won't let you stop us this time. You'll all finally be eliminated. I'll make sure of it."

I push her mystifying gibberish out of my mind and go into survival mode. Predator meets predator, not letting her make me the prey. My hand shoots to my Glock, but Shira's quicker. Her hair flies out around her again and within a breath and the snap of her fingers, Athena and I are pushed back against the headboard. My muscles strain and my back arches as I push against whatever force is holding me down. I try to yell out for help, but Shira merely shakes her finger at me before turning around. When I try to yell, my throat closes up, and I barely get a breath down.

This panic is sickening and striking me down.

While we're struggling for our lives, Shira drinks the other few jars of liquids and sparks of energy zap around her. If I wasn't seeing this with my own eyes, there's no way I'd ever believe it. Calling her a witch was too kind. I imagined some screwy forest witch shit from one of those fairytales or weird movies the girls made me watch over the years.

But this? This is petrifying and envelopes me in a raw fear I haven't experienced before. Shira stands as a demon goddess cloaked in torrents of power, and I have a strong feeling we're not going to enjoy what comes next.

"H-how will you m-make sure of it?" Athena whispers, her teeth chattering.

Shira is rummaging for something on the towel. She slowly turns her head, baring her teeth.

"May the Sairn bless your souls for eternity," she growls before appearing next to the bed in the blink of an eye and plunging daggers into our hearts.

Time slows for me. The tip of the icy blade glows a dark purple. It moves through skin and muscle, sinking into my chest. A sticky black substance oozes out, sliding down my sides onto the bed. Horrified, I use the last of my energy to peer at Athena, who is convulsing while a green light glows from under her skin. Her eyes are closed, and she looks asleep. Peaceful, even.

I don't get to consider what this might mean—my time has run out.

Pain latches onto my heart and squeezes until I'm bursting with agony, and my vision tunnels into black and red. The last thing I see is Shira's snarling mouth, the same black substance smeared around her lips.

THIRTY-TWO
Nyx

If you can't set a boundary with yourself,
how will you ever set them with others?
-Note from a professor, taped on Athena Lilar's office desk

I wipe away the last of the black residue smeared on my lips, savoring the smoked, chewy meat I nearly inhaled while walking briskly into the crisp night air. It's one of the tastiest travel foods one could bring with them, but it leaves your lips and teeth stained black if you're not careful. Ivar catches up to me, matching my pace, while finishing his own piece of meat. I made everyone take a few bites before leaving, in case the night turns long, and we're left hungry. That never leads to anything favorable with our restless beasts.

"Don't you think you were a little harsh?" Ivar asks me while we head over to Eliina's tent.

"No," I reply without looking at him. "She needs to learn to control herself. When any of us tell her to, not just me. But I'm the one who can put her in her place when my beast is on a tight leash. I'll do what I have to."

"But she isn't *all* bad," Ivar continues. "She's connected to *solliqas'* emotions and highly responsive to them. If she can get a better handle on her demonic self, she might be suited to work with the healers or manipulators. To help *solliqas* manage their emotions and connect with their inner sensuality."

"The key word there is *might*," I say firmly. "In the meantime, all she's done is cause trouble. I'm fair and patient, but when I tell someone to get in line, I absolutely fucking mean it. Even if Eliina wasn't here, we're not in a position to be messing around. If she does anything again, she's being sent home. *No arguments.* If she can't follow a simple command, she won't last five minutes back in Rioa around the Council."

I turn to face Ivar before we enter Eliina's tent and clasp his shoulder. "A large part of me cares about her. So much that she's permanently molded to what's left of my heart. It's the reason I hooked up with her in the first place. An even larger part of me is scared for her. What you saw back there is *nothing* compared to what the Council would do to her for resisting a command. You know this is true. She either adapts and works on herself, or she'll be better off left behind."

Ivar nods, his expression grim yet understanding. We've both experienced the horrors of the Council personally.

"Now," I breathe. "Let's go see what fresh shit awaits us."

Ivar's lips pull into a smirk. "I thought that smell was you."

I playfully punch his shoulder and push through the tent opening. I make it two seconds before I'm hit with a staggering pressure. I get the overwhelming need to scream, emotions surging through my entire body, my soul leaping with fire. As quickly as the sensation came, it's gone. I struggle to control my breathing, uncomfortably aware of various eyes watching my every move.

"You okay?" Ivar whispers next to me. He narrows his eyes and scans the room, alarmed and tense, his hand already reaching for his transparent bow. It was a gift from his father, made from the translucent trees in Wyndera, and he managed to bring it with him before he was shunned from Rioa.

"Yeah, I—"

My heart stops.

No, my entire existence stops, and I cease to be.

I notice my group surrounding me and the presence of others in clusters around the tent. But my entire focus is on the striking silver and blue eyes from across the way, our gazes locked on one another. The air is sucked out of me in a vacuum, and for a moment, it's only us, frozen in time, aching to be closer.

"*Shit*," someone mutters next to her.

I blink out of my daze and take in the others in this space. There are souls I don't recognize, but I know the shifters flanking the *solliqa* I dreamed of. Who wouldn't? Daya, Daru, and Del. Some of the fiercest shifters in Rioa, let alone the realm, and it's quite fitting they're teaming up with Eliina. Even more fitting that she tasked them with a mission this damn important.

Daru takes a step toward me, half-shielding this *fim* behind him. *Eira. Her name's Eira.* His face is set in a murderous snarl, his body already surging with power. The other two look equally poised to fight, but there's something different about Daru. He's acting entirely too protective of a soul he's just met, even if she's supposed to be a queen. An ugly flare of jealousy thrashes through me, settling like acid in my throat. *Is he also her almaove? I know there are solliqas who have more than one, depending on how powerful they are. Will she prefer him over me? He sure doesn't have the black markings of the plague.*

Eira's face is blanched and ashen, clearly unsettled with our presence. If she's new to this realm, I can barely imagine what she's feeling right now. Still, even as the scent of her fear washes over me, she straightens her back and nudges Daru in the ribs. He turns to face her, and her expression morphs into a scowl. I fight back a smile. Not an ounce of fear when she's facing one of the most lethal shifters in our world. A fluffy feline winds around her legs, seemingly glaring up at Daru with the same ferocity and displeasure.

"Would you cut it out?" she hisses. "You can't act this way with each soul who interacts with me here."

The sound of her voice, even when annoyed, nearly sends me to my knees.

"Don't presume what I can or can't do," he flings back. A brisk breeze rushes along the floor, pushing against the tent walls and causing them to billow outward. "You don't know the first thing about those creatures. A darkness so barbaric consumes their souls, they'll—"

"*Those* creatures?" she replies, her voice thick with sarcasm. She barks out a laugh. "As if you aren't one, too? At least they're not fluttering around like birds, flapping their wings in greeting. And don't even start about darkness right now. I'm quite aware of what it does to the soul. Remember I was a therapist?" She knocks on the side of his head. "Or does your birdbrain only hold so much information at once?"

Daya snorts next to her and Del smiles, clearly enjoying her reaction to Daru's protectiveness.

And I'm standing here, unable to take my eyes off her. I'm essentially a demon prince, but I'm a demon prince who might be swooning for the first time in my life. She's feisty and agitated and fearless. My fingers twitch, eager to touch her smooth skin and explore her fiery energy. See if it'll rise to meet my own.

Daru opens his mouth to respond and then closes it. He looks ready to strangle her and clenches his fists by his sides. Eira doesn't give him a second thought before turning back to assess me. Her energy throbs around her akin to a beating heart and a brilliant blue fire dances in her eyes. Beneath that, though, she is also alert. Assessing. Shocked. Lips as soft as petals twist to the side of her mouth as she chews on the inside of her cheek. Her fingers tremble as she tucks her hair behind her ears. *Is she scared of me?*

"Well, this is not at all how I planned this introduction," Eliina sighs. She glowers at Del. "I thought I instructed you to go *right* to the healers with Eira before coming here."

He merely shrugs. "She was anxious to meet you. And it doesn't help that the healers effectively swarmed her as we approached. Between her arrival, the marking, riding an *alklen,* meeting Hauke of all *solliqas*, and having a bunch of glowing creatures smother her with attention and questions, I thought it was best to find you first. Clearly, I didn't think there'd be this many, ah, others here." He glances over at me. "Or *them*."

Eliina ignores him and walks briskly over to Eira. She leans down to whisper something in Eira's ear, quiet enough that none of us can hear. Eira turns toward the back area of the tent while they continues to talk. She stiffens, anxiety bleeding out of her pores. Eliina glances behind her shoulder and calls out, "Naeva. Paloma. Both of you will escort her to the private healing area next to the waterfall. *Only you* will go with her." She pauses. "And Isa. She could do with your pacifying nature and level of powers tonight."

Isa and Paloma bow slightly before walking toward the tent entrance. Paloma appears to be healed with new robes on, and she doesn't falter even a step when she passes Ulf. Naeva smiles and shoots a wink toward Daya, who's grinning from ear to ear. I forgot how close of friends they are. I suppose not everything has changed since I've been gone.

Eira warily glances at Daya, Daru, and Del. Del and Daya nod encouragingly to follow the healers and Isa. Daru is rigid but motions her toward the entrance. He narrows his eyes at me, a clear warning to not interact with her. I smirk. If I'm willing to suffocate one of my own to teach them a lesson, I'm capable of anything. Does he think I'll heed his commands?

The feline scratches at Eira's worn clothing, and I find myself irritated that no one's bothered to give her new clothes yet. She bends down to pick it up, and it scans around the room until its gaze lands on me, its tail swishing wildly. Green and blue eyes stare me down, and I'm struck with an odd sense of familiarity.

Eira starts off walking hesitantly toward me and then rolls her shoulders, straightening her back. I admire how she still keeps her chin up, not outwardly showing her obvious fear. The connection between us is palpable, and I long to stroke her face, to twist my hands in that luscious, long hair. As she nears, smoke tendrils dance along my skin, excited by her presence. She gasps and almost as if in response, light flames crawl up her arms. Stunned, she glances down from her arms and back to me, and if I wasn't so amazed by meeting her, I'd laugh at how surprised her face looks. Eira blows out a breath and quickens her pace. She stops next to me before exiting and turns her face toward mine. I can't bring myself to move away.

"What's your name?" she breathes. The silver and gold in her eyes crackle like lightning, a mirror to my own.

Having her full attention this close to me sends shivers down my spine. I take half a step closer to her, my shadows and smoke mixing together and reaching out to her hand, giving it a gentle caress. Her eyes flare slightly with light, and I'm a second from pulling her into my arms when someone clears their throat. I glance away, and of course, it's fucking Daru. *I already hate the fucker. He has no idea that she's already mine, and I'll burn my own kind just to keep her to myself.*

"Nyx," I whisper. Brown meets blue. A color I'd willingly drown in. "My name's Nyx."

"Hi, Nyx," she whispers back. Her voice surrounds me in a cloud, fogging any sense left in me. "I'm Eira. Perhaps we're finally meeting. Or is this another dream?"

I'm falling back into the shadows before Eliina can even grab for me and scatter out into the night air. I hear her yell a warning, but all that's left behind are whispers of smoke. Now that I've found Eira and felt our connection, I can't let her out of my sight. Not yet, anyway.

The healers guide Eira to a different tent, the sounds of a small waterfall becoming louder the closer we get. Isa is walking next to Eira and using one of her gifts: relaxing the body into a state of serene peacefulness. Eira glances up while they walk and asks quietly, "There are two moons here?" Her feline follows Eira's head movements, taking in the clear sky.

Isa nods. "The moons cycle out throughout the year. These are currently lavender and navy. There tends to be a celebration for each change in cycle, especially in Rioa."

Eira hums to herself, not asking more questions. I blend into the dark air and keep from the small globes of light.

"How are you feeling right now?" Isa asks her, keeping her tone low.

A beat of silence and Eira responds, her voice tight and raspy, "Brittle."

Naeva and Paloma look at each other and pull back the tent opening. "We're hoping we can help with that," Naeva responds, keeping her voice easy and gentle.

Eira pauses before entering and peers around her, searching for something. Her eyes move past where I'm standing, and I let out a breath I didn't realize I was holding. Whatever she sees must be deemed okay because she nods to herself before entering. Her feline is staring right at me, and I edge closer into a patch of darkness to my right.

"I'll be right in," Isa tells them. She waits until the entrance closes behind the feline before lowering her hood, cocking her head to the side. "Nyx," she whispers. "This isn't a wise idea."

I hide myself deeper into the shadows against the cliffside. Isa walks slowly toward me, her eyes turning burgundy. "I *see* you, Nyx," she says. "And I'm not afraid of the likes of you. I meant what I said—there's no judgment of your actions here. But you're the reason Eliina sent me with Eira. She knew what you'd try to do."

"I need to be with her," I grind out, struggling to keep my impatience at bay. "I met her in a dream, saw her in a dead child's body, and now she's *here*, in the flesh!" My nostrils flare, taking in her scent. "Even her smell is decadent, Isa. Sweet and smoky. I *need* to speak with her, to be next to her, to hear her voice again."

"And you will," Isa says kindly. Lost in the scent of Eira, I didn't even see how quickly Isa snuck up on me, standing an inch away. "But not tonight. You might have made connections with her previously, and truly, your souls might already be intertwined. But this is her second perceived day here. She's frightened and isolated from her loved ones back on Earth. She doesn't even *know* you. I know you're used to doing what you want, when you want. And before now, you were brought up as a warrior prince, able to seek desires at your will. That's not how things work where she comes from. You need to go slow. As... friends."

I scowl at her in the dark. "*Friends?*" I ask. "I meet my *almaove,* and you want me to be her *friend?*"

"Well, *yeah*," Isa responds, barely controlling her eye roll. "Put yourself in her place. She learned there's a realm of magic right next to Earth. She has been having horrible nightmares before transitioning here and now needs to get help with the bear marking on her arm—"

THE LIGHT WITHIN

"The *bear* marking?!" I interrupt, growing uncontrollably agitated.

"Did you not see her arm? Or hear what Eliina warned us all about before?" Isa sighs, throwing her hands up in the air.

"Yes, she has *the* marking on her arm. Which is alarming for multiple reasons, since we all thought he was dead. And beyond this, she's *alone* and *isolated* from her loved ones. Imagine not knowing this place and realizing you have *maji* flowing through your blood. Don't even get me started on what it must have been like to wake up to Del and Daru. *Ugh.*" She makes a face. "And *then*, she meets you! The person she's been having dreams about and still doesn't understand why she feels uncontrollably connected to you. Can you even begin to imagine?"

"But I can—"

"*No*, Nyx," she says more firmly. "You can do all those things when you develop an actual relationship with her first. Start with friendship. If you can control yourself, I'll allow you to stay outside the tent while we get her situated. That way you can have peace of mind that you're close enough if anything goes wrong. But make no mistake, Nyx." Isa grows a few feet taller, her voice lowering. Luminous antlers grow from her head, little flames on the end of each tip. A pure white substance morphs onto her body. "If you cross the line of that tent, you will have not me, but *all* of us to deal with."

I gulp, remembering the hidden powers a soul as small as Isa manages to carry. How easily they can break through my fog of smoke and slithering shadows. She hasn't been able to find a cure, but she doesn't have any problem with handing my ass to me.

"I'll be out here," I mumble. "If it's deemed safe later on, please let me come inside. I—I need her."

Isa searches my eyes for a moment longer and swiftly transforms back into her usual humanoid form. Her skin is back to its light brown with white markings, like someone painted splotches of white along her body. Her eyes are still that merciless burgundy, though, which tells me she's ready to strike at any minute.

"And what is it that *she* needs, hmm?" She walks toward the entrance of the tent, so quiet on her feet that only a *solliqa* trained in the art of shadows would be able to hear her.

I'm left alone in my thoughts once again, hoping the one soul I want seeks my own.

THIRTY-THREE
Eira

Trauma is moldable and takes the shape we give it.
Until it's too late.
-Correspondence from Rei, High Soul Reader

Seeking any grasp I have left on reality, I try to massage my arms as I'm guided into the tent. Me. As in, I, Eira. I'm the one who journeyed on something called an *alklen* with three shifters. I've now arrived at a base in the valley between cliffs where many magical beings saunter around. *Me.* I'm the one who came face-to-face with that soul, if I can even call him that when he was half drifting into shadows and smoke. The one I dreamed about and saw while I was in the hospital. What's crazier? That smoke flitted off his arms and hands or how I felt a power surge under my skin and flames traveled down my arms.

Flames!

If I wasn't in such a state of shock, there's no way I'd still be standing, let alone interacting with magical beings called healers.

I suppose I'm relatively grateful that Daru was acting like such an overprotective asshat. It must be all my years of dealing with the guys back home because all it took was his obnoxious tone, and I was ready to throw hands. If he does that again, I'm going to whip out the self-defense moves that Athena, Astira, and I learned. *Punch him right in the beak. That oughta shut him up.*

The tent I'm standing in is incredibly beautiful and ornate. Miniature globes of dimmed lights float around the ceiling, and the walls are covered in layers of intricate scarves, billowing out into the chilly night. The colors match the lavender and navy moons shining brightly in the sky. One side of the tent has tables lined up next to one another, full of tools and ingredients. Orange and red mushrooms, or at least, I think that's what they are, glow on the middle table, and delicate herbs and twisting glass jars with mystery liquids surround them.

Zaya stalks over to explore this table and Isa hastily guards the mushrooms from my too curious cat. In the other corner, there's a natural hot spring, beckoning me with its steam. I feel disgusting from not bathing the last few days, and oh gods, *my teeth*, that I don't even care how there's a hot spring in this tent. I only know that I need to be inside of it right now.

And I'm still beyond clueless about what I'm supposed to do about the bathroom situation. We went pretty much nonstop on the *alklen*, and the few times we stopped, Daya insisted that we go "the natural way" until we arrived. Well, now I'm here. My bladder is nice and ready, eager for anything resembling a toilet.

It must be obvious that I have some physical needs because Naeva laughs at my antsy dancing and careful steps toward the hot spring.

"This is precisely what we are starting with and why Eliina wanted Del to bring you straight to us," she says with a grin. Her smile is beautiful and accentuated by her gray eyes and wavy, strawberry-blond hair. "I'm pretty sure he knew to come to us specifically, not the healers as a whole, but you'll find that he fancies causing trouble. Of all sorts." She winks, and her freckled cheeks heat.

"Let's get you settled in the bathroom here, and then, perhaps, you can soak in the hot spring while we talk," Paloma suggests. She moves with grace, the air parting for her as she walks. Long, curly black hair sways against her dark skin with the movement of her hips. I see a room hidden in the back of the tent, and when she pulls back the entrance, my jaw hits the floor. *Are they serious? That bathroom is three times the size of my own back home.*

"You look, uh, shocked," Paloma says, her dark brows scrunching together. "Is this not what you have back on Earth? I know that we haven't been there in ages, but we do remember the toilet, sink, and tub system. Or I think we do—Isa, is this right?"

"No, no," I insist, forcing myself to recover. "This is absolutely *amazing*. It's even nicer than what I had on Earth, and after peeing in the woods the last few days, I didn't realize you even had something like this."

Naeva laughs again, the sound as soft as bells. "Of course we do! Keep in mind where many of us come from. I'm sure this hasn't been explained to you yet, but we have full, expansive libraries back in Rioa detailing the histories on Earth. Our system works differently here because we don't use electricity. We use *maji* for almost everything."

"There's that *maji* word again," I mumble.

"Mhm!" Paloma nods with a smile, her dark eyes lighting to a swirling gray with excitement. "It's everywhere and comprises everything in our world. Think of it as magic. Some of it is drawn from the elements and creatures around us, which I'm sure you've seen with Daya and her companions. Other parts of it are drawn from abilities our souls were naturally born with, such as *solliqas* connecting to and being able to manipulate others' thoughts or what we do with our ability to heal soul-deep wounds. The way we live is also dependent on *maji*. This ranges from what we wear to food preparation—no, you don't have to be human to appreciate and thrive on delicious food—to our lights and heating systems. Everything is fueled and created by *maji*. We'll definitely illustrate more of this later, but I must insist that you take care of yourself first. I have an affinity toward bodily functions and pain stored in certain areas of the physical form, and I sense that you need to relieve yourself, take care of your teeth, and bathe."

My eyes widen, and I'm completely consumed by embarrassment.

"Way to be creepy," Isa mutters before pushing her way through the bathroom entrance. "Come on, Eira. Let me show you what we have here, and if you need anything else, I'll go get it for you."

Now hyper-aware of my body's needs, I hurry into the bathroom.

"Sorry about her," Isa whispers. "She's extremely talented in this field, and as I'm sure you also observe on Earth, unnaturally smart and talented individuals can be a bit..."

"Odd? Eccentric? Quirky?" I finish for her.

She grins and breaks into a full smile when she hears, "*Hey!*" from outside the bathroom.

"This is the toilet, which I'm sure you'll be familiar with. We have a variety of soaps and lotions around the basin you can use to wash your hands and face. We don't use what you'd call toothbrushes here. We found a different, more effective, way to clean our mouths, and you'll find the natural remedy next to the glass of *lipva*. Swallow it with a sip of *the lipva* and voilà, clean mouth. Over here, you'll find towels, more soaps, and the tub. I'll turn on the water for you; it doesn't take long. Call for us or come out when you're done." Isa dips her head before leaving me alone in this extravagant space.

I quickly take care of my business and explore the different soaps. I might be testing out all of this for, you know, science or whatever. I press the herb-scented pill into my mouth and take a sip of the *lipva* before I can change my mind or think too much about what I'm doing. *It'll take some time for me to get used to all of this.*

My hand glides along the stack of lush towels, and I turn off the faucet by the tub. It takes a few minutes to take in the size of it and decide which soap I want to pour in. I pluck the first few glass bottles of liquid soaps, and each scent is better than the last. Lavender, mint, eucalyptus, rosemary, lemon, and more swirl around me. I settle on the minty lemon scent and gingerly step into the now bubbling water.

A moan breaks free as I settle into the water, my toes uncurling and ankles rolling as I bask in the heat. I lean my head back on a cushion by the edge of the tub and let the heat soak into my worn and tired body. *This is the first time I've been alone here.* The thought eases a coil of tension inside me, the kind that always tightens up when I'm around people for too long. It also feels unsettling. I know the healers and Isa are in the tent, and I'm more than aware of Nyx and his shadows creeping outside, but still. I'm gloriously *alone* and can finally take a full breath.

Above me is a fancy shower head, the kind I imagine rich people having back home. I tell myself that I'll get up in another minute to scrub my body and wash my hair, but I think that minute turns into an hour. The next thing I know, Isa is gently tapping my shoulder.

I groggily open my eyes and peer up at her. "Hey," she says. "I'm sure you're tired enough to sleep for a week. But I came to check in on you, hoping you hadn't fallen asleep here. We don't want you to drown, do we?"

I stifle a snarky retort that I can drown if I want to and instead nod my head and push myself up out of the now cooled water. Isa doesn't stay—she is definitely one of the best *solliqas* here by far. She's here with me, but she doesn't disrespect my space or hurry me. "Come out when you're done washing up, okay? We're eager to check out your arm," she calls out before leaving me alone again.

While I'd much rather take my time exploring the different shampoos and sponges, I force myself to wash quickly with a shampoo I plucked at random. I make quick work of drying myself off with one of the fuzzy towels. It's strange that I didn't think much of the bear marking, but my body was *so* tired, I couldn't focus on anything but the warm, soapy water engulfing my body and senses. Isa's reminder gives me the push I need, and before I know it, I'm stumbling out of the bathroom, wrapped up in the fluffiest robe.

"Ah, she made it!" Naeva beams at me from the worktable. Zaya is nuzzling into one of her hand's. "I was worried you found a way to swim somewhere else in that tub."

Paloma elbows her ribs. "*Hush*. Don't give her any ideas."

Isa shakes her head and tells me, "Don't worry about it. You'll learn what your *maji* can do soon enough. Let's get you looked at." She guides me toward a bundle of plush patterned cushions lined up on the ground. They're surrounded by a pattern of rocks, crystals, herbs, and candles, and I decide that I don't want to know what that means quite yet.

Isa has me lay down on my back and fluffs the cushions up around me, a look of concentration hardening her face. "You seem worried," I tell her.

She meets my eyes for a second before turning back to the pillows and tinkering with the crystals near my head. "There's nothing you have to worry about," she says. "This is a rather big moment for us all. We don't know what we'll find. Will we be able to see who harmed you? What will the bear marking do to your body and soul? How long will it take to find true healing? There are many questions, and I have a feeling we'll be left with even more by the end of tonight."

THE LIGHT WITHIN

Isa peers over at Naeva and Paloma. "She's all ready to go. I'll situate myself at the crown of her head."

Anticipation rushes through me like a river breaking through a dam. As soon as anyone tells me not to worry, I immediately do the opposite.

Don't worry? You mean worry about everything and anything all at once. I'm a professional worrier.

My hands clench into fists, and I try to unwind my muscles, but I'm scared. It rumbles in my chest and wrings out my stomach. Isa gently places her hands on my shoulders and exhales deeply out through her nose. My muscles immediately relax from my neck down through my shoulders and out to the tips of my fingers, forcing them to stretch out. Fear still has me in its clutches, but I'll admit that having Isa helps me feel more at ease.

While I'm getting situated, Isa watches me intently. "Do you remember what you had with Nyx?"

My heart stutters at the mention of his name. I'm reminded of the way his smoke and shadows swept across my arms, so immensely gentle it was unnerving. Bright blue flames responded to his touch, answering his call. Do I remember this? *No, not at all.*

But do I remember his eyes? *I'm not sure my soul will ever let me forget.*

"I don't remember my time here in Majikaero," I say. "Before crossing over, a healer on Earth told me she thought I was having past life memories. They weren't appearing solely as dreams or nightmares—it was as if I was physically going back into the moment, waking up exhausted from it all. Some of my dreams have involved a man that appeared different from Nyx, but he had his eyes. Those crackling, dark eyes."

Her eyes flare in interest. "You soul was remembering his own. You must have seen his eyes in your dreams more recently. They're part of his soul's form, a window into who and what he is as a *solliqa*. As souls go through different human lives back on

Earth, they don't always keep their true eyes, the one physical trait connected to the soul. Each part of them will change over time, whether it's their skin or gender or hair color, until they get closer to crossing over to Majikaero."

My eyebrows furrow in confusion. "Daya told me about our soul forms changing. How do I change how I look?"

Isa arches an eyebrow. "Is that what you wish to do?"

Laying on my back, I stare up at the orbs dancing along the tent's ceiling, considering her question. No, perhaps I don't want to. At least, not right now. My flowing white hair falls around me in waves. My chest is small but allows me to move more freely. My skin is pale, a reminder of how my family looked on Earth.

I might not truly want to change my soul's form right at this moment. But I suspect that will change as I explore more of my *maji* and bond to my true self.

Isa moves her hands to the top of my head and takes long breaths. I stare up at her closed eyes and her eyelashes that fan out against the top of her delicate cheekbones. My eyes widen when her body changes into a different form.

This is *nothing* like the bird shifters. They're changed into a new form in a flash, so quickly that you'd miss it if you blinked.

Isa's form changes slowly as she grows into this new creature, an extension of herself. Light, bright fingers morph into longer white fingers with lethal claws at the tips. The whiteness spreads up her arms and onto her face. Parts are as smooth as silk and other areas are woven, intricate patterns lacing up to her head. Her hair is replaced by thick white and silver antlers, with crystals dangling between each one and flames glowing the end of tip. I get the sense that she's grown taller, but with her kneeling above me, I can't be sure. Isa takes one more inhale and opens her eyes, a dark, glittery burgundy peering down at me.

No, not at me. *Into* me. I perceive something thrash about wildly inside me, eager to climb out to Isa.

"That's your soul," she says in a throaty voice. "I'm calling it to the surface to give Naeva and Paloma a better chance at healing any festering wounds. Do you feel any pain?"

I open and close my mouth, unsure of what to make of this new form of Isa above me. I push myself to blink and clear out any cobwebs of shock. "N-no, I'm fine," I breathe.

Isa leans down further, her red orbs boring into me. "*Good*," she hums. "And now we begin."

Nothing could prepare me for what happens next. Literally nothing, not even my new shifter companions. Naeva and Paloma's eyes turn a milky white and buttery light extends out of their bodies. One of them places their hands on my chest and stomach, and the other places her hands on my legs. My soul slinks and pushes against the barrier of my skin, gravitating toward their hands. Liquid gold pools out of them and soaks into my robe. As my skin greedily absorbs it, a scream tears from my throat as my soul retreats and batters against my insides. A putrid smell bubbles out of my pores, and one of the healers brusquely removes my robe.

I already know it's the same thick, tarry substance, especially as I watch dark liquid pool in the crevices of my body.

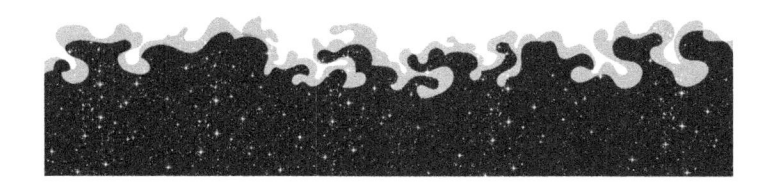

THIRTY-FOUR
Nyx & Eira

Embrace the ones meant for you.
No matter their light or darkness.
-Berlind, God of Healing

Nyx

My body has gone stone-cold and motionless, burying my need to be next to Eira as deep as I can. I've been near her for less than a few hours, and our connection is already maddening. The springy sound of someone pressing their foot into the moist earth breaks me out of my spiraling thoughts. My nostrils flare, and I don't need to look to know who is approaching me. She stops next to my seated form and cautiously lowers herself, leaning her warm body against my side. Silence builds around us like an invisible cage, pushing against my personal space.

"So, that's her," Fraya whispers.

The initial tide of emotion has crashed into the cliffside, diminishing into subdued ripples lapping against my feet. Her voice is hoarse from raging, her eyes bloodshot from inconsolable sobbing. Ivar's spirit can lull her into a more tranquil headspace, but even he can't completely mend heartbreak. And I can't give her the one thing that can. I never could. That's going to be a different wave that she needs to ride by herself and will be found within her own heart.

"It is," I respond, not breaking eye contact with the healers' tent.

She sniffles and leans more of her weight into my arm and shoulder. "I knew this was coming. I thought I could convince you to pick me."

With a heavy heart, I turn to stare down into her hollow eyes. "Fay," I say. "I never have picked you. It was you who thought I did."

"But—"

"That was my inner beast. The dark version of myself, drowned in turmoil. A shadow of who I am. A subconscious manipulation of our friendship. That's what we are and what we should have stayed. *Friends*." I turn back to gaze at the tent, mulling over the theme of *friendship* in my life now.

"But I feel such a strong connection to you, Nyx," she says, her voice breaking. "I know that we're meant for more."

"I'm telling you *no*," I say, more firmly.

Fraya runs her nails up my arm and chest, inching toward my neck. I lash out with my right hand, gripping her jaw hard enough to bruise. Even through my anger, I can sense her demon's influence on my actions. I lean forward and press my lips against hers, letting them melt together. She hums a small sound, and I back away, a growl making its way through my chest. "I said *no*," I growl. Before she can respond, I sink my nails into her cheeks. It doesn't matter how forceful her *maji* is—I'm finally pushing through her barriers, and she's muffling a scream into my palm.

Eira's pretty face flashes behind my eyes, and I instinctively know, without a sliver of doubt, that she's the reason I have the courage to push back against Fraya. I've always been powerful, but there's a special type of strength that roots itself in you when you realize you might not actually be alone.

Smoke slinks from my fingertips into her skull, wisps coming out of her nose, ears, and eyes. She's thrashing in my arms, and I taste her fear on my tongue. I give one last squeeze before pushing her down to the ground, and she crumbles into a ball. There's no anger in her eyes this time. Solitary sadness. Fear. Rejection.

"That was goodbye," I snarl. "You continue to push past this boundary, and you'll be *gone*. Do you understand me? That was your last chance. You do not touch me. You do not seek me out. You do not even *think* of suggestive comments. You respect me and my choice, or I'll show you the meaning of disrespect."

I'm seconds from snapping off her limbs, suddenly overtaken by the need to rid this damaged creature from my life. But I catch a swarm of feathers swooping in the moonlight out of the corner of my eye. A sharp caw echoes against the cliff walls. *The crows. Jade.*

My attention is drawn away from them and back to the ground. The grass is moving and what feels like a gust of air is approaching us rapidly. Conflicted and throwing her a disgusted look, I leap in front of Fraya, since she's in no shape to defend herself. I might be a violent asshole, but I tend to be a chivalrous, violent asshole when push comes to shove. I crouch down low, gathering smoke under my skin and forming cords with my shadows. Readying myself for the translucent form making its way toward me.

"No need for such dramatics," a voice hisses from the ground. "Unless you're planning to whip me. I have been rather bad."

Huffing out a laugh, I release my *maji* into the open air. "What took you so long? And you're one to talk about dramatics. What's with the snake form again?"

The translucent serpent rises and gathers into a plume of smoke, coming eye-to-eye with me. It opens up wide, showing off its fangs, before swirling into the shape of one of my favorite assholes.

"Not a fan?" Hadwin smirks. "And I'm doing great—thanks for asking. Mission was a success, and I'm alive."

"Splendid," I grunt. "And I love snakes. You're just growing attached to this creature, and you could have arrived another way."

He shrugs, glancing around at the different tents. "I jumped between forms on my way here. I liked this one the best. It kept me hidden, but not camouflaged enough if *you* could see me."

I punch him in the arm. He cringes slightly, telling me I still have pent up rage from dealing with Fraya.

"I take it lovers island turned into one filled with volcanic activity," he mutters, peering down at Fraya huddled on the ground.

I roll my eyes. "Don't even start with me. There's a lot to update you about, much more important than her."

He cocks his head to the side, indicating that I should continue. "Not here. Later, after I'm sure Eira's okay."

Hadwin makes a garbled sound, tongue-tied for once in his life. "Did you say *Eira*?"

"Yes, her," I say, sharpening my focus on the tent again. I feel a surge of tension coming from it, and I'm unsettled by where this is going. "She's my *almaove*, I'm sure of it."

His eyes bulge slightly, and he clears his throat. "So, uh, yeah. You do have a lot to tell me. If she's that strong of a soul connection to you, what are you doing out here?"

I whirl on him, antsy and hyped up all at once. "Because of fucking Isa," I sneer. "Insisting that we start off as friends and that I give her space while the healers work on her."

"I mean, that's not the worst—"

A wild scream pierces through the night, cutting Hadwin

off. My muscles coil, and I launch into action, not stopping to think. How can I when that was Eira? Fuck Isa and the healers.

I'm coming, sweetheart.

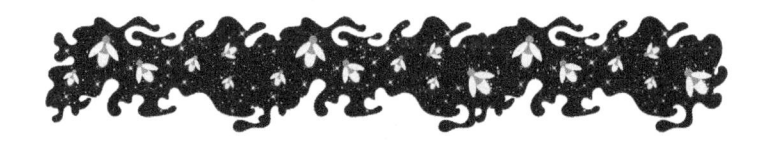

Eira

There's no time to act shy about my exposed body—I want this gross liquid *out* of me.

Naeva curls her fingers into the space between my stomach and hip bone. "We're about there," she grunts. "A large portion will be released from you tonight."

"Yeah," Paloma pants, pressing into my shaking feet. They're dripping in the sticky substance. "The poison is fighting us, but we'll get most of it out for now."

For now? I have to do this again?

Both healers and Isa tighten their hold, and I can't control the tears flowing down my face. A sob catches in my throat and my mouth opens in a silent scream. Something sharp slashes through my organs and burns my ribcage. I'm heaving and coughing and in the midst of losing my mind—

"I told you not to come in here," Isa growls out.

"And I told you what she is to me," Nyx snaps. "Move over. *Now.* I'm going to help her." His tone leaves no room for argument. Commanding. The voice of royalty.

A cooling blanket of darkness settles over my sweaty skin, spreading soothing relief down my body. The poison continues to push out of me, and I'm coiling my body in different directions, desperately trying to escape.

"Shh, sweetheart," Nyx whispers, the voice completely at odds with how he looked before, cloaked in smoky shadows with those demonic eyes. "You're safe. This marking on you, this poison, will eat away at your soul if we don't get it out. It's cutting you from the inside out to trick you into wanting us to stop. You can't listen to it. The more that comes out right now, the easier the rest of your healing journey will be." He pushes back my still-wet hair and cups my cheek. "Feel my hand. Now notice the smoke leaving it and allow your fire to meet it. You have so much power, Eira. That power, that healing light, will help drive this poison out of you."

A smoky haze covers me, and my soul ripples against the surface of my skin again. Calmer. Humming with excitement.

"That's it, sweetheart," Nyx murmurs. His other hand brushes against my lips, and my tongue darts out to lick his fingers. The smoke and shadows jerk around me, and he huffs out a laugh. "Not now, Eira. Use that energy to push as much of the dark poison out as you can. We've got you."

Energy jolts through me, causing my breathing to quicken and my muscles to seize up. I take a huge breath in, and on the exhale, I imagine all of my air and energy forcing the poison out of my pores. There's a stinging sensation in the middle of my forehead, but I keep going. Telling myself that nothing lasts forever, and I *need* to get this out.

Nyx grazes my marked wrist, and my whole body locks up. Smoke smothers my whole forearm and by my next breath, a blinding fire rushes up to meet it. Both the fire and smoke bind together and squeeze along my arm, the rest of my body littered in goosebumps. A vision suddenly sends me shooting out of my mind and into a different time and space. *Fuck, fuck, fuck. Not now. Please.*

It lasts all of a minute but has me shaking to the core.

One minute, I'm in my body experiencing the worst pain of my life. In the next, I'm floating above Athena and Tryg, watching a knife get stabbed into their chests by the *last* person I'd expect. Athena's mental voice calls out to me, curling around my own, begging for my help and to find them. As quickly as I'm thrown into this vision, I'm snatched back out, surging into my current reality.

My body begins to violently shake, and a full-blown wail pours out of me. I feel myself sobbing and trying to tell the others what I saw, but no one's listening. I'm engulfed in a fire, not entirely my own, and then... *release*. Sweet, beautiful release. My body releases onto the ground, a broken, disgusting heap. A rejuvenating sense of restoration fills up parts of my body, and the light and flames dance and weave along my skin. Free from the poison's chains and able to explore.

Everyone releases their hands from me and backs away. Except Nyx. His smoke is still gliding down my body, and when I crack my eyes open, I see him frantically searching each part of me. He brings his attention back to my face and blows out a breath.

"Eira?" he asks attentively. His voice echoes around me.

"We have to help them," I rasp.

Nyx's eyebrows furrow, looking perplexed. "Help who?"

"Athena and Tryg. Someone has hurt them, and they need my help," I croak through my dry throat. I peer toward the others, pleading with my eyes. "Please tell Eliina. Daya, Del, and Daru. We need to help them. *Now.*"

More tears gather in the corners of my eyes. Furious that I'm lying here while my friends are in trouble, I try to push myself off the ground. I'm met with Zaya jumping on my chest, pushing me back down. She gives a little hiss and kneads into my chest, and then she abruptly turns to leave, swishing her big tail in my face. I sputter, more annoyed than anything that my cat prevented me from getting up. Zaya glares at me, full-on *glares*, while she slinks around Nyx's feet. *Traitor*.

"I'll tell them," Isa offers. "But you will not be going

anywhere right now. Before you argue, feel free to take a look at yourself. Then tell me you're in a state to search for your friends."

Narrowing my eyes at her, I shift my gaze to the rest of my body, and my breath hitches.

A horrendous amount of sticky tar is smeared along my skin and in pools all around me. Naeva and Paloma appear to be utterly exhausted, with dark bags under their eyes.

"We did our best," Paloma says, chest heaving. "We got most of it out, and I can't believe I'm saying this, but a part of that is due to Nyx here. There are still buried shadows and poison in your wrist. We won't be able to mend that tonight."

I hesitantly glance down at my arm and regret doing so. Bits and pieces of my skin look charred, and the marking is still there, even if it appears to have faded slightly. My eyes take in the rest of my arm and chest and—wait, my chest?

"Oh!" I squeak, covering my chest with the tattered robe next to me.

Nyx's eyes glitter with mischief, but he manages to keep his eyes on my face.

"Yup," Isa says with a loud pop. "I'll make a deal with you. I'll go tell Eliina about what came out of you, how Nyx helped, and that your friends need help. You'll go to the bathroom and bathe again, since I sincerely doubt you want to stay soaking in all of this. Naeva and Paloma will help get you there. And *you*," she says, whirling on Nyx. "You'll be coming with me."

I can tell Nyx wants to argue, but Isa's eyes flash a brighter red, and he closes his mouth. He nods his head curtly.

Before leaving, he kneels next to me and brings his lips to the shell of my ear. Shadows slither over my collarbone in the shape of a heart.

"We'll go slow," he whispers. "But don't think I didn't see what your tongue did or felt that hot flame of desire, sweetheart. We'll be discussing *that* later."

THIRTY-FIVE

Eira & Tryg

You're only as strong as the friends by your side.
Don't make the mistake of believing you're the strongest.
-Correspondence from Captain Iletei Miwona

Tryg

Later, I might think back on this moment as incredible. That I traveled through veils in time and existed in a space so vast, I was both my previous selves and current self all at once. Light and dark astral views surround me. I'm engulfed in knowledge and perspectives I didn't realize my soul had been storing.

But I sure as hell don't enjoy it right now.

"Fuck," I groan, rolling onto my side into a fetal position. Scratches line my bicep from *who-the-fuck-knows-what,* and I'm bloated in misery and depletion.

"Tryg?" a familiar voice calls out from far away. The scent of lavender and lemongrass floats in the air. *Huh.* "Tryg, are you there?"

Ah, that's Athena. Has she always smelled that way? What do

I smell like? Never mind; I don't want to know. Can't be anything good.

"Regrettably, yeah, I'm here," I call back. I sigh, trying to coax my eyes to open. As the girls would joke, *I ain't no bitch.* Let's get it over with.

My eyes are heavy and take forever to open, and once I do, I'm met with a brightness I was not prepared for. I went to sleep with the howling winter air, and I'm waking up to the land basking in a summer glow. Wait, no. This place looks different. The actual trees and grass have the same shapes as what I'm used to, but the colors are all wrong.

Grumbling, I push myself into a seated position and immediately experience a surge of pain in my chest. I rub it, hoping it's a strained muscle, but feel the puckering edges of a scar. Glancing down, I see a jagged line near my heart, and a rush of memories batter through my mind. *Ah, shit. I didn't go to sleep. I'm fucking dead. In a world of vibrant colors when I practically specialize in wearing shades of black. Even my room and decor are darker than the rest of the house, much to Eira's chagrin. Yeah, this makes sense. Of course, I would end up in some trippy world, my personal version of Hell.*

"Tryg," Athena mumbles, significantly closer than a few minutes ago. She's crawling toward me, a similar scar etched on her light brown skin. She lays down with a huff next to me, acting as exhausted as I am. Her lithe body dips at the curve of her lower back and swells into a plump ass. *Woah, we're naked? Apparently so, if my dick is any indicator. Alright, fucking chill. This is Athena.*

"You're naked," I say like the dumbass I am.

She rolls over slightly, covering her ample chest with an arm, and narrows her eyes. "Yeah, so are you. You don't see me riled up, do you?"

Damn. My ego dives right off the metaphorical cliff.

"We have bigger problems to worry about," she continues.

"Such as not having any form of protection or clothes in an unknown place. Or figuring out water and food. Maybe even figuring out what the hell just happened with Shira and why we ended up here. *Together*."

A beam of sunlight breaks through some of the leaves shading us. Athena's green eyes are positively dazzling. An exotic garden full of lush flowers. I'm being pulled into them when she barks, "Have you always been such a dumbbell?"

I shake my head. Hard. "Dammit, I'm sorry. You've never been *not* beautiful, but you're a real sight right now, Athena. And I don't even know where to begin. I want to go back to sleep."

She arches one of those delicate eyebrows. "I don't need to be told how marvelous I look—I already know it."

She peers around at the multicolored trees, and one of the dark blue birds flying in between them. "I don't think we should go back to sleep. I think that's what Shira wants us to do. I couldn't stop her from stabbing us, but I did see the dagger was coated in a gray and milky substance. I think she wants us to give up, specifically here, so that something finds us. And I'm not going to wait around to see whatever that is."

With a strength I wish I had, she jumps upward and crosses her arms. She cocks out a hip, her fingers tapping rapidly, and more actively watches the birds swooping above us. "Alright, Muscle Man," she says, throwing me a look over her shoulder. "Now's your time."

Confused, I stumble to a standing position and am momentarily blinded by pain. Biting into my fist, I search the rest of my body and see other dark scratches strewn about my ankles and calves.

Athena heaves a sigh. I shoot her an exasperated glare. "Would you give me a minute? Why are you fucking annoyed of all damn emotions?"

"Because we're both obviously struggling, and you're the

one who can't get his head out of his ass." She points up at the huge leaves in the towering trees, scowling. "Yeah, we're in pain. But this is the hand we've been dealt, and I'm choosing to not wallow in self-pity. Now listen up. I'm strong, but I'll admit you're *physically* stronger. Think you can manage climbing up for some of those leaves?"

Rolling out my shoulders, I evaluate the nearest tree more closely. "Yeah, I can get up there. What do you want the leaves for?"

She flashes me one of her cunning smiles. "Time for one of your favorite activities: arts and crafts."

Eira

"I can't believe with a few words, Eira convinced not only Eliina, but the rest of us to go after these *friends* of hers," Ulf mutters.

Daru snarls quietly, and I fling one of the bready crackers at his forehead.

"And how lucky are you that I'm rested enough to come with you!" I chirp, plaiting my hair back in a thick braid.

Ulf narrows his eyes at me, but Ivar and Hadwin grin behind him.

"I like her already," Hadwin says to Nyx.

Nyx tries to hide his smile while organizing a pile of supplies. I'm not convinced that we need *that* much food for a few days of travel, but his smoky look had me shutting up quickly this morning when I pointed that out. I also told him that I don't need someone to fuss over me, and he simply shrugged and responded with, "I prefer the words *caring and attentive*. Will it really bother you if I carry extra food with me?"

I still have mixed emotions about where I'm currently at and all these new creatures. Especially the ones with darkness seeping around them similar to a shadowy, creepy fog. My heart involuntarily jerks. I wonder when the spike in adrenaline and survival instincts will die out, and the trauma responses will kick in.

Shaking my head, I decide I'll take what I can get for now and will try to go with the flow. Now more than ever, I need to get a grip. I physically sense the presence of Athena and Tryg, and after Eliina spent time meditating and connecting with the earth last night, she confirmed she felt two distinct souls enter this realm and are currently all alone. Isa was rather prickly when I announced that I'm going with. She insisted that I need to rest and have more healing sessions, but Eliina had cut her off, saying that Isa can't stop a queen's decision any more than she can.

Daya loops her arm around my shoulder, brushing the lacey fringes of the shirt Paloma loaned to me. She envelopes me in her snarky, yet adorable, aura, which I'm grateful for. Daya and Eliina are the ones fully supporting what I want right now. She managed to stifle Daru's irked retort by saying my desire to explore the area and search for my friends is encouraging, showing I'm adapting more to this new home.

"You bet you like her," Daya says, winking. "Wait until you meet her fiery side—literally."

Nyx snorts. "That's how I prefer her."

I scowl at Daya, annoyed that she's rooting for an instant relationship with Nyx. I don't care if I've seen him in dreams or past lives or during the spine-chilling experience of taking over a dead child's body. I don't *know* him. No matter how persuasive Daya might be, I've got my brick wall firmly in place, ready to ignore his flirtatious ways.

"What's the plan for travel?" the *solliqa* named Odin asks.

He looks more creature than human right now, with his reptilian eyes and long, glossy hair framing a devilishly handsome face. When we find Athena, she's going to die when she meets all of these males, or, I suppose, *misns*.

"A mixture of *alklen* and *drekstri*," Delano says, waltzing into the tented space. "I don't care who rides with who, but don't force me to ride with *her*." He casts his sister an irritated glare.

Daya giggles and pokes the tip of his nose with a slim finger, causing it to wrinkle. *Reminds me of Lyk and Liv.* My heart clenches at the thought of my friends still trapped on Earth.

"What's wrong with riding with me?"

"You might as well be flying," he snarks. "It's a crazy notion, but I want to help Eira find her friends, not crash and die."

Ulf's eyes flare with evil joy. "You can ride with me, then," he purrs. "I'll make you soar."

Daya looks him up and down and then turns her head in disinterest. "I'll travel alone and one of her friends can ride with me. If they're anything like Eira, they'll be fine."

I bite down on my lips, trying not to laugh at Ulf's startled face. Not many females—*fims*—must deny him. *Yeah, he definitely is a full misn. Huge alpha energy radiates from this creep.*

"Fraya will ride with me," Ivar says, collecting the last of his arrows. I'm finally noticing now how the tattoos swirling up his arms match his arrowheads.

Fraya peeks out from behind him, acting mopey. I quickly glance the other way. Every time we've made eye contact this morning, she's smiled a little too wide and is quite eager to chat. When my gaze lingered a second too long on her lilac and onyx earrings, she was quick to take them out and offer them to me. *No, thank you.* I'm sort of adjusting to this new home, but that doesn't mean I want to talk to all of them.

I'm surprised we're even in the same tent right now. From what I gathered from Daya, Nyx and his shadowy friends have all been banned from the capital, Rioa. She said that they didn't used to be bad, but something happened to various creatures in the realm a while back. Daru described it as a disease, infecting the body subtly before striking the major parts of the soul and causing harmful behaviors. I asked if they'd be okay working with those who've been shunned, and Delano snarled softly, saying there wasn't much of a choice. If Eliina deemed them important in aiding me, then they would be there, whether they like it or not.

His words make me even more wary of interacting with any of them, including Nyx. If their aid is not built on trust, I can't be sure what any of their true intentions or behaviors will be.

"If she's interested in trying out a *drekstri*, Eira can come with me," Hadwin says, his mouth pulling into a smirk.

"No," Nyx says firmly, his eyes shooting daggers at his friend. "It's already been decided that she'll stay with me. My shadows will protect her."

My face twists into a scowl, and I open my mouth to argue, but Daya nudges me with her shoulder. "Just go with it," she whispers. "He's promised to behave himself, and if you do truly have the connection I think you do, you don't want to antagonize him right now, okay? I'm surprised you're also not overwhelmingly protective of him. It's the norm around here—the stronger the soul connection, the more fierce each *solliqa* gets in the beginning. Even for the connections that are solely friendships."

She looks unnaturally serious, and for that reason alone, I agree to keep my mouth shut. For now. *I'll antagonize whoever I want.*

Delano arches a brow at Erika, who's been soaking in the hot spring for the last hour. "You want to ride with me? I don't bite."

Erika's mouth peels back into a sultry smile. "Oh, but I do."

Delano flushes and clears his throat. "I'll, ah, g-get the *alklen* ready for us then." He shuffles toward the entrance, his face burning up.

Giggling, I whisper to Daya, "Poor Delano. He's about to get more than he signed up for."

"I told you that you can call me Del. You don't have to be so formal," he shoots at me before meeting Erika's now reptilian-gaze and stumbling out of the tent.

I shrug. "I prefer Delano. And it gets him all riled up." Daya laughs and finishes strapping closed her bag.

"Erika, *behave*," Nyx hisses at her.

She gives him an innocent look. "What? I am. I didn't actually bite him or anything. It wouldn't be polite of me to give him unclear expectations about me." Erika examines her nails and mutters, "And it'd be a crime not to tease him a bit. I sure savor the taste of ginger."

"Yeah, and you won't be doing anything related to that. Keep your focus on Eira's friends."

Erika flings her other hand out of the water. "Yeah, yeah," she sighs. "You're changing by the second, princeling, and now I'm not sure I like it. Maybe one of her friends will be interested." She cuts a glance at Ivar. "Did you pack those herbs I told you about?"

"Mhm," he hums. "I cut a few bundles and have them safely stored in the front of this bag. You've got a keen eye."

Erika smiles, her face smug. "I know. Which is why I know Del will come around, eventually."

"Erika..." Nyx begins. He stomps over to the hot spring, all agitated and ruffled.

I tie up my bag and bite back another smile. It should terrify me that *both* of my friends would be into Erika, but I keep that thought to myself.

"Alright, so..." Daya trails off, motioning toward us. "Del and Erika. I'll be alone and ready to take one of her friends. Nyx and Eira. Ivar and Fraya. Ulf, Odin, Daru, and Hadwin—what are you doing?"

"You said there's an extra *alklen*?" Odin asks Daru.

He nods, barely keeping a lid on his irritation. He's shown the most resistance so far. Daru insists that Nyx's shadows and smoke will infect me, even after the healers said he's the reason a lot of poison burned out of me in the first place. I won't push him, though. There's no sense in arguing with someone who's got their mind made up. If he's sure he can't trust any of Nyx's group, then for him, that'll be the truth.

"Great. I'll take that one. We can ride next to one another," Odin says, either oblivious to or ignoring Daru's attitude.

"I guess I'm stuck riding with the big, bad wolf," Hadwin dramatically sighs. He points a finger at all of us. "If I don't come out alive, though, know that this is all your fault for not picking me."

Ulf grumbles indistinguishable words that I'm sure is offensive, making Hadwin flash a toothy smile.

Isa pops her head through the tent entrance. Her features appear even more graceful in the daylight and at odds with her edgy, antlered form from last night. "Is everyone ready to go?"

We all give varied affirmative responses, and she promptly opens the tent wider, showing the different animals we'll be riding today. Nyx stalks toward his *drekstri*, the scales glinting like volcanic rock in the sun. I take a step toward him, and Zaya leaps onto my shoulders, giving me yet another heart attack. Her eyes flash gold, and she meows brightly, appearing eager to search for our friends.

"You ready for the next adventure?" I murmur to my cat, scratching behind her ear.

She gives one of her cute silent meows and marks my face, which I'm sure she knows always improves my mood. We approach Nyx's *drekstri,* and he holds out a hand to help Zaya and me up.

"This is Ambra," he says, patting her mane. "She's one of the fiercest creatures you'll meet in this realm. And she's insanely loyal once you develop a relationship. I have no doubt that she'll sense what you mean to me and will warm up to you quickly."

Ambra and I side-eye one another, and I audibly gulp, feeling intimidated to ride this thing. She blows out a huff of smoke from her nostrils and playfully nips at my braid.

Nyx laughs, and I'm laser-focused on his body, moving with deep belly laughs. I didn't realize I could feel immense joy by someone's laugh, and the thought is nauseating, as if I'm a hopeless romantic. *Argh. I don't want to fall for him. Not yet.*

His eyes are still shining, and the sunlight shows swirling browns and shades of black mixed with the silver and gold crackling streaks. Nyx's coverings match his eyes today and strain deliciously against his muscular body. He takes my arm and lifts me up with ease, Zaya startlingly jumping up to Ambra's mane and comfortably burrowing herself in it. My cat is infinitely more comfortable with all these new creatures and *solliqas* than I am.

Nyx positions me in front of him, locking his hips against the swell of my bottom. His breath sends shivers circulating down my spine, and I find myself naturally leaning back into his sculpted chest. I see Nyx's hand move, and a pocket-sized design made out of shadows appears on my shoulder, this one in the shape of a cat. I have to hold back a squeal of joy.

Uh oh. I'm in trouble.

THIRTY-SIX

Nyx

Our souls grow brightest when our maji blooms around us.
Our hearts grow brighter when a friend is in need.
-Page 77, Understandings of the Soul, Volume III

I sense trouble coming to greet us from miles away. It bubbles up from the soil, like quietly simmering water, causing all the *alklen* and *drekstri* to prance around every few minutes. While holding Ambra steady and readying myself for the incoming humans, Eira's frantic energy pelts around her. It causes flashes of light to heat against my torso and arms, in any place that touches her. It's simultaneously dazzling and distracting, but I can't fault her. I know she's anxious to get to her friends.

Someone, or rather *something*, sent these two humans to our realm, and solely the most powerful *maji* can do this. To send two souls tumbling into a new world with no other creatures nearby to greet them? That means the individual is not tremendously powerful but also wicked and unfair. Cruel. Even more than me, which causes quite the identity crisis.

We passed the pathway out of the valley soon after the

blazing suns rose into the violet sky. The only sign that we cleared the secret cliff trails and made it out into the viridescent hilly pass is the silver dust still smattered across my black boots. I pluck out tiny rocks that got stuck in Eira's woven hair and she sends me a look mixed with irritation and gratitude, causing me to laugh. My darling is rather layered, and I can't wait to explore each level on my way to her molten core.

A convulsion seizes through Eira, and she tenses up, her shoulders rigid and tight as a bow's drawn string. I greedily watch every muscle in her back flex with tension, her bare skin on display. Black, gauzy material and lace wind around her neck and in a thin pattern around her shoulders before it skims down her sides, crisscrossing in thin straps along her lower back. Leaning forward, my lips graze against her ear. I ask, "What are you thinking about that's got you wound so tight? It certainly can't be me."

Satisfaction rolls through me when I hear her suck in a breath. A pretty rose blush paints her skin, and I have to fight the urge to trace the outline of her neck with my teeth. Eira bites down on her bottom lip for a second, enough to tell me she feels our connection, too. Then reality sets in, and her eyes are bulging, and she's coughing on choked air. "I-I nothing," she stammers.

She clears her throat, obviously flustered. I am *delighted*. "I'm thinking about what the healers shared with me last night after you and Isa left. That's all."

I don't have to be facing her to know she's avoiding all eye contact with me. Laughing, I let my right hand drift to her arm and lazily draw a line with one of my fingers. Smoke spurts out in the shape of a sun. "And what did they say, sweetheart?"

Eira shakes her head and belts out a loud *ugh* before turning slightly to face me. Daya's laughter sails around us—she's equally as excited about what's going on here. A purple bird of prey swoops between us and her, swerving to loop around Daru and

Odin. Odin gives a little wave at Hauke, completely unfazed by his attention-seeking antics. Daru, on the other hand, gets more rattled by the minute. He's either glancing at Eira and I, muttering in annoyance at Odin, or glaring at one of my shadow members or, presently, Hauke.

Daru's always rubbed me the wrong way, and it brings me sick joy to watch him getting so bothered by the littlest of things. Although, nothing is little about Eira's and my soul connection. Or me.

"They told me what they saw about the bear marking on my wrist," Eira says. This gets my attention real quick.

"And?" I ask, slightly more forcefully than I intend to sound with her.

She hesitates, glancing at Daya nearby. Daya gives her a nod, a silent urge to share this with me.

"When Naeva and Paloma were healing me, they were able to peer inside at certain memories. Not all of them. Only the ones relevant to the pain sticking to my muscles and bones like tar. Even though you were the one to grip my forearm, they could still see the memory associated with the marking." Eira pauses, gathering an uneven breath.

"The bear design matches the bracelet I used to own from Tryg, one of the friends we are going to rescue. They said that he unknowingly bought it from one of Shira's workers at a small shop in town. Shira is a health provider and yoga teacher where I come from, and I—she might be bad. It doesn't make sense to me, but Naeva said that Shira recognized Tryg and put the curse on it when she heard him say my name. This curse was meant to cause me pain, death, and prevent me from leaving Earth, especially with Tryg's intentions of wanting to keep me for himself." Eira chews on her lip, lost in thought. "I wanted to ask them more questions about what they saw from the marking and the significance of the bear, but they were too drained after the session. Eliina and Isa said they needed to rest after having their energy zapped, that our *maji* lasts as long as the energy in our soul does. So... that's all I know right now."

I'm not sure I've ever put this much focus into controlling my breath, even after all the breathing exercises Eliina used to push on me while visiting her in Rioa. *Fuck, his name is* Tryg? *And he brought this pain on her?* A tremble racks my body, and I take as much of a breath as I dare, not wanting Eira to see how angry I feel. How *out-of-my-mind terrified* I am that she's been around this piece of shit and still doesn't even see how much he can harm her.

It was rumored that the Sairn were the ones to strike our Queen of Light down. Yet the more information that Jade has brought to me, the more it's become crystal fucking clear that they weren't working alone. Or were even the ones to initiate the idea of destroying Eira's soul. I was taught about the infamous soul family Tryg, a deadly manipulator, was connected to and his relationship with the Sairn. My mother taught me the importance of recognizing our different soul connections and why we must respect each of them differently. She used Tryg as a prime example of what can happen when a soul does *not* do this.

"I know everyone thinks he's bad," she continues, "but he's one of my best friends. I love him." Eira finally glances at me, her eyes lined in silver.

"Please give him a chance, Nyx," she breathes. "You say we're meant for one another, but I can't be with someone who won't even give my best friend a chance."

Is she pulling this guilt card on me right now? *Yes.* Am I going to unconditionally support her? *Unfortunately, probably.* As sure as the air that I breathe, I know that she's the one who can tame my tortured soul. The one who will dig out what's left of my love and kindness, even if it means she needs to crawl on all fours in my grave, her nails covered in poisoned dirt, as she unburies the forsaken light.

Isa saves me from having to respond right away. She's in her full deer form, shimmering in white as bright as the moon on Earth. A faint light outlines her body and matches the burgundy glow of her eyes. The jewels dangle from her antlers as she trots alongside us, angling her head up to face Eira.

"They shouldn't have shared that so soon with you," she says, concern radiating out of her.

"Why shouldn't they have? It's about my body and friend," Eira snaps. Displeasure coils around her in thick cords of flame. She doesn't enjoy being left in the dark, even if the news will harm her. *Noted*.

"Because we don't have all the information yet," Isa responds with gentleness. "This makes it sound as if Shira manipulated Tryg and that he is part of the reason for your pain. As much as I dislike how similar he is to, ah, a certain creature previously from this realm, I don't want to spin stories about your friends that might not be true. To cause that kind of chaos."

"But that kind of chaos is half the fun," Ulf grumbles. Not for the first time, I get the sense to shield Eira from him. We all might carry the burden of shadowed beasts, of monsters trapped in our souls, but he wields a special kind of evil. While I've grown to love my shadowed friends as family, my relationship with Ulf has often been one out of necessity. It can be difficult to befriend a soul who eagerly throws themselves into carnage and pain. It's even tougher to truly love them when you know they'd do it to spite you, even after everything you've given them.

Two other healers pull up next to Isa, distracting both Eira and me from Ulf's comment. I recognize them from Rioa. Rada connects to small critters found both in the forest and in *solliqas'* homes, and Daglo draws his *maji* from our suns, simmering in their healing warmth. They're usually in Rioa, training new healers, especially those who are also shifters.

"Try to keep your focus on your friends for now," Rada says. She's currently in her small weasel-like form, laying on top of Daglo's back. She's white with scarlet markings on her face, feet, and spine, and has a glow along her body, similar to Isa and Daglo. Although, that's certainly not a surprise. Blazing rays slither out from Daglo's paws as he stalks next to us, causing my shield to slink back in alarm.

Eira's transfixed by Daglo's form, which also isn't a surprise. He resembles a mythical mountain lion, moving steadily, full of lethal grace. Even I'm taken aback by his golden fur and swishing tail, a small flame flaring on the end of it. Daglo strikes me as the kind of creature who would counter my demon, my monster, my twisted side. *If only he could*.

Eira asks no one in particular, "Can I turn into an animal form?"

Rada and Isa glance at one another before Isa says, "Perhaps. It'll depend on your *maji*. We won't know until we get more of the poison out of you or if this part of your power decides to make an appearance sooner." She shrugs, or what I imagine a shrug to be on a deer's body. "Everyone is incredibly different."

Eira furrows her eyebrows. I practically see her brain whirling a million miles per hour. I nudge her, catching her gaze. "Don't worry so much right now, sweetheart. It's coming. All in due time."

Scowling, she pushes lightly at my chest. "Stop calling me that." She peers down at my wrapped shirt and looks distracted by the sleeves. "Why do you have these black markings?"

I swallow, not wanting to answer her. To say it out loud is always a bruising reminder.

"It's the marking of the plague," I mumble. "Each of us who've been infected has it. The confirmation the Council needs that normal soul pain has transformed into the dreaded disease."

I feel her hand tense on top of mine. Fighting to keep her hand there, to not flinch back from me.

"Is it safe to touch me?" Eira's voice trembles.

My eyes meet hers instantly. "Of course it is. That's not how the disease spreads. I'd have to physically, emotionally, mentally, or spiritually harm you. And I don't plan on doing any of that."

I don't break eye contact with her, urging her to see how serious I am. That I would *never* knowingly harm her.

She becomes mildly uncomfortable the longer we stare at one another. Eira shifts her focus back to my coverings.

"And what's with all the clothes here? They don't look, um, normal."

Now it's my turn to be confused. "Normal?"

"Yeah," she says, absently tugging the bottom of my sleeve. "The clothes here shimmer in the light and are gauzy. They all look so, um, so *pretty*. Magical. Unreal."

I huff out a laugh. "You *are* in a magical realm. And wait until you get to Rioa. These coverings, as we prefer to call them, are for practical use while traveling. When you get more in tune with your *maji*, you'll be able to create all sorts of intricate coverings."

"Oh, yes," Rada says dreamily. "They can be quite exquisite the more one practices making them. They also typically go with whatever your main powers are. You'll probably be a healer, but *maji* and coverings also change if you're a soul reader, an elemental, a shifter, a manipulator, a protector, an intellect—"

"Okay, okay, let's not push her into overdrive," Daya says hastily, steering her *alklen* in our direction. "Eira might be venturing out to help her friends, but she's still new to this realm. Baby steps, Rada."

Rada's critter form rolls her little eyes. "Well, she's got to learn *sometime*. And she isn't meeting these creatures yet. Only hearing their titles."

Eira breathes out a heavy sigh in front of me, and I can tell even this amount of information is a lot for her to take in. I'm both curious and dreading the moment it all comes crashing down on her. "There's, um, even more types of *maji*?" she asks, her voice meek.

Rada happily hums. "Yes! Without going into detail," she chirps, glaring over at Daya. "I'll tell you that there's *maji* connected to what you know as the arts, languages, mechanics, and all sorts of foods and resources connected to nature. And there's plenty that we still don't know. There'll be time in Rioa to show you the ancient library and get you more acquainted with everything. I think you'll especially be interested in what *solliqas* have learned from Earth over the years and how that's impacted our realm."

Cocking her head to the side, Eira says, "Hmm. I *do* love to read. I'm sure there's quite a lot to learn about this new world."

"New to *you*," Rada corrects her, not unkindly.

Eira hums and peers toward the mountains, now visible. Dense fog covers most of the range but breaks free toward the top of each peak. I guarantee Eira hasn't seen mountains like these before. The crests curl toward the sky, similar to sharpened claws ready to sink into the billowy clouds. Even Ivar avoids this range, fearful of the creatures that lie within and of the *maji* layered on every mountain like a scar. It's where the Council originally wanted to send me. Through her subtle manipulation, Eliina was able to convince the others that even they weren't cruel enough to send one of their own to a place where catastrophic nightmares exist in the flesh.

Then again, I'm sure they never counted on me teaming up with Ulf.

We trot down the curving hill, the suns budging closer and closer to the horizon. We'll need to set up camp soon if we're out much longer. My own team will want to continue, no doubt, but I'm not risking Eira's safety. She doesn't have the faintest idea what exists during the night. What monstrous creation exists right behind her and might want to come out to play if we continue into the tree line up ahead, surrounded by growing darkness.

Clearing my throat, I push myself to ask Eira more questions.

"Is there anything in that beautiful mind of yours you wish to ask?" I whisper against the shell of her ear.

She scowls again in my direction. I'm beginning to think this might be how she permanently looks at me.

"Yeah, now that you mention it, there is. Why the hell am I paired up with *you* of all *solliqas*?"

I swallow down a laugh. "First, by *hell*, do you mean Cudhellen? Because I approve of that new name."

Eira turns fully to face me and squints her eyes. "Ignore my question long enough, and I'll *show* you what I mean by hell. Perhaps my powers will burn you like the fires there and demons will come to torture you for eternity."

I raise a brow, instantly intrigued by her flare of spicy irritation. *Yes, give me your strongest emotions. I want to feel their heat.* "These might be the same realms that we'll most definitely need to discuss later. But you forget, my soul is already suffering." I trace my fingers down the top of her leg, not breaking eye contact. "I'm already a demon, inflicting pain on myself and others."

She maintains her stare, and for a brief second, it's as if I'm peering into a reflection of my own hardened glare. Yet as much as I want to test the different sides of her soul, I also don't want to ignore her or push her over the edge so soon.

"Do you mean why are you my *almaove*?"

This breaks her out of our heated staring contest. Throwing a hand out, Eira says, "Yeah, whatever you call it here. Why are we together?"

Her question is valid but throws me off. I honestly don't know why our souls are drawn together. Panic swells up inside of me, and nervousness I'm not used to tickles my breath, causing it to stutter out of me. I don't want to disappoint her, especially about this kind of topic.

"You're asking the right questions, Eira," Isa jumps in beside us. "It just might not be the right time or with the right souls." She sighs, clearly not wanting to dive into this topic while we're searching for Eira's friends. "I can give you some insight, though. Information you can mull over before we get to Rioa."

Eira's eyes are wide and curious, drinking in everything that Isa says.

"*Almaoves* are strong soul connections. It doesn't mean that you don't have other soul mates, simply that this *solliqa* is who aligns with your soul the most. It typically involves love, attraction, and fierce protectiveness of one another. You balance each other out, fill in any cracks made along your souls over time. There are a number of theories of how souls become destined to be together and what kinds of purposes we're given and from who. What I can say with certainty is that both you and Nyx spent time in the earth realm and were able to transition to Majikaero after you learned your life lessons. What those lessons were, I can't be sure right now."

I watch as Eira chews on her plump lips while she takes in this information. It's too easy to become mesmerized by her actions, no matter how small.

"You both then played significant roles in Majikaero before your souls were destroyed," Isa continues. "I'm almost positive that Eliina doesn't want you to think about this yet. I personally believe the more you understand *why* you were called the Queen of Light, the better off everyone will be. This plague of darkness technically started spreading over our realm a long time ago, and fortunately, it was able to be contained and somewhat handled at first. We weren't at a point of monsters or demons. You, Eira, had the ability to reach these poor souls before you were destroyed. Before the sickness turned into the plague. Nyx was able to help you bring them back from the illness. Or he could destroy them if they were beyond repair and needed to be released into stardust or sent to another realm that could potentially help them. You also had a team of *solliqas* with you, and none of you were actual royalty. Not even you, Nyx. You all went in search of these poor souls and helped heal them the best way you could or sent them in rips between the realm to other worlds. You were quite the love story."

I mindlessly curl my hand around Eira's waist again, bringing her close to my chest. She doesn't even push against me. She's too transfixed in our history and what this could mean for us now. I would be, too, except I care more about her physically being in my arms and how fucking incredible she is.

Pride blossoms in my heart. Of course, I've heard the stories of our lost queen. But it's entirely different learning that you're connected to her, and you both had the ability to prevent a fucking plague from destroying your home. It also brings me to that moment I learned I had the ability to destroy a soul. The Council framed it as evil, but what if I was meant to use it for something good? *To set a soul free?*

"So, who knows? This might be why you and Nyx are destined to be together, your souls tied from the very beginning with the purpose of preventing plagues of darkness. I'm sure we'll find out the longer you're here with us."

Silence sweeps around us, leaving Eira fidgety in my arms. I'm dying to ask her what she thinks about our history together, to hold her even closer. But it's also hitting me that she doesn't remember being in Majikaero; at least, not yet.

As if sensing her discomfort, Daya brings her *alklen* to a trot, making her way to my other side. Their souls have already bonded in a way I don't think Eira can see yet.

Eira peers over at her, looking devastatingly lost. Her voice is a whisper on the wind as she works through her tumbling thoughts. "If Nyx and I were preventing the plague from spreading in this realm, why would anyone want to destroy our souls?"

"Because souls that support the Sairn don't have the same

definitions of good and evil as the rest of us do, friend," Daya whispers back. "They thirst for power. If any *solliqa* gets in the way of their fucked up definition of it, they do what you've seen so often happens on Earth—they destroy and eliminate their designated enemy. If the Sairn, and anyone else who supports them now, viewed what you and Nyx and your other close soul connections were doing as damaging to their plans, then they must have been pretty desperate to hunt you down."

Eira shudders. Sparks of cold fire line her body, and I can tell her thoughts are taking a negative turn.

I glance down at her body, trying to find a change in topic. I see that bear marking again. It's intensely dark against her fair skin, especially without other tattoos.

Clearing my throat, I ask, "You don't have other markings on you."

Eira turns back, seeming seconds away from going haywire. "Huh?"

"Markings," I say. "Tattoos. Designs. You only have this bear marking seared into your skin. I don't see anything else on you."

Her eyes spark like a shooting star. "You haven't seen *every* part of me." Giggling to herself, she continues. "I also didn't want to get any until I could afford full sleeves and huge pieces. They cost a fortune where I come from."

My thumb moves in small circles by her hip. "I could always tattoo you," I murmur into her ear.

"And the price?" she asks.

My imagination ignites in all the ways I could charge her for a tattoo. But it stops as quickly as it starts.

Zaya lurches me out of my thoughts, causing both Ambra and me to stagger at the bottom of the hill. She immediately perks up, standing at attention on top of Ambra's head with her pointed ears moving wildly. Before I can ask Eira anything, her cat leaps off of Ambra and bolts toward the nearing tree line, her fur standing on edge as if lightning hit her.

Shocking me with the stupidity of it all, Eira scrambles off Ambra and runs after Zaya. One second, she's safely in the arms. The next, she's somehow squirmed her way off and is fucking running after her cat. Without considering *where* Zaya is running and *what* might be awaiting us. *As I said. Trouble.*

Growling, I heave myself off Ambra mid-gallop, knowing my shadowed form will find her faster than anything or anyone in our group will. I urge my smoke toward her, as if gnarled hands reaching out, hoping to singe her covered back enough to compel her to stop.

But it doesn't. Her light absorbs my smoke, swallowing the darkness whole. And I'm nearly trampled by Ambra when I see how fast she runs, darting into the trees like fragments of light. I'm stopped by a mixture of awe and growing fear that clutches me firmly in its hold.

THIRTY-SEVEN

Eira

A bond of love can become violent when threatened.
-Valencia, Goddess of Fire

Holding my breath, I'm propelled forward by fear and adrenaline. A sliver in the back of my mind whispers that I should not have stormed after Zaya. That it's best to stay firmly in Nyx's arms on top of Ambra. But I've never claimed to make the smartest decisions. When the only other creature from my home world goes berserk and runs toward an unknown forest, then *dammit*, I'm going with her.

I'm vaguely aware of the others catching up to me, and I'm more amazed than anything that I'm still going faster than them. One of Nyx's tendrils of smoke sparks at my back, a detail I'll be harassing him about later. I surge forward, letting what I think is my *maji* take care of it for me. It's liquid fire pouring through my veins, and a brilliant light flashes behind me as I push myself forward.

If Zaya is following our friends' scents, then I need to be the first one there. I'm hyper-aware of how they've reacted to Tryg's name: the glints in their eyes, the way their shoulders tense, the snarl barely hidden behind their words. I'm not worried about Athena—she'll dominate in whichever realm she's in. But Tryg will need my support. My protection. And hopefully Zaya's while we're at it. Especially if she stays in her larger form.

Streaks of ignited orange light blend into new colors throughout her fur with each tree that we pass. What I think is a tiny bird swoops down in front of her, and she snatches it in her teeth mid-leap. *My enchanting, ferocious kitty.*

The air burns in my lungs as I continue to hurdle over spiky bushes. Zaya and I are thoroughly immersed in the colors of the forest now. I'm borderline disoriented by this dream-like environment. None of the colors match what I'm used to in my home world, and I know I've seen only one type of forest so far —but this is completely different. These leaves are dark blue and splashed with magenta. The bark on the trees, thin and tall as they tower above me, is a vibrant yellow. Each strand of grass has shades of blue and pink and green, as if I'm splashing and waving through a scintillating sea. Every color is vibrant, intensely fresh and full of life, and I feel myself spiraling into its magical hold.

Focus. I can't stop to let this new reality sink in. I need to get to my friends. *Now.*

Reeling from my jagged breathing, I try to peer within and find more of my *maji*. *It would have been so very chill if someone taught me how to use it.* I have zero clue what I'm doing, but I'm hoping I can fling particles of my magic toward Athena. It might be a gut instinct, or maybe a desperate hope I'm clawing at, to try to connect with her. To latch onto her scent as Zaya has done quite naturally. I throw whatever I can of myself outward like a beacon, flaring it high and wide for my friends to see. Hoping that Athena, the more sensible of the two, will see it and call out to me. Spending the two seconds to concentrate on this, if it even works, borderline costs me.

I trip on a fallen branch. The yellow tips of it sink into the grass, tickling the tops of my calves. I brace myself to crash face-first into the ground when a wind gushes below me, forcing me upright to keep running. I don't have to look back to know that was one of the shifters, probably Daru. Annoying, yet endearing, with his intense protection.

Something vibrates against my chest. Startling me and throwing my attention back to the task at hand, I narrow in on this sensation and cling to it, holding it like a thick cord. It goes taut, and in my mind's eye, I see a dark emerald-green light flare at the other end, pulsating brightly. I *know* in my heart that it's Athena. It's healing light, the kind she's often spread to me with her hugs and raunchy jokes and goofy smiles. It's my best friend wrapped up in the light of the forest—or the forest from home, at least.

I use this green light as a guide and chase after it. Running, jumping, sprinting for my life. I'm not sure why, but it feels urgent that I get there first, as if this might change the course of the entire future if it's me who finds them and not the others.

I'm hurtling past tree after tree until, finally, Zaya and I land in a small clearing and the green light subsides. I tumble over Zaya's tail and snatch her up, hugging her to my chest as I fall into the grass. My teeth clash and grind with each skid mark and bruise added to my skin. *Not my finest moment.* And no one saved me from this fall, which means I must be far enough ahead of the others.

Gasping, I convince my hobbling body to get up. *Where are they? Are we lost?*

When my eyes land on the far side of the clearing, I almost laugh at what I see. Athena and Tryg are on the ground, wrestling with a *solliqa*. The soul held down has streaks of different colors patterning their skin with talons for their feet, each covered in bright teal feathers. My friends are both draped in the huge blue leaves, tied around them with pieces of the long grass. *Ha, clever Athena.* Her hair is tied back with one of the strands, too. The thrashing creature gives off fragile and frantic energy and is shrieking in fear.

A giddy laugh escapes me, and I can't help punching my fist in the air, beyond stoked that my friends are alive and here. *My brave, incredible, foolish friends.*

My laugh turns louder and a bit unhinged. "Hey!" I yell out to them. "I didn't know we're attending a wrestling match."

Athena's big green eyes meet mine, widening slightly in surprise and relief. The *solliqa* jerks beneath her, and her lips tug into a smirk. "This creature happens to be the bird we hunted for food."

"This *creature* wants to live," the shifter sputters.

Tryg pushes brutally into his collarbone, causing the shifter to gasp. "And you will, if you'd just answer our fucking questions."

My whole body trembles with the need to be next to my friends. *Of course,* they would go into fight and interrogation mode rather than balk in fear. I'm not sure what happened to their clothes, but if they came here without them, then Athena would be clever enough to create her own coverings and search for food. Tryg is smart enough to do this, too, but if I know him, he was in a state of utter shock landing here. They might both be used to managing people's pain and trauma, but Athena? She's a true protector. Fierce. Ready to jump into any situation to help. Able to shake off her own fear if she senses others are in greater need.

I can't take it anymore. Zaya weaves in between my feet while I run toward them, and a large part of me wants to throw her into a lake for trying to trip me at a time like this. *Ugh, typical cat.* I leap onto my friends and the random shifter. I hold Athena particularly close, and her body melts into my own.

"I love the new outfit," I whisper in her ear.

"Thanks," she responds with a sniffle. I don't realize that

we're both crying until I taste salt against my lips. "My friend told me that leaves are totally *in* this year."

Cackling, I crash against her again and give her a tight hug. Needing to feel her flesh against my own. Eleven-year-old me might have been the person to teach her this while we went camping in the woods years ago.

Keeping one arm looped around Athena, I pull Tryg up to join our embrace. A dull pain unfurls from my bear marking, and my wide smile falls into a tight grimace. I force it into a strained smile, but it's too late. Tryg already saw my expression when I hugged him. He went from semi-delirious to alert, searching my face and body for any signs of pain.

My heart aches that his touch harmed me. Scrambling for a way to convince him I'm fine, I shove myself forward to plant a peck on his cheek. An act of affection, yet quick enough to avoid any blistering pain.

"It's *me*," I tell him. "This is real. We're all here together."

"This is so fucked." Tryg's voice is hoarse and strained. The poor shifter half beneath us looks hilariously disoriented while he manages to wiggle free of us. "I knew not to trust yoga."

I shake my head in dismay. Only one of *my* friends would make that kind of comment right now, as if that's what led them here. *As if every yoga instructor tries to stab you.* I shiver, remembering the vivid scene of Shira wielding two daggers at my friends. Zaya marks their legs, acting all cute and innocent while she tangles around their ankles. As if she didn't just try to inadvertently kill me.

In a beat, she jumps in front of us and lets out a low growl. She hunches down and bares her teeth, bringing me back to reality, her eyes flashing bright gold while her body grows larger by the second. *Oh, right, the others. This will be a joyful reunion.*

No sooner do I think those words than a hunk of *maji* and muscle are lunging for Tryg.

"*No!*" I scream. But it's too late. I go to dive in front of Tryg and am tackled by a shadowy mass.

Straining against my captor, I call out, "Daya! Don't let anyone manhandle Athena!" My voice cracks, and adrenaline is surging through my body. I'm scrambling to find a way out, to figure out *any* way to protect my friends. Part of me knows they'll be safe, but the other part of me can't be reasoned with. I still barely know these creatures, and my friends—I can't leave them alone.

A different kind of heat simmers inside, starting below my rib cage. I can already tell the light building is not the same *maji* I used before. It turns a frightening bright blue, coating my exposed skin in liquid rage, and thrashes against the shadows holding me down.

"Fuck," Nyx grunts, loosening his grip on me barely. I try pushing out of his hold again, but it's no use. I'm not trained enough with this *maji* yet.

I bare my teeth at him, knowing his face is hidden in there somewhere. "Let me go!"

Smoke curls around us violently, and his dark, beautiful eyes appear above me. They're way more sinister than the other times he's looked at me. Like the Devil incarnate. Gulping, I edge back an inch, slowly realizing that I might be in danger but refusing to completely back down.

"No." His low voice scurries down my skin. Waking up other feelings that are entirely inappropriate for this moment.

I scream as loud as I can, up to the treetops. "Why are you doing this?"

"Because your safety means more to me than whether you're angry," he grunts, holding me tighter. A lick of smoke curls around my marking. His words blunt the edge of my static emotions.

"Besides." He pauses, and I feel the slickness of his tongue trail up my neck. "Your anger tastes *so* delicious."

I spit in his face and try to ignore the way his tongue quickens my pulse.

"You said you'd give him a chance," I growl. Although, even I hear how half-hearted it sounds.

"I never said such things," he whispers. He lowers his lips for a heartbeat against my collarbone and chuckles darkly. "You asked me to give him a chance. I haven't seen if he's worthy of one yet."

"But—"

"Shh," Nyx whispers. He suddenly has one hand threading through my hair and the other snaking around my hips. Caging me against his body. "I said *yet*, sweetheart. I'll take a closer look once we get back."

I find myself willingly leaning into Nyx, my back arching as he trails featherlight touches at the base of my spine.

Writhing in his arms, I whimper, "This isn't fair. Why do you have to be all growly and protective? I can't be falling for you already."

Those menacing eyes soften at the edges. "Of course you can, Eira. Our souls are tied together by the threads of this universe."

"You don't understand," I whisper. The fight within me vanishes with each caress of his fingers. "The closer we get, the more likely you'll leave me when given the opportunity."

Spirals of ocean-scented smoke tighten their hold on me at my words. They crawl around my chest and spread down the dip of my belly. My mind is rattling against my skull, irritated that my body is betraying me, yet I can't stop the small moan that breaks free. The mixture of pulsating shadows and smoke and waves of Nyx's heat is intoxicating and for a second, I forget to breathe. Forget to feel upset and push back against the *misn* embracing me. *Yes, he has that* misn *energy, and I'm loving it.* His scent batters around me, knocking me senseless. My hands wind around his neck, and I pull his face closer, absolutely aching to taste his—

"Alright, I think you made your point," Daru grumbles.

A sharp, whirling wind breaks me free of Nyx's spell, sending goosebumps skittering along my skin. His shadows fall back to expose his whole body, and he still has his hand placed firmly on my hip. Nyx snaps his gaze toward Daru, his lips pulling back in distaste. If looks could kill, I'm sure Daru would be a pile of ashes and burned feathers right now.

Nyx leans down close to my ear, whispering softly enough that I can barely hear him. "I'll never leave you, Eira. I can already be sure of that, even if this prick throws a tantrum whenever we touch."

Still dazed, I catch Daya's eyes and realize she and Athena are *both* ridiculously smug. *Excuse me.*

"You have *so* much to tell me about," Athena says, her eyes glowing with mischief. I'm mildly concerned that she's not running for the hills after watching Nyx devour me in his shadows.

I hastily untangle myself from Nyx and try to put as much distance between us as possible. The key word there is *try*. The second I go more than a foot away, his shadows strike out and curl around my feet and hips, tugging me closer.

Narrowing my eyes, I jab a finger into his chest. "That was unnecessary and—and *rude*."

He arches a dark eyebrow. "Rude?"

My whole face is as bright as a cherry. I feel everyone watching us, and all it takes is a fraction of a second to see both Tryg and Daru heaving like caged animals. *Great.*

I get up into Nyx's face. "You knew what you were doing," I grit out.

Smoke gently caresses the outside of my hand. "Of course I did, sweetheart. But do you?" Nyx winks before turning to the others, leaving me in a frazzled mess. "Let's get back to the base.

This took less time than anticipated, but we can't travel to Rioa quite yet. Eliina needs to get a good look at both of them, especially *him*."

I don't miss the way Nyx's lips curl when he focuses his attention on Tryg.

Nyx takes three large strides toward Tryg, his darkness beating in sync with each step. Even Daya and Delano, who are both standing near Athena at this point, are clearly on edge. Ulf is the only one who appears unsettlingly excited.

To Tryg's credit, he doesn't break eye contact with Nyx, even with the shadows and smoke spewing out of his body. His eyes dart to me but quickly go back to Nyx when he lets out a feral growl. He firmly takes Tryg's chin in his hand, *actually grabs his face*, and stoops slightly to eye level.

"Let me make myself crystal clear. You might have been Eira's friend in your home world. But you're not on Earth anymore. You're in Majikaero. I could recognize the rot in your soul in any realm and know *exactly* what you are. I now *know* you were there when Eira was torn apart, just as I know you've somehow slinked your way back here time after time to harm others. Always forgetting to hide your eyes; we remember who the fuck you are. You even breathe in Eira's direction, and we won't wait for Eliina's evaluation. The Council won't even need to convince me to use their *best-kept-secret*—my *maji*—I'll kill you again myself. You have nowhere to hide this time."

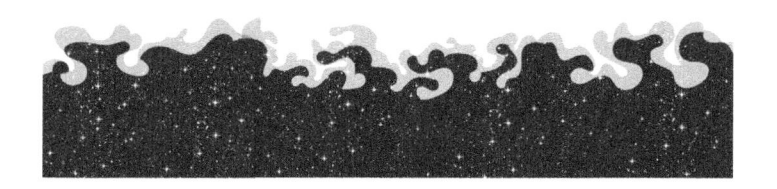

THIRTY-EIGHT

Tryq

Magic is often thought of as fantasy, as nonsensical and seen in books. It's a pity so few see the magic in their own bodies, in their hearts. Or it might be considered a blessing.
-Dr. Antonio Piernt, Founder of Seeds of the Lotus

Time isn't on my side right now. I'm still reeling from seeing a fucking bird change into a grown-ass man. I'll go to my grave saying I held the creature down first, but Athena knows the truth. Give me a worthless, pathetic murderer or thief, and I'll chase them down myself, ready to pull the trigger. All this magic bullshit's something else entirely. I can practically taste the fear coming off Athena, yet she acts fine. She talks as if she was made from this new land and is destined to be here. *Maybe she's been called home.*

Athena fucking threw herself on this creature without a second thought and sent me a judgmental look. As if this is all normal, and I'm the weirdo for not wanting to touch whatever this *thing* is. I manage to get a fucking grip when Eira, of all the people I could see, comes flying through the trees with Zaya. I have a million questions, my mind is still spinning from

THE LIGHT WITHIN

watching them. It was like watching an angel wrapped in fire spread her magnificent wings, flying from running so fast. And don't even get me started on her fucking cat. Only Eira would have managed to bring her cat into a magical realm.

I'm still processing a million emotions after seeing her. Even more so after watching her beautiful face, full of bliss after hugging Athena, drop in misery when she held me. Those silver-blue eyes crackled into blazing fire after she kissed my cheek. Unsurprisingly, she was determined to pretend as if everything was fine, but her body was clearly ready to fight me.

And holy fuck, what are all of these creatures?

One minute, I'm reunited with Eira and her fucking cat and the next minute, we're all surrounded by a number of creatures. A gyrating mass of shadows and smoke engulfed Eira and pushed her out of the way. A red-headed male scooped up a flailing Zaya. What looks to be his sister twirled off one of those terrifying deer creatures, the one that I saw a day ago, and landed in front of Athena. Neither of them were too threatening, especially since the female said to Athena, "I'm Daya. We'll chat more later, but my brother and I are friends of Eira. We're here to help you stay safe."

Although Zaya acts less than thrilled about the situation, hissing and thrashing and pretending the male is burning her alive. *Dramatic*.

The others are frightening enough that I'm forced to bite down on my lip to keep it from trembling. I refuse to show more fear, especially with how strong Athena appears. *Women*. My eyes dart from creature to creature, soaking in their forms. A group of what I swear to be actual demons, reeking of terror, spread out along the tree line, effectively blocking any chance of escaping. I count six different outlines of darkened creatures with shadows seeping from them, but they are shifting and pulsing so fast, I can't be sure how they look in the light. Fragments of eyes litter the space in between the trees surrounding us, giving me all the more reason to stay put where I am.

I'm starting to think I might be drugged because the biggest fucking bird skids to a halt in front of me. It aggressively clicks its orange beak centimeters from my face. A group of other creatures, equally paralyzing in their own ways, stalk the other area of trees where Eira was tackled. One makes my eyes widen in awe; a shining deer with pure white antlers and dazzling burgundy eyes stares into my soul. A ferret-type creature shifts around in the tall grasses and jumps onto what could be a mountain lion. Except it swallowed the sun and is twice the size of a normal lion from back home. *Jesus, save me.*

When I don't think I can take anymore, a male with golden hair and dark green eyes lets out a thunderous snarl and immediately has me thrown to the ground. One of the demon-looking monsters slithers over through the grass and wraps tightly around my ankles and knees. The huge bird uses its fucking *talons* to yank my shoulders up, forcing me to peer up into the golden male's seething face.

Woah, woah, woah. The fuck did I do? Why are they all posed to strike at me, *and Athena is being treated like a rescued damsel in distress?*

Grunting, I'm about to ask what their problem is when I hear the sweetest sound I've ever heard in my life. It's quiet enough that I'm surprised I could hear it above all these shitheads snarling at me, but I know what I heard. Eira gave a soft moan, and an irrational sense of jealousy tightens its hold on me. I must not be the only one because the male in front of me grunts in disgust and says, "Alright, I think you made your point."

Wisps of smoke and shadow fade away, revealing a rather intimate image of Eira with whatever that male is supposed to be. I can't bring myself to care *what* he is, just that he has Eira pliant in his hands, and their mouths are a breath apart. When she realizes that we can all see them, she looks exactly how I'd imagine her to: red-faced and frazzled. I'd laugh if I wasn't fucking jumbled and foaming at the mouth with envy.

The piece of shit she's with? He doesn't give a fuck. He swivels his dark eyes to me, and the male in front of me. A shard of glee pierces through me when he glances at the golden male, but when he stares at me, it turns into hardened malice. I can tell he's trying hard not to morph into a full *demon-monster-whatever-the-fuck-those-things-are*. His eyes are switching back and forth from swirling layers of brown with silver and gold to a piercing black to a staggering opal. The same opal as that monster in my nightmare. Teeth as sharp as daggers grow longer, the tips dipping below his upper lip.

He's a haunted soul brought back from the dead, and I already know that I'm his next victim.

"Let me make myself crystal clear. You might have been Eira's friend in your home world. But you're not on Earth anymore. You're in Majikaero. I could recognize the rot in your soul in any realm and know *exactly* what you are. I now *know* you were there when Eira was torn apart, just as I know you've somehow slinked your way back here time after time to harm others. Always forgetting to hide your eyes—we remember who the fuck you are. You even breathe in Eira's direction, and we won't wait for Eliina's evaluation. The Council won't need to convince me to use their *best-kept secret*, my *maji*—I'll kill you again myself. You have nowhere to hide this time."

Without a chance to respond, the golden male presses his thumb into the middle of my forehead, and everything goes dark.

I manage to peel my eyes open and have to actively fight against the draining grogginess. My chest can barely get a breath in, crushed under the weight of shock and denial, as well as whatever that male did to my head. *Rot in my soul?* Instead of being greeted with warmth and any form of hospitality, I've been thrown onto the back of what might be a scaly, horse creature. If the swinging movement doesn't kill me, the horrendous smell of magical horse shit will.

Multicolored vines are wrapped around me and prevent me from moving even an inch. Truly. I flick my head to the side to get a better view of who I'm riding with, and the vines tighten against my skin, squeezing until circulation is cut off at points along my arms and legs. *Wait, they're cutting into my skin?* Careful not to move my head, I glance down and realize with horror that I'm completely naked. *Mercy.*

I don't know how many minutes have passed and how much longer I'll be wrapped up like a breathing sausage. It takes more energy than I'm capable of, but I manage to calm myself down enough for some of the pressure to release. Enough to temper down the waves of rising panic.

Athena's voice beckons me from nearby, brushing against my ears. The reminder that I'm not alone keeps me still and focused. *If I cause trouble, what will happen to my friends?* Although, I suppose I shouldn't worry too much about that yet. Eira has a demon clearly wrapped around her finger and a group of creatures willing to defend her. Athena might feel terror deep down, but she's doing a damn good job of keeping it there, hidden from maybe even herself. She laughs at a comment the red-haired female makes and, being the brilliant woman she is, jumps immediately into asking questions. No, *demanding*.

"So, let me get this straight. You're saying that time works differently here? It moves... slower?" Athena asks, her voice heavy with skepticism.

"Err, sort of," the red-haired female answers. "A lot of it has to do with perspective, while time also overall moves at a constant pace. I'm sure you've heard of time being an illusion back at your home? It's a construct. On Earth, especially. In this realm, I suppose you could say it overall moves slower than on Earth, but it can also be manipulated by different souls here. The closer you get to a thinner part of the veil between our worlds, such as at the capital in Rioa, the more warped time and reality becomes. It's all about perspective."

I don't have to see the conversation to know the look Athena's giving right now. Sucking onto my teeth, I bite back a laugh, picturing the expression she's given me a thousand times.

"I know that's difficult to process. Even those of us who study this practice still find it unnerving and challenging to imagine. I'll connect you with a manipulator when we get to Rioa if you'd prefer. They might be able to answer more of your questions."

"Doubtful," Athena mutters. "Alright, what's the deal with Tryg?"

A hushed silence whips around the group at her question.

"What? You don't have to act so damn sneaky about it. You've already got him tied up like a hog and creepily insisted he should remain fully exposed. I want to know what's going on." Athena pauses. "Oh, fuck, this isn't a sex ritual, is it? Because I did *not* sign up for that shit."

"No, *no*!" someone else interjects. "It's nothing like that at all. We don't, ah, want to say too much until Eliina looks at him first."

"Yeah? Eliina can do all the looking she wants. Similar to what you've forced the rest of us to do by keeping him naked. I want to know what all the fuss is about with his rotting soul or whatever that guy said," Athena snarks.

The red-haired female lets out a heavy exhale, clearly twitchy and on edge. *Excellent.*

"I personally think this is a perplexing mess," she says.

"While you and Eira don't exactly know who or what you were previously, you've been adapting to this realm. You, especially. Anyone can see that Tryg is rattled, his eyes as wild as a caged animal. He doesn't know about his soul and what he's done in the past. Which is troubling. *Enormously* troubling. Considering the damage he caused, one would think he'd know *exactly* where he is and what his relation to Eira was before. It's rather confusing. Everyone who ends up crossing over here makes that kind of connection."

"But death is often its own mystery, Daya," another creature says. "Much of it's unable to be solved until it's experienced."

"Sure, but I thought he didn't exactly *die*," Daya responds. "His soul should have been shattered into millions of shards and pieces, scattered across different realms and universes, unable to be put back together."

"I mean, that kind of sounds like death to me..." the creature mumbles to themself.

"This endless debating makes no difference," the *shadowy-smoky-demon-who-touched-my-Eira* says sharply. "We've arrived. Eliina will know what to do."

"Who the fuck is Eliina?" I mutter. I instantly regret this. The vines grow serrated thorns and pepper my throat with unbearable cuts.

Alright, that's it. Giving someone this many paper cuts should be an act of war.

One of the shadowy creatures lifts me up, swinging me on their shoulder, treating me like a sack of potatoes. I smirk when they stumble for a second, enough to show me I'm heavier than they expected. *Maybe they wanted my body on display for more than one reason.* I'm carried quickly through a series of lavish tents. When my head swings upward, I see we're walking in a valley between two major cliffs. The low roar of a river can be heard in the distance. I might not be able to speak or move, but that doesn't mean I won't soak up any bit of information I can.

THE LIGHT WITHIN

My captor pushes through a large tent opening and unceremoniously dumps me on the ground in front of them.

"We'll be getting everything settled for Rioa," they grunt before giving a quick dip of their head, shoulder-length blond locks skimming their shoulders, and dashing out the tent.

The vines disappear in a flash, and I sigh in relief. Blinking as the blood rushes back to my head and extends out toward my fingertips and toes, I peer around at the serene space and orbs of eye-catching lights. A woman wrapped in black gauzy material approaches from the shadows. Her swirling green and black eyes peer through me, and while she doesn't appear old, I sense her ancient wisdom. A chill rolls through me when I realize she reminds me of Shira. But much lighter. Different.

"They didn't have to humiliate you," she murmurs while pushing back my wavy hair. "Hadwin?" she calls out quietly enough that I'm sure no one will hear her.

The same creature who dumped me in the tent steps back in, as if he materialized from thin air. "Yes, Eliina?"

Ah, this is the woman they were all talking about. I guess I can see why they'd want her opinion on things.

Eliina sends Hadwin a stern look. "While I thought it potentially excessive to send so many of you with Eira to find her friends, I understood the desire to protect her and ensure her safe return. What I *don't* understand was why you felt the need to mangle and expose one of Eira's *friends* and in front of her at that. Surely you didn't think after being thrown into our realm and encountering all of your shadows that he would do anything to harm her. We all have different strengths and weaknesses, but I was quite sure you didn't lack intelligence."

Hadwin has his head lowered slightly and seems properly chastened. Almost fidgety, reminding me of a kid being scolded by their parent.

"We just, you know, wanted—"

"I clearly don't," Eliina says wryly. "That was shameful and will not be tolerated again. And if I'm right with the sense of heat and anger flaring around Eira, she'll have some choice words for you now that she knows you won't outnumber her."

Hadwin clears his throat and looks away. When he glances back at Eliina, his green eyes are dark and remorseful. "It won't happen again, Eliina," he murmurs. "You know what he was like last time. We felt such rage seeing him appear in the realm again and wanted him to pay for what he's done."

"That isn't your justice to serve," she says. "We'll all be having a conversation before we get to Rioa to establish this isn't *any* of your responsibility. Tryg will be well monitored and in the care of my fiercest protectors. He will also have access to his friends, receive regular meals, and for the sake of everyone, he will remain properly clothed."

As Eliina continues to speak, the tent becomes smaller and smaller. The earth shakes ever so slightly. As if to emphasize each of her pointed words.

"You and your group should know better than anyone how easily the soul can sway when faced with harsh environments and aggressive, cruel individuals," Eliina continues. "How much one's perspective plays a delicate role in the fate of a soul. There's clearly still good in Tryg, or he would have already harmed Eira on Earth during their last living cycle. We don't know the circumstances of him returning to this realm and what pieces remain. Eira and everyone's safety will be prioritized, *and* Tryg will not be shamed for existing here. Understood?"

Hadwin mumbles an incoherent acknowledgment and nearly sprints out of the tent when Eliina gives a dismissive nod. I have the insane urge to stick my tongue out at him.

"Now, this is no way for us to have a conversation," Eliina says with kind eyes. "Let's get you bathed, fed, and very much clothed, and then we can talk."

THIRTY-NINE

Eira

Never underestimate the power of Earth communication.
The soil knows more than the oldest soul alive.
-Neta, Goddess of the Earth

"Talk? What does she want to talk to *me* about?" Athena asks incredulously. As I figured would happen, now that she doesn't need to act tough in front of everyone, she's crumbling in front of me. She's one of the strongest people I know, but even the strongest need time to process and take in major change. And I would consider waking up in a magical realm after being stabbed by someone you trusted to be *quite* the major change.

"I know that I've only been here a little longer than you, but I assure you that talking with Eliina is nothing horrible," I say gently. "Plus, we'll be together. I'm sure she wants to check that you're okay and answer any questions. You didn't exactly have the best arrival experience."

"Yeah, no kidding," Athena mumbles. She blows out a sharp breath while fiddling with the thin orange, pink, and yellow coverings Eliina gave to her last night. "This feels fucking unreal.

I'm not sure which is crazier. Tryg and I getting *stabbed* in the heart or realizing I'm in a world with a million different colors and creatures who can shapeshift and control the elements. Don't even get me started on the idea that time moves slower here, we arrived fucking naked, *and* there are different perspectives of time depending on who or where you are. *Sweet Jesus.* Consider me *shook*."

Chewing on my lower lip, I consider the scenarios Athena shared. A piece of me buzzes loudly when I think about what Shira did. It grows louder and louder, similar to a swarm of hornets erupting in anger, causing me to grind my teeth in distress.

Fuck, I've got to stop thinking about this. This isn't about me right now. I rub soothing circles on my friend's back. There's nothing I can say to ease her worries or make processing this new world any easier. The best thing I can do is be here and show her that she's not going to be alone during any of it.

"Let's go talk with Eliina. I think Tryg is still in there with her. We can have whatever conversation and then head to the capital," I tell her. I'm not sure she's even listening at this point. Athena nods her head absently and pushes off the smooth rock we were sitting on. We walk the short distance to Eliina's tent. Before we go inside, I grab Athena's hand and squeeze.

"Remember, you're not alone in this. We even have Zaya with us," I whisper. She worms around Athena's calves, a silent act of love.

Athena gives me a watery smile and huffs out a laugh. "Yeah, that furball of a cat is even here. Maybe things will be okay. Alright, let's get this over with."

Eliina's earthy scent greets us when we enter, filling me with a sense of ease. Athena must feel this, too, since her shoulders visibly lower, and she stretches out her clenched hands. We spot Eliina toward the back of the tent, speaking in a low voice with Tryg. The poor guy is already frazzled and mentally scattered, I can't imagine what this realm will now do to him. It'll eat him alive, I'm sure, if Nyx has anything to do with it.

Eliina whips her head in our direction as we tiptoe our way in. "Ah, this is favorable—you're both here," she says with a smile. "Come back to my work area."

We weave our way around lavish seating arrangements and tables of varying liquids. "Are you going to take all of this with you to Rioa?" I ask.

"Oh, no, not at all," Eliina says. "Half of the *solliqas* you see around here will be kept at this base and will have access to these antidotes and potions. I don't need to take much with me, anyway. Everything I need is all in here." She points to her head and to her heart, a white light flaring under her hand. "The rest of us will travel to Rioa together in a bit from now."

"Right, we're traveling," Tryg croaks. He's wearing all black today with some kind of gray boots. His gaze catches mine, and he looks at a loss for words. "I, um—"

"Don't worry about anything right now," I tell him. "I'm sure you learned a lot of information. Maybe *too* much."

He nods his head slowly and has the same look he used to get when I would chatter his ear off after finishing a favorite book. I let myself smile at the memory.

"We did have a lengthy conversation," Eliina confirms. "At various points from last night through this morning. I shared with him some of your history, why your new friends might have responded rather inappropriately to him, and more clarification about Majikaero. We've finished talking about *solliqas* and the Council members."

"They seem like charming old fucks," Tryg mutters under his breath.

I bark out a laugh. He might appear scared out of his mind, but it puts me at ease to hear his snarky response.

Eliina gives him a wry smile. "I'll admit our Council in Rioa has taken a turn for the worse." She glances at Athena. "You'll be much easier to communicate with."

"*Me?*" Athena asks. Her eyes are as wide as the floating orbs above us.

"Yes, you," Eliina chuckles. "I already sense your type of *maji*. You connect with the earth as I do. It'll make it easier to show you my thoughts instead of speaking everything out loud. You'll have more of an innate understanding."

"Um... like telepathy?" Athena whispers.

"Not exactly," Eliina says. "It might be best if I show you what I'm talking about. Here, come sit in front of me." She pats the rug in invitation.

Athena gives me a wary *what-the-fuck* look but proceeds to sit in front of Eliina. Luckily, she doesn't have to sit in worry and tension for long. Eliina takes both of her hands, and a green light flashes and travels up both of their bodies until they are sitting in an outline of buzzing light. The color mixes with Athena's sparkling coverings, giving her the look of an ethereal spring goddess. Athena gasps and Eliina holds onto her hands even tighter. I'm sure she's prepared for this to freak Athena out and doesn't want to break the connection. Athena's eyes flutter under her eyelids, and her expression morphs from fear to concern to genuine interest.

There are no fucking clocks here, but forever passes by us. Tryg and I silently watch Eliina and Athena in front of us, in awe of their glow and ability to communicate by touch. At least, I'm in awe. Tryg is as baffled as a frantic chicken.

Finally, Eliina releases Athena's hands and they both open their eyes. My friend still looks mildly confused, but I can also sense that she's more settled. Ready. Focused.

"That was certainly new," Athena breathes. She lets out a little yelp when the earth below the rug grows underneath her.

"We can also communicate through the earth with one another," Eliina shares. "You'll find that you'll be able to do this

THE LIGHT WITHIN

with those who have similar *maji* and most likely with Eira, since you're so close with one another."

Athena gazes down at her hands and slides them over the rug and ground below her. Her mouth opens and closes, as if she wants to speak, but she keeps any thoughts to herself. She shuffles back toward where I'm sitting and silently leans against my shoulder. It takes way more patience than I thought I had to not explode with all my questions and test out if she can communicate with me already. But that isn't what Athena needs right now. No, she needs reliable support. Someone who isn't going to push her with questions while she sits with all the new information bubbling in her mind.

Eliina turns to face Tryg again. "Now, I know that we spoke at length about this realm. When I communicated with Athena just now, I was also able to read her soul and find any traces of darkness inside her. Considering the work she's done on Earth, I'm surprised by the clarity of her system. Although, pain can bury itself in the deepest areas of a soul, hidden from even our own self." She pauses and assesses Tryg. He's slumped against the base of a chair and looks utterly, tragically lost.

Narrowing her eyes, Eliina continues. "May I try to read your soul, Tryg? The last time your soul was here, you were a mass of darkness. I need to know where you currently stand with everything. I had told you that you'd be near your friends going forward, but I can't be sure until I deem you safe."

I'm not sure he really has a choice, but the therapist in me appreciates Eliina framing it this way to him. Giving him the option to voice his concerns. He simply shrugs, and Eliina doesn't give room for any pushback. Her light surges forward, and she places her hand on his chest. Hard.

Immediately, Tryg convulses onto the ground and shrieks with agony. I can sense a force is crushing him from the inside out. His fists clench the scattered rugs, and his body jerks left and right while his feet and hands stay put, as if chains have shackled him to the earth. Tryg lets out a groan and garbles a sentence to Eliina, but it comes out more as a savage growl.

"Hmm, try again, Tryg," Eliina murmurs. Her own body is trembling from keeping her hands on his thrashing chest.

"*What* are these parts of me," Tryg grunts. He bites at the air, spit flying out of his snarling mouth.

Like a man possessed, he arches his back and forces his stiff neck upright. He turns his face toward Eliina, imitating a mechanical doll. Athena and I automatically grip each other's hands, and I can't be sure either of us is breathing at this point. Tryg's golden-brown eyes have turned to a dirty mud color, as if he trudged his soul through soil and ash. Black veins bloom down his jaw and neck all the way to his fingertips. They trail up to his chest, giving the illusion that Eliina has her hands dipped in a sticky web. Trapped by the leeching darkness.

Eliina doesn't flinch, not even a millimeter, when Tryg seethes at her. "What the *fuck* is going on with me?" he spits. "There's two parts waging a war, and I'm stuck in the middle of a battle I didn't even start. One side continues to crash into me as a shadowed wave, willing me to drown in my misery. The other side whispers it's my true self, who I was in the beginning, and is begging me to not give up yet."

Tryg chokes a strangled sound. I lift a shaky hand to grab him, and Athena pulls me back down, silently telling me no.

He rasps in a voice not his own. "I should let go. It's pointless to fight the inevitable."

"But then you'll hurt Eira," Eliina says in a low voice.

"I don't care about our fucking history here. I *love* her. I would never hurt her, and whoever did that before was not *me*."

"Oh, child," Eliina whispers. "Even if we love a soul fiercely, we can harm them in irreparable ways if our love is self-serving." She leans back slightly, taking some of the pressure of her light and *maji* off him. "You left your family mark on her soul. An imprint of what you are, so that you would never be apart. An act of control. Is that truly love?"

"If she can't be mine, she can't be *anyone's*." Tryg's eyes bulge. "It was best that I helped them destroy her. Then, if anyone found her, they'd hardly have one tiny piece. There's still one winner here."

Tryg grunts again and tenses his muscles, but he also doesn't break eye contact with Eliina.

"Who did you help, Tryg? Was it the Sairn?" Eliina breathes.

My friend spits at her before his eyes roll to the back of his head, his body continuing to endlessly shake.

"I was promised true love," Tryg grinds out. "It's all I ever wanted. It will be delivered to me one way or another."

She abruptly releases him, and he sags onto the ground in a heap. She shakes her head in dismay, her eyes shining with disappointment.

"I'm afraid he'll need tighter care and security than I originally anticipated," Eliina shares with us. "The darker part of him lashed out at me with such ferocity, aiming to kill. While there's no doubt that a large part of him loves you, Eira, we can never underestimate the power of selfish love. Its sickly sweetness turns into rot and will drive every action, no matter the good intentions behind it. I hope you can understand."

I find myself nodding, not knowing what else I can possibly say or do. Who am I to argue with a *solliqa* who has seen millions of souls and can connect with the earth in such a powerful way? Who has witnessed darkness spread in the form of a disease here? Glancing down at the mark on my arm, I notice its lines darkened since last night.

"This is his family mark?" I ask, tracing the edges of the bear with my finger. The mark no longer hurts, thanks to Nyx and the healers, but it appears to be permanently etched on my pale skin. A tattoo, a branding, smothered in dark splotches; one that was forced onto me.

"Yes," Eliina responds. "His lineage is formidable. Dominant. Striking. There are positive traits, such as his protectiveness, bravery, and loyalty. When Tryg or anyone from his family line connected with someone, they loved fiercely. I'm sure you found all of these traits admirable while on Earth. Yet he is stubborn and will not hesitate to attack if he deems it necessary, even if that means harming the ones he loves in the process. His aggression and territorial behavior have been his downfall. And I'm afraid it'll continue to be if he doesn't get a handle on the darkness unfurling in him as we speak."

I swallow past the lump in my throat, suddenly overcome with emotion. I'm not sure what's happening, but what I *do* know is that I can't let my friend succumb to his inner demons. I'll have to at least try to find a remedy. And not only for him, but for every other *solliqa* suffering right now. *Like Nyx.*

"Well," Eliina claps her hands firmly together. "Understanding this is a fragile situation, I don't think we should linger and ruminate on what's happening with Tryg. It's best for us to head to Rioa. That's where we can find more extensive levels of care for him and, more so, for *you*, Eira. We can discuss this issue more after we arrive."

Athena and I manage to use one another for support and stand on shaking legs, similar to newborn colts. We're obviously not okay—that's as clear as fucking day. What's worse is that I insisted that a conversation with Eliina isn't horrible. *Amazingly cool, Eira. Let's continue the trauma fest.*

"Go get some *lipva* and food from the main healer tent," Eliina urges us out of the tent entrance. "Everything else is packed up. I need to gather my belongings and get Tryg settled in for the ride."

I want to go back to ask if we can travel with her, but I come face-to-face with smoky tendrils that wind their way through my disheveled hair. Once Nyx has me enveloped in his shadows, which are unsettlingly comforting, he takes a quick assessment of my entire body. As if even in Eliina's aura, he can't be too careful. One of the wisps falls down my neck. It morphs into the shape of a hare, and I can't help giggling at the cuteness.

"Do you forcibly inspect *all* of your friends like this?" I tease him.

Nyx snorts and arches an eyebrow. "Would you prefer me to, sweetheart?"

He steps impossibly closer. "Or do you desire all the attention?"

He lowers his head, the dark markings on his neck twitching with the movement. His lips graze my reddening cheek. "Thriving from the knowledge that you've already got me at your beck and call?"

I force my lips into a smirk, not wanting Nyx to know how much he already affects me. Time moves vastly differently here, and it's possible I'm falling for him after a few days, or perhaps it's been months or years or lifetimes. "If that's the case, I'll take my *lipva* and breakfast by Ambra. Something fresh. A piece of meat with a tantalizing flavor, if you can find one." My gaze flickers down to his waist and back up to his scorching eyes.

I swear I feel the smoke tighten their hold in my hair, pulling hard enough to show me I got under his skin. Nyx's eyes take on a darker look, his face morphing for a second into a cruel, hungry demon.

"At once, my queen," he purrs, backing away until the shadows and smoke creep out of my hair and release me from his hold. Taking the salty breeze of the sea with him. *So similar to that memory I had of us.*

Licking my lips and instantly starving, I turn to see a gaping Athena. We've been joined by Delano, Hadwin, Ivar, and Erika. Zaya's lounging on Delano's shoulders, her fluffy tail swishing in his face. They're all watching Nyx saunter off to gather my breakfast with raised eyebrows, a hint of shock rendering them speechless. Erika faces me and her expression transforms into one of amusement.

"You've already got our terrorizing, demented prince preparing your meals? I *totally* call dibs on sharing a room with you when we get there. I want to see what else you can do."

Ivar slaps her arm. "Can you not control yourself for one minute? You're beginning to sound like Fraya. Look at you, frothing at the mouth."

Erika makes a face and what I'm assuming to be a rude gesture at him.

"It's the least he can do," I smirk. "He's existed for *ages*. He should know by now that food is the way to a girl's heart."

Hadwin's head falls back with hearty laughter. "Our souls are a bit old, aren't they? Don't forget yours is ancient, too, little queen. You're just comparing Nyx to your latest human life."

Athena interrupts whatever questions I'm about to hurtle at Hadwin. "I'm sorry, did you say... *prince*?"

The word bulldozes through me. My brain thought Erika was simply teasing him, but could he seriously be someone in royalty? *Fuck no. I haven't even eaten yet, and I'm still trying to find coffee here.*

Erika's smile widens, and she's frighteningly elated. "Oh, ho ho! You've got yourself shacked up with the Prince of Darkness. Many say he's not really a *solliqa* because his hidden monster has eaten away at his rotten *soul*. But he's pining for you, little Queen of Light, brimming with fire and hordes of *maji*. But wait until you..." She mimes little explosions, flexing her hands in the shape of fireworks as she trails them down her body.

I can't tell what I'm more disturbed by. Her psychotic behavior or that I'd already willingly throw myself into the fire with Nyx. Even though he has the same kind of darkness that I saw in Tryg. The same kind of darkness that I know will smother my burning light.

FORTY

Eira

Are we not gods to man?
-Council Member Namid, Grand Soul Reader

Lights from the nearing city flicker on the horizon akin to glittering diamonds. They're reaching out with their greedy hands for the twinkling stars above us. The sight is both captivating and relieving. We've been riding for multiple days with not nearly enough stops. Eliina gave the command that we *must* arrive at her section of the Council living quarters as soon as physically possible. Nyx gave up arguing with me long ago about flying on Ambra instead of riding on land. He insisted that we'd get there in half the time by sky. I pushed back, *naturally*, and asked if time is a perspective here, then what's the difference? He couldn't find a good enough retort, so we've been riding in a strained silence for the second half of the journey.

I wouldn't mind flying. I've never had a fear of heights and am the one in our group most likely to seek an adrenaline rush. Athena, though. She doesn't have many faults, but her fear of heights leaves her stunned and incapable of even basic speech. She nearly begged me to keep her on the ground. And there's no way they're separating Athena and me now that we've been reunited. *Nope.* Not a chance.

Besides, I needed a break from Nyx's questions. We had fallen into easy conversation while Athena and I took turns describing our childhood and recent lives together. Even Tryg cracked a few smiles when we talked about the wildly inappropriate and hilarious shenanigans we've gotten up to with our friend group over the years. But after a lull in the conversation, Nyx asked me more detailed questions about my life on Earth. He's been pushing me for information about my family and deeper interests, saying he can't be my friend if he doesn't know anything about me. I'm still torn between not wanting to expose personal information, wanting to be his friend, and wanting to skip all of that and jump straight to climbing him like a tree. The latter sounds more appealing each second. At least it doesn't require me to peel back purposely forgotten layers about my life.

I finally broke the silence when we passed damaged homes and land on the outskirts of Rioa's borders. Buildings made of shiny stones and sleek, colorful wood, now dilapidated and crumbling to the burned ground. The entire scene is a smudge of gray in this vibrant world. My heart hiccups, feeling such sadness that hundreds of *solliqas* were attacked for no reason. But a plague doesn't follow logic; it only follows the scent of despair.

I asked Nyx if there was this kind of damage everywhere in Majikaero. He didn't respond right away and had waited so long to speak that I didn't think he would say anything at all. Completely lost in the sea of charred homes destroyed by the *solliqas* who used to live there. Who never would be themselves again after caving into their monstrous forms. Nyx finally sighed heavily and stated that the plague has infected thousands of souls in random clusters around the realm. But that he isn't convinced specific groups of souls aren't being targeted.

The creatures we're riding quicken their paces to a canter,

aching to arrive and be done already. Tryg is barely restraining himself from lashing out at everyone. Eliina agreed to no bounded vines, but he would need to be surrounded by protectors and travel with a fellow *solliqa*. He's coiled up tightly and appears rather disturbed. Although, I can't blame him. Hadwin volunteered to travel with him to get back in Eliina's good graces, yet from what I can see, he has used this as an opportunity to provoke Tryg nonstop.

Daya rides up beside us. The shadows cast from dusk paint her hair a silky shade of brown.

"I'll get you and Athena set up in our rooms and then take you to meet some other healers," she says.

Nyx grumbles loud enough for everyone to hear. *Embarrassing*. Daya gets a teasing glint in her eye when she peers at Nyx. "Oh, no, am I interrupting your attempts at wooing her tonight? How will you manage to keep the romance alive?" she coos.

"Eira's supposed to sleep with me," Nyx grinds out.

Daya snorts. "Yeah, that's exactly what you'll be trying to do. She'll be staying with Athena and I these first few nights. And before you get all growly on me—Eliina might have gotten to you first, but did you seriously think the Council would allow you to sleep near us?"

Nyx's arms tighten; the only sign this question got to him.

"They wanted you to sleep in the dungeons," Daya continues. "But Eliina convinced them that if they want any of your, um, assistance going forward, then it'd be best to treat you with more kindness and respect."

"Ah, let me guess. We're sleeping outside," Nyx says drily.

Daya winces. I wonder if that's happened before. "Not quite. You'll be staying in rooms in between ours and a few of Eliina's main elementals and shifters. Each of you will also be required to stand in protection of Eira's door in shifts. I don't think that was the Council's demand, though."

Nyx huffs a laugh, his breath warming the back of my neck. A few loose strands blow to the side, and he carefully tucks them back into my braid.

"I figured as much. We would have one of us guarding her either way." He leans in closer and places a soft kiss where my neck and collarbone meet. "We won't let you out of our sight, sweetheart."

"And what if I need the bathroom?" I ask.

"I'm not one to judge someone's kinks."

I throw back an elbow, making Nyx chuckle. The low sound of his voice has my heart leaping and tickles something inside of me.

I'm hesitant to initiate another conversation with Nyx, but considering we're close to the city at this point, I suppose it won't hurt. And just because I'm asking him a question doesn't mean I have to reveal information about *me*. I reach out to feel the shadows at my side. With each step Ambra takes, they twitch in response, moving in their own dance pattern. It still surprises me that my hand can pass through them like smoke, but in a flash, they slink along my skin as if a liquid serpent.

"Have you always had the smoke and shadows?" I murmur.

Nyx stiffens, causing Ambra to jerk to the side. He clears his throat. "Yes, and no."

I arch an eyebrow and peer up at him. "Now who's being difficult about opening up?"

He rolls his eyes before setting Ambra on course again. "It's a sensitive topic for me. For any of us impacted by the plague. Consider how an illness feels in your body. You're constantly weighed down by fatigue and heavy exhaustion, your body hurts, and there might be specific symptoms you require a healer for. That is how this plague reacts except multiply the agony by a million. And it's not a mere weight in your body—it warps who you are, what you can even do with your *maji*. The plague connects to the darker forms of *maji*, such as the shadow work and smoke powers you've seen me use." He laughs to himself. "It's oddly fortunate for me, since I had the ability to wield shadows and powers of the night before the plague found me. I strongly connected to my mother's *maji*, though, and the ability to use fire. As you can see, all that's left of that is fucking smoke."

Nyx's eyes turn sadder by the second. "You miss your soul mother," I whisper.

His mouth twitches, fighting to stay neutral. "Who doesn't miss their soul caretaker? Although, I should consider myself blessed. Not everyone has found theirs or has been lucky enough to be born into their soul family, and they go their whole lives in other realms searching for this connection. I'm told it can turn any soul mad."

Before I know it, we're crossing a gold-plated bridge decorated with swirling black designs. The head protectors of our group take us down a side road that slopes away from the city's center. I can't bring myself to look away from the huge, suspended orbs and the few *solliqas* I see standing outside of flashy and vivid shops. A sweetened, savory smell wafts toward us, and the whole scene lures me toward it. I debate jumping off Ambra to go explore, but Nyx is ready for any escape attempts this time. He tightens his hold on me and gently turns my head to face the narrow road in front of us.

"All in good time, sweetheart. It's been ages since I've been here, but I still know this place like the back of my hand. I'll take you wherever you want to go. But not tonight. It's too dangerous."

"What's dangerous?" I ask, whispering against his hand.

"Your existence," he answers. "And what it means if you're connected to me."

Nyx swerves Ambra into a near-hidden tunnel branching off the side of a huge stone building. The outside of it thrums with iridescent light, power emanating in currents. Our tunnel is concealed between thick, winding trees. While they're not equally striking in colors, an ancient breeze whooshes through them and sends shivers scurrying through my body.

"We're taking a side entrance into the head Council building that can only be accessed through Eliina's quarters," Nyx mutters. "Most of this building has exceptional protective shields around it that would lash out at anyone in my group before you can even blink. We need to go to the door where Eliina can momentarily shut down the shield for us to enter safely." He lifts a finger, pointing to the trees looming above us. "Keep a mindful eye around these. They have eyes of their own and are *always* watching you."

"Then won't they tell the Council we've arrived?" I ask. *Of everything I've experienced so far, I can't believe I'm being so nonchalant about trees watching us. My breakdown is oncoming.*

"Depends on whose side they're on. Since they opened a pathway for us to follow, I imagine they're communicating with Eliina. But you can never really know who to trust here," he says.

How comforting.

We approach a multicolored, mossy doorway that flashes out of nowhere. A small scream catches in my throat, and Nyx has to catch me before I fall. Eliina materializes into her humanoid form from pieces of grass, soil, and twigs. She must have jumped from one piece of earth to the next the whole journey here. All it takes is pushing her hand against the doorway for it to yawn open for all of us to enter. I swear we enter an actual mouth with serrated teeth above and below us, waiting for the command to tear us to shreds.

Another few steps into the next tunnel, and a power erupts out from my core like a bomb. I helplessly fall back into Nyx's awaiting arms. My *maji* appears as a sultry light, buzzing around me and extending out, similar to the rays of a sun. Nyx's *maji* is a smoldering fire encased in shadows, dancing with the edges of my own. I giggle as if I had one too many glasses of wine. The top of the arched tunnel spins until it meets the earth, causing me to laugh even harder at the lunacy of it all. I hear a few other startled voices and rich laughter from behind us.

Daya and Delano are quick to swarm us, their eyes soaked in concern. "Shit, we forgot to warn you about that," Daya murmurs. She urges her *alklen* to stand even closer to us, her gaze sweeping over both Nyx and me.

"Are you both okay? Other parts of the Council building dim your *maji*, so Eliina created a spell to amplify it in her quarters. A few other Council members have done the same thing."

I'm too dazed to respond, drunk on the liquid power swimming through my veins. There's a roaring in my ears, and the only thing I can do is look at Nyx. My insides are shaken up, frothing and foaming over, and I'm overcome with an urgent desperation to jump him. His shadows aren't covering us. No, they're tangling with my light, his embers chasing my own.

A brisk wind eddies around us and doesn't dim the desire, but it snaps me back to focus on our current reality. My light settles back under my skin, and Nyx's shadows and smoke wrap closer around him. We don't break eye contact for several seconds, peering not at one another but into our souls. Into our higher selves. I'm met with a hardened wall of darkness, a challenge I'll have to tackle another day. I don't know what he sees inside me, but I imagine peeling one layer back, showing him flashes of my other friends from Earth. They're snapshots, but Nyx's eyes flare wide. He can see what I've chosen to share.

Nothing can dull the sea of feelings that have been awakened.

A small hand holds my wrist, and I know it's Daya without having to look at her. "I'm not trying to interrupt anything here. But we're still exposed in this tunnel and need to get to our quarters before anything else happens." Her voice is unnaturally soft, and I realize she doesn't want to offend. At this moment, Nyx and I must appear how they've imagined us—a banished prince and a lost queen.

I finally take in the rest of the tunnel. The healers and protectors and other *solliqas* we've traveled with, even Hauke, have their heads bowed slightly, baring their necks to us. Even Ulf and the other banished *solliqas* have fists placed over their hearts, giving us their undivided attention. *Eeek*. Eliina has one hand placed up against the next door while turning to face us. Her eyes shine with an emotion I can't place.

There are three people not looking at us. One is Tryg, who is actively staring at the opposite wall. *Alright, you don't have to bow down to me, but acting like a toddler? Really?* The other two are Athena and... *Hadwin?* They're both thrumming in green light and have the same bewildered expression on their faces. A few seconds must pass by before Athena abruptly turns to face me and offers me a grim smile. I arch a brow and give her my best *we-are-totally-discussing-this* face.

"I'm sorry about that," I tell Daya. "I didn't realize we were so lost in our power surge and connection. I know it's been a few minutes—let's keep going."

Daya smirks. "Time is never what you expect here, Eira. A few minutes can turn into hours for others."

Realizing her implication, a furious blush heats my face. *Were we seriously staring at each other for hours? Ugh.*

Nyx doesn't say anything, not even a snide remark, and Eliina and the protectors guide us to an area we can leave the *alklen* and *drekstri* to eat and sleep. He unloads both of our bags of supplies, slinging them on either shoulder, before plowing through the others to get to Eliina. He's acting jittery and uneasy, and Eliina gives him a knowing smile. *Why am I always left with more questions than answers here?*

"Nyx, I'll show you where your group will be sleeping," Eliina says, back in full business mode. "Daya, our team will bring Athena and Eira's supplies up to your room while you take them to meet the healers. The rest of you—you know where to go and what to do."

"Where will Tryg be? And supplies?" I ask her.

"He'll be in a special room next to where I sleep," Eliina says. Her voice is kind, yet her tone is sharp. On edge. "I refuse to lock him in a dungeon when he hasn't done anything wrong, but I want him near me, so I can keep working with his soul. He'll be safe, don't worry," she assures me. "And we had new weapons and coverings created for you."

Ah, weapons. Pointy, dangerous weapons. I suppose I'll have to get used to those. Right after I figure out my maji.

Athena loops her arm through mine and drags me in the direction Daya is walking in. She's acting a little *too* nonchalant. Narrowing my eyes, I tell her, "Don't think I didn't—"

"Don't," she says, keeping her body deceptively loose. "Not here. Let me figure it out first."

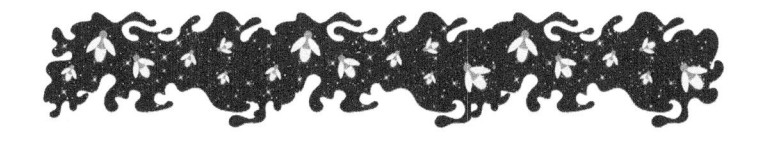

"Alright, these are some of our most powerful healers," Daya announces, pride evident in her tone. "We've got Stefanie, Takisha, Daglo, Daiki, Jasón, and Ebele. You've already met Daglo. And over there, I believe, are Lyo, Nomusa, Rahim, Cadence, and Alyosha. I'm not sure what they're working on, but you can meet them later."

Humanoid *solliqas* give us warm, welcoming smiles. The *solliqa* named Stefanie steps forward, encouraging Athena and me to come closer. Her flowing hair mirrors Astira's in its shades of red and gold. She peers at us with light green eyes, unable to hide her joy that we're finally here. Purple and red sparkling coverings drape in layers over her freckled skin, and I notice she's not wearing shoes. None of them are.

"Welcome to our healing quarters!" Stefanie says, her eyes lit with excitement. The area is enormous, full of natural hot springs and bathing pools, all enclosed in what might be a greenhouse that shields us from the outdoors. Tables and cushioned seating areas are scattered throughout, with supplies and books neatly organized on top of them. "Eliina sent a message that you were on your way. I can't believe that not only do we have our lost queen here with us but *two* healers. These are harsh times, and we need all the help we can get."

The others nod solemnly. It's obvious they're all weighed down by exhaustion.

"We don't mean to intrude," I say. "We can come meet you another—"

"No!" Stefanie interjects. "No, *please*. Please stay. It'll take time to learn our healing practices and how each of your specific *maji* works, and this is a perfect moment to start. We were about to immerse ourselves in the healing water to subdue our aching and overworked souls." She shakes her body slightly, as if she's willing the heaviness to leave her.

"All you need to do is enter the natural pool with us. These have healing, magical properties in them. It's said that the God of Healing, Berlind, and the Goddess of Healing, Eliina, joined the Goddesses of Water, Deniz and Derya, to construct areas in our realm where all *solliqas* could heal their souls. Not to get confused with our leader, Eliina, of course. She certainly seems to be a goddess at times, but she's not the Goddess of Healing I'm referring to. The one reason you wouldn't enter one of these pools is if you truly did not want to relax or heal. It's crazy, I *know*, but some *solliqas* resist restoring their souls to the point they won't even enter the healing pools to rejuvenate themselves. I'm not getting the sense that's the case for any of you. If you enter the pools by force, the water will scald your soul. It's meant to ensure that those coming here want to heal by choice. Oh, and don't worry, it won't take long to dry off in this heat. Daya, you can join us too, if you'd like."

Daya beams. "You bet I am! This is the best."

"Daya is a fiery shifter, but she also has secret healing talents." Stefanie winks at me.

Athena and I follow Daya and the others into the nearest natural pool. I gingerly roll up my silky black pants and remove my borrowed boots, not wanting soggy shoes and pruney feet. *Gross.* We ease ourselves into the pool, and I'm surprised by how warm the water feels. It's already working its magic on my sore muscles—riding all day has me wanting to knock out.

Stefanie strides toward me and kneels behind me. "Before we begin, I wanted to warn you about how entering the healing waters might impact *you* of all *solliqas*, Eira. I can't emphasize enough how impressive your healing powers were before. There's a high chance that you'll leave here restored, and at the same time, your *maji* will thrum wildly under your current skin. As your powers slowly awaken, don't be surprised if your emotions become untamed and feral. Your *maji* will present to you a range of surprises." She beams at me. "We can get started as early as tomorrow with healing sessions and exploring your *maji*. You let me know when you're ready."

I feel a surge of doubt and jitteriness waver within me. Athena squeezes my hand under the bubbling water, and I breathe out a sigh of relief. *I'm not alone.*

Nodding my head, Stefanie gently touches my shoulder before moving to another spot in the water. She and the others hum quietly and place their hands in front of them, keeping their palms up. Her lilting voice flows and twists around me while she chants.

"*Through our light, we make love possible. Through our love, pain can heal. Can be accepted. Can be set free. With both our light and love, we can meet the darkness where it's currently at. And show it that it can, too, be at ease."*

Between the warm, soothing water and the hushed chanting, their voices melodic and reverberating, I find myself fighting the urge to drift off to sleep. My *maji* flashes in small bursts around me, causing the water to glow, and forms a glove of protection around my abdomen and forearm. As if it senses where a lot of my physical pain festers. We all have a light around us. Even Daya has a red glow around her body. Smiling, I allow my eyes to close, taking in the feelings of acceptance and belonging this group of *solliqas* has already given me.

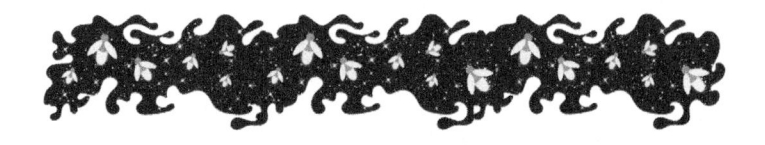

"Okay, I'll admit, that was amazing," Athena says on our walk toward our sleeping quarters.

"I *know*. I don't even remember when I last felt this relaxed," I say. "Not even yoga settled me like this."

Athena huffs out a laugh. "Yeah, well, maybe some of that had to do with our lovely *friend,* Shira."

Furrowing my eyebrows, I come to a halt. "Oh, fuck. Do you think the others are okay?" A smashing force of emotions barrel into me, especially when I consider how I last reacted toward Morgan. Spite had formed blisters along my heart, and now I crave to heal them. To tell Morgan we all make mistakes, and I still love her.

My friends' faces appear one after the other in my mind. Liv. Lyk. Jace. Astira. Ruse. All of them are still in the same realm as Shira. Not even realizing the danger they're in, the predator hiding underneath a lamb's skin.

"I haven't let myself fall down that rabbit hole yet. Tryg and

I were fortunate that you managed to find us. My heart won't be able to take it if she's harmed the rest of our friends, and they're trapped somewhere else. Or worse, born again into another life cycle during a time of war."

I grasp her hand, and we start to walk again. I refuse to respond, to even tread down that line of thinking. She's right. We're surviving, at best, in this new world, neither one of us succumbing to our heightened fears. If I think too hard right now about our friends dying, the sanity I've worked so hard to reconstruct will smash again into a million pieces.

"Ah, so the rumors were true," a coarse voice says. My *maji* immediately bristles, ready for a fight I wouldn't know how to win. I let out a low hiss. The bear marking throbs and prickles in pain, warning me I'm near an entity so nefarious and wrong.

Athena and I turn sharply to our left and see a *solliqa* walking toward us, a slight swagger to their gait. We were hoping we wouldn't see anyone. Even though Daya had stayed behind to talk more with the healers, she insisted that if we went quickly enough, we would be fine. She didn't sense any other *solliqas* out tonight, and the healing quarters are close to where we're staying. We're mere steps from Eliina's doorway.

This *solliqa* has an air of importance and is draped in navy-blue and purple robes. A shooting star flies across the cloth stretched across their chest. *Woah*. Sleek black hair cascades in waves down to his shoulder blades, matching his eyebrows and even darker eyes.

"The name's Namid," he says with a smirk as he approaches us. I have the urge to slap him from his condescending tone alone. "I get to meet the Almighty Eira, Queen of Light."

Athena goes rigid next to me, and I could kiss her for her unrelenting bravery. She places her shoulder a fraction ahead of mine.

"Cute," Namid snickers. "You have even less power than our lost queen, and you think you could protect her?" He gives her a cursory glance. "Although, one mustn't have wits to have beauty."

Snarling, I bare my teeth and feel heat simmer along my skin. Namid's eyes flare ever so slightly, his sole reaction.

Tsking, he says, "Careful, careful. You wouldn't want everyone knowing your weakness, now would you?"

Oh, yeah. I'm totally slapping this creep.

A bird flies in front of us, its feathers dark red flames. It morphs into a violently pissed off Daya. I notice her coverings have changed from the ones she arrived in—she's now wrapped in delicate white material with rubies shimmering under the floating orbs above us. Within seconds, Daru skids to a halt in front of us, covered from head to toe in gauzy green and brown. Both of them taking a fighting stance against Namid.

"How did you—"

"Your boyfriend," Daru grunts. "I also felt a sense of urgency, but he was going absolutely feral up there all night and insisted something was wrong."

All night? How long have we been out here?

"And I have superior senses," Daya says airily. She throws me a wink. "Namid, darling. What a surprise. Did you miss me?"

It's baffling to watch petite Daya facing down a *solliqa* so... towering. Intimidating. A creature clearly with a role of power and influence.

Namid cocks his head to the side. "This is rather interesting," he mutters.

"What are you doing here all alone? Surely you didn't think I'd be waiting for you," Daya continues, batting her eyelashes and tiptoeing toward him.

"I'd drown you, if I could," Namid sneers. "And someone needs to stay here. Not all of us can go slinking off on secret missions like Eliina. Everyone else is scattered around the realm to help mitigate fears before the Moons Cycle Festival. You can taste the nervous energy from this plague of darkness spreading. But that doesn't concern you."

Daya manages to look down her nose at him. "I *know* you're not saying the protection and care of our realm doesn't concern me. That you're not implying a *solliqa* not directly on the Council is beneath this information. Not *you*, who stated we're all equals, that the Council implements what's decided by us all."

Namid narrows his eyes. "Watch that tongue of yours."

"Or what?"

"Alright, stop it," Daru snarls. "Let's get back upstairs. It's been a long enough day—we don't need to invite more trouble."

Namid shifts his eyes to me. The darkness is frighteningly different from Nyx's. There's no smoky embrace. Just an unrelenting, tunneling night sky. A black hole without even one twinkling star to be seen.

"Be careful who you surround yourself with, little queen. You were already betrayed once by a close friend. I'd hate for you to make the same mistake again."

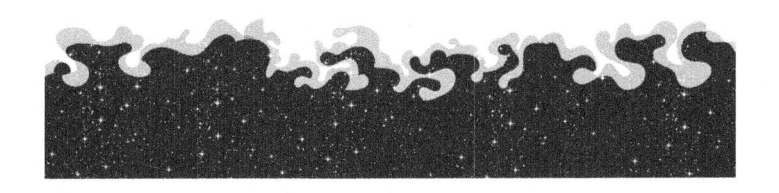

FORTY-ONE
Nyx

Darkness isn't always bad. But any rot that it's covering will always be found by the light.
-Queen Tyxmia of Rioa,
Land of Natural Cities & the Capital

Again. I've lost her again. The terror rips through me, tearing apart my human form.

After we were shown to our rooms, which I'll admit are more lavished than I thought they'd be for the likes of my companions, I felt a momentary calm wash over me. We'd fucking made it. And we were given a handful of Council-worthy suites to share. Each room is made of stone with colored branches snaking through the crevices, and the plush, black beds can easily fit three or four *solliqas*. Rugs of every color cover the smooth floors and are thick enough that my feet easily sink into their softness. I allowed myself to breathe deeply and soaked in the humid night air. Even my shadowed beast thrummed with its own twisted form of happiness, knowing Eira isn't too far from us.

But that all went to shit the second my shadows felt her

energy grow agitated. I wasn't able to process the fact that we're already this deeply connected because I was overwhelmed by her fear. Breathing in the knowledge my shadows shared with me, I was able to sense when a *solliqa* brimming with the wrong kind of darkness appeared too close to her. My instinct was to race out of this room and toward my Eira, but Odin, Ivar, and the others held me back. They insisted that making a rash decision and hurtling down the hallways to find her wouldn't end in anything good.

Erika had disappeared briefly before returning with Daru and Del. I'll never admit it out loud, but I'm thankful as fuck for Daru's obvious protectiveness of his queen. He took one look at me and gave the slightest nod before shifting into one of his many bird forms. Daru soared out the window, not caring if anyone stopped him. Just another reason for me to resent the fucker—he can come and go as he pleases, not impacted by the plague.

"Nyx, you've *got* to calm down. What are you going to do if Eira comes up here and sees a raging monster of shadows?" Ivar scolds. His black and gray coverings wrap tightly around him, and with each movement of his arms, they give him the very illusion of one of these shadows.

"You don't understand. I felt her in danger. I *experienced* the danger of someone else. I'm fucking *feeling,* and it's not anger, and I can't take this, I can't—"

The door pushes open and fuck, shit, fuck, *shit*. Eira is standing there with Athena, Daya, and Daru, but all I see is *her*. I sink to my knees in relief, parts of my deranged soul still swaying wildly around me. Eira runs to me and holds my head against her stomach, her beautiful, stunning light moving down my head and back.

"I'm back," she whispers. "And I'm okay. I'm safe."

My shadows wrap around her on their own, quivering slightly when they find fragments of her light. I distractedly trace the outline of her hand while my smoke forms a few critters along her fingers. Aching to bring a smile to her face, proof that she's here and happy.

"For now," Daru says. The rest of them walk into our suite, Daya promptly jumping onto a cushioned bed and waking up a dozing Zaya. She flashes her pointed teeth in response and burrows under one of the pillows. I swear if a cat could grumble, it'd be her.

Fraya goes impossibly more restless, and Ivar shuffles her to the other room. Neither of us want to cause a scene tonight, and he knows the closer Eira and I get, the more savage I'll become if I think she's threatened. My eyes dart around, taking in where everyone else is getting situated. Such an unlikely bunch of souls. A twist of shadows and burning light, coming together like two halves of a whole. Movement catches my eye, and I see Athena standing oddly in the corner, away from Eira and the others. She's backed up against the wall as if she's suddenly overcome with discomfort. *Weird*.

Daru gruffly shares what happened with Namid. "I don't trust any of this," he continues. "The biggest of the Moons Cycle Festivals will be happening here. I'm wondering why Eliina chose *now* of all times to come back here. There'll be no escaping it. We'll have to be vigilant and work together as a team to keep Eira safe."

"Ummm and Athena. And, you know, all of us. Like *me*," Daya huffs.

Daru rolls his eyes. "*You'll* be fine."

Daya sniffs dramatically. "Namid did act rather troubled to see me tonight. He might decide the festival's the night to rid himself of me for good."

"He'd be doing all of us a favor," Delano says dryly.

Hadwin clears his throat. I'd almost forgotten about him back there with him tucked away by our bags, especially with the way his dark coverings keep him hidden. "Daya does have a point."

Daya waggles her eyebrows and flashes Eira a smile, sticking her chest out. "I actually have two."

Odin snorts and pushes Daya over on the bed, making room for him and Erika to sit next to her. They're matching in their new black and blue coverings, a gift from Eliina, and they look striking with their dark hair and cerulean eyes. A terrifying team, yet Daya's not the least bit afraid. I'm not fully understanding these budding friendships, but I also don't give a fuck. If they all befriend each other, that's easier for Eira.

"So, um, why don't we talk about this with some drinks or food?" Hadwin suggests. "I have an idea why Eliina would want us in Rioa for this festival, but before talking, we'd be better off with something to take the edge off. Odin? Daya? Ulf?"

While they scatter around the room in search of hidden goodies, Eira gives me a questioning look. "Hey, where did Hauke go?"

Possessiveness startlingly deluges me. Erika knocks into my hip, breaking me out of my thoughts. "She didn't ask to fuck him. She asked where he *went*, Nyx."

Rolling my eyes, I turn back to face Eira. "Eliina likely sent him on a different mission. He probably traveled with us to help with protection and left immediately for the coast. The last I heard, he typically gets sent to check in with other members there and to deal with those leading Shymeira and Sunnadyn, the Lands of Tropics and Sunlight."

She opens her mouth to ask more questions, which now that I think about it, I should have told her more about the other regions here. *Dumbass. I find my* almaove, *and all my thinking goes straight to my dick.*

"I already found a few bottles," Ulf smirks and shakes a few large bottles in the air in victory. "It'll be the best part of our stay here, no doubt."

"Rude," Daya sings while she plucks a bottle out of his hand. "Alright, queeny dearest. Time for you to taste the wonders of *veina*. You might compare it to your, ah, what's it called? The drink made from grapes?"

Eira giggles, her laugh reverberating through me. "You mean wine?"

Athena slinks forward and throws an arm around Eira's shoulder. "We're pretty familiar with that." She winks, and Eira throws her head back with a hearty laugh.

It's incredible how open and carefree a soul can be when it's near a true soul mate.

Eira reaches for a glass of the *veina*, which means, regrettably, I have to untangle her arms from around my neck and release her. I'm nestled between her stomach and core, so close that I feel her heat luring me in. *Soon.*

She takes an extra glass and hands it to me. "Are you drinking some?" Her voice is more good-natured. Playful. Eira takes a sip and lets out a moan. She licks her lips, savoring the complex flavors of our *veina*. It has its own magical component, causing flavors of fruits and sweetness and sin to explode on your tongue. To awaken your senses.

Eira opens her eyes, a smile playing on her lips, already mischievous. I adore this side of my queen.

"I can," I whisper.

A low growl grumbles in my chest at the way she's staring at me. I can't help myself. I take her unmarked wrist and bring it to my mouth, letting my tongue roll gently over her veins. We don't look away from one another, and I see her breathing hitch.

"This drink is meant to infiltrate your veins with liquid passion, to free you of inhibitions. I'm not sure I need it when I can taste you myself."

Slowly, gently, overwhelmingly so, I push my teeth into her skin. Just enough to taste a drop of the blood thrumming through her veins. I savor the pleasant tang along my tongue. My cock jerks uncontrollably when her breathing increases, and she doesn't pull away. *Oh yes, I'll be worshipping your soul in more ways than one. So soon.*

I release Eira's wrist and stand to my full height, taking the glass from her. Swishing the *veina* before swallowing it in one gulp. Imagining it's her addicting blood.

"You're such a freak," Erika mutters and nudges past me, putting herself in between us.

"You're one to talk," Odin says. "Remember that *solliqa* bathing in the river? She undressed, and you used the water to—"

"That was different," Erika says quickly. "At least we were alone."

"Well, clearly not, if I had to watch you."

"I don't remember inviting *you*, but if you're into voyeurism involving your *sister*, then don't let me stop you." Erika looks gloriously ruffled, and I can't help but laugh.

"As much as I enjoy this conversation." Hadwin laughs, obviously loving how easily Erika can get riled up. "Let's try to stay focused."

Athena muffles a yawn. "Yeah, *let's*. I have an appointment in dreamland. Like, right now. It's been a horrifically long day."

Hadwin arches an eyebrow. "Who said it's been only a day?"

Athena squinches up her face and appears utterly perplexed, but no one offers an explanation. There's not a clear-cut definition we can give her. Time is a perspective, in Rioa more than other regions in Majikaero, an illusion draped over our senses. I'm not sure any *solliqa* can explain it to Eira and her friends sufficiently. They will need to explore their *maji* and experience the differences in time themselves as their souls continue to wake up.

"I think there are a few reasons we're being drawn to Rioa right now," Hadwin continues. "Remember, the Council wants us here. Eliina managed to find us first. They might be drawing our group here to unleash something on us or to see what we do with the heightened energies during the new moons cycle. *Solliqas* are often lost in chaos during this festival. And remember how we've all been losing control recently? All at once? This might be connected."

"Sure, I see your point," Odin says. "But why would Ellina want her team and Eira here?"

"Because of the heightened energies," Daya says. She's absently poking at Zaya's little paws, sharp claws curling around her fingers. "They can bring out our true selves and enhance our *maji*, so it's even more powerful and intense. This would be an advantageous reason to put Eira here, if she's now returned and is trying to figure out her abilities. Rioa is the most energetic location for the festival because of its proximity to the thinnest veil in time and space between multiple other realms."

"Yet Eliina risks placing Eira here when it's this dangerous?" Daru mutters.

"She would do this if she thought it's worth the risk," Erika says. "I don't know Eliina as well as Nyx or the others do, but it's clear that she cares for us and how we're treated. The fact that we're not locked up in the dungeons says it all. I don't believe she would place Eira and her friends here if it wasn't for a good reason."

"She might want to see what Tryg can do, too," Ulf grumbles.

Eira looks alarmed. "What do you mean, see what he can do?"

"He's not here with us, is he?" Ulf throws back another drink of the *veina*. "We don't know what'll happen. Eliina might want him near her when the moons change to the next cycle. See if it brings out his real soul."

"Enough. You don't know that for sure," Daya reprimands. "I agree with Erika. I think Eliina might want Eira here because she's the lost queen. And with the plague wreaking havoc across the realm, she *needs* her to find her healing abilities." She shoots Eira an apologetic glance. "No pressure, friend. But the darkness started sweeping across regions the second you left. It'd make sense that Eliina wants to find a remedy."

"And let's not forget the blessed word, *and*," Athena says softly to Eira. "Eliina can want to find a remedy *and* still care about you."

Eira screws up her face. "*Blegh*. We truly were meant to be healers. On Earth and in other realms."

The low murmurs of arguing can be heard from the other room, taking my attention away from this conversation. I try to stay focused, but irritation boils in my stomach. Ivar and Fraya should be out here listening to this. He shouldn't be having to babysit her because she's having an outburst. *Fuck it.* I need to take care of this before it undeniably escalates. I nudge my arm against Eira's and mumble something about returning soon.

"Keep talking, I'll be right back," I grunt at Hadwin. I shuffle past him and walk directly to the other room connected to this living area. By the glint in his eyes, he knows what's about to go down.

I block the rest of their conversations out, turning my focus on the scene in front of me. *Just as I fucking thought.* Fraya is crawling on the ground, her purple jeweled coverings now ripped in thin pieces. She's growling at Ivar, who has one of his arrows drawn and pointed directly between her big, glassy eyes.

"She's out of fucking control, man," Ivar breathes, keeping his eyes locked on his target. "She was completely fine before, even when you and Eira were eye-fucking each other in the tunnel. Out of nowhere, Fraya went *hysterical*. Eira came in after meeting the healers, and the new energy set her off. I forced her in here so we could talk about it, since there were no issues on the journey here. But *look* at her."

There's nothing for me to look at. I made myself crystal clear the other night outside the healers' tent. I don't *care* what kinds of emotions Fraya picked up from Eira and the others. I cast a net of shadows over Fraya's body, willing them to clamp down over her mouth. With a snap of my fingers, the net molds into smoking embers. My monster *craves* her screams, for her to wish she'd never met either of us. I squeeze my hand shut, and the smoldering net sinks into her skin. I'm going to cut her into a million pieces and serve her on a platter to the Council myself. Maybe to the *solliqas* attending the festival as a special treat. I'm going—

"Stop this," Eira says firmly. She places a hand on my shoulder blade, heat building under her palm. "All this power you throw around, like a child having a violent tantrum. I don't know what she did, and it doesn't matter. *No one*, human or *solliqa*, acts the way she's acting and is okay. Fraya needs help and to be treated as if she matters. Not abused and flayed."

"You don't know her or—"

"And you don't know *me*," Eira says, her voice coarse. "I'm still gathering my bearings here and am a little dazed from this magical wine, but I'm still me. I've often been described as quiet and too kind, and some might even say I let people walk over me like I'm a dirty, used rug. But I'll *not* tolerate this kind of abuse. You don't treat friends with such hatred because you're frustrated or angry or fed up. You said our souls are connected? Fine. Then show me you're not a sick abusive fuck. Make the right choice. Because this *is* a choice, Nyx. It's you giving power to your negative emotions. We all have the power to choose the right reaction. And listen closely—in no realm will I be tied to such a vile creature."

Each word slams against me harder, her voice being wielded as a weapon. I'm rattled to the core from the whiplash of her anger after laughing and teasing moments ago. I cower away from her overpowering brightness. Eira moves to stand with no fear before me, outrage and righteousness fueling the confidence it takes to fight against a creature such as myself. Her eyes are icy shards of fury, and they're targeting *me*. I'm stuck somewhere between festering shame and maddeningly lovestruck.

Athena darts out behind Eira, fearless in her own way. She wraps her hand around Eira's arm, pulsing with light, with the courage and trust only a true friend would have.

"Winter fox," Athena whispers. "Take a breather. Remember what Stefanie told you. You're fierce when faced with others' trauma, but that doesn't mean you usually react this sharply. Not without clarifying what's going on first. We don't know what Fraya has been doing, but she isn't necessarily the battered women we've worked with." She runs her hand down Eira's shoulder at a leisurely pace. The pulsing light dims just enough to see the outline of her arm again. "Your emotions might be kind of haywire right now, friend. Let's not fight how Nyx does."

"Athena's right. You shouldn't even be in here. I have this taken care of and said I'd—"

A stream of golden light slashes out at me. Athena shoots me a look full of exasperation and irateness. Horrified yet frozen in place, I watch as my monster extends out of me in a wave of darkness and makes the mistake of lashing out at Eira in retaliation. As if she's been doing this for decades, Eira raises a hand, and hot blue flames form a shield around her. *That same healing light will burn me. And damn it all, I'll gladly embrace the pain if it comes from her.*

Her shield starts off tight around her, fitting her body like a glove. It quickly morphs into a raging, turbulent barrier of flames. It rises higher and higher, unable to be contained, until even Athena has to dive out of the way or risk getting burned. The pillows and decorative chairs surrounding us are likely already catching fire, and the plush bed next to my right isn't far behind. Eira's blue flames roar around her, and I'm sure any *solliqas* wandering past the Council building can see them through the open windows. I find myself taking a step back, wincing as she focuses those crystal eyes of fury on me.

"Ah, so you're a coward, too?" she mutters. She might as well have slapped me.

Eira inhales deeply and blows out a breath. Light as shimmery as the night sky breezes out of her and swirls together with her flames. It coils and twists into the shape of a fox with crystalized arctic-white fur and bright gold eyes. I hear a gasp in the background, vaguely alerting me that we now have a full audience. The little fox stretches and leaps and is mesmerizing until I realize it's charging directly at me.

There's nowhere I can hide that won't end in agony; either I burrow myself and let my demonic beast take the hit or I embrace the animal running toward me. I already know, deep in my shredded soul, that if I turn away from Eira's healing light, she'll do whatever she can to break our soul connection. Even if it means hurting herself in the process. *And that will not do.*

If I can't accept her light and truth and face what I've become, then I don't deserve her.

Baring my soul, I ready myself for impact. Yet... it never comes. I don't sense anything at all. Her fox passes right through me, a piece of her spirit colliding with mine. My monstrous form is *screeching* around me, the ends of its grimy claws charring into nothing.

No, that's *me* screaming.

I jab my hands into my hair and pull as hard as I can. Seeking any form of pain as a distraction. Eira has me on the ground, thrashing and rolling in misery, in the unending pile of feelings I've buried. I give myself over to the raw pain. I choose this. *I choose her.*

The torture finally subsides after minutes, hours, days. It doesn't matter how long. Pain this excruciating doesn't follow a timeline. I manage to glance up at Eira, my queen, and am flooded with relief to see her eyes are not as hard now. Her skin is flushed with the glow of *maji*. Her hair falls in thick waves down her back, the tips still flickering with blue fire.

She's a fucking goddess, bathed in a fierce storm of radiance. She's what will set me free.

Athena lunges at her friend. Daya and Daru dive from the other side, and I watch, helpless, as they send any soothing and healing *maji* they can into Eira while Athena holds her still. She continues to glare at me, still not backing down from this fight or her heightened emotions.

"Look at you. A *solliqa* without a soul. But you're not powerless, Nyx darling. You're not something to be rescued. You can funnel all this power you use to hurt others into saving yourself. But you can't become what you should be because you're too attached to what you've been for so long," Eira whispers. Her voice cracks at the very end with distress. She's finally seeing what lays behind my physical form.

Eira manages to break free of her friends' hold, her breathing slowing down by the second. She crouches down next to me and gazes into my eyes. Such sadness wraps around her. Her stunning eyes are shards of pain and guilt and grief as she comes down from an emotional high. A force completely outside of her control as her *maji* was unleashed from within her. I long to hold her, to soothe her turmoil, but I can't even lift a finger.

"I won't apologize for the way my *maji* reacted tonight or for stopping you. It doesn't matter what Fraya has done—you don't give in to your darkness. I'm glad I saw your demon. Your monster. Whatever you want to call it. Nyx, I need you to really hear me. The longer you resist your pain, the longer you'll stay a monster. And the longer it'll take for you to have me."

FORTY-TWO
Eira

To heal is to cleanse the soul.
Both yourself and the one in your care.
-Page 11, Healers of the Light, Volume I

Me. I'm the one who can shield myself with light. It now takes the form of the stars, blue fire, rays of sunlight, and a fox. If I didn't wield the *maji* myself, I would never believe this. Ever. It felt as if my magic had a mind of its own—all I did was fuel it with my intentions and scattered emotions. I had no idea I could call a shield of blue flames or create a fox of light.

It was originally startling when that graceful fox formed from the *maji* thrashing and gathering in the pit of my stomach. She was *stunning*. I didn't fully feel like she was created out of magical powers—it was more of a piece of my soul connecting to a higher version of myself. I suppose I shouldn't be too surprised that a fox, of all creatures, made an appearance. It's what my closest friends have always called me. As if they've always known the importance this animal would have for me after Earth.

I'm lying in one of the most comfortable beds with blankets, the texture of pillowy clouds. Yet I only fell asleep last night out of pure exhaustion. Nyx passed out in that room, writhing shadows covering him. *As if that could hide him from me.* Ulf and Hadwin crowded around him while Odin, Erika, and Ivar checked on Fraya. Nyx didn't quite slice deep enough with his net, thank the gods. I get a weird vibe from the *solliqa*, but I don't want her soul destroyed.

And the more I think about it, the more confused I become. What did Fraya do to Nyx to warrant such a reaction? How did Nyx manage to break that poor soul and was it even him who did it? He said he's the Prince of Darkness, but something else nags at me. I wonder if it's possible that his darkness is covering his true abilities. If he has the power to *completely* destroy a soul from existence. And does that mean he could reverse it? Save a *solliqa* from total destruction?

Guilt gushes through me as I consider what Athena said to me last night. She was the one brave enough to try to stop me as my *maji* burst uncontrollably around me. Shame covers me in another blanket when I realize I *didn't* ask clarifying questions. I saw Nyx about to cut Fraya into tiny pieces, and my *maji* broke free of me in vengeance. It never occurred to me that I might be so used to going on the defense for a helpless *fim*, I didn't even stop to consider if the roles might be reversed here. If Nyx, my fucking soul mate, is the one who has been harmed. *Fuck. Ugh, I need to check myself more, especially if my emotions continue to throw me around in a tornado here.*

Round and round the thoughts go. I absently scratch at the bear marking. It hasn't gotten darker, but it certainly isn't going away. A sick part of me is glad for this, since it connects me to Tryg, and maybe that means he's okay. Most of me, though, is ready to rip off the skin itself if that means I'm set free and no longer in this vexing pain. I had a brief period of bliss when I first entered Majikaero, where my body wasn't hurting from invisible pain. Tryg's marking has made the blanket of fatigue return in full force and wrap around me tighter. And I'm *sick* of it.

I'm sick of a soul-deep ache that manifests as chronic pain. The burden of it weighing me down, carving right through me just below the surface. It better hide from the world while it can. Because it'll soon be smothered by my flames as if it never existed.

Zaya is waking up, grooming her delicate paws. Her form changed multiple times throughout the night. My favorite was when her fur matched my light blue flames, and she peered up at me briefly with eyes of molten lava. Her current eyes dilate, and before I can prepare myself, she pounces on my chest with playful energy. Not quite playful for me, though, when her sharpened claws dig into my skin. I yelp, scooting her off me, and the sound must wake Athena, who's curled in a ball next to me. She stifles a groan and rolls into the blanket, effectively cocooning herself.

"How are you awake?" she grumbles.

"Would you prefer for me not to be?" I ask.

"Don't be dramatic. I want us to sleep for another few hours."

"You already have," Daya calls out from the other bed.

"Time's a perspective, *yeah, yeah,*" Athena mocks under her breath.

"She's not a morning person, is she?" Erika asks from our shared bathroom. She's been in here for the last hour. Nyx was supposed to guard our room, but given his condition and the incessant urge I have to kill him at the moment, Erika switched out with him. She spent most of the night outside of our room and finally snuck in when the suns first crested over the distant mountains. The mixture of light sprinkled into our room like spilled oil, bathing us in dawn's greeting. I spent time gazing into the suns, mesmerized by their dual colors and the way everything sparkled under their rays.

Erika had gone right to the bathtub, unfathomably used to the beauty of this realm. I believe Nyx mentioned she has an affinity for water and needs to have contact with it every day.

"Why'd you let the mermaid in?" Athena mumbles into her woven pillow. Zaya's gnawing on the frayed edges. *Guess she doesn't need breakfast, then.*

I stretch my arms up above me and arch my back, mimicking my cat. "We better find you some caffeine before you insult the whole realm."

"I'm not insulted," Erika says loudly. "And Odin says breakfast will be sent up shortly."

"Odin? Where's he?" I ask. I'm sure I would have seen him.

"Oh, he told me up here." Erika taps her forehead. "It's a twin thing."

Athena is at least sitting up now and staring at Erika like she's turned into one of those leggy insects she despises. Her slow blink says enough, and I burst out laughing. "Come on, you. Let's clean our teeth and change."

"Change into *what*? I don't have a wardrobe." She brushes the ends of her glossy hair, the color matching the tattoos still decorating her dewy skin. She's still wearing the borrowed coverings from Eliina and glances down at their wrinkles in annoyance.

"And soon, you won't need one. Once you get comfortable practicing your *maji,* you'll be able to manifest your own coverings," Daya explains. "But in the meantime, you can have some of mine. This green dress will bring out your eyes, I think."

Athena huffs and untangles herself from the blankets. "I'll be in the bathroom. Tell me when the coffee arrives."

"She does know that we don't have coffee here, right?" Daya asks me.

Erika makes a face. "We still have ways to wake up in the mornings. She'll be fine."

Snorting, I shake my head. "Yeah, right. That'll be one of the first things Athena learns how to do here. Forget the coverings—she'll go straight for the coffee. Or better yet, if our friend, Jace, makes it here, that'll be his expertise."

Erika wiggles her eyebrows. "Oooh, who is this Jace friend? And I can think of a few *solliqas* who wouldn't mind if she's without coverings."

"I can *hear* you," Athena barks from the bathroom.

"Thank the gods," Daya chirps. "Then you can hear that I need you to go a little faster in there. We don't have all day, you know."

I playfully slap her arm. "Stop it. This is an adjustment for everyone but especially us. Show me what I should wear today."

Daya gives me a coy smile and holds up a matching shirt and pants set. Narrowing my eyes, I snatch them from her and quickly throw them on. *Good grief.* I can already tell this is revealing.

"Daya?"

"Yes, Eira?"

"Why do you want me dressing like a stripper?"

"I don't know what that is, but I totally approve if this is what it wears," Daya says.

Our room is at the top of Eliina's quarters and has huge circular windows facing the curving eastern mountain range. On the stone wall with our beds is a floor-length mirror framed with iron flowers and leaves. The woman, or I guess *solliqa*, staring back at me is *not* Eira. My skin is still glowing from using my *maji* last night. The white in my hair now has tiny streaks of bright blue and my eyes are blazing like the rising suns. This blue top changes shades in the light and I'm not even sure I'd call it a top. It's a scrap of cloth covering my small breasts and crisscrossing between my shoulder blades by mere threads. The pants hug tightly to my hips and slink down my legs, fitting snugly, similar to my favorite yoga pants and leaving little to the imagination. *Oh, that's a shame. I miss those.* When I shift, the coverings ripple with shades of blue.

Daya has me dressed as a living blue flame. And unnecessarily provocative.

"I don't want to argue about this," I sigh. "I'll wear this, but don't get used to it. This is not an outfit for a healer."

I keep staring at myself and swear I see Nyx's demon form peering over my shoulders. Shuddering at the memory, I try to turn to see how my ass looks in these new pants, but I still see him. He's a creature I couldn't even come up with in one of my incessant nightmares. Black pits of hell glower at me with smoke rising out of his curling nose and vicious mouth. There's no specific shape of his head and body, which is terrifying. Endless swirling movements of shadow and smoke, shifting rapidly in the air around me. Able to transform into razor tentacles or whetted claws, ready to shatter my soul. Even though it's shapeless, there's a thin lining of what could be skin where I see darkened blood moving as an oily, viscous substance.

I have no idea how I pulled out my *maji* or the fox last night. But for all our sake, I hope I can find them again today.

"You can heal people *and* look exquisite while doing it," Erika says with a pout, shaking me out of my thoughts.

A sharp knock at our door forces me to turn away from her and Daya. Which is fine. They're nothing but tiresome right now.

"Is that breakfast?" Athena calls out, her voice full of despair.

"Has she always been this needy?" Erika whispers to me.

I shake my head, not acknowledging her, and heave the bulky door open. Its tangled and knotty wooden edges nearly hit me in the face. Scowling, I expect to see Odin with scrumptious food and anything resembling some form of caffeine. Instead, I come face-to-face with a towering demon prince, fidgeting and avoiding direct eye contact.

It takes all my energy not to laugh. *Is this him stressed?*

"Um, hi," he croaks out. He hastily clears his throat.

Crossing my arms and cocking out my hip, I raise my eyebrows. It's good to make them squirm sometimes.

"I, uh, I wanted to come apologize," Nyx mumbles.

"For?"

"For last night."

"Which part? Being a violent dickhead to your friend or not participating in a conversation about my safety and then leaving to be said dickhead."

Nyx closes his eyes, his jaw spasming from how hard he's clenching it.

"I never apologize, you know. A prince can do what he wants, and a prince filled with terrorizing darkness simply takes and moves on."

"Thanks for the lesson. I'll be sure to remember that when I come across princes filled with darkness. You know, normalize the terror."

He breathes in sharply and exhales. When he opens his eyes, they're a dazzling combination of melted dark chocolate and caramel, threatening to pull me in. *But I can't.* One of the best things my eldest brother taught me before he vanished was to have respect for myself and that *no one* but me could demand it. If I want Nyx to take whatever we have seriously, and to truly value what I am, he must show respect. We both need to.

I let him continue to simmer in his thoughts. I already laid out all my moves; it's up to him to change the course of this game.

"I'm sorry," Nyx finally says. He's stiff as a board, but his eyes are earnest, full of panic and sorrow. "I'm so sorry. I didn't mean to hurt you or place *anyone* above your safety and well-being. There's a part of me, a large part, that doesn't care what happens to Fraya. She's taken advantage of me for years, even if you want to call it her own version of a demon, and I can't take it anymore. *Any* of it. Her behaviors, the stinging grief, the constant complaining and need for blood and the thrill of death. It's all too much."

An inky tendril of smoke curls around my pinky. Testing my reaction.

"I'm sorry if it seems I wasn't taking the conversation seriously. I just..." he trails off, shoving a hand into thick, dark locks. "I'm all over the place. Fear is driving a lot of what I do at this point, which, unfortunately, feeds the demon within. I *know* I fucked up. But I want to fix this and get better. Eliina and the healers tried before I was banished, and I'm telling you, *nothing* has worked. I don't know what to do, Eira. But I'll do it." He grabs my hand, his palm surprisingly clammy with nerves. "*Anything*. Everything. Name the price, and I'll pay it if it means you'll give me a chance to make this right."

My heart twists at what I must ask of him. But I need to know.

"What if the payment is what you think you are? Every drop of blood from your damaged soul?" I ask.

"Then it's yours," Nyx rasps. He steps toward me, and I instinctively take a step back, leaning against the stony wall. Layers of ivy twist and zigzag under my uncovered spine.

"I'll prove it." His voice skims down my neck, stroking my sensitive skin. "You can take me to the healers' pools today. Right now, if you want."

The tightness around my heart eases a bit at his willingness to get better. I know the process of discovering my *maji* is out of my control, but I want to show him that I'm willing to work on myself, too.

"I'm sorry, too," I whisper, not breaking eye contact. "It wasn't right what you did, but I should have asked you more questions before attacking you. I'll work on restraining my *maji* when my emotions jump off the cliff into insanity."

Nyx has an unreadable expression on his face as he watches

me. He gingerly twirls a lock of my hair around his fingertips and shadows, keeping his mask in place.

"But maybe I want to jump off that cliff with you," he whispers.

Someone huffs up the stairs near us, and when I peek over Nyx's shoulder, I see Odin precariously balancing trays of food and decanters of bronze liquid. He gets to the last step and lets out an exasperated sigh, shifting his weight to keep the trays upright.

"Oh, yes, please continue to watch at your leisure," Odin mutters. "Feel free to not help me carry this obnoxious amount of sustenance my equally obnoxious sister requested."

Nyx's previous sincere expression morphs into a hardened mask. He stares blankly at his friend.

"Really?" I ask, squirming out of his arms that cage me in, careful not to touch him. I gingerly take the two glass decanters off the top tray.

"What? It's not my fault he didn't ask for help before. I was with him before I came to speak with you," Nyx says.

Odin shoots him a scathing glare. "That's because you left while I was talking mid-fucking-sentence, you loon."

Nyx's lips tug into a devilish smile. "Then maybe next time you'll ask me quicker." He takes one of the decanters and steals a twisting roll-shaped item before Odin or I can stop him, shoving it into his mouth.

"You're impossible," Odin mumbles. "Good riddance to you. Eira, you'll need all the luck you can get."

I push my shoulders into the massive door and find Athena, Daya, and Erika scrambling to get out of the way. *Of course they were pushed up against the door, straining to hear anything juicy.*

"I come bearing gifts," I announce, shaking the decanter lightly.

"What's that?" Athena's vision homes in on the liquid.

"Similar to your idea of coffee," Odin says. "We call it *einral*.

It tastes rich and creamy and helps you shake away any remnants of sleep or exhaustion."

Athena pounces on me and plucks the *einral* out of my hands, rushing to the tables next to the huge windows. Snickering at her caffeine obsession, I turn to take the tray from Odin and promptly push Nyx out of the door. *An apology doesn't mean he gets to share my food.*

"I picked out the best food I could find," Odin tells me. "The twisted ones are like your bread rolls with spices. These here are a tangy fruit wrapped in both dark and lean meats—don't give me that look. You need to try it before you judge it. The ones right here are made from grains and thick sugary liquids. There should be another few savory options with what you'd call vegetables and eggs, I think." He shrugs and sets the few steaming trays down on the long wooden table between our beds and the doorway. "I'll be down in the library with Eliina and the others. She said she didn't want to disturb your first night of sleep here, and you can come to her whenever you're ready."

Odin turns to leave but stops. "Oh, and don't worry about Fraya. We already informed Eliina about what happened. Fraya will be fine—she's with the healers right now. Eliina was, dare I say, overwhelmingly thrilled to hear about your fox. We asked if she wanted to see you, and she said she would at some point today and preferred for you to rest first."

Nyx waits a beat before stepping forward again into the room and handing me a wrapped parcel. I'm trying to figure out where the hell it came from since he's dressed in ridiculously skin-tight black coverings and doesn't have any bags with him, but he doesn't give an explanation.

"I, um, also brought this for you," he mumbles, acting shockingly shy.

Giving him a suspicious glance, I regretfully put down the sugared citrus roll dipped in honey and lick the few crumbs off my fingers. *Divine.* I delicately unwrap the parcel and find a thick, leathery bound book. The title is written in looping, polished writing: *Healers of the Light.*

"It's one of my favorite books Eliina had me read in the Council's library," he explains. "When we stopped to rest during the journey here, Athena had mentioned that you adore books."

I glance over at Athena chugging down the *einral,* and she gives me a shifty look.

"But if you don't want it, I understand," he adds hastily. "I thought you'd like to read about some of the powers you used to have and what's been written about you."

"It's... this is lovely. Yes, thank you," I reassure him. "I adore reading, and maybe a chapter in this book will help me when it comes to healing you."

Looking relieved, Nyx nods and backs away toward the door. "I'll be around the downstairs quarters. Let me know when you want to go to the healing pools today."

He abruptly leaves, as if any more time spent in this obviously *fim*-dominant room would push his nerves over the edge. I decide to dig into the breakfast Odin brought, so I can get on with the day and figure out what I'm doing with Nyx at the pools. I don't take more than a step before Daya and Erika squeal like little piglets. *Those sneaky gremlins.*

Squinting my eyes, I give them both a once over. "What?"

"He brought you one of his *favorite* books," Daya sighs.

"The big, bad demon prince wants you to learn about your past and how to heal his bleeding heart," Erika says dreamily.

"And he didn't even punch the wall," Daya adds with glee.

Oh, sweet gods. They're swooning as if hormonal teenagers.

"Alright, you busybodies. Attempt to get a grip. Tell me which roll I should try."

FORTY-THREE

Nyx

*The deeper the level of hurt, the worse it will feel.
But it will result in longer lasting healing than
simply skimming the surface.
-Correspondence from Stefanie, High Healer of Rioa*

"Try to go in with an open mind today," Eliina urges me.

I'm pacing a hole in one of the downstair rooms, doing everything I can to get a fucking grip on reality right now. I purposely chose this room because of all the damn plants and the crystals hanging from the starry ceiling. Anything to soothe the rising anticipation of going through the healing process. *Again*. Eliina walked into the room rather briskly, her white and gray robes shimmering under the crystals, claiming she could feel my nervous energy from the archives of the library. She left the others to continue researching any information about previous plagues of pain and darkness and any connections to their special *maji*. She said they could explore more of Rioa after acclimating to her quarters and the enormous library first.

I personally think she brought us here for a specific reason, and touring the Council building and city center is not on the schedule.

"I don't want to fuck this up again," I grit out. "I didn't think it would be *easy* to rebond with her soul, but gods, she's giving me hard lines not to cross. I'm not perfect. There's no way I won't screw it all up. And her *fucking maji* was as fervid and manic as I felt."

"She knows that, Nyx," Eliina says gently. "But she has to lay down firm boundaries of what she can and can't accept. She needs to see that you're serious about changing and diving into the healing process. As I'm sure you saw last night, it's one of the most painful experiences you'll ever endure. Even more so in this realm. Your soul is already stripped bare in Majikaero, and no amount of abilities or disguises or coverings can fool a healer. Especially not one with her level of *maji*, even if she's in the midst of discovering what that level is. It'll take her some time to master her powers and the intensity of them when she's upset."

"I'm scared," I whisper into my hands. The sound is muffled, but I know Eliina can still hear me. "It felt like she was dragging out my soul into the open."

"Which I'll continue to do until you're healed," Eira says from the arched doorway. Her long locks are plaited back in a series of braids, woven into a messy bun. The light from the suns causes the blue streaks in her hair, eyes, and new coverings to shimmer the same as flames.

How is it possible to be wildly scared of someone's strength yet simultaneously want to bend her over and fill her with my dark power?

"That's the tone of a queen," Eliina says. Her face is smug. Hopeful.

Eira chuckles and shakes her head, her matching blue earrings dangling like chimes. "We'll see about that." Zaya weaves between her feet, staring up at me with her mismatched eyes. "What will you be up to today? I thought I would be with you more. And I have many questions about this cat of mine."

Eliina scoffs and rolls her eyes so hard, I'm surprised they don't get stuck. "We will be spending quite a bit of time together, fear not. There are many Council matters I must attend to, and heaven forbid Namid has to do *anything* on his own."

Snickering, Eira asks, "Bane of your existence?"

"His attention-seeking is the bane of the realm."

Eira barks out a laugh and sweeps her crystal eyes back to me. She peers up at me, and a no-nonsense look is now plastered across her face. "Let's go."

We walk in silence through the winding golden stone and dark crystal halls that lead to the rest of the Council building. Zaya's paws barely make a sound, and she stays alert at Eira's side. The maze-like design can be suffocating, even for a *solliqa* formerly living around here, and I can scarcely imagine how Eira is feeling. Smooth, marble floors turn into a stony path that takes us outside into the muggy air. It's the kind that sticks to your skin, a warning that a blistering heat is on its way. We continue through the haze, both of our bodies drinking in the morning sunlight before it becomes too much to breathe, let alone be outside.

I send a plume of smoke toward Eira, this one taking the form of a running *alklen*. She swats it away but can't hide the washed-out smile tugging at her lips.

Silence can be nice. Comfortable. Easy. The key word is *can*. I used to enjoy it, but ever since the darkness afflicted my soul, I long for any sound that isn't the cold silence my demon forces through me.

Reaching for anything to say to Eira, I, *of fucking course*, choose a question I most certainly don't want the answer to. "Do you think I'm a villain?"

Stupid. You don't want to know that. You could have asked her literally anything *about her interests and you chose that? You deserve the pain coming in those healing pools.*

Eira twists her mouth to the side, lost in thought as we approach the healers' quarters.

"You know, forget I—"

"I think the better question is, do *you* think you're a villain?" she asks.

"Why would that be better?"

"Because why else would you ask me if you didn't already think that about yourself?"

Flustered, I try to turn the conversation back on her. "But I don't care what *I* think, I care—"

"Maybe you should," she says softly. "If you care about *you*, it'll be easier to plunge into your resistance to healing."

"How did you—"

"I'm a therapist," Eira winks. "Call it my superpower."

A small group of healers are working with *solliqas* afflicted by the plague in some of the pools, the heated multicolored water churning around them and swishing rapidly. I immediately feel self-conscious and regret my offer to do this today.

"Heya, Eira!" A healer with red, wavy hair approaches us. "Oh, and look at this cutie." She bends down to pet under Zaya's chin, the cat purring in pleasure. Her small eyes glow like a sun, and her form grows bigger for a split second, and then she settles back down again.

"Stefanie," Eira greets her with a nod and bright smile. "It turns out our meeting last night was rather fruitful. New abilities have already awakened, and I'm here to see if I can work on Nyx."

Nodding with a knowing smile, Stefanie glances my way. Her light green eyes like glowing suns from a faraway world. "I thought that might happen. The longer you work with us, the more that you'll discover. What did you experience last night?"

"Oh, you know, the usual magic. Forming a shield of blue

fire around my body and sending a fox made out of *maji* through the Prince of Darkness."

Stefanie makes a choking sound. "Oh, yeah, the usual indeed."

She points to a more secluded pool in the corner of the building with pink and orange plants forming a border around it. "Maybe let's try out that area today. If this is one of the banished ones, we don't want to place him in such an open and vulnerable space."

Eira stares at her for a second before Stefanie clarifies, "Oh, we're all going to do this together. It'll be your first healing session, after all. While you'll continue to learn healing chants and ways to cleanse yourself with the rest of us, I or another highly trained healer will be with you during any one-on-one sessions. Each healer's *maji* is *quite* different, and we'll unravel what you can do together."

Eira gets a guarded look, but it's gone in a flash. She rolls back her shoulders and lifts her chin. I don't notice the forced determination in her eyes because I'm too focused on the way the movement makes her chest rise. Her covering doesn't leave much to the imagination, and I'm practically salivating at the chance to lick her unexposed skin. The thought sends a surge of heat down to the tip of my cock.

Stefanie clears her throat, her eyes lighting up with mischief. "You might want to get your thoughts in order before going into the pool with her. And she's, ah, she's waiting for us."

Embarrassment flares against my cheeks. I'm not usually this hyperaroused, but *fuck,* do I need to taste her. I'll take any part of her at this point. Even the part of the human body I'm most disgusted by—the *feet.*

I adjust myself and head toward where Eira's standing in front of the rising plants. The tips of the leaves curl above her in an arch, framing her like a picture. She gives me a curious look, obviously unaware of my thoughts becoming dirtier and dirtier the more I'm around her. *Thank fuck for that. Or this pool experience will get awkward incredibly fast.*

Stefanie follows behind me as I make my way toward Eira. My queen turns to fully face me, definitely eager to get started.

"I'm not sure if you practice this concept here, but I was thinking of us trying out some breathing exercises together," she says while assessing the glimmering pool. Streaks of colors melt together like a swirling portal.

"Exercises on how to breathe? I mean, we're already—"

"Shush," she slaps my arm. "Exercises on how to calm our minds. We can talk about that at a different time, when you're not acting like a dumbbell." Stefanie snorts next to her. "Take your shirt off and get into the water."

"Yes, my queen," I purr. I shuck off my shirt in one fluid motion. "Want my pants to come off, too?"

Eira audibly gulps and tries to avoid looking at the hard-earned muscle down my chest and abs. *Adorable.* For a blissful few seconds, I don't even notice that I'm showing her all the swirling black vines and veins that cover my whole torso.

"That won't be necessary," she says stiffly.

"Yet," I add with a wink.

Chuckling at how ruffled she acts from taking my shirt off, I take a few steps into the circulating pool and let myself sink down. It's warm enough to ease any tension from my soul but not hot enough to burn me.

"When you're done drooling, feel free to join me," I call out to her. Inhaling sharply, I float on my back in the middle of the pool, letting the small waves lap around me. It's a good thing she's here with me. This water is acting as a lullaby, and I could see myself drifting off to a permanent sleep if I focused my destructive *maji* on myself.

Eira releases an exasperated sigh, and I crack open one eye to see what she's doing. I can't help but smile. She's standing next to Stefanie with her hands on her hips, sending me a scathing glare. Zaya followed us to this spot, her tail swishing in annoyance at me. With each passing minute, I'm more and more convinced that this cat is a spirit guide for her. Or maybe a guard, ready to lash out at any attackers dumb enough to approach Eira.

Stefanie guides them both over to where I'm soaking in the water. Her light blue coverings barely cover her shoulders and glide down to just above her knees. They're much more conservative than what Eira's wearing, but they shimmer in similar ways. As if they're two flames dancing together toward the healing pool.

"We all connect with the earth and our *maji* in special ways," Stefanie begins. "Healing *maji* can take the form of different elements or abilities. It's not about the element that's used, but rather the natural ability to sense any kind of pain in the soul and be able to eliminate it. I believe one of the reasons yours has always been exceptionally strong is because, historically, you connected to the lands of fire and sunlight. You have the capacity to physically burn the pain and damage from a soul. Other *solliqas* can also connect with fire or sunlight, but I haven't met many who can connect with *both*. Let alone use blue fire."

Eira hums in response and frowns down at her hands. She's examining them as if she's waiting for something to come out of them.

"So, how do I tap into my *maji*? I didn't call for it last night. It came to me as I became more heated with emotion. And I had almost *no* control."

Stefanie takes Eira's hands in her own. "It will become easier as time progresses and you adapt more to your *maji*. It needs to become an extension of who and what you are, not a separate piece of your soul. I'm going to have you breathe in and out a few times for me. When you breathe in, notice the buzzing of energy under your skin, trying to break free. When you exhale, focus on breathing out this energy."

Eira gives her an annoyed glare for a second before closing her eyes to start the breathing exercise. *She doesn't like to do them either, huh?* Nothing happens for the first few minutes. She breathes in and out, the tight lines around her face smoothing out with each exhale. Time stands still while I watch her take a final deep breath in, and as she exhales, sparks of light and a flash of blue flame pushes out of her skin.

"I did it!" Eira squeals excitedly.

Stefanie beams. "We're going to practice this a few more times before you get in the water with Nyx." She looks at me over her shoulder. "You just keep floating there. Don't bother anyone."

"Who am I going to bother? The plants? The water?" I ask.

Stefanie rolls her eyes. "I wouldn't put it past you."

We watch in silence as Eira continues to connect with her *maji*, controlling how it comes and goes with her breath.

"This is you tapping into your magic," Stefanie tells her. "You need to become one with it. Before you know it, you'll be able to call it to the surface in one inhale, in a heartbeat. You'll merely think of what you want to do, and it'll move with you."

"How do I even know what to do with it right now? How can I help Nyx if I'm only now learning how to manage it?" Eira asks.

Stefanie giggles. "I have a feeling you won't enjoy this next part. Part of the reason it's important to become one with your *maji* is because your soul will sense what a *solliqa* needs, and your *maji* will then create it. For example, do they need to heal a minor bruise from a loved one's words? Are they overcome with anxiety? Are they infected with the plague and need support not spiraling deeper? Their situation will determine what you'll do with your *maji*. Fortunately, you've already worked as a healer on Earth, so you should be able to pick up on what a soul might be needing in that moment. It also never hurts to ask them." Stefanie turns Eira toward the pool. "When you enter the water, peer inside your soul and see what it recommends for you to do today. No day is ever the same. Really ask yourself what you think Nyx would benefit from the most right now."

"What if I fail?" Eira whispers.

"You never fail," Stefanie says. "There will be more successful healing sessions than others. Your intuition might steer you in the wrong direction at times. The *solliqa* might communicate what they want, and it turns out they didn't fully understand what their own soul needed. Regardless, you'll learn something new each time and develop a closer relationship with the *solliqa* in pain. You'll learn together what needs to be changed, if anything, and how they want the next session to go."

Eira steps into the warm water, ripples of it dashing out to greet me. She sighs in contentment for a moment before peering at my floating body. Stefanie crouches down near the edge of the pool.

"Continue to take deep breaths in and out. Remember, you won't harm him. Your *maji* will strike out at his pain, and in Nyx's case, his monstrous form hidden within. He'll scream in agony, and for once, that's *good*. Your *maji* will sweep through his current form and can do a number of things, such as detangling the different pain, triggering memories that need to be addressed, burning through the trauma, and healing his soul scars with warm sunlight. The healing water with all of its mysterious properties will absorb into your skin and amplify your own healing abilities."

Eira wades further into the water and stops a few feet away from me. Clearing out my thoughts, my stomach rises slowly with the breaths I take. An uncomfortable pressure tugs at my core. It takes a moment to process, but I hear Eira muttering to herself, and there are lights and colors changing around her, as if I'm staring through a prism. I angle my head to get a better view of what she's doing, since the more time that passes, the more unbearable this feeling gets.

"*Good*, Eira," Stefanie encourages. "Keep breathing out your *maji* and light toward Nyx. It's connecting with him and seeking out which pain to address first. Trust in your powers. Doing so will allow them to trust in you."

The fox I saw last night peeks out from around her and leaps off her shoulders. I wince, preparing myself for it to jump through me again. Except, *fuck me*, it doesn't. It stands on the fucking water peering up at Eira while she moves the water with her hands.

"I think I understand what my *maji* is telling me," Eira says in awe.

The water rises and bubbles and forms into the shape of a creature. *Shit*. Eira's hands roll in a circular motion until glistening yellow and blue scales lock in place in the form of a hissing snake. It leisurely rises above the water and opens its mouth wide at my fucking feet.

"You must allow yourself to be swallowed whole, so another piece of your pain and grief can be destroyed and released," Eira says, her voice melodic. "You need to shed a layer of your darkness and be *willing* to let it go. To thank it for what it has taught you and to release it into the water. To let my snake take the misery with it."

"Very clever, Eira," Stefanie whispers. "Keep going with it. Allow your *maji* to travel to Nyx now."

The snake slithers up my buoyant body, and I watch my body lock up as its fangs glide along my dark skin. Not quite grazing me, yet entirely too close for comfort—toying with my nerves. Its scales glint in the reflected sunlight, giving the appearance that it's smoldering from the inside out and will breathe fire down my body like a horrific sea dragon. The moment it covers my face, my body jolts in panic. *I'm inside a fucking snake made out of water. The* solliqa *I've already fallen for and am connected to has created a snake out of water. And instructed it to swallow me.*

"Calm your breathing, Nyx," Eira's voice skitters over me. "Allow yourself to let go. What has this next layer of pain taught you? Why are you holding on to it so tightly?"

I highly doubt my breathing is even remotely controlled, but I center my thoughts on her question. The first thought that comes to me is that I *deserve* to feel pain and to be a monster. This could be teaching... *fuck*. This could be teaching me that if I believe the pain is deserved, then a part of it might be trying to hold me accountable for an atrocious thing that I've done.

Well, many atrocious things. I've harmed *so* many since I was first declared a liability by the Council, a sinner with no ability to repent. I've given in to the rage and thirst for revenge more times than I'm willing to count. I'm not sure if it's something specific or not yet, but I know that this view of myself isn't going to serve me anymore. It *can't*. I have to at least *try* to hold myself accountable while not being this cruel to my soul. And to others. And gods, not to Eira.

The snake suddenly meanders up above my head, and I sense it's taking a layer of my skin with it. At first, this feels relieving, as if it removed the oozing pus from an infected wound. Then lightning strikes my soul. I experience the full brunt of Eira's burning light against my raw, exposed skin. My soul. The pain is tremendous, yet brief, before I let go completely, sinking to the bottom of the pool.

Muffled voices waft around me in hushed and urgent tones. I might still be alive and resting on the sandy floor of the pool, nestled in its warmth. Yet I don't feel suspended in water. No, that's firelight rippling against my skin. My face. The heat is nice but different from the healing water. Fire can burn, wild and uncontrollable, but it can also cleanse and purify. It can remove the rankling infection most can't recognize until it's too late, until their spirit's anchored down by its unremovable weight.

The voices become clearer and must be nearby. Squinting my eyes open, I can tell I'm in the healing quarters still, and I'm wrapped tightly in a bundle of blankets. I feel like a swaddled fucking baby. The others will never let me hear the end of it, and if I know my sassy queen, it'll be one of the first things she tells them.

Eira's outline comes into focus first. She's huddled close to a few of the other healers, and snippets of their conversation carry over to where I'm lying.

"... *maji* must be connected to multiple elements if you could move water *and* the light at the same..."

"... try using sounds similar to Cadence next..."

"... light amplified by suns or moons..."

"... mark... on fire... won't stop and horrible..."

"... healing yourself must be... it's a priority..."

"I always... hard to focus on me... will try... afternoon."

Their words funnel around me until I'm dizzy, the world swaying even with my eyes squeezed close.

"Eira?" I rasp, coughing.

Eira flies to my side in a heartbeat. A mixture of worry and a feeling akin to affection crystallizes in her eyes. The fact that she's concerned makes my heart flutter. Her previously plaited hair lies in a damp heap down her back.

"How are you doing?" Eira asks. She brushes a few strands of my hair out of my face and retucks a blanket against my side.

"It's—It's hard to describe," I say. "I think a part of the weight has been lifted. I'm starting to recognize how heavy the rest of the darkness feels inside of me."

Eira looks momentarily overjoyed and beams down at me.

Between her smile and the fire reflecting in her blue and silver eyes, my breath catches in my throat. *She's so beautiful*.

"Healing is a heavy battle," she says, nodding her head. "But the fact that you feel that way is promising."

I try to sit up, and Eira hastily removes the outer blankets, the ones she meticulously tucked against my body. No longer bound by them, I realize that I'm different. It's like I can take a full breath.

"So, a snake?" I ask suspiciously. *She and Hadwin are going to get along just fine.*

Eira looks nothing but amused, and her laughter echoes around us. "You bet! I called to any spirits connected to my *maji* that could help you shed one of your layers, and she immediately slithered forward. Wasn't she precious?"

This *fim* does nothing but keep me on my toes. If she described *that* as precious, I can't wait for her to see what Erika and Odin can do with their *maji*.

"And can you believe I did it?" she squeals. "I know it'll take time to do more with my powers, but I was able to remove a thin layer of your pain on my first time."

I smile up at her. *Of course* I can believe she did it.

"What time of the day is it?" I try to glance outside, but the healers purposely designed this part of the building to remain dim and well-hidden.

Eira snorts, shaking her head in amazement. "I think it's about evening, but I can't be sure of time in this realm. You and your friends continue to remind me of this." She sticks out her tongue at me, and I'm struck with the sharp need to suck it.

"We still get morning and evening here, sweetheart. The way time moves depends on the one viewing it," I tell her.

"Oh, yeah, that's easy enough to follow."

Smiling, I push myself up and reach my hands overhead, stretching out any kinks in my humanoid form. "I know it's only the beginning, and maybe part of the reason is because you're, well, *you* and not part of the Council. But there might be some hope for me." I take one of her long strands of glowing hair in my fingers, letting it run through them like fine silk. "There's a lot to share with you about who I was before all of this started. Who I dreamed to be on the island of Drageyra and what I'm hoping to change with the Council."

Eira cocks her head to the side. "You have sway against the Council?"

I bark out a laugh. "Not as much as I thought, or I wouldn't be in this position. Before the plague consumed me, I was leading a proposal to change who gets to be on the Council and whether they must be Elders. A number of *solliqas*, including my soul parents, supported my views. I understand that souls don't necessarily age as they do in the earth realm, and time moves differently here. But other *solliqas* should have the opportunity to be a part of this kind of leadership. Or at the very least, there needs to be a change in how the decisions are being handled. I was told to prepare for the eventual position of King of Drageyra. Yet, what good will that do if I can't make changes where it counts?"

Eira grips my hand and gives me a small smile before reweaving her hair back into a braid. "One step at a time. We need to move backward and heal all your layers before we can jump back to this present moment and then to the future with these plans of yours."

I nod my head and roll my muscles out again. "Yes, my queen," I say with a wink. "*Presently*, I'm feeling oddly refreshed, my little fiery queen. May I take you to see one of my favorite places in Rioa? With the moons coming out soon, it'll be glorious. I'll take you there quickly."

Eira glances at her attire warily. It's completely unnecessary. She could walk around caked in mud, and she'd be as lovely as the vibrant moons tonight. "Where will we be going? Should I go change?"

"No, there's no need," I scoff. "We'll be sweaty soon after arriving and you are beyond stunning the way you are."

A pretty blush colors her cheeks, and I wonder if it tastes as good as it looks on her.

"You, on the other hand, might prefer to stay back," I lean down to tell Zaya. Part of me feels incredibly stupid for talking to a cat, but the larger part of me knows there's no way she would be here if her soul hadn't awakened. There's more to her than we know, and I'm determined to figure it out.

Zaya leans against my hand and nips at my fingers before rubbing her head against Eira's legs. I'm rather smug that she already approves of me. She stalks off toward the other group of healers, which I'll take as her trusting me with Eira tonight.

I take Eira's hand before she can change her mind and pull us toward the healing quarters' entrance.

"What about dinner?" Eira whines. My queen has quite the appetite, not that I'm complaining.

"You can have *lipva* and other goodies where we're going," I tell her. I try to clamp down on my excitement to keep it at bay, but it's already bubbling over.

"Nyx, where are we goingggg?"

Chuckling under my breath, I pull Eira tight against me as we weave through the *solliqas* setting up the night market. Eira's eyes widen in awe and interest as she passes the arched wooden stalls, each painted with luminescent colors to draw souls in. Some already have the scents of decadent food drifting toward us, while others have intricate coverings and flashing jewelry and dozens of other items crafted from different *maji*.

"I'll take you back to this market another night. Athena and Daya will surely want to come," I say into her ear. "Tonight, we're going *dancing*. To rejoice. To celebrate the healing we've achieved so far. To let go of that tension you carry so close to your heart, sweetheart."

FORTY-FOUR
Tryq

The manipulation of a soul is the most dangerous when it's
being done in an act of love.
It's a heavy curse to place on any heart.
-Wrathiala, Goddess of Manipulation

"You carry this so close to your heart, don't you?" Eliina murmurs across from me.

I scoff, fighting the urge to snap another chair into pieces. The irritation I feel at this point is maddening. And while I'm buzzing with nervous energy, the agitation pulling me in a million directions at once, Eliina is looking peaceful as fuck. Casually leaning against her wall of swirling plants. Twirling a vine around her finger as if she's got all the time in the world.

"Of course I do. I'm the one being fucking *accused* of wanting to harm my best friend. The soul I love. My heart is going to be a little strained."

She hums in response.

There's nothing in this room except a few chairs and a table, each intricately carved, a plush bed with entirely too many pillows, and a wall of colorful plants. They bask in the blue and yellow sunlight that filters through the open window. On the wall opposite the plants, a thin veil of water trickles down the stony surface. The sound is soft—a low hush in the background.

I'm sure this is meant to soothe me. To placate any normal soul. And maybe it would if I wasn't isolated from my friends. Fucking forced to be alone. *They're already pressing charges against me, like I'm some low-life criminal.*

I choose not to respond to her. Eliina is pleasant enough and easy on the eyes, but I've said everything I need to say. No, I don't remember what my soul did to Eira in Majikaero. No, I don't believe that a demonic part of my soul was clawing its way at me when we were in her tent. No, I don't know what a Sairn even is. And *fucking no*, I don't want to undergo a healing session where they'll put me into magical special water, thinking they'll cleanse me of my pain.

Fuck. Them. If they can't accept or handle me as I am, then I'm not giving them the satisfaction of cleaning my soul or whatever fucked shit they want to do to me.

Ah, shit. Liv and Lyk would be having a field day right now. This is probably a fucking cult.

Eliina sighs, snapping me out of my thoughts. It only annoys me further. Thoughts of friends, even creepy ones, are what keep me sane.

"How about this?" I offer. "I'll try your magical pool nonsense if you tell me how we can get our friends back home, away from Shira."

Her extraordinary black and green eyes soften around the edges. They match the silky coverings that wrap around her shoulders and plunge between her heavy breasts. "I already told you that it's a complicated task, Tryg. Some of our *solliqas* and your friend Athena have been looking into this in our library. The type of *maji* it takes to send a soul over to our realm, and certainly when they're not ready to do so, is out of my wheelhouse. The creature who did this also managed to send you and

Athena to the exact same timeframe as Eira, which means they have the power to manipulate time."

"Well," I sigh in response. "Then I guess we're at a standstill. Because I don't believe one word of that shit. There's no way you're this all-knowing Council woman and don't know how to move a soul over here. Eira was able to do it."

Eliina nods to herself. "Eira has been ready for a long time."

I scowl. "Eh, fuck off. Go on, leave and feel free to *not* return."

"Tryg, I'm unbelievably worried about you," Eliina says, her tone growing more urgent. "I want to take you to a safe space to work on your healing, so that I can trust you around Eira and the others. But our pools don't work like ordinary water. You must enter them willingly or they'll scald you until your physical form is in a burnt heap. I also believe if you try to work through any amount of your pain, and especially anything that relates to Eira, that some of that darker part of your soul will come out. And then we can work with it, work with *you*, and make everything okay."

"You want to make this okay?" I shout. "How about you even just *show* me Eira and Athena? Let me speak with them. You should know how healing friends can be in a time of distress. Why are you not thinking about what *I* want right now?"

"Because this is infinitely bigger than your wants or needs," Eliina says. Her voice is unnaturally calm in the midst of my belting voice. The silence in between our voices is deafening. "All I'm hearing from you is your concern about yourself. And a lot of the time, that's okay. It's natural for us to prioritize our own well-being. I need you to step outside of that framework, though. I *know* this is hard. But I desperately need you to look at the situation as a whole and find it within yourself to work on even a drop of your pain. If you can start there, I can meet you."

A ferocious growl unleashes from me. Untamed. Feral.

THE LIGHT WITHIN

Crushing the air around us in its animalistic sound, the tone ringing in my ears.

We stay this way for minutes. Maybe hours. Eliina, staring straight through me, her eyes a vortex drawing me in. Me, hunched against the wall, my chest heaving, my pale coverings long ago shredded out of rage, the air too humid and lush to fully breathe down.

"I understand that you don't remember what happened with Eira. From what I saw in my tent and what Eira has shared with me and shown the healers, I believe you've followed her from lifetime to lifetime. You've ended her precious life in each one. Was it for personal gain? A grudge from when you were both in Majikaero together? Another demon of darkness moving your body and will like a mere puppet? I wish I could tell you for sure, that I could pluck it out of your memories. That happens in severely drastic situations, and I refuse to put you through that unless you give me permission. What I *can* tell you is that you're resisting even remotely working on your pain. And it's chilling how similar it is to when Eira, when she was called our Queen of Light, begged you to do this for her. You were out of your mind, attached to her soul. It's part of why I'm trying to convince you to come with me to the healing pools. This act of resistance is scaring me."

"I told you that I'm not going to the healing waters," I rasp. I swear I see a wisp of smoke comes out of my mouth, but it's gone when I blink.

"Then it hurts me more than you could ever know that you can't leave this room yet. I'll leave it unlocked for you, but the *maji* I've woven around the door won't permit you to leave unless you have good intentions and will try healing. I can't risk Eira's safety. I *won't*. When you're ready, Tryg, we'll begin your healing journey. This is the only way."

FORTY-FIVE

Eira

You're such a bundle of stress.
Muscles coiling so tight, you might as well be doing flips!
No wonder you can't shit or sleep or talk straight.
-Thoren Karlson, Brother of Eira Karlson

The only way I can describe the scene before me is *electrifying*. As we enter the Crystal Trance, the beat of the music edges into my skin, flowing in my veins. I can't keep up with everything around me, from the millions of crystals dancing in the firelights to the smoke cascading down the walls made of woven branches. The smoke is soft and pillowy, but even as I gaze at the tendrils making their way toward us, I see there is nothing soft about this. It looks *alive*, writhing and snaking its way along the skin of each newcomer. Tempting us with the hammering beats and raucous laughter.

I wanted to argue when Nyx said we are dancing tonight. Truly, I did. My heart brightens in happiness that he feels this ecstatic about his first real session of healing. Especially that he wants to celebrate with *me* exclusively instead of staying in Eliina's quarters and telling the rest of the team. But he still has

THE LIGHT WITHIN

quite the distance to go if his expansive and wandering shadows are anything to go by. It'd be smarter to keep us both isolated until he survives a few more healing sessions, and I go to a few of my own.

Tomorrow. Tomorrow, I will meet with Eliina and the healers to break this warped bond with my Tryg.

I push those lingering thoughts from my mind. I'll let myself be free, even if it's just for this moment.

My eyes dart up, and my breath hitches; I see the lavender and navy moons above us, with lanterns hovering around the nonexistent ceiling. The brisk evening air travels down to us, but with the number of souls here, my body is already heating. Groups of *solliqas* are sitting along shimmering, thick branches that part of the Crystal Trance balances between, and I wonder how they even got up to such heights. They're all wearing different forms, some half-animal and others more human with different textured skin.

A *fim* throws her head back in laughter at something her friend said, her burnt-red and blond tendrils cascading down her scaly, iridescent back. Bright light akin to electricity is crackling down her slender neck and arms, all the way to her burgundy nails holding a clear glass with turquoise-colored liquid. The smoke is buzzing around her, and I can almost see the color of her eyes: pure glowing violet.

I must have made a ridiculous sound because Nyx can barely contain his laughter. He intertwines his fingers with mine, and my gaze finds his. *All the angels better be with me tonight.* We haven't even entered the actual club, and his dark toffee eyes are swirling with mischief and mirth, little crackles of light soaring across them as shooting stars.

His smile looks carefree in this moment, and my heart stutters in my chest when his hair falls against his forehead. Nyx's face becomes more feral as he holds my full attention. A hysterical laugh bubbles from my lips as he tucks me closer into his side. Shadows slither out from beneath his leather jacket and stroke my arms, sending another addictive spark up my spine and filling my senses with rich smokiness. *Have I walked into the wolf's den?*

Nyx leads us past the entrance hall, still laughing as he drags me to the landing of the main stairway. I've never seen so many crystals in one place before, and my brain can barely register their constant shimmering.

"Where are you taking us?" I yell out to Nyx.

"To get something to loosen those tight coils in your muscles," he says with a wink. "Unless you want to give me a try?"

A furious blush rakes down my cheeks and neck, and he pulls me again as he cackles loudly into the night. He takes me up a winding staircase, and I swear, I must be flying with how quickly we maneuver around everyone. His shadows tickle my skin again, and my body lurches forward, flush against his back.

"Try to keep up, my fierce firefly," he calls back to me.

Firefly.

I decide that I like it. Better than *queen*, at least.

Even with the magic tingling around me, I'm not enamored enough to ignore his annoying jabs and roll my eyes for what must be the hundredth time. I huff a breath as we climb a staircase covered in ivy and vines, a few leaves tickling my neck as he pulls me up higher and higher.

"At least if I'm a firefly, I can fly away from your idiocy," I yell back to him.

He abruptly stops, and I trip into his hulking form. Nyx uses this moment to catch me and cradle me close to his chest, peering down at me with that stupid, smug smile he often wears.

"But if you're a firefly, that means I'll always follow your light in all this darkness," he murmurs into my ear.

I suck in a breath as his shadows dance around both of our faces, and my skin lightens and pulses in response to them. His brown eyes are mesmerizing, with their own shadows and what appears to be specks of stars instead of lightening tonight. Being this close to him gets me all flustered, and the shadows pull me closer to his body, like a magnet melting in a fire. *Eira, what the hell are you doing? Absolutely not.* He will not win me over this easily, especially after that vicious stunt he pulled with Fraya. No matter who's the victim.

Scowling, I push him away with as much force as I can muster, which causes him to break into another fit of laughter.

Males. Misns. Idiots. Buffoons. They're all the same, in this realm or the next.

"Okay, my Shadow Prince, Prince of Darkness, whatever you're called—where have you taken us?" I shout over the noisy room now that I'm safely a few feet away from him.

Even with all his jokes and smiles, I can tell he doesn't like that I moved away. His shadows become sharper, and his eyes take on a slight glint that wasn't there earlier. Nyx eases his way toward me and guides us to what is the biggest and most colorful bar I have ever laid eyes on. *Ruse and the others would die seeing this.*

This room, if you could call it that, balances in the crevices of different branches that curve upward in the shape of an inverted dome. I see through the branches to the front entrance Nyx and I were just at, noting that there is still no ceiling above us; only the millions of stars twinkling down beside the radiant moons. There are no walls except the weaving branches and the illusion of separation from the outside world. Each branch is adorned with shimmering flowers—inky blue and indigo—that drift with the wind. Yet I can't feel the room move with the branches, and I'm presuming we are swaying in the breeze. *Why are none of the drinks spilling?!*

My attention is pulled in different directions, starting with the bar, which is made up of black and brown stone and molds into the tree branches. I thought I would see *misn* or *fim* workers, but I barely suppress a gasp when I see who is making all the drinks.

Shelves of many-hued containers in various shapes and sizes are lined up behind three creatures who, at first glance, I thought were *fims*. Their skin is made of tree bark, and their hair is a flurry of marine-blue and purple petals, trickling down their backs. They have the same faces with slightly different coloring —eyes made out of crystals and leaves, noses of small acorns, and lips of rose petals. Their lengthy arms reach back to grab different glasses and liquids, and for those on the higher shelves, a few branches bring the items down to their outstretched fingertips. The creatures are wearing jeweled bracelets and rings that match the colors of their crystal eyes.

"These *solliqas* are shapeshifters with a special affinity to trees," Nyx whispers in my ear. "Their names are Xylia, Narina, and Bianka. Xylia comes to work here during special occasions. Tonight through the Moons Cycle Festival, you will see her on the Council's grounds. You can recognize her by her multi-crystal eyes and ability to shift into any kind of tree or plant. Be mindful of her, though. She has a fierce and vengeful nature."

I can't tear my gaze away from all three of the shapeshifters and am particularly lost in their crystal eyes. I think Xylia is the one who suddenly peers out at me. Eyes of pink, white, yellow, and orange stare so sharply into the core of my being, I quickly fumble for Nyx's hand in fright. She doesn't look away, and I'm drawn to her, despite my immediate terror, and before I know it, Nyx is pushing us both forward toward the bar.

"Nyx, it's been some time since I last saw you here," Xylia calls to him in an entrancing, melodic voice. Even though she speaks to him, she does not take her eyes off of me. I can feel myself want to draw closer to her, to peer further into those mesmerizing gems.

I hear Nyx chuckle behind me. "With how you treat my guests, what would you expect of me, Xy?" he yells back to her.

"Come back to me, *my firefly*," he says to me, and Nyx twirls me around to face him.

The room sways slightly and instead of jewels, I'm met with smoldering eyes and the coolness of shadows and smoke, slithering up my arms and around my neck and hair.

"Xylia doesn't mean any harm, but when she gets curious about people, she can be quite... fixated and difficult to leave," he says, his shadows still creating a buffer between us and the rest of the room. "What kind of flavors do you enjoy? I'll get our drinks, and we can leave before she finishes pulling you into a trance," he says with a wink.

My senses are still battered, so I can barely find the strength to answer his simple question. "I enjoy most flavors... surprise me," I whisper back to him.

I can't believe he can hear my reply in all the chaos of this bar and over the rhythmic beats of the music, but he grins slightly and turns to order our drinks from Xylia. I notice that he doesn't turn me back around to the bar and leaves his shadows to slink up and around my skin, like a protective shield. *Is this his way of being kind and careful?*

Within a moment, Nyx is back in front of me, that mischievous light in his eyes. He is holding two crystal glasses in the shapes of tulips in front of him, filled with two different colors. In his left hand, he is holding a glass filled with turquoise liquid, and in his right hand, he is holding a glass filled with a deep plum color.

"Don't be fooled by drinks in this world, *firefly*," he says with a smirk. "The turquoise tastes of sweet apricots, and the purple tastes of cherries. Which do you fancy tonight?"

My body must have a mind of its own and instinctively takes the turquoise liquid. As I peer down into the glass, it's as if little diamonds are sparkling throughout, and I risk a glance back up to Nyx before taking a sip. Dark eyes find my own, and he suppresses a grin.

"You look cute when you are unsure about the new foods and drinks here," he says.

I wrinkle my nose and glance back down at my beverage. "Are you playing a trick on me tonight?" I ask him, hoping my insecurities aren't shining through.

I expect a sarcastic comeback, but Nyx simply smiles down at me. He surprises me by playing with a few strands of my hair and tucking them behind my ear.

"I would never trick you, Eira. I want to help you feel even more alive tonight and explore the fun this world can offer," he says quietly. "I've hidden enough in my shadows, and you've been sheltered behind Eliina's power squad your whole time in Majikaero—we'll let go and embrace the magic tonight."

His glass clanks against my own before he downs his drinks in two gulps. Similar to a cat crouching before a curious toy, Nyx's eyes dilate, and his smile turns feline. *Here goes nothing.*

I toss back the turquoise liquid, something I don't even have a name for yet, and it skates down through my body. I briefly wonder if I should have at least told Daya and the rest of them where I'm at and what I'm putting into my soul. *Oh, fuck.* Athena is going to kill me for not including her.

A powerful *whoosh* streams through my veins. There is no more time for thoughts—not as the magic from this drink drips into my bloodstream like a sweet venom.

My senses are heightened, and I sense the magic under my skin bubble to the surface, ready to come out and play. My face feels flushed, and my muscles loosen to the point that I could be gliding in the air. The shadows are still tickling my neck and face, and as Nyx's smile grows wider, I can tell my night is about to take a crazy turn. Suddenly, the shadows are gone, and I'm thrown back into the room's lights, sounds, and chaos.

Nyx pulls me impossibly closer and looks ready to burst; you'd think he was the one with powers of healing and light.

"It's time to dance with the stars and the moons, *firefly*," he excitedly yells to me.

I know I'm resisting the flow within myself, and I hesitantly ask him, "When we are dancing with the stars, are you going to let me fall?"

Nyx walks backward, pulling me gently into him, and he whispers against the shell of my ear, "I'll never let you fall. You are the light the moons and stars and suns envy. You are the shooting star I long to fly with through the skies. And while we dance, it might be *you* who drops *me*, tumbling back into the shadows."

FORTY-SIX

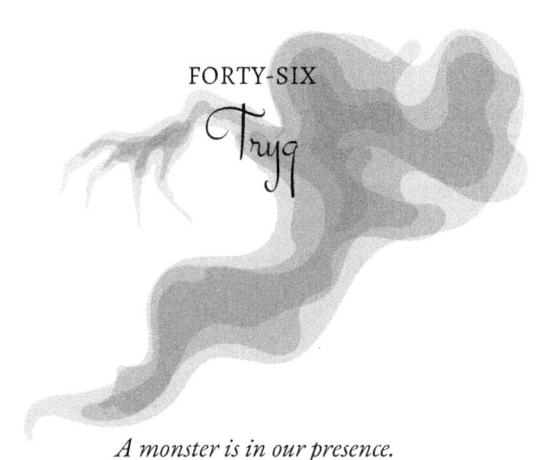

Tryq

A monster is in our presence.
And delightfully enough, it's me.
-Correspondence from Erika Sylvan, High Master of Water

Shadows claw at my insides, begging to be set free. They're resentful that we're trapped in this room while everyone else gets to explore these new living quarters and the Council building—antagonized that we're left alone with disturbing thought after thought. I can't blame the shadows' reaction. I, too, am furious that I was sent to a new world to be discarded like the piece of trash they all view me as.

They're not trying to isolate you. They're trying to keep Eira safe. To keep you alive.

I discard the pulsing thoughts as quickly as they come. I don't give a fuck about their reasons anymore. The truth is that I'm not allowed to leave this room while everyone else gets to roam freely. They get to research any connections between their shadows and beasts and the plague, as well as previous sightings of this disease overtaking the realm. Athena gets to look into ways to connect with souls on Earth, a task I've expressed a hundred times already that I'm *dying* to help with. Desperate, even. But I guess even these precious, enlightened *solliqas* can act inhumane.

Technically, Eliina said I could leave if I wanted to. There are no chains preventing movement. I have a fresh supply of coverings, my own extravagant bathroom, and a mixture of drinks and foods sent here throughout the day.

But I *can't* leave.

Eliina cast some kind of spell on the door that will allow me to leave if my thoughts are safe and intentions are good. And while I keep telling myself that I'll be fine if I can leave this fucking room, my inability to break the damn door down proves otherwise.

I'm about to try one of those stupid breathing exercises Eira's made me do when I've gotten angry before when I'm hit with a wave of inner turmoil. It starts as a spark, but then my wrist and forearm are thoroughly on fire. White flames engulf me, and I physically feel my soul departing from Eira's. Separating. I'm not sure what is more gut-wrenching for me: the fact that I unknowingly *forced* Eira to tie herself to me or how much I loathe Nyx.

I *know* he's the reason she's leaving me.

Somewhere inside of me, I'm distinctly aware that this isn't necessarily wrong. But it's wrong to *me* and my soul. It's a punishment I didn't know I deserved and am futile to fight against, but goddamn, it's also a mistake. Eira's been a part of my life for years, for lifetimes apparently, and it's not fair I'm being punished for my past selves' crimes. Not when I'm willing, begging on my fucking knees, to do whatever it takes to not lose her.

But could I simply be her friend?

Flashes of memories pass by me, pulling me into the ones seared in me forever.

A moment of chasing Eira around when we were kids, being introduced to a giggling child version of Athena.

A scene of us studying with Lyk, Liv, and Astira under the willow in my backyard.

Another memory of Jace and Ruse playing video games with me, Ruse letting out a loud whoop when he destroys us.

The image of holding Eira as she cries and cries. Her tears threatened to drown my whole world after she walked into her home, and her entire family was gone. All their items were taken, too, as if they never existed.

Flash forward to another memory of watching Eira and the girls dancing at a local bar and a herd of guys slowly moving toward them. The anger that split me in half, and the realization that I might love her as more than a friend.

An image of making food with our friends and watching Eira drink wine with Athena. Both howling with laughter and falling on top of each other on the tiled kitchen floor. I had tried to pull her up, and she took me down with her by accident, causing me to land on top of her. We had a moment where there could have been more.

So much more.

I'm twisted up on the floor, squirming in pain and the harsh reminder that I never took that next step with Eira. Yeah, she could have done it, too, but I'm the one who knew I loved her. Who wanted to take things further. Even a kiss. *Anything*.

Chest heaving, my heart rate doubles and pounds against my ears. My body radiates violent tension, and I'm shaking from the forced control. I crawl on my hands and knees to the floor-length mirror across the room and, trembling, manage to push myself to a standing position. Clenching and unclenching my fists, I seethe at the image before me, at the soul glaring back with a look of vengeance.

I scream, half wondering if the sound itself will shatter the windows and shake the ground I stand on. It doesn't, leading me to rage even more with irrational fury. I punch the mirror without thinking about what could happen next. It doesn't matter. I know I'm not damaging and cutting my hand but the outline of my soul. I know it's better to feel pain than to accept I'll never have Eira. Not in the way I want her, at least.

As if lightning of pure, undiluted hate strikes me down, I'm lost in the thought of what would happen if I eliminated the males who love her. Who she thinks she loves. Who can't possibly care for her better than me. Who tear her far, far away.

The idea shatters me in the best way possible. It hurls me deeper into the darkness building inside me. Breaks me free of my consciousness, of lingering thoughts of regret or apprehension. It shows me the glorious path I can take if I want to. All I have to do is take the first step, and the shadows will guide me the rest of the way. *Give in*, they tell me. *Just a peek won't hurt.*

Everyone is saying I'm a monster. Their thoughts are as clear as day on their faces, cursing and haunting me. Their actions speak even louder, keeping me confined as a beast in a glorified cage. I *know* that even Eira believes this shit.

If this is how they view me, then fine. I might as well start acting like the monster they think I am.

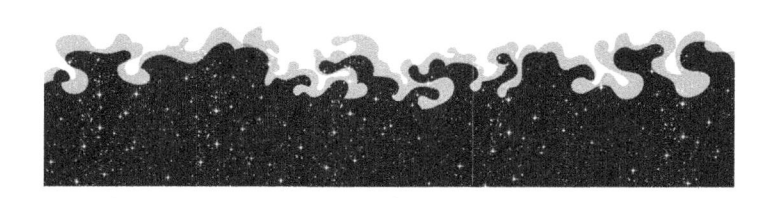

FORTY-SEVEN
Nyx

You can't heal darkness from the soul if it benefits them.
-Message from Council Member Namid,
Grand Soul Reader to
Council Member Eliina, Grand Healer

One thousand percent, watching Eira dance will forever be one of my favorite memories for as long as my soul continues to exist.

We had weaved our way through the thickening crowd of *solliqas*, all of them here to break free and soak in the lavender moonlight before the next cycle is upon us. I'd kept Eira tucked into my side as we ducked under sturdy branches until we arrived at the main room. Here, I nearly threw her out of my arms onto the pulsing dance floor, eager to set her loose. To let her experience the pounding music and beats and throbbing souls all here to escape.

Eira's body moves with the rhythm, her movements fluid and enrapturing, the music contained in her very skin. She doesn't stumble at all and is feeling herself and the *solliqas* surrounding

THE LIGHT WITHIN

her. Her slender hands begin at her ankles and snake their way up her legs and around those swaying hips. They move up her sides and glide under the curve of her breasts. Her shoulders are rolling to the throbbing base of the *maji*—*solliqas* are gathered on a stage nearby, manipulating sounds until they form a mesmerizing beat.

As Eira moves like liquid sin, I nearly stumble and go crashing to the ground. I see her in her current form, and then she's... something else entirely. Her hair and movements are the same. She has that carefree smile I haven't really gotten to see yet. But in flashes, each image pulsing with the beat, I swear on my soul and to all the gods, that she's moving in another form in a completely different world. In one second, her skin turns a leathery black. In the next, she looks taller, with iridescent scales and water weaving around her. And then I can't breathe as the next scene unfolds and I'm watching her grow wings that extend the length of her lithe body. I can't be sure if what I'm seeing is a terrifying reality where she's moving between realms, if these are actual memories, or if that purple liquid is affecting me more than I realize.

Eira's body moves faster, jerking me out of whatever the fuck just happened. Her arms raise above her head, seeming to shake out the strain that's been weighing her down. She's a fucking goddess sent here to destroy me. And she's got her hands in another *solliqa's* hair, rocking to the beat together.

Shit.

I pounce on her and pull those wandering hands toward me, spinning her into my arms. Eira's mouth opens in a tiny gasp at the impact. The outer rims of her eyes are lighting up, but her pupils are blown wide. Her gaze locks with mine, and the connection between us pulls taught. It's a mixture of bright light and roiling darkness and a flash of colors I don't understand. Pulling us closer and closer together until I can't take it anymore, I have to feel those lips on me.

"Firefly," I grumble into her ear. "Can I take you somewhere private?"

Her eyelashes flutter at the tone of my voice, and she winds her arms around my neck, pulling me down to her level. A kaleidoscope of shadowy butterflies flutter up and down her arms.

"Yeah," she breathes. "But when I say stop, we stop."

I have to fight the urge to flinch backward, swallowing down any anger. *She dares think I would force her?*

A growl works its way up my chest. *Has someone else forced her?*

Eira watches me intensely. Stuffing down the rest of the rage, I cup her cheek and tell her, "Sweetheart, I'll *never* force you to do anything. You can say the words right now, and we'll be back at Eliina's quarters in a heartbeat. I swear it to you. I swear it on our soul connection. You're my *almaove*."

She peers at me for another few seconds, and I mentally prepare myself to whisk her back to the safety of her room. I'm bold, but not this level of rash, and would never dream of harming the sweet soul in my arms. This, I realize, is a testament to her healing powers. My previous self might not have been so kind.

But Eira surprises me and nods her head before taking one of my hands. "Then lead the way, my panther darling."

Arching an eyebrow, I huff out a laugh. "Panther?"

"Oh, yes," she says with a smirk. "All black and sleek, with that feline grin of yours. Prowling at me. Lethal as hell. Or a demon from Cudhellen, as you call it. It's exactly what you are. You'll see." She winks. "Now take me where you'd like before I change my mind."

I bare my teeth at her, and of all responses, Eira cackles in the cutest way.

I'm going to absolutely devour her.

Our fingers intertwine, and I lead us to one of the many private rooms tucked away in the base of the enchanted tree.

There must be a hundred of them scattered around here. People use these for a million different purposes, ranging from hanging out with friends to private dances to anything the soul can conjure. There are no rules here. There is one room in particular that I'm searching for, and I can't wait to see Eira's expression when she enters it.

I drag her with me, passing by a number of other hidden coves. Some are dazzling with amethysts; others are earthy with the scent of moist soil and fresh rain. Eira's eyes wander the spaces in wonder, and I can practically taste the excitement coming off her.

Skidding to a halt, Eira crashes into my side. She shoots me an irritated glare, and I can't help but chuckle at her lively expressions. The potion I drank a while ago is still snaking along my body, and I'm brimming with ecstasy, readying myself for my *almaove*. We have to take a short walk further underground to reach where I want to take her, but it'll be well worth it. I feel Eira humming with nervous energy, and right when she's ready to explode, I pull her with me into our room.

We both marvel at the thousands of crystals and jewels glimmering throughout the space. There is raw quartz that strikes out like stalagmites. Others are various pastel colors and smooth as marble. My personal favorite is the crystal forming along the back walls that is so pure, it resembles a mirror. It's so clear, I can see Eira's astonished face peering back out at me. I stay back toward the entrance, watching her tiptoe her way around the room, her breathing uneven with excitement.

"This—this is so—"

"I know," I whisper.

"How did you—"

"It's my favorite place here. The music still finds us, but we're hidden away in a sea of light. Where I can briefly experience peace."

Eira cuts me a look soaked in pity. *No, this isn't the direction the night's taking.*

I stalk toward her, letting my shadows writhe around me. I make sure she knows exactly what my intentions are.

"This is why I wanted to take you here, firefly," I rasp, so close to her that I feel her breath. I grip the back of her neck and arch her face toward me. "To show you the light you bathe me in—why I'll easily fall to my knees and worship your soul."

My thumb gently traces her lips, and she lets out a small whine. I smile, eager to show her what she does to me.

"But I wanted to dance," she mumbles with a pout. Her half-lidded eyes have a glint of mischief, and she darts her tongue out to lick my finger.

I crash to my knees in front of her. "Then dance, my fiery queen. Perform for your prince."

Eira's light flares around her as a glowing orb, reflecting off the crystals. She rolls her body to her own rhythm, the music fading far away in the background. It's her long, wavy hair that steals my breath. She loosens her braids until her hair is free, cascading down her back like a waterfall made of white flames. Beads of sweat glisten down her arms and chest and it takes all my restraint not to dive on top of her and lick them off.

She gradually lowers herself to the glittering floor, and I'm lost in her trance—in the way she sticks her ass out toward me and sends me a sultry glance over her shoulder. *Oh, gods.* Eira's bewitching, and I'm willing to give her all my power if she'll take it.

My firefly continues to amaze me. She slinks down to her hands and knees and turns to face me, a hungry look in her eyes. And this little minx decides to *crawl* toward me. With each inch closer, my body threatens to fall back and surrender to her. There's a piece of my mind that's actively forcing my hands to stay put, to not make any sudden movements. I don't want to shatter this image of perfection in front of me.

Eira... oh, my sweet, precious soul. There's a fire-fueled sass that orbs around her, but most of her soul bleeds innocence. Yet here she is, crawling into my lap and pushing me back onto the floor off my knees. Grinding her warm core on top of my still covered cock, driving me fucking *wild*.

She loops her arms around my neck and stares me dead in the eye. "But I don't want to perform for a prince, Nyx," she says, her voice dark and husky. "I want to dance for my *king*."

I swear on my soul that still lives, her words have cleansed me of another layer of darkness. Like the predator I am, my shadows wrap around her wrists and slam her backward onto the ground. A growl rips through me, and I'm diving down, stopping a breath away from those luscious lips that are *begging* to be kissed. I look up at her through my lashes.

"Tell me I can kiss you," I pant. "I beg of you, firefly."

Eira fucking *smirks* at me, a wild look igniting in those silvery eyes. "Just how I prefer you. Ravish me, my king."

It's a simple push forward. That's all it takes to brush my lips against hers. Once. Twice. On the third time, she pushes back, molding her mouth around mine. She tastes of smoky sweetness, a savoriness melted in rich, dark chocolate. Tangs of fresh fruit with the airy sugar of whipped cream. Delicious, addicting, the most exquisite taste and sensation. Eira's tongue dashes out to meet mine, and I'm fucking gone.

The kiss becomes needy and desperate, her hands managing to break free of my shadowed restraints and grip my dark hair. I sink myself lower toward her body, making sure to hover enough not to hurt her. The beast is still lurking inside me and craves to taste her blood. I try to push the urge down when Eira stops, reeling back. Her beautiful face is flushed, her mouth puffy.

"Stop holding back," she breathes. "I can feel you restraining yourself."

"My beast. I don't want to—"

"You won't," she says confidently. "I *know* you won't hurt me, Nyx."

Before I can protest, Eira pulls me back to her and crashes her mouth against mine. On instinct, I bite down on her lower lip, drawing a few drops of her blood. She moans loudly and somehow moves even closer to me, as if urging our bodies to morph into one. A shiver rolls down my back, and my entire body trembles with desire. The mixture of her scent with the taste of her kiss and her blood has my eyes rolling back with a husky groan.

I continue kissing and nipping down her neck and collarbone, marking a path to her heaving chest. I look up at her for permission; Eira gives a firm nod, and I peel away the blue covering. Peaked nipples greet me, and I feast upon them, starting with slow, torturing licks that have Eira squirming. I bite down, applying just enough pain to push her pleasure closer to the edge. Her hips keep reaching for mine, and I chuckle darkly in between her tits.

"Eager, are we?" I ask.

She doesn't respond. Eira simply sends a bolt of fiery light from her hands down my body in thrilling bliss. I tuck that knowledge away for the future.

I work my way to the top of her tight pants and roll them down. Eira lifts her ass to help me shove them down her thick thighs, and my heart nearly stops in my chest.

"No under-coverings?"

"You didn't think I'd ruin the surprise, did you?" she asks, smirking.

I spread her legs open, but a jerky movement stops me. Glancing up to check if she's okay, I notice Eira is watching her wrist with the bear marking intently.

"What is it? Are you okay?" I ask, a sense of urgency filling me.

"I—I, yes, um, I am," she stammers. "Look. Quick. Patches of the mark are fading."

Sure enough, part of the bear fades away like a force of *maji* is wiping her arm clean.

"I think... I think I'm choosing you, Nyx. And that means I have to let pieces of Tryg go. My soul innately knows this," she whispers.

Hope surges through me at both her words and as half of the bear marking stays erased. "Does this mean I'm the cure, then?"

Eira goes quiet for a moment, and I wonder if my joke was taken the wrong way. I'm still inches from her soaking pussy, and while it pains me, I keep my eyes focused on her face.

"I think it means you're the drug that I'll surely become addicted to," she says quietly, staring into my eyes.

"Perfect," I grunt, not breaking eye contact. "I'm already addicted to your soul and will die if I don't get a taste."

I don't give her a chance to respond before I use my tongue to trace all the way up her slit, pausing to swirl around her glistening bud. Her body goes tense below me while she simultaneously cries out. Out of the corner of my eye, I notice her hands jerk, as if to stop me, and she pushes them down onto the ground. There's a sudden hint of jumpiness wafting from her, and I take one more delicious lick before pushing up to face her.

"Your body feels different now. What happened? Do you not want me down here?" I ask. I urge her to see the true concern in my eyes.

Eira's gaze flitters around me, not quite making eye contact.

"It's, um, it's not that. No, no. *No*. That felt incredible," she breathes. "I've never had someone, um, do that to me before."

Arching an eyebrow, I barely contain my disbelief.

"You, this glorious creature, have never had *anyone* go down on you?"

"No," she squeaks. "I, um, I have a lot of problems with this part of my body. It always takes too long, and I don't want to waste anyone's time and—"

Growling, I lunge forward and cut her off with a searing kiss, letting her taste herself on me. "You will *never* be wasting my time, firefly."

I caress the side of her face and move my hand into her hair, lightly massaging her scalp. "If you're not comfortable, then I won't force you. We can stay here or go back to the dance floor, or, as I mentioned before, I can take you back to the sleeping quarters."

Eira stiffens slightly, and, still avoiding any eye contact, she says, "But it felt so good. I—I want you to, um, continue. If you'd like."

Taking her chin, I force her to face me. "Look in my eyes, sweetheart."

Slowly, so slowly, Eira raises those incredible eyes to peer up at me.

"Now tell me what you want."

Her eyes widen, but she's remarkably brave. She keeps her eyes trained on me as she says, "Nyx, I want you to lick me."

"Where?"

She swallows, looking as if she'd rather be burned alive than have to say the next words. "I want you to lick my... my pussy."

I smirk. "Good girl. My queen shall receive what she commands."

I cradle her in my arms and move us to one of the mirrored crystals. Pushing her back down to the ground, I lift her hips and wrap her legs around my shoulders. Her still-wet pussy is an inch from my mouth, and I'm already salivating.

"Why did you move us here?" Her voice is breathy. Winded. Aroused.

"I want you to see what it looks like when your *almaove* pushes you over the edge. When you watch me worship this pussy how it deserves. When you fall apart and see that I'm the one who'll catch you."

I dive in without another thought and ravage her dripping cunt. I can't decide which taste I prefer—her mouth or her sweet pussy. My tongue dips from top to bottom and teases her entrance enough to make her thrash below me. Glancing up at her, the sight nearly makes me come undone. She's moaning and writhing on the floor, her chest swaying slightly with each heavy breath.

Her eyes are closed, though. That simply will *not* do.

"Eira," I growl her name.

She cracks her eyes open, lust swirling in their depths.

"I told you I wanted you to watch. That wasn't a request. It's a fucking demand from your king," I snarl, her juices smeared around my mouth. "Now open those pretty eyes and *look*."

The moment she takes in the sight of me ravaging her, I sense a thrill roll through her body. *Oh, yeah. She's absolutely getting off on watching us*. Her moans build into screams, and I'm loving every second of this, every moan I can coax from those full lips. If it takes her a while? *Excellent*. She can take the entire fucking night if she needs to. I'll keep lapping her up until she tells me to stop.

"Nyx," she moans. "I'm so close."

"Don't you dare cum yet," I growl. "Not until I command you to."

Light flashes behind her eyes, her control wavering. She can deny it all she wants, but she *is* a queen. And I don't think she's as submissive as she thinks.

"Nyx," she pants. "Please."

I've been avoiding her bundle of nerves and finally clamp my mouth down over them. Eira lets out a strangled sound and free falls over the edge right into my greedy mouth. I drink every drop of her in, golden and turquoise light traveling from her shaking body into mine. The light reflects off the surrounding crystals, bathing us in its healing glow. Diving deeper than I have in the past, I hurl the pieces of my soul that are healing toward her, hoping she'll catch them.

She does. Our souls' connection strengthens even more. A sensation that's both anchoring and has my spirit soaring into the starry night. By the look in her eyes, I *know* she feels the same. I place a few kisses on either side of her thighs and delicately unhook her legs before lowering her down in front of me.

"That was—"

"I know," I say. I school my face into sternness. "Next time, you'll wait until I tell you to cum."

Eira's eyes gleam with a mixture of rebellion and elation.

"Gods, you're breathtaking when you come undone like that," I murmur. "And it's okay if you don't listen yet. We have time." My eyes dart to the half-faded bear marring her creamy skin. "And each will be a part of your healing, sweetheart."

Confused, Eira furrows her eyebrows. "Part of my healing?"

"Mhm," I hum. "Learning to accept and love all the parts of yourself. Embracing this stunning body and pussy of yours. Dominating me with it all until your soul breaks free of this slab of darkness."

FORTY-EIGHT
Eira

Canielors. Avoid them if you can.
Unless you want to become another lost soul.
-Message sent from Ivar Freqa, High Master of Wind to
Prince Nyx of Drageyra

Darkness might as well be taking me over because that was the most delicious and explosive form of sin I've ever experienced. And I plan on doing it again and again and *again*.

The very thought is jarring. We must indeed have a soul connection if I'm willing to give myself again to him freely, knowing that he'll have the power to abandon me when I'm at my most vulnerable with him physically.

Nyx's gaze is scanning the length of my body, as if he's trying to memorize this image for the rest of his existence. He swipes my hair out of my face, sending tingles down my spine. My body is insanely sensitive, and any touch is sending me careening out of my skin. Each breath is still labored, my heart fluttering from the aftershock of the biggest high of my life.

He is still playing with the ends of my white hair and brings his other hand to trace my collarbone down to my exposed breasts. The dark markings that cover his smooth skin make my hair and body shine even brighter among the surrounding crystals.

"So beautiful," he murmurs.

The intensity of his gaze sends a string of goosebumps up my arms. The part of my soul that normally functions takes back over, forcing my arms around my chest to cover myself. I don't know *what* that was tonight, but it certainly couldn't have been me. It's not that I'm not sexual or have fantasies that trickle from my jumbled mind down to my heated core. The girls and I have gone to countless bars and clubs, losing ourselves to the provocative flow of the music. We all can be sensual, some of us more than others.

But I've always had a complicated relationship with my body. A chest I feel is too small with, and much to my dismay, one boob is ever so slightly larger than the other. I shudder at the memory of an asshole telling me I'm as *flat as a semi* before puberty fully hit and my body bloomed. And my vagina? *Ugh.* My uterus has always given me awful pain, at least on Earth. It either makes me bleed enough for a crime scene or turns anything sexual into a horrifically uncomfortable event, my muscles coiling into tight vipers from hell.

So, I don't know what the fuck happened. It could have been Nyx's sultry voice. Maybe it was him *commanding* me that sparked a deep-rooted release in my soul. That tugged on that part they call *queen,* causing me to rise to the challenge.

Whatever it was, Nyx will have to coax it back out another night. That steamy side of me has scuttled back to the hole it hides in. And it's left me in a heaping, jittery mess.

Oh, *fuck.* I should touch him back, shouldn't I? That's what people do, isn't it? Or I guess *solliqas* in this case.

Blowing out a shaky breath, I hesitantly reach out to Nyx's solid chest, letting my fingers slide down the ridges of his abs. I stop briefly at the top of his pants and ready myself for this next part. It's nerve-racking for me, but if he was able to worship my body in such an unbelievable way, then *dammit*, I can do this for him.

Nyx's hand darts out and grips my wrist firmly.

Shaking his head, he says, "I don't think so, sweetheart. I promised that we'd go slow."

I scowl at the idiotic prince before me. "Yeah, going slow as *friends.*"

"This isn't what you do with your friends?" He smirks, basking in my frustration.

Nyx's laughter bounces off the jewels as I lunge up at him, tackling him to the ground.

"Oh, my firefly," he murmurs. He grants me a rare smile, full and brimming with wonder, making my heart stop for a second. There's a soul full of light trapped under his darkness that I'm determined to set free. "You can do whatever you want to me. But I want you to be fully ready when you do."

Humming, I lower myself closer to him. "And what if I want to burn right through you until there's nothing but a pile of ashes?"

"Then do it," he whispers. "Because if you're not happy, then I don't want to continue to survive in this realm."

His words dance around me, my skin sizzling with delight. The crystals closest to us pulse in time with my heartbeat, but it's short-lived. Like a dark whisper on the wind, any and all light is snuffed out in our room. I'm learning that I'm strong and can take care of myself, but Nyx wastes no time in rolling me underneath him. He throws himself over me in an attempt to shield me from what's coming. The stiffness of his body and predatory stillness confirms what I already suspect: this isn't supposed to be happening.

I shove one of his arms off me. He growls, but I couldn't care less. My soul is *not* made of suffocating darkness, and I need to see what the hell is going on. Light bursts from my hand and my eyes go wide, fear locking up my body like a corpse.

Floating above us is a deformed creature with no eyes and tiny slits for a nose. A gaping hole takes up half its patchy face, a tornado ready to suck us in. It lifts a mangled, ropey arm and raises one of its bloody talons over my face, a few drops dripping into my hair. Milky, peeling flesh brushes past my arm, snapping me back into reality.

A scream tears out of me, echoing off the crystals in a series of waves. The creature reels back for half a second before echoing my wails. A scent of rot carries from its mouth with each garbled scream it makes. Nyx instinctively tries to cover me again, and I regretfully have to force him off me.

"No!" I yell. He reels in shock at my tone. "You need to *move*. The creature is caked with blood and might be a worse version of the plague. It's here to break *you* with more darkness."

I don't wait for him to respond. Using my *maji* is still new to me, but I trust my soul to know what to do. It has always known how to protect those I love, how to heal and connect. This fucked up demonic being might be drenched in this disease, but it won't be able to penetrate my shield of light. I know it won't. Because I won't let it.

I push my *maji* forward and sheath my entire body in the blue fire. I'm absolutely petrified, a small sob sticks in my chest as I try to breathe in. Once this creature lunges at Nyx, though, a snarl works its way out of me, and I widen my shield of fire on the next exhale to form a wall between them. One of the flames licks at the creature's mutilated feet, causing it to howl in misery. I urge myself forward, knowing full well that if I let myself pause, I'll panic. Tunneling far down inside my soul, I search for anything I can use to take down this creature. I grasp onto a beam of light. It's like smooth suede and feathers in my phantom hand. I know something so full of love will destroy the vicious being in front of me.

With all the strength I can manage, I swing that beam of light out at the creature, slashing as if it's a sword. It cowers and whines and roars its terror at me, but I refuse to back down. Blazing forward, I use my *maji* to coat its decaying skin with my light.

Snarling, I tell it, "I won't let any more of you take the soul that belongs to me. I'm no queen, but I'm certainly not going down without a fight when the ones I love are in danger."

I melt the creature down, its darkness pouring similar to the liquid we tried tonight, going from black to bright colors with sparkling bits and pieces. I know in my heart that I'm watching myself melt the darkness out of it until all that's left is the brightness of its original soul. Guilt gathers in my gut, urging me to question if even a creature this horrid is worth saving. If I should have stopped earlier and focused my energy on healing rather than destruction.

Yet I don't stop. I could. It's gone from this realm. But I let the light flow freely from my arms, the fire overtaking me for another moment before I crumple it in my hand. Glancing up into one of the crystalized mirrors, I catch my reflection. The terrifying gleam in my eyes. The curling smoke and lingering blue flames churning up to the ceiling. Making me appear as a demon wrapped in sunlight.

And I have to wonder if the path to healing is only through destroying the heavy darkness, or if it is also being aware when it becomes a part of the light.

"Why the *fuck* are you naked?"

"Why have you both been gone for the last few days without telling anyone?!"

"Do you have any idea how worried we've all been?"

"Zaya clawed up the entire couch, and it's your fault."

"Yeah, okay, we were worried, but what I want to know is *why* we weren't invited?"

Their questions pummel my brain. Nyx and I weren't the sole ones attacked by, what Nyx has now clarified, a *canielor*. A creature the Council thought Nyx and his group would quickly deteriorate into considering the intensity of their shadows and violent tendencies. I've personally explored the depths of Nyx's disease and witnessed the way it tangles around his limbs and crevices. Even with the trauma he's endured, he's not even *close* to becoming a *canielor*. He explained that since each soul is impacted differently by the plague, the progression of the disease and their final monstrous forms are all equally unique. The *canielor* is apparently the form the illness takes before the *solliqa's* demonic transformation is complete, and the gruesome creature resembles the pain and trauma the soul endured.

Nyx covered us in his shadows and kept us out of the way of any Council members or protectors coming to assess what happened. We snuck our way through the few alleyways and safely arrived back in Eliina's quarters. Except my fire burned all our coverings. And my hair is all knotty from Nyx tangling it and then going into full fight mode. Oh, and the small detail that I reek of blood, melted *canielor*, smoke, and sex. And we entered my room to find our group looking distraught.

Daya hastily chucked her cozy robe at me as soon as I walked in, at least having mercy on my humiliated self. She knows I don't normally walk around in this way. Ever. She smirked at Nyx and threw him a plush pillow before turning her concerned eyes back to me. Typical Daya fashion. I quickly jump into explaining our situation before Daru scowls Nyx to death.

"Alright," I begin. "I guess let's dive into the lunacy. We're naked because we were attacked at the Crystal Trance by a *canielor,* and I used my light to destroy it. And consequently, both of our coverings. You'll have to fabricate more, Daya." I wink at my friend. "Last few *days*? It felt like we were there for a night, so I don't know what you're talking about. I'm sure everyone's been worried, but we were supposed to be there for a night after successfully healing a part of Nyx." I pause, letting them digest this for a minute.

"As for Zaya—she can do whatever she wants, when she wants. There's no stopping a cat; that should be obvious." Zaya blinks slowly at me from one of the dyed cushions under the floor-length window. *Ah, yes, the queen of felines has given her approval.* "And Nyx can explain why no one was invited, since he's the one who dragged me there."

Erika snorts. "I'm pretty sure it's clear why he wanted you alone, if your scent is anything to go by."

Fire races to my face, causing a frenzied blush to spread all the way down to my chest. Nyx is no help. He keeps one of his huge hands on the pillow in front of his dick and drapes his other arm around my shoulders. Looking entirely too smug.

"Don't get too riled up, sweetheart. Erika's just jealous, is all. She'd happily join us if you asked her."

I shoot him a bewildered look, mortified beyond repair. I get the idea that maybe I should've burned more than his coverings.

"Reckless, daring Eira," Delano tsks, wagging one of his fingers at me. *The nerve.* "First, I see you riding off on that motorbike. We must not have scared you too much, since you went running after your cat back in the forest without a second thought to the *solliqas* residing within it. I learned recently about your, ah, adventures back on Earth with what you call wine. And now running off to go dancing with a prince known for darkness without telling anyone? You've got quite the flair for danger, little risk taker."

Flickers of light buzz under my skin, begging to be set free on this judgmental feather-brained blockhead in front of me. "I'll have you know that *plenty* of people go on adventures with wine," I huff. "And *of course* I'd run after my cat in the face of danger. And—wait. Excuse me. Did you say motorbike? Y-you've followed me on my bike?!"

Athena must sense I'm going to erupt because she swiftly takes control.

"Daya and Erika, let's get the bathroom ready for Eira. While even *I* can smell what they did together, I also can smell corroding blood on her. That can't be sanitary for anyone. The rest of you, out you go. Especially you, Del. Fly far, far away. My bestie needs some time to decompress after what sounds like one hell of a wild ride."

"You're presuming to order us out?" Hadwin barks, his usual easygoing vibe gone.

Scowling, Athena turns on him with hands on her hips. "You're presuming that I *can't*? Wait around and watch what happens."

"Maybe I will," Hadwin retorts.

"Yeah, of course you will. You're a magical, earthy stick-in-the-mud. The dirt is the one place that'll accept your level of stupidity."

Hadwin rolls his shoulders back and puffs out his chest, looking ready for a fight. "I'm incredibly smart. I'll have you know that Eliina tasks me with quests only the most clever can handle."

Athena simply rolls her green eyes. "I'm sure she does. Anything to get you out of her hair. The farther away, the better."

"Can I stay to help?" Fraya interjects. Nyx stiffens next to me, but a violent glare from me has him behaving. Besides, Fraya has a ray of lightness twirling by her ankles and wrists now. If the healers have been working on her, I don't want to diminish any progress by turning her away.

"That'd be great," I say warmly. "Maybe you can help me with that small plait you wear."

A slight blush graces her sharp jaw, and she walks over to Erika, who's glancing at Fraya with a guarded expression. *Hmm, suspicions noted*.

"The rest of you follow me," Nyx grunts. Hadwin starts to open his mouth and freezes when he sees Nyx's stormy expression. "That wasn't a request. Let's leave the *fims* to rest. Eira doesn't need to be harassed by *all* of us."

"Yup, especially not when she has me!" Daya chirps. "And we need to have a chat about the term *fims* later. Just because my tits and ass are banging doesn't mean a little *misn* isn't in me."

The *solliqas* all gape at her, stunned, and I can barely take it anymore. Exhaustion is hitting me. Hard.

"Nyx, march your naked butt back to your sleeping quarters. And take the rest of these idiots with you." I send a spark of light at his exposed butt cheeks, and he yelps. Faint amusement glimmers in his eyes, though, and a promise of retribution. They snake out of the room, all grumbling about *controlling* solliqas, and I slam the door on Ivar's back for some extra emphasis. *Bye*.

Athena immediately hands me a steaming mug of tea. "I thought they'd never leave," she huffs. "Although I'll admit that Nyx is growing on me. And so is that weak-ass coffee drink they've got here."

Giggling, I take a sip of the herbal tea. It reminds me of a mango peach tea I used to drink on Earth.

She throws a nasty glare at the doorway. "I'll be real with you, Eir. I'm not convinced of all of them, though." Athena shakes her head, like she's clearing her mind of cobwebs. She quickly looks at my wrist and gasps. "Your marking!"

Daya, Erika, and Fraya scramble over to us. "Half of it's gone?" Daya asks in awe.

I nod, not sure what to say. I'm relieved that the others left, even Nyx, but that doesn't mean I'm ready for a million questions from the others.

"Do you think Nyx is the reason it's going away?" Athena asks.

"I have a theory," I say. "I think it's part of it. Nyx is enough to crack the seal between Tryg and me because of the love that he pours into me. But as with any soul, how we've told our clients back home, Athena, I'll need to be the one to sever it completely. Along with any of the other darkness already festering inside of me."

Daya hums and takes the mug of tea from me. I'm about to take it back when she says, "That might be true. But that's certainly nothing you need to focus on right this second. Let's get you cleaned up and rested. Erika got the bath ready for you."

I send Erika a grateful smile, and she responds with a smirk and nod. Athena guides me to the bathroom, and I realize I haven't even asked her about her healings or what she's been up to.

"Do you want to show me the library first? Or do you want me to peer inside you to begin the healing process?" I ask.

Athena snorts and shakes her head. "Girl, you're crazy as fuck. If you can barely handle our questions, what in the world makes you think you can handle healing me or traveling down to that expansive library? Yeah, that's right, don't bother answering. Focus on bathing and resting and then we'll go to the library and talk with Eliina. Don't worry about any trauma and pain sticking to me. I'll be okay."

Not convinced, I ask, "How do you know that?"

Smirking, Athena responds, "Let's just say I've found my ways. You'll have to wait until later to find out."

Before she can leave me alone with my thoughts, there's something I'm anxious to ask her. "Hey Athena?"

"Hmm?"

She looks at me with wide eyes, a wariness bruising the

corners of them. Her body is tense and ready to spring into action, even with a blanket of exhaustion covering her body, nearly pulling her to the ground. It's not the time to ask her about Hadwin. I switch gears, hoping to distract her from whichever thoughts are eating away at her mind.

"Why was Daya the one to throw her robe at me?"

She flashes me one of her radiant smiles. "I think it's rather refreshing to see you walking around without coverings. I don't want to jinx it—maybe you'll continue to embrace your body. And keep working that clingy tension out of you while you're at it."

I throw one of the lemon vanilla soap bars at Athena, barely missing her hair, as she cackles like her usual self and dashes out of the doorway. Leaving me alone for the first time in days, apparently.

FORTY-NINE

Eira

A life without stories is meaningless.
-Old sign hammered into the brick walls of the Sweazn
Capital Library

"Apparently, we *all* needed our beauty sleep." Daya yawns.

After I stumbled out of the bath, my muscles sufficiently looser and ready for a nap, I burrowed myself in the mountains of blankets. Athena soon joined me, looking equally exhausted. It could be from whatever she's been doing in the library or related to the other *solliqas*, but I believe she was legitimately worried about me not returning right away. Anxiety can easily weigh a soul down.

Much to my surprise, Daya, Erika, and Fraya also curled up on our double king-sized bed. A wave of nausea passed over me at their closeness, how they each pressed into some part of me. All of them seeking physical reassurance that I'm in the bed and not carried off to an otherworldly club plucked from the wildest of fairy tales. I can't say that I blame them. If one of Nyx's friends scooped up Athena without telling me, I'd be tearing down Rioa's streets in a frenzy.

"Of course we did." Athena nods in agreement. "It's been an unsettling few days."

Erika hums and pulls Fraya up with her. "Let's go find a snack and get back downstairs with the others," she mumbles. Her jet-black and inky-blue hair is sticking up all over the place.

I don't respond, too lost in my scrambled thoughts. Ideas leap into the next, pulling me along for the ride. My *solliqa* body is indeed hungry, and I'm hit with the stark realization that I haven't eaten in a few days now. That takes me to wondering how the fuck time works here and why it didn't feel like multiple days passed when I was with Nyx. Leaping to the next thought, I'm spiraling through feelings of dread, yet I'm equally eager to see this infamous library everyone's talking about, wondering what I'll find there. I wonder if I can research concepts about time and space and where my soul fits into it all. Flashes of the *canielor* move like a film through my mind, making me—

"I know that look." Athena taps my nose with her slender finger.

I scoff. "I don't know what you're talking about."

"No?" she muses. "Considering you tell me *all* the damn time how lost I get in my cluttered head, I'd surely thought you'd see it in yourself."

I choose not to respond, not wanting to go into what demonic being now permanently lives in my mind.

"Eira..."

Ugh. "The last thought I had was that I haven't had any nightmares since coming here."

"Silly queeny. Of course you wouldn't," Daya says, snickering. "How can you have nightmares if your soul has woken up?"

Pursing my lips, I manage to stand up and find new coverings to wear. I find a lacey and sheer jumpsuit threaded with violet and deep navy-blue tones. It matches the theme from the

Crystal Trance perfectly. *I guess Athena is getting her wish. Time to show more of this body.*

"I'm not sure nightmares work like that," I mutter.

Daya leaps off the bed and flings herself around me, almost causing us to topple to the floor. I'm forced to take a step back and accidentally step on Zaya's tail. She hisses at me with disdain before stalking off to the torn-up couch she's claimed.

"What do you mean?" Daya asks. Her eyes are innocent, as if she didn't nearly kill us both.

"I think nightmares can find us anywhere. In our homes, in our bodies, in our memories. Back on Earth, in the form of war. Here in Majikaero, as the plague of darkness. In the dreams our souls dare to have." I turn back to the mirror, tying the top of the jumpsuit together.

"Does that mean we haven't truly woken up?" Fraya asks quietly.

I meet Athena's eyes in the mirror. She's my soul sister, the one I know like the back of my hand. Without a doubt, she knows what I'm thinking.

"Maybe it's similar to peeling back layers," Athena says, her voice hushed. "We're awake enough to be here in this realm. But there's always more, always a step we can take to reach a higher level of understanding and enlightenment. This might only be the beginning."

Daya raises her eyebrows to the top of her hairline, her interest altogether piqued. Fortunately, a knock at our door saves me from having to provide more answers that I'm not sure I have.

Erika tugs the wooden door open and barks out a laugh.

"Are you here to escort all of us down to Eliina? And are these for *me*?"

"Fuck off, Erika," Daru grumbles. His forest eyes find mine, and he visibly relaxes. "I brought you something to munch on before dinner. Since I'm sure that asshole was more concerned about getting his dick wet than he was about taking care of you."

I feel my eyes flash with heated annoyance. I'm grateful for Daru's support and friendship. And I know souls make those kinds of asinine comments out of spite and jealousy, but he's got another thing coming if he thinks he can talk about Nyx like that.

"I assure you, *friend*, that Nyx took exceptional care of me." Daru winces but maintains eye contact. "He didn't even let me touch him and focused all his attention on me. It was incredible, in fact. And considering multiple days have passed by, you might want to consider how long he was using his mouth and hands on my body. Just think about how powerful it was, since half of the bear marking is still miraculously gone."

I step forward and pluck one of the pear-looking fruits from the basket he's carrying. "Thanks for the refreshment, though. I surely needed it after being *so* exquisitely ravished."

Taking a bite into the tart fruit, I let some of its juice drip under my lips. My tongue snakes out to wipe it clean, and I let Daru see the blue fire simmering in the depths of my eyes.

"Come on," I call back to the others. "Let's head down to the legendary library. And don't forget to take a piece of fruit on your way out the door. Daru is kind enough to share with *all* of us. Since we're all, you know, *friends*."

He keeps his raging gaze locked on mine as I shuffle past him, his body going rigid. A brisk wind twirls through the ends of my hair, and I ignore him. Athena loops her arm with mine and laughs into her fruit, giddy as can be now that she's officially growing fond of Nyx.

"I warned you," Daya says behind me. "I told you to take it easy."

"She could also be mine," Daru snarls back at her.

She slaps him right across the face. Zero hesitation. No fear of retaliation.

"She *could*," Daya hisses. "But she certainly *won't* if you act like an entitled brat. You're completely reacting off emotion right now. You don't even know what kind of soul connection you have with her or if it's anything near being an *almaove*. She doesn't show up for a few days and you go into a wild, feral mode, not even thinking how your comments and actions will impact Eira."

"And it doesn't help that you insulted her *almaove*, especially right after they physically bonded," Erika adds.

"Or that you didn't offer to share the food with all of us. Even *I* know how much that matters to Eira, and I'm just getting to know her," Fraya mumbles.

"But when we couldn't find her, I felt the pull—"

"Then it'll still be there when she's *not* still adjusting to a new home. Or bonding to her *almaove*. And integrating herself into Rioa while learning she has the power to heal those suffering from a plague of darkness meant to doom us all," Daya barks. "Now stop acting like a moron. You're falling for her? Great. Show her that. With respect."

"For someone who was such a loon when it came to guys back on Earth, I'm absolutely loving how you've already got two hunks fighting for you," Athena whispers in my ear.

Snorting, I elbow her in the ribs. "Wait until it happens to you. Or, oh gods, Astira, when we eventually find her soul. If this is happening to *me*, imagine what'll happen to the likes of you and the others."

Athena merely smirks and gives me one of her classic side-eyes. *Keeping secrets, I see.*

I'm guided down the winding hallways that switch from gold to dusted in white and black. The irony isn't lost on me that this Council building, more of a palace than anything, is represented by the very colors that symbolize light and dark. *Except they haven't seen my fire and glacial blue. All the other colors of healing*. Athena pulls me down a hallway that is dimmer than the rest, with a handful of orbs hovering above us.

"Brace yourself," Athena mutters. "You're about to meet your kryptonite."

"A library that could kill me?" I snark.

"There may or may not be a bet placed on how quickly you'll pass out."

Rolling my eyes, I place my hand on the obscured wall, letting it glide along the smoothness as we walk. The damp cold seeps into my fingertips and causes a shiver to roll through me. I was so distracted by the bickering behind us and the shining hallways, I didn't realize we traveled this deep underground. There have been no stairs, only slight slants to the floor, enough not to notice. Yet each turn has clearly played a trick on me.

"And I unleash you!" Athena chuckles as we turn into an enormous arched doorway.

Holy. Fucking. Shit.

I sway on my feet, staying upright because of Athena's firm grip on my arm. She continues to laugh at my utter amazement. Orbs flicker similar to candlelight above glazed wooden tables, surrounded by an array of cushioned chairs and benches. Luxurious woven rugs litter the marbled floors, adding splashes of color to the earthy atmosphere of the room. Multi-level baskets sit on either end of the tables filled with books and more lights.

No, not exclusively books. Tomes, scrolls, ancient pictures, and artwork. Notebooks and quill pens for note taking. I'm dazed out of my mind, peering from table to table with building excitement at such a space for reading and learning. Athena gently tilts my chin to look up beyond the tables, and I let out an obnoxious gasp. Rows upon rows of bookshelves extend forever into the darkened area near the back of the library. Orbs float along the rows next to impossibly tall ladders. They must be a good twenty feet high or so. And above us? Glass windows surrounded by painted beams showcasing the brilliant night sky, the full moons flooding us with their light.

Now *this* is a library.

"You weren't kidding. She looks like she's been made queen of the whole realm," Delano snickers.

"Uh, *no*," Athena scoffs. "That would be a look of terror."

"We better chill her out a bit. She's going to brim over with that fire of hers and burn our books," Odin mutters. He walks quickly in front of me and places both of his hands around one of my own. I manage to bring my gaping eyes down to him and am instantly mystified by his mumbling.

I'm suddenly filled with the cooling sensation of liquid, reminding me of when I've blissfully drank icy water during scorching days back on Earth. It spills into my veins and winds up to my face. The kiss of the sea breeze playing on my skin.

"There we go," he mutters.

I must appear disoriented because he adds, "Erika and I have a connection to water. I used my *maji* to cool your light and fire. You were getting a little too excited." He chuckles and offers me a smile.

I narrow my eyes at Erika. "If you both have this connection to water, then why didn't *you* help me?"

"Sometimes I like watching chaos ignite," Erika purrs before stepping past me and heading toward the tables, where the others are hunkered down with books and supplies.

"That's my sister," Odin sighs. "Come, join us. We're rather impatient to show you what we've found so far."

Following Odin, I find he's situated between Hadwin and Ivar. Ulf is sitting opposite them, acting agitated with his shadows rolling off his back in sharp movements. Fraya moves to sit next to Hadwin, followed by Daya and Athena. At the table next to them, Delano gives a small wave before going back to the large tome in front of him, scribbled notes stacked around the table. Daru gives an irritated sigh before plopping down next to

Delano, followed by Erika, who's acting oblivious to Daru's attitude.

It occurs to me that Daru's bitterness has pushed the others to cram together at one table, anything to escape his mood. Except for Erika. She looks positively elated by getting into his personal space.

"Come hither, Eira," Delano says without peeling his eyes from what he's scanning. "Come learn about ancestral curses and how to pacify evil shadows with the strength of a strong soul connection."

"Or she could see what I've gathered about past life experiences potentially impacting this plague," Daya suggests.

"I personally vote for what Athena's been tirelessly researching," Ivar says, giving her a small smile. "She's been focusing on how to find your friends' souls, and she thinks she can use her budding *maji* to connect with them through the earth from this realm."

Athena blushes and glances down at her notes but can't hide her smile. My heart inflates with pride, so much that I risk burning with light again. Of course my talented friend thought of that idea.

While I'm leaning toward wanting to hug Athena and shower her with love, I find that I don't have to choose where to sit. Bronze hands wrap around my waist, and I'm pulled back into a sea of shadows, thrown onto Nyx's inviting lap.

The second I land with an *oomph*, his crackling dark eyes lure me in until I'm leisurely pressing my mouth against his full lips. I tell myself just a taste, but then I'm twisting and pouting my mouth against his, hungrily taking what he has to offer me. Nyx releases me, and I'm dizzy with lust. He chuckles lowly and tucks my hair behind one of my ears.

"I was going to come right back to your room," he rasps. "But I wanted to give you some space. I knew you would come down when you were ready."

Nyx sends a galloping horse made of shadows toward me, and I marvel at the increasing amount of details he adds each time.

He pulls out a wrapped parcel that smells *divine*. "I got you a piece of grilled meat from one of the local market stalls," he says against my lips. "I know how much you enjoy food that's this juicy." Nyx pushes a piece of the thinly sliced meat, still fresh off the fire, into my parted lips and throws me a saucy wink. I chew it slowly, hoping he'll lick the grease off my lips. But we're broken from our trance as quickly as we entered it.

"Eliina!" someone gasps. "You're here."

FIFTY
Tryq

How we treat other souls is the biggest indication of how we treat ourselves. Honor this or perish.
-Faramond, God of Spirit

"Here is where the fun begins." Her scratchy voice curls around me.

Shards of who I used to be threaten to make an appearance. They twine through the throbbing form of my soul, imploring me to reconsider my next steps. Even though I'm not alone in this. Not by a long shot. The lines between love and betrayal will be blurred by more than one as the moons change to the next cycle.

And those new moons will be quite the fucking good omen for me. One will be a harsh crimson, as if submerged in the very blood we seek to spill. The other will slice through the night with the color of steel. The image of the blade I'll use to splinter their souls into such insignificant fragments, no amount of *maji* will be able to mold them back together.

"We'll grind them to dust and inhale their sweet powder,"

she murmurs. "Spread them over our roasted food and relish in their flavor."

Uneasiness crashes through me at her bloodlust. I'm not sure this is me. I'm not fucking sure of anything anymore. Just that I want out, to be *free*, to be unleashed from the sorrow that clouds my ability to think.

"It's the only way," she whispers, her voice sickly sweet and dragging down my senses like whetted iron nails. "Do you want to stay locked away? Exploited for crimes you haven't yet completed?"

No. Of course I don't. I want to go home.

I want my job as an investigator, even with its crushing responsibilities and impossible tasks. I want my friends. For Ruse to feed my coffee addiction and share those dirty jokes. I want to feel the rhythm of Astira's skin against my own and wrap my hands in that hair of blazing fire. I want to take Eira to that new coffee shop and feed her tart strawberries dripping in her favorite dark chocolate. To tell her how I really feel, about the love that's so strong, I've felt it for eternity and in each passing life.

"Love?" she spits. "Where has that gotten you?"

Flickers of memories rush toward me, all those memories with my unruly family and wickedly fun friends.

To wrestling with Eira and Athena, landing blow after blow on my stomach, as if their childlike punches could have truly harmed me.

To Jace handing me a literal goblet of wine, betting his next paycheck that I couldn't drink it all without passing out.

To Lyk and Liv plotting something troublesome, their sly smiles being their sole warning.

To the team who works religiously and gives their entire hearts to find those lost children and families.

To the therapists at my friends' clinics who always greet me with warm smiles, no matter the leaden exhaustion lining their eyes.

In both small and big ways, I've been surrounded by that remarkable feeling of love my entire life. Perhaps in multiple lives, especially if Eira has always found her way to me. There are few that love as faithfully as my darling Eira. Few that can light up the entire room with a simple smile.

Those sizzling eyes of crystals and ice that have any man crumbling to their knees. And women, if I'm being honest. Any human can find themselves caught in her healing web of love.

"But she isn't choosing you," the voice rasps. She sounds ravenous, her stomach rumbling, her breathing labored. "What's the point of being surrounded by love if they don't even choose *you*?"

Delicate hands pry into my mind. They're so frozen they could blister, piercing the thawed parts of my heart. Sending them scattering into a bitter wind and coating them in a sheen of frost. It's hard to remember what the cozy heat had felt like or meant. All I detect is hostility, hardening into a layered shell of contemptible disgust.

"No one ever chooses *you*, Tryg," she sighs. Regret and despair billow up and around me. A miserable speck inside me thrashes around violently, still resisting the pull to self-hatred.

"You're awfully rigid. What are you protecting?" The voice eddies from different directions. "Don't you see how you'd *thrive* in chaos? How it was created for you?"

Chaos. Chaos is the murkiness I'm used to wading through. It's one of my secrets, a card I hold close to my chest. I'm at one with chaos. It's why I deal with a high-stress job and fucked up emotions from my friends.

"I have my own secret to share." The voice is alluring, dripping in heat. "You *are* chaos. I'm simply asking you to embrace yourself."

Yes. How did I forget?

A coppery taste fills my mouth, tangy liquid dribbling down to my chin. I smear a little off and am mesmerized by the bubbling black and red blood that continues to pool at my feet. No, at my knees. Curdling around the *solliqa* in front of me. *Or is it me?*

I don't think. I *feel*. Submit to the growing urge screaming to be released from the confines of my soul. Bending forward, I lick another mouthful off the ground, savoring the undiluted power it sends through my veins. I can't stop, even if a tiny fraction of who I once was wants me to. That part doesn't matter. All that matters is how this *fuels* me, and I fucking crave it.

More than nicotine. More than my past life. More than Eira.

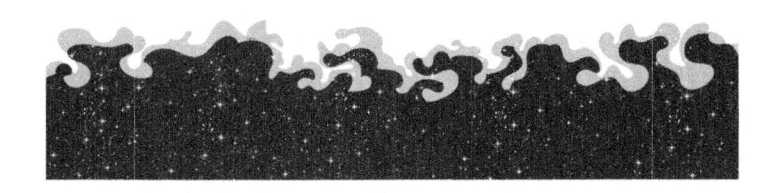

FIFTY-ONE

Eira

Who does the body belong to?
At what point is it no longer attached to the soul?
-Course notes from Lyk Ainjin, Child & Trauma Therapist

"Eira, my dear, you're who I've been looking for," Eliina mutters.

Nyx's shadows creep back, and I'm awkwardly left staring up at Eliina from his lap, his fingers still moving in small circles along my hip bones. Her strained eyes assess me once before she turns her flustered stance on Nyx.

"*You*," she seethes. Nyx has the good sense to flinch back. "And *when* were you planning on telling us where you were taking Eira? And to one of the most sensitive areas in Rioa where souls can get lost to time and space, no less."

"Our souls call out to one another. She was safe with me and—"

"And nothing!" Eliina shrieks. "You could have *both* vanished to another realm, one completely unknown to us all. Eira is still acclimating to her healing *maji,* and you have begun the process of recovery. That is not acceptable, and so help me, and all the gods *will* help me, I'll have you buried in the earth for the next full moons cycle while you finish your healing. Do you understand me?"

"Yes, Eliina," Nyx mutters. His eyes remain downcast, the scent of embarrassment rolling off him.

"Look me in the eyes," Eliina demands.

Nyx immediately raises his gaze to hers and says, rather earnestly, "I vow to not take Eira somewhere without informing you first. I'll not go forward with plans if you deem them inappropriate or unsafe."

Eliina doesn't respond but nods curtly, seemingly satisfied at his display of remorse.

From the corner of my eye, I can tell Daru is looking fucking smug, which sparks a flare of annoyance in me. The bastard didn't take me anywhere, but he sure as hell offended me.

Without missing a beat, Eliina whirls on him. "And *you*, Daru," she hisses. "I can't believe how disappointed I am in you. You better wipe that smile off your pretty face."

Daru gapes at her in dismay.

"I have eyes and ears *everywhere* in this realm, especially in Rioa. I'm more than aware of how insufferable you've been acting. Eira had a rattling, traumatic experience, is having to learn as she goes with healing, and has made the decision to physically bond with Nyx. Amongst other changes as a new *solliqa*. You dare to place any level of pressure on her when she's barely managing one soul bond as it is?"

Eliina continues to mutter under her breath in a different language my mind isn't privy to. But from the harsh blush on Daru's face, I'm sure it's merciless.

"Now, you either support Eira fully, or I'll assign you a new task elsewhere." Eliina doesn't give him a chance to respond, either not caring or feeling confident that he'll follow her command. Wide and frantic eyes meet mine. "I need to steal you away for a few minutes, my dear."

I clamber off Nyx, and he places a gentle kiss on my wrist, where half the bear marking has faded, before letting me go. The motion reminds me of Tryg, except this time I'm filled with a molten heat. Eliina takes my other hand and tugs me along. I nearly trip into one of the bookcases as she clutches my hand tightly and jerks me back, back, back into the furthest corners of the library. The fact that she's holding me closely, my hand cramping from her numbing grip, and that we're heading into the spooky, hidden corners of the library is rather alarming.

At last, when I'm trying not to choke on the dusty and obviously long-abandoned section of this library, Eliina lurches to a stop. She makes quick work of constructing transparent vines around us, keeping us safely tucked away from the others under her ward.

"That should do it," Eliina states. She ties her hair back in a bun, the tops of it reflecting under the one purple orb she conjured above us. "I do apologize about the, ah, rush of everything. Things have been a bit complicated."

I settle onto my knees before her, waiting for her to continue. Eliina gracefully lowers herself to the floor, her gossamer robe smudging in dust. I settle myself against the base of the bookcase, being careful not to disturb any of the books. Even if they're untouched, I have no doubts they're hidden back here for a reason. And I have no plans to find out why.

"The Council has been dispersed everywhere," Eliina says. Her eyes are pools of murky emotion, pleading with me to see past her words. "As with any plague, there's been a surge in infections, and what I'm afraid have been... deaths. For as long as I can remember, it's been near impossible to completely destroy a soul, which even applies to you. Such few *solliqas* have this capability and burdensome talent. Some of the Council's behaviors are now being driven by fear, paralyzed by this notion that souls are vanishing." She blows out a breath, twisting the intricate rings on her fingers.

"I'm not convinced," she murmurs. "My sources don't make it sound like these are actual soul deaths. I think they might be possessed. But I can't be sure for what purpose and by who. I don't know why any *solliqa* would possibly want to control souls who are demolished to the point of sheer ruin."

The hairs on my arms rise at her words. A creak echoes in the eerie silence. My muscles and tendons clench, as if readying for one of these *solliqas* to spring out from behind the bookcase.

"I fear you'll need to be extra careful during the festivities and celebrations. I'm not saying you shouldn't go. Your *maji* will sing powerfully under the last evening of our moons. This current cycle represents serenity and confidence, the ability to find peace in the choices our souls have made. But you must stay close to Nyx and the others and be sure not to wander off." Eliina pauses and gives me a searching look.

"Nyx had given you a book not too long ago. Yes, I'm aware of the one he chose. I'm the one who introduced it to him many years ago. I'd recommend that you read this, as well as a few others I've found for you." She pulls out a few worn books from a satchel I swear was not there a second ago. "A few of these contain detailed information about the regions in Majikaero and chants from the earliest known healers. This one has lists of herbal and liquid remedies that you should also practice. Don't fret; Stefanie and the others will teach you what they know too. And this last one"—she waves a small, leather-bound journal at me—"is all about *you*. A *solliqa* had written down the power they witnessed you wield, and I'm hoping this can guide you on your current journey."

She hands me the tomes, each feeling heavier and more fragile than the last. I linger on the journal, its near-translucent pages the same as the wings of a butterfly. *Accounts of what I've done, who I've been—who I am and have forgotten.*

"These seem rather important to only be giving them to me now," I say quietly.

"I didn't want to pull you down here, not to one of our most beloved resources that can siphon even the most indifferent souls in, until you explored healing more. You needed to meet some of the healers, experience a cleansing in the healing pools, experiment with Nyx, and acclimate yourself. With your type of *maji*, you will be more sensitive to the energies around you. I wanted to ensure that you had a little time to yourself before jumping in with the others."

This *solliqa* before me is incredibly thoughtful and maternal. *So similar to Morgan*. A prickle of pain wrings a few tears out of me, and I hastily wipe the traitorous tears away.

"It's okay to miss them," Eliina says. "You have soul connections to them, too. They might not be like Nyx, but that doesn't mean that you don't share a dynamic level of love."

Sniffling, I shove down those emotions, stuffing them anywhere I can to avoid their presence. I have more pressing questions to ask Eliina.

"Speaking of Earth," I whisper. "I've been thinking a lot about Shira."

Disquieting grimness dims Eliina's usual bright green glow. Out of the corner of my eye, the vines shaping the ward writhe in agitation.

"That wretched fool will eventually splatter before us in her own warped idea of a sacrificial death," Eliina snarls. "The moment she chose the Sairn was the moment she cut herself off as my sister."

Sister?

"How—I... how is—"

"The Sairn started as a small group of *solliqas,* wishing to worship angelic creatures of death from another realm entirely. Since they'd never wounded the souls who've awakened in our realm, we never had cause to worry about them. Unlike on Earth, no matter the strangeness or unorthodox beliefs some might have, we don't believe in controlling what souls believe in.

They are drawn to those ideas for a reason, and who are we to decide what they can or can't think or believe? While I still don't condone limiting what one believes in, we have recently learned of the group's unhealthy obsession with you. They are convinced that your 'death' was an act from the creatures they serve. When word got out that your soul might have survived, they took this as a direct threat against their gods' plans. They've been scavenging multiple realms in search of you. And, I'm afraid, in search of your closest souls."

I can't bring myself to respond. It's like a crack split down my center. One side of me is debilitated by shock that this group even exists, and the other side of me is distraught for my loved ones still on Earth.

"Shira never used to believe in the Sairn," Eliina continues. "She actively teased them for following such destructive gods in realms the Council couldn't even contact. Her *almaove* became interested in the group, and while she and I have been soul sisters for centuries, you'll find that this type of connection can be rather... captivating. Your other half can persuade you to do even the most peculiar activities, and before I knew it, Shira was enthralled by this group. She became *obsessed* with finding you, Eira. I tried so hard to reason with her, but we eventually had to go our separate ways. In the name of love, at that. You'll find that love will often lead you to light, but it can also hold you down in the most frightening of ways."

"I'm... I'm speechless, Eliina," I whisper. "You say this all easily, even though she's your *sister*."

Eliina hums to herself. "That could be true, but I've learned over time that the souls who refuse the light, even those you are closest to, need to be let go. Or you risk following them into the dark."

I clear my throat. "I'm nervous to even ask you this, but does this mean we need to, um, take Shira down?"

"Oh, my dear. Shira will take herself down because a soul can only bring so much pain to the universe before they're at its mercy. This will be a much bigger conversation with the whole Council, specifically addressing the growing numbers of the Sairn. You should focus on your own healing for right now. We have to start with healing ourselves before we can heal others."

"Will that be the goal? To heal Shira?" I ask.

"Always," Eliina says, but the confidence in her voice doesn't quite meet her eyes. "It's always the goal to strive for healing. That's how to truly drive out the darkness, and it has a ripple effect out toward others. If you can master healing yourself, then we can talk about the next steps, including understanding your *maji* abilities and how that relates to other parts of this realm. It'll also serve you greatly in your mission to heal Nyx."

"Is this why you wanted to find me before the other Council members?"

"Yes." Her voice is more hushed. "You need to begin the healing process first, before you meet everyone. I suspect there's at least one person on the Council that has caught this dreaded plague and would have scooped you up with the plan to use you for their own personal gain. Even here. *Especially* here." She looks around rapidly. "You must be brave when conquering yourself and your fears, Eira. And I strongly encourage you to get more healing work done before you continue to work on Nyx; especially if you want to extensively awaken more of your *maji* during the festival."

Questions upon questions curve through my mind. But I narrow my eyes on Eliina. "Why are you acting so shifty right now?"

Paranoia floods her stunning eyes. "Truthfully, the Council can now sense when I'm alone with you, since we aren't in my private living quarters. They've been recruiting certain *solliqas* with *maji* that can connect to and feel another soul's energetic charge. They claim it's to help monitor which souls have caught the plague, but I've yet to see any other soul getting pulled into their chambers other than myself. I can't meet with you for long or it'll raise suspicions and draw some of them here into the library."

Oh, gods. "They don't come in here anyway? They wouldn't be suspicious of the others working together as a group?"

"Not at all; not right now. They want nothing to do with the banished ones and ate up my lies that I'm having them do busy work for me—the kind most of the Council deems below them." She scoffs. "But let's head back. I'm sure the others are getting hungry, and I think my kitchen is whipping up something new for everyone tonight. You'll love it, I'm sure. It's a similar texture to potatoes."

Her different moods and responses are giving me whiplash. I numbly turn with her as she gathers up her satchel and unweaves the earthy ward around us. Eliina places her hand on the small of my back, urging me to move back to my friends, when a scrap of darkness catches my eye. A strangled sob sticks in my throat, and I stumble into Eliina, startled from head to toe.

Oh, no. No, no, no. Not another canielor.

The monstrous form lurks next to a nearby shelf. Even from here, I see slimy pus leaking out of its pours. Fragments of what looks to be bone stick out of rotting tissues. I have to fight the urge to gag from the stench of decay settling in the air around us.

Yet Eliina appears unfazed. She catches my eye and heaves a sigh. This was evidently something she wanted to keep secret.

"Before you assume anything, know that not all of them are as dangerous as the one you encountered," she whispers lowly. "I allow some of them to hide here. They might look grotesque, but believe it or not, their souls have not caved to the torturous disease yet. I keep them hidden in my wards, and since their souls are still seizing most of the power over the disease, the Council can't fully tell that they aren't 'normal' and should be banished."

"Wh-what?" I sputter. Simmering rage makes me turn on Eliina while still keeping a watchful eye on the *canielor*. "How is *that vile creature* allowed here but not Nyx and the others? How can you protect *that* but not the others?"

"Well, *this vile creature* wasn't making a fuss against the Council. And wasn't a prince. And hadn't honed its *maji* into a lethal weapon. And I'm not sure why everyone keeps thinking I have a special command over the rest of the Council. I'm one *solliqa* with only so many abilities of my own."

I make a choking sound as it suddenly floats toward us. Bile threatens to spew out of me, and I'm close to screaming out for Nyx.

Eliina twines her hand with mine, keeping me grounded to the spot. My body starts to shake violently, and I'm full of terror, a small part of me whispering that Eliina is about to betray all of us. But the *canielor* propels toward me, and I'm thrown into a tunnel of memories. It's eerily similar to when I was shown previous past lives and memories; I instinctively fight whatever it's about to show me.

Wait, it's a *she*. She strokes the side of my face before leaping through one of the thousands of memories spinning past me. And I'm dragged down with her.

At first, I'm confused. Puffy clouds the same as scoops of vanilla ice cream breeze past in the light blue sky. Fresh rays of sun chase away the clammy air from the back of the library. I inhale and am met with the scent of wildflowers, and peering around me, I see I'm in a field of them. No, wait. *We're* in a field of them.

What was once a monstrous, hideous creature is now a young woman. She's sitting amid the flowers, light brown hair moving in the breeze, and eyes of cinnamon stare back at me. Her summer dress has poofy short sleeves and cinches at the waist, the rest of it lies around her like a blanket. This woman is as beautiful as a painting.

She continues to stare at me, and I get the sense she's insisting that I keep watching, that I pay close attention.

The memory we're in speeds up, and I'm wishing she never brought me here. A man walks up to her from a nearby trail, and they're clearly friends. He leans down to peck her cheek and slides next to her on the grass. They talk with animated hands and expressions. It's beginning to feel similar to a horror film. All calm and happy-go-lucky, and then—*bam*—someone dies.

I think she wishes she did die here.

This friend of hers starts to kiss her neck and slinks up to her mouth. The woman pushes him away, laughing. He smiles back, but there's a sinister glint in his eyes. Dark and all-consuming in the worst possible way. He forces her down and continues to kiss down her collarbone, all while she's frantic to escape.

A sinking sensation hits me. Another man wanders their way, and this poor woman, she thinks he's come to help her. All he does is hold down her wrists while her *friend* tears open her button-up dress. He discards the material while keeping his weight on her knees, forcing her to stay trapped. I can't believe my eyes when *another* man makes his way toward them at an agonizingly leisurely pace. This one has the smile of the devil, and the woman instantly locks up, her body freezing in panic. Bleak acceptance shudders through her breaking body.

I can't bring myself to look away. I watch, even as tears well up in my eyes, as each man takes his turn with her. Using their hands and fingers and repulsing cocks to fracture her into nothingness.

When I can't take anymore and try to release the memory, I watch in horror as a woman marches her way to this group, dressed in a matching jacket and skirt business suit. Managing to hike her way up to them in light pink heels. I think for a moment that this woman is a professional, maybe working for the police or the government. But *gods*, she simply stares down the beaten woman and nods in approval, motioning the men to carry her to a nearby van.

Cinnamon eyes greet me once more, full of harsh emptiness

and depleted of all life. Except for a faint spark. That lingering spirit in her soul desperately wanting to still live.

I'm instantly released from her memory and fall into Eliina's arms, sobbing uncontrollably. She gently brushes my hair and holds me. Silent as the woman in the memory. Because what can she possibly say?

It's at this moment that I vow to find a way to heal these poor creatures, especially if the root cause of the plague is related to trauma stored in these tortured souls.

FIFTY-TWO

Nyx

It starts with us. Or it starts with no one.
-Page 47, Healers of the Light, Volume I

"Souls are often anchored to a diverse combination of other souls, each carrying its own lesson to be divulged when deemed ready," Delano reads aloud. "The process can take anywhere between one and a hundred life cycles until the designated soul is perceived ready enough to receive the lessons. Some may be construed as positive, while others are meant to cause heartbreak and unimaginable pain. Each is life-altering in its own way."

"So, you're thinking we're all lessons for our little Queen of Light?" Ivar asks.

"I'm thinking it's possible," he says. "I'm thinking, at the very least, we all have a designated connection and bond to her."

"But we're riddled with corruption," Erika scoffs. "How can we possibly be connected to Eira, of all souls? *Look* at Ulf."

"We haven't always been this way," Fraya murmurs. "And even if we're drowning in pain, that doesn't mean there can't be a connection to our queen."

"*Our* queen?" Ulf scowls. "I never said I'm following her."

"Then you better make peace with the idea of death," Daru snarls, beating me to a response.

Ulf chuckles darkly. "You fool. I *am* death."

"Alright, enough," I cut in. "The point is that we all have a connection to her. I'm guessing when we figure out what that is, it'll be easier to protect her from whatever is behind this plague and wants her gone."

Athena nods, staring off into space. "You better believe she'll be protected. Even if it has to be from one another."

I don't like the direction her thoughts are going in. Not in the fucking slightest.

Everyone stops talking when Eliina and Eira's footsteps emerge a few rows behind us. My queen shuffles through the bookshelves, a lantern in my smoky shadows. But her luminescence has lost some of its luster. Eliina has an arm draped around her while Eira wipes fervently under her puffy eyes. *The fuck?*

I'm not the only one who notices Eira's demeanor. Almost everyone jumps up to greet her and, I'm sure, smother her in affection. Everyone except Ulf, which makes sense. Even Fraya appears concerned, her body lurching backward as Eira passes by, and *that* raises quite a few suspicions.

My spirit tangles with Eira's, and I find it flailing in distress at whatever she saw and the amount of *solliqas* approaching her right now. Before she can even blink, I curl into my shadows, willing them to portal me to my love. Wisps of smoke linger where I was sitting, and in a surge of *maji*, I'm enveloping Eira in my arms before whisking us to the library doors.

There's momentary confusion from everyone except Eliina. She regards me with a shrewd look before she nods, giving me permission to take Eira away from the others. I wrap my arms around her tighter and portal us back to one of the shrouded rooms in Eliina's living quarters. Here, I know the Council won't be able to get to her, and it's hidden enough that neither can our friends. She'll be protected and draped in comfort, able to pick from one of the many fur blankets and cushioned seats surrounding the fireplace.

I grasp Eira's chin, turning her to look up at me. Eyes as dull as a rainy sky peer back at me, a shadow suppressing her usual spark.

"Let's get you something to eat," I murmur. "Even souls here feel better with food in them."

She absently nods, not entirely seeing or hearing me. She doesn't even respond to the shadowy Zaya illusion I create and send her way. With a snap of my fingers, a plate of sizzling meats and roasted vegetables and roots appears before us. I throw in a bowl of spiced bone broth with fish caught fresh this morning at the nearby river. Surprise lights me up, amazed that these abilities I had so long ago are coming back. I know Eira's not here with me mentally when she doesn't react to the portaling *or* my ability to summon food. *That's okay. She has time to learn all I can offer.*

When Eira doesn't move for either option, I pick the large chair closest to the fire and pull her down onto my lap once again. I carefully bring a spoonful of the flavorful soup to her lips. It takes a moment, but she finally parts those pouty lips and swallows down a mouthful. I repeat this a few more times and keep her held steady against my chest. After the fifth or sixth spoonful, a dash of color brings light to her pale skin, and she turns to face me, pushing the bowl away.

"I couldn't save her," Eira whispers.

I do my best to keep a firm hold on my mask, not wanting to discourage her from speaking. But I have no fucking clue what she's talking about.

"Save who, firefly?" I ask.

She swallows. Her eyes dart to the plate of vegetables, and she grabs one of the roots, munching on it before responding. "I couldn't save the *canielor* in the library."

There's a what *in the library? Where we've been gathering?!*

"That poor woman," she continues. "Held down against her will. Betrayed by her own kind." She shakes her head sadly. "I have to be better, Nyx. Queen or not, I can't let this plague continue to destroy the innocent."

"What about those who are already depraved?" I mumble against her hair.

"A healer doesn't distinguish between those who are innocent and corrupt. It's not our role to handle justice."

"But what if you're the queen of healers?" I rasp.

She stares me dead in the eyes. "Then I would be contaminating souls rather than healing them. My loyalties would be misguided."

Eira jumps off me and plucks another root from the plate. I take note that she's been favoring these.

"Where are you going?" I ask, tumbling after her. She hurriedly cloaks herself with one of the blankets, unbothered that it's still humid and scorching outside.

"To complete more of my own healing," she calls back. "The new moons will be upon us and there's no time to waste."

"Surely you want to eat first," I tell her, matching her hasty pace as she speeds through the hallways.

She shoots me a peeved glare and marches forward to the healing quarters, looking ridiculous in her sheer jumpsuit and wrapped up in a thick blanket in this toasty weather. At least we don't have her cat following us. I swear Zaya's goal is to trip us and send us to a swift death.

Eira speeds to the door, light stirring around her body. She pauses before pushing it open and glances back at me. "I'm not sure what they'll find," she says. "Be mindful that you might not like what you'll see."

"I'm not leaving you," I say firmly, leaving no room for negotiation.

Eira shrugs, and I rush inside with her.

"Our queen," Stefanie greets her with a small bow and beaming smile. "Eliina sent word that you might be coming our way. Any pool in particular you'd prefer us to work on you in?"

Eira glances around and points at a pool in one of the corners. This one isn't wholly turquoise but also bright rose and mossy green. Exquisite yellow flora bloom around its edges.

"Those waters can lull you to the deepest, sweetest dreams, but they can also break your worst nightmares right open, making you burst with an aching pain. Are you sure you want this pool?"

"Absolutely," Eira says. "I have an inkling which part of me needs to be healed next. And I won't be able to face it if I'm not forced into doing so. Take me there, and let's begin."

I follow Eira and the healer, who beckons another to join them, and alertly watch as she throws the blankets off to the side and dives straight into the water. No hesitation. Whatever Eliina showed her must have truly set her off if she's willing to dive right into one of her worst memories. I'm almost afraid to see. *Almost.* I'd be lying if the remnants of my beast weren't ecstatic at seeing her nightmares. *Gods, I'm still so fucked.*

"Only two *fims* are here to work on her?" I ask. My tone comes out harsher than I meant, betraying my building uneasiness.

"Us *fims* will be fine," Stefanie responds with a smirk. She throws her curtain of hair up into a messy bun. "And besides, we've got the big, bad princeling here, just in case. Isn't that right, Alyosha?"

The chosen healer, apparently a soul named Alyosha, snickers and leaps up to the stony edge of the pool, climbing one of the surrounding boulders with ease. She walks with a tranquility I envy, her bare feet gripping each stone as if she's done this a million times, not a care in the world as they prepare for whichever horrors are released from the queen with a shattered soul.

Stefanie gets to work chanting, wading far enough into the water that her shoulders are covered. All three colors swirl around her, reminding me of spring and lush green gardens. The other healer stands off to the side with her shoulders squared and her weight on the balls of her feet. Dark tendrils of hair sway against her shoulders in soft waves, her warm brown eyes staring right where Eira dove into the water. Readying herself for the mayhem spiraling to the surface.

A minute passes. And then another. Eira is still under the fucking water. Unease convulses in my core, causing my muscles to twitch in agitation. The demonic beast within that was ready to relish in her nightmares is now frothing at the mouth, antsy to make sure she's okay. *What a sick, protective fuck*. I inch closer to the edge of the pool and remove my top and shoes, discarding them off to the side; I want to be as prepared as possible, if this takes a turn for the worse.

Like a volcanic eruption, molten water bursts from the center of the pool. Eira's delicate form rises as if in slow motion, levitating above the pool's surface, her mouth open in a silent scream. Her snowy and icy-blue hair ripples down behind her. Her limbs hang loose, gravity not letting her out of its clutches. I'm stricken with terror and jog a few steps forward. I don't know what the *fuck* this is, but it's not what she did to me. And I'm not about to wait around for these healers to dictate what will happen to her next.

One, two, three lunging steps, and I'm pushed into the side of a wall of rocks. Alyosha stands on the opposite side of the rising waters and sends another beam of light at my shoulder, immobilizing my whole upper half. *Shit*. I look up, ready to slash out with my shadows and smoke, but the healer merely gives a small smile and shakes her finger *no*. She proceeds to turn her attention back to Eira and molds her golden light into a ball.

Growling, I struggle against the confines of her *maji*,

wondering who the fuck she thinks she is to stop a prince. That's my *queen* suspended in midair, and I'm not about to—

Eira unleashes a heartbreaking scream. Her chest draws in ragged breaths until they grow into gut-wrenching sobs. Stefanie's voice grows louder, booming against the wall of rocks and nearby glass windows. The yellow flowers shake, almost quivering in fear. The healer I'm ready to strangle shapes her light into a number of strands and rays and weaves them into various leaves and vines. She sends them drifting toward Eira's body as scenes of memories flash above her.

My jaw practically hits the floor. I didn't know all that pain and suffering could be seen *outside* of our bodies. *Does that mean Eira saw mine?*

Repressed memory after memory flies by at an unwavering speed until the images pause. It shows a younger version of Eira crying uncontrollably in a house. Alone. Overwhelmingly alone. Her small body shakes with grief.

"Abandoned by your family. A deep-rooted sense of unworthiness. Hollowed out. Release these feelings to the waters, Eira." Stefanie's voice takes a dominating tone. Something tells me her *maji* is connected to a wealth of creatures unknown to even me. "Release this first layer, and you'll come back again to delve into the next one. You don't have to do this all at once right now."

Eira's body violently trembles and those leaves and vines of light wrap more tightly around her. As each muscle slackens, I realize Alyosha is pouring a power that can alleviate such traumatic torment. Eira slowly becomes more and more veiled in the light until it abruptly stops around her abdomen.

"Interesting..." Stefanie murmurs. Grinding her teeth, she directs more of her *maji* into Eira, her arms visibly shaking even under the vicious movements of the water.

Another image flares to life above Eira. Her body changes from incredibly young to the current age before her soul had crossed over to our realm. Back and forth, the size and form of her body lengthens and shortens, but one thing stays the same. She's bent over in anguish, clutching at her stomach. *Oh, no. No, it's her uterus. What does this mean?*

"For years you have suffered." Stefanie's voice rises again. Alyosha is shaking with exertion, her muscles cramping and beads of moisture rolling down her face. She throws more golden plants gliding into the air, wrapping around Eira's hips and throbbing with healing light.

"All of this negative energy writhing like angry vipers around your uterus. They've lashed out at you for many lifetimes. Trying to protect you from the pain you've always known. What would that be, Eira?"

Tears roll down her lovely face, rivers of sadness breaking through a breathtaking mountain pass. *My poor firefly.* "If I resent my uterus, I'll avoid sex." Her voice cracks. "If I avoid sex, I can't possibly have kids. If I don't have kids, there isn't the risk they'll feel abandoned. There isn't the option for me to *fail*."

A tear falls down my own face. I ache to cradle her in my arms. To protect her from her brutal demons.

"But have you ever failed, my queen?"

Sobbing, Eira responds, "N-no. I'm not-t a f-failure."

"That's right," Stefanie continues, her voice becoming tender. "There's pain that can weigh us down, pain that no one else can see. But even with this, consider how you've survived, Eira. Look at how resilient and strong and beautifully brave you've been. Building your own family. Pushing through numbness. Not succumbing to those turbulent thoughts that are set on convincing you to throw your precious life away."

Eira's body is entirely swathed in the lustrous leaves. All bundled and cozy in the healers' love.

"I'm going to lower you back into the water," Stefanie continues. "We'll come back to this memory another time. You made great progress by removing the first layers, showing such tenacity. When you fall back into your soul, ask yourself what you've learned from this. And what you can finally let go of."

Eira gradually breaks the surface of the pool, the waters becoming still once again. The moment she falls under, I tumble into the water, nearly knocking Stefanie over with my foot. *Wish I could say I was sorry, but this demon doesn't change overnight.* I gather my firefly in my arms and bring her close to my chest. Over and over, I murmur how I feel into her ear, placing soft kisses over her face. I wade through the water until we get to the rocky border. I might intentionally smash some of the petals in my blind aggravation.

"Be gentle with her," Stefanie says, catching up to me and placing a shaking hand on my arm. Her skin is slick with perspiration. I pull Eira closer to my chest, baring my teeth at the healer. She laughs and flicks the pool water at me. "I'm not going to take the queen from you. Take it easy with her, okay? She's carried around some hefty trauma and damaging thoughts for what must be lifetimes. I'm not sure how she'll respond when she wakes up."

I grunt out confirmation and make a beeline to one of the seated areas with a roaring fire. I nab the nearest bundle of white, gauzy coverings and when we get to the puffed-up sofa, I hastily throw down blankets and essentially swaddle Eira up like a newborn in the sheer material. Sitting down in front of the fire, I keep Eira curled up against my chest, rocking her slowly. The stars on the coverings shimmer in the firelight, reminding me of the glow of her *maji*.

Time passes. I can't say I know how much or that I care. My focus is on my queen still breathing in my arms, and her body is getting warmer. I never thought I would want this, but I'm desperate for her to light up with her blue flames, even if it burns me in the process. Anything to confirm that she's truly okay.

I find myself gently combing out the knots in her hair while she lays in my lap, eventually plaiting her hair in a number of braids. Cringing at how they fall, I unweave them all and settle for a small braid near the top of her head. Just enough to keep the strands from covering her pretty eyes.

Eira coughs and stretches out her neck. She looks adorably cranky and disoriented. Her eyes flutter open, and I'm met with vibrant blue and silver. I release a breath I didn't even know I was holding.

"Nyx," she breathes.

"Firefly." I offer her a smile. Or I hope that's what I do. You act grumpy enough for decades, your face might rebel against the idea of looking happy.

"You're here. You stayed with me." She burrows in closer to my chest.

I scoff. "Of course I stayed with you. I'll be here for as long as you need. For as many layers as you need to break through as you search for your light."

She gives me a watery smile that grows even wider when she reaches up to pat the braid I finished. "I appreciate you. Fighting your own demonic beast and still being here for me."

"I'm here *with* you, sweetheart," I rasp. Shadow flowers spurt out of my hands and bloom around her cradled head. "We're on this healing journey together. Lifting each other up, no matter how challenging."

Another tear travels down her cheek, and I swoop in to kiss it. Eira giggles, her joy tickling my cracked heart.

"There's still a long way to go," she sighs. "But I now know that I already have the light within me to heal. I had to trust myself enough to search for it, to find it."

I kiss the tip of her nose, relishing the sound of her voice.

"And I'll walk with you through the darkness each time, my firefly, as you remember your light."

FIFTY-THREE

Eira

Time is unsettling. The perception of it. The misunderstanding of it all. How ridiculously impactful it is on everyone. Yet not at the same time. What even is time? Does it actually exist? Or is it just my perception that it does?
-Written musings from Athena Lilar, Novice Healer

Lights twinkle from the swaying orbs and incandescent lanterns, each one placed delicately along the pink and green branches lining the main road in the capital. Stall after wooden stall lines the cobbled street. Some booths are filled with the rich smells of roasted meats and freshly baked pies or syrupy, candied sweets. Others come to life in a flurry of colorful coverings and lavishly created artwork and sizzling potions that sputter on small fires. They go on for what could be forever, winding down the main road and following the curving river that loops into the grove of trees.

Flickering lights and sounds spill out all around us, leading us down the path of what's to come—of the unknown, awaiting our buzzing souls.

"Next one, please!"

I've been tasked with helping the healers finish off the last of the decorative preparations. Ebele insists these aren't decorative fairy lights but are designed to radiate rejuvenating *maji* meant to soothe those attending the festival tonight. Jasón and Nomusa explained there's a number of heightened feelings at any of the festivals, especially when the moons change cycles. The healers will be attending the festivities while also being ready in case any behaviors escalate. Their goal is to be as preventive as possible, so they can also enjoy all the fun.

"Eira, hellloooo, next lantern please," Lyo sings to me. Her earrings made of seeds and petals dangle in the wind.

Shaking myself out of my cluttered thoughts, I carefully hand her the next lantern to hang. It's taken a few days to recover since Stefanie and Alyosha used their *maji* to heal parts of me. The experience was rigorous enough that I'm still feverish and dazed. It's unsettling to be aware of how physical and heavy the trauma weighs against my soul, realizing only now how there's so much more to uncover. I'm grateful it's not the plague, and I'm not currently at risk for turning into a *canielor*. Daya thinks part of why this healing knocked me out so thoroughly has to do with the moons changing tonight and that something big will happen to me. *I really fucking hope not. I'll take an enchanting celebration where I can finally unwind in peace, thank you.*

"Are you feeling alright?" Daglo asks. His black and yellow eyes still make me jump, especially when they're wide with concern. They're all-consuming, like a sun bursting in the galaxy.

"She'll be fine," Daya chirps as she waltzes by. "Our beloved queeny is, what did Athena call it? Just a little bit *discombobulated* today."

I snort, half laughing and half wanting to wring her slim neck. I'm not sure who her *almaove* will be, but I sure am sorry for them.

"How are you holding up?" Erika whispers next to me. She can be alarmingly compassionate at times. "The fresh air doing you any good?"

I nod, never quite knowing how to respond to her. We both have blue eyes, but hers remind me of an iceberg in the middle of the sea, ready to pierce your soul if the wrathful waves don't take you first. I fumble with the next lanterns on the table, hoping no one notices how strung out I am. Eliina instructed us to take a break from researching or learning about the realm and our *maji* abilities. She warned us that doing this during one of the biggest celebrations of the year instead of integrating ourselves will only draw unwanted attention. But I can't snuff out the anxious feeling grating under my skin. *Whose attention are we drawing? The Sairn? A* solliqa *on the Council? Something else entirely?*

Athena tackles me with a side hug, the breath getting knocked out of me. I laugh, shoving her off me playfully. "Since when did *you* become so strong?"

"Since when did you become so *weak*?" she retorts. "Come on, you've gathered enough lanterns for a hundred Moons Cycle Festivals. Let's find a snack."

Chuckling, I allow her to pull me away from the others. "Same as always, Athena. Sneaking away for treats and snacks."

She raises an eyebrow at me. "And? I don't see you complaining."

"We can always try new *veina*," a new voice chimes in. We both shriek like hyenas, Odin bent over laughing in between us. He is starting to take some sick joy in scaring the living fuck out of us—*me* in particular.

"How do you even do that?" I screech, still laughing and half crying, my heart thundering in my chest.

"I'm called to both the wind and the sea." Odin winks. "It pays to have many talents. Especially when I get to use them in such fun ways. Such as blending in with the air around you, knowing you can't sense when I'm right here."

"Yeah, yeah, whatever," Athena mutters. "Where's this *veina* you were talking about?"

He laughs and points to one of the booths. "We need to go get it. Hadwin—"

Odin turns around in a circle, looking hilariously confused. "Hm, that's strange. He was here a minute ago."

Athena rolls her eyes. "Yeah, that's rather typical of him. Disappears when he's most needed."

"Not to fret, I can show you how to get the goods," Odin whispers to us, as if he's letting us in on a big secret.

"I prefer to show them." I know it's Nyx before turning around. Smoke cascades around my shoulders, honeyed and charred and mouthwatering.

Odin scoffs. "Alright, you can come with us."

Athena and I giggle at Nyx's incredulous look, and the four of us meander our way through the stalls. The dusky sky washes over us with its purple and blue gradient, mirroring the rising moons ascending above the forest. The shades remind me of the indigo and lavender fields in the countries south of Sweazn, flourishing under the single sun of our solar system, their petals like gemstones scattered on the rolling hills. I let myself take in the colors, memorizing them, to remember this rare moment of hope budding inside me. To keep it tucked away when I'm too lost to see the beauty of this realm.

Odin hooks his arms with Athena's and mine, much to Nyx's dismay, and tugs us to a stall with freshly baked treats. A mixture of sweet tartness and savory spices batters my senses, and I'm not too proud to hide my eagerness for food. Athena is acting as starved as I am, even though I definitely caught her shoving berries and pillowy-looking bread into her mouth less than an hour ago. *Some things will never change and* this *I'm totally okay with.* Scrunching my brows, I turn my head to face Nyx.

"How are we supposed to pay for this? Come to think of it, I don't think I've ever seen *solliqas* use coins here," I whisper.

He chuckles, his hot breath tickling my neck. "That's because we don't. If we've learned anything from the realm of Earth, it's that money is one of the roots of all evil. And we don't need any of *that* mixing with souls like Ulf here."

"Huh," Athena breathes. "So, how are we supposed to buy these?" She impatiently taps her foot on the ground, and I can't help but laugh. When we're hungry, we're *hungry*.

"We trade services or *maji* here," Odin says. "Watch."

He greets the *solliqa* working the booth, a stout, curvy *fim* with luscious black locks pulled back out of her dark eyes. She's wearing gloomy shades of coverings that are in total contrast to the flashing symbols and painted designs of her booth. She glances at Odin expectantly. He points to four of the pies, two savory and two sweet, and she glances around her stall.

"I could use more herbs, some of that *maji* you add to *lipva*, and is that a healer? These burns are ruining my concentration." Her voice is hoarse, as if she's been yelling over the clanging sounds of a kitchen all day.

Odin nods his head and sends a flare of *maji* at a huge jug of *lipva* in the corner of her booth. "Athena, think you can gather any herbs for our chef here?"

Athena hesitates but ultimately closes her eyes, keeping her palms facing upward toward the *solliqa*. Green light coats her arms and tiny leaves crawl down to her fingertips before gliding up to the *solliqa's* hands. Giddiness seeps from Athena as the clerk snatches up the different herbs. She *totally* owes me an explanation of where she learned to do that. Everyone turns to face me, and I realize it's my turn. *Ugh. Similar to presentations back in school. All those eyes watching me, seeing if I'll mess up.*

I reluctantly press my hands against the *solliqa's* outstretched arms, focusing on connecting to my breath and being mindful of the blistering burns welded onto her skin. I send the smallest trickle of *maji* I can, not because I don't want to give her more, but because I don't want to send her careening over the edge wrapped in my flames. This must do the trick, since new skin weaves on top of the burns in a matter of seconds.

She smiles, looking pleased at the *maji* she received. "That was *very* nice," she says. "Here, take an extra pie. I haven't been healed like that in years."

I flush with pride, overjoyed that I completed another healing session, even if it was brief. Nyx kisses just below my ear, and hazy shadow hummingbirds fly out from his fingers and travel all around us.

Athena nudges my ribs. "Fancy healing queen with a prince who gives you fancy shadow pets. I need to get you a sign."

"Oh, please don't," I mumble. "You know how I feel about attention."

She flashes me a wicked smile. "Or maybe we can all get matching coverings. Promoting your healing services."

"They can have Eira's embarrassed face on them, bright red for special effect," Odin says around a mouthful of pie.

Nyx laughs, the sound free and contagious. "I vote for making hats."

By the time we make it back to the others, I've been fed a sliver of each pie, and am ushered toward a bouncing Daya. This is *never* a good sign.

"Why are you bursting with excitement?" I ask, narrowing my eyes.

"Erika and I made you something to wear tonight!" She's bubbling like a glass of champagne, and I'm ready to bolt in the opposite direction.

"You mean coverings with the least amount of fabric possible?" I mutter, getting more flustered by the second.

"Absolutely," Erika says, peering at me over a glass of *veina*. "It's a night to embrace our bodies, no matter their shape or size.

Our soul forms burn their brightest under the change of the moons."

I make a face and turn to Athena. "Where's Zaya? Still back in the quarters?"

"Mhm," she hums. "I know she's a rather adventurous kitty, but I didn't think she'd want to explore a festival with so many souls fluttering about."

"Yeah," I agree. Although I'm wishing she was with me. Zaya manages to give me the strength others can't.

"We can take her back some fried fish as a treat," Nyx whispers to me. I grin, grateful he realizes what she means to me.

"And where's Eliina?" I ask.

Ivar pins me with his inky-blue stare. "We were just debating this."

"It appears she's given each of us a different reason for why she can't be here," Delano jumps in. "She's at a Council meeting before the festival is in full swing."

"Or tucking away our resources in the library," Daya adds.

"Communicating with one of the healers," Daru says.

"Sending messages to her base."

"Preparing security for plague attacks coming our way."

"Securing extra lodging with Namid."

"Taking care of a conflict between angry manipulators and shifters."

I stop hearing the words they're saying, too lost in the jarring discontentment. This isn't the first time there's been conflicting information shared with me. There's been bickering between our two groups of companions, especially during that long journey to Rioa. Disagreements about the order of previous battles, which power is from which region and why, where 'gods' have traveled from in other realms. The list goes on and on.

I originally chalked it up to different upbringings, since not everyone comes from Rioa. Any time the conversations turned into fuming confrontations, I thought there's obviously going to be contention. Some of them suffer from a soul-deep disease and were banished for an illness out of their control, while others have been favored by the Council.

I'm sure my close confidants and someone like Eliina, who's been extraordinarily benevolent, are telling their own truths. They *have* to be. I won't accept another answer.

But Eliina's connection to Shira is dubious.

They're *sisters*. I glance over at Athena, spitting a slew of sass at Hadwin. There's no way, in any timeline or realm or life, that I would let her go. We're not related by blood. Our connection is the kind of bond that never breaks. For Eliina to act so nonchalant about letting her sister go... it's unnerving.

And now Eliina is giving different reasons for not being here? After corralling us all together, including those of us taken from Earth? I don't understand and have an unsettling suspicion we'll all find out sooner than later.

I gasp, overtaken by sudden regret.

"I haven't even *thought* about Tryg," I groan.

Everyone exchanges pointed looks. *Um, no. I don't think so.*

"What are you all not telling me?"

Nyx turns me toward him, his eyes laced with remorse. His lips tug up in a subtle smile. Shadows frame his haunting face, from his tousled hair down to his sharp jawline, and lash out toward me, soothing in their own ways.

Gods, he's devastatingly beautiful.

"We aren't telling you theories and suspicions that we have. Nothing concrete. There's no official confirmation of what's been happening with Tryg, and without proof of our concerns, we didn't want to worry you, sweetheart."

"*Your* concerns?" I scoff. "Since when have you been concerned about Tryg?"

"Since I realized that to adore you is to embrace those you care for," Nyx murmurs. "To care for you is to acknowledge that I might've been wrong. For you're the one filled with light, clearing away my demon. How could I possibly see what Tryg is through the dark?" He chews on the inside of his lip, his eyes darting around my face. "I still have my reservations about his soul based on what he's done before, but if you're willing to still see the good in him, then I'll have to learn this, too."

Squealing, I throw my arms around him. I'm too blown away by his admission and willingness to see what makes Tryg my friend to continue focusing on why no one has told me their concerns yet. I'll save that qualm for another day. If I've learned anything so far in this realm, it's how quickly the world shifts under your feet and tempers with the very nature of a soul.

"Not to interrupt a mushy moment here," Daya says, sneaking her hand around my waist. "But we've got a festival to get ready for. *Now*. So, run along shadow boy, we've got hours of work to do in mere minutes. Chop, chop!"

I'm turned around by the *solliqas* in a matter of seconds, being hurled away to an empty stall to change into whatever coverings they've cooked up for me this time. Nyx sends a trickle of smoke across my neck before I'm shoved into the booth, surrounded by chortling lunatics who have wormed their way into my heart. And into Athena's, by the sound of her laugh.

"Buckle up, queeny," Daya snickers. "You're in for a wild, bumpy ride. And you're not getting off until you've been successfully beautified for this festival."

"Who decides whether it's successful?" I mutter.

"*Us*." The *fims*, and to my horror, some of the healers, cackle. And it begins.

FIFTY-FOUR
Nyx

When we give ourselves over to our maji,
we can find our true purpose.
-Page 460, Understandings of the Soul, Volume I

"Beginning with the first strike of the chimes, the *solliqas* will be driven by the untamed manifestation of their given *maji*," one of the Council members announces in the center of this section of stalls. "We have created these chimes so that as soon as the new moons' light touches them, their music will resonate across the capital. We give many thanks to the healer Cadence for her innovation. When you hear their melody, that will be your opportunity to seek shelter. Not every soul wants to, or should, be around the havoc often seen at this festival. Especially during such dark times."

I snort, immediately pretending to cough to cover it up. What deranged fools. This is one of the few times a year our *maji* controls *us*, when true bliss ensnares even the youngest of the souls.

"Are you ready?" Ulf huffs beside me. He is covered head to

toe in pitch black, the gleam in his nearly soulless eyes and his savage, wolfish smile showing.

"Very much so," I say. "You know, you're probably the reason they even need to give this stupid warning."

"As if you haven't joined in on the fun." Hadwin chuckles next to me, bumping into my shoulder. He's wearing a black and green mask that highlights his alluring eyes.

Ivar and Odin approach us with grim faces, each wearing dark coverings. I'm the only one wearing a mixture of black and white tonight. Eira's healing light might have inspired the white covering I grabbed instead of my usual black or gray.

"You good?" I ask.

Ivar stabs his fingers into his hair and looks away, blowing out a hard breath. "Things will be," he mutters.

Odin doesn't respond and keeps his gaze on the ground. I want to push, want to ask what in Cudhellen they're not telling me—on a night such as this, of all times.

"Our prince asked you a question," Hadwin grunts.

Gods, he really picks the best times to stand his ground. He's been such a prickly fuck lately.

"Hadwin, it's—"

"Then he can fucking punish me for not wanting to talk right now," Odin sneers.

I lay a hand on his shoulder, a flicker of dread snagging my heart. He doesn't get easily irritated. Not unless something is terribly wrong. "Hey, it's a celebration tonight. Let's—"

"Do me a favor, Nyx," Odin mutters, as quiet as the calm wind. "Keep your queen close to you tonight."

That puts me on high alert.

"Alright, enough with the cryptic shit, what's—"

"Hellooooooo friends!" Daya announces from behind us. She weaves her way around another group of *solliqas*. "Feel free to personally thank me for my deviously gorgeous work." She tosses me a wink and skips over to Delano and Daru, who've been keeping a healthy distance from the rest of us. Probably because we look as if we're on our way to assassinate someone. Daru's eyes go wide, and his jaw slackens. I follow his line of vision and—*oh my*.

Erika slithers by us, barely concealing herself with azure scales practically painted onto her skin. She whispers in Fraya's ear, who's wrapped up in sheer black coverings that sparkle as she moves. Behind them, Athena is wearing a matching white and green mask and skimpy dress set, the colors making her eyes blaze under all the lights. Her dark hair is plaited in many braids, wrapped around her head like a crown. The whole look is incredibly fitting and arousing. But it's the white-haired beauty next to her that has me choking on air.

Eira doesn't even have to try. She's a goddess sent from the demon gods the Sairn worship. Her stunning hair is left down in loose waves, only part of it pulled back out of her face. Instead of a mask, she opted for blue, silver, and black face paint, accenting those captivating eyes of hers. She's wrapped in a flimsy covering threaded with black, blue, and silver. Its thin straps crisscross up around her neck, leaving her shoulders deliciously exposed.

I'm most surprised that she's walking barefoot toward us.

"You're impeccable," I whisper. "A dream come true."

"Good," she says with a smirk. "I like how the colors match those shadows of yours. Thought we could play tonight."

Licking my lips, I nod, unable to form words. I'm not sure who this smoky knockout is and what she did with my Queen of Light, but I'm glad she's saying hi.

"No shoes?" Hadwin asks from behind me.

Eira tilts her head to the side. "How will Nyx chase me if I can't run?"

My beast uncoils, shaking slightly with mirth.

"Careful, prince," Ulf murmurs. "She might be healing you, but you're surely corrupting her."

Eira responds by taking my hand in hers and guiding us

along the row of stalls and different booths. The winding streets are bustling with *solliqas*, each brimming over with delight for the festival. Night has crept up on us by this point, but the moons won't be rising for another hour or so. We take our time wandering around the different shops, Eira being pulled occasionally by the *fims* or Delano wanting to show her a fascinating book he's found. I have a hand on her, no matter where we go or who we talk to. Odin's warning is still rattling around in me, but he's nowhere to be seen now.

Fuck. I want to warn the others, but I don't even know what I'd say. That Odin is acting mysterious and temperamental on a night when our *maji* turns particularly wicked? That's nothing new.

Eira moves in front of me, grabbing another earring to try on. Her and Athena's excitement about the dangling jewelry is endearing. The ones she's currently trading *maji* for are dancing spirals of black with splashes of gold and silver. She turns to face me, switching them out with the ones she has on.

"These remind me of you," she says.

"Yeah?" I ask.

"Yeah," she says with a small smile. "They remind me of your smoke and the light moving around in your eyes."

Cute in the best possible ways. I loop my arm around her waist and pull her flush against me.

"Are you enjoying the festival so far?" I ask her.

She peers up at all the floating lights and down toward the booths we have yet to explore. "I think it'll do. For a festival controlled by the Council."

"So sassy," I tease, tapping her nose. "What else is on your mind?"

Eira's quiet for a moment. "Everything and anything," she sighs, playing with her new earrings. "Our strengthening connection. How I'm brimming with discomfort. I'm fraught with anxiety about, well, *everything*. How beautiful I look for a soul still processing such bleak emotions about my body. The fact that I forgot about Tryg, a soul who's supposed to be one of my best friends." She heaves another sigh, shaking her hair out behind her. "So, you know. Everything. All at once."

"So much going on in that gifted mind of yours," I murmur. "There's a lot to still work through. Tryg will take a while, I'm sure."

She glances away, shifting restlessly on her feet. *Fucking bare feet. It will be so arousing to chase her, yet she's such a weirdo.*

"Hey," I say. I turn her chin to face me again. "Don't be so hard on yourself about Tryg. There's also a lot of anger surrounding his soul that you've been privy to lately. Despicable things he's done to our families from a time long ago. Such dreadful acts that would make Ulf look like a saint. It's bound to rot not only his soul but the rest of ours as we continue to mourn."

"Hmm," Eira hums. "That makes sense. I just... it's hard for me to conceptualize and fit all these different pieces of Tryg together in my mind. There's the friend I grew up with, who essentially took me in when my family vanished. There's the version the others told me about, who apparently helped 'them' destroy me, whoever 'they' are."

Huh. "And his soul has been destroyed each time he's brought pain on a *solliqa* here."

"So... he keeps coming back?"

I'm not sure which response I can give her. His soul could be returning. Or there could be another reason, yet why does it seem there are many sides to him? And how are they such close friends that her soul is in agony over this when he tried to have her destroyed?

I can't worry too much about this right now. Because there goes that melody.

Chimes envelope our senses for a few brief minutes. The sound is loud enough that it has our bodies gyrating.

And then chaos ignites around us. *Solliqas* of all sorts cheer and woop in deafening excitement. The ascending moons grow even brighter, and Eira stares at me in wonder.

"Do you think this is what those shifters experience in the movies back on Earth?" she whispers to me.

"What?" *Shifter movies?*

"Yeah," she says dreamily. "Bathing in the moonlight and their bones morph into another creature entirely."

In a blaze of smoldering embers and bright blue light, Eira lets out a howl of joy and soars over one of the stalls, landing as a crystalized fox. One so similar to the one that jumped through me, except this fox is vibrating with brightness, ready to ignite. It has Eira's exact eyes and stares straight into me, right to my winding beast. She snaps a translucent golden whip into my beast's face. It snarls at her in retaliation, but she's already gone.

"Catch me if you can, panther darling. Find me in your shadows." Her voice is velvet, a faint caress.

I'm smoke in the wind before my brain can catch up to what my soul urges me to do. I don't dare portal. I'm finally getting my bearings with that particular talent again, and there's too high of a risk that I'll lose her scent. That distinct mixture of sparkling snow and sunlight on a beach and sweetness buried in fire—all forms of light that I know I'll follow to any realm, wherever she chooses to go.

I match her speed, getting lost when we get to the trees. She's a clever *fim*, my firefly, figuring out how to change the color of her fox to match the passing colorful trees. But she hasn't spent as much time here, doesn't know these woods like the back of her hand. *I do.* And for that reason alone, I'm going to win.

Breaking away from the forest, I fling myself toward the edge of the river. I know *exactly* where she's going to go. From this new angle, I see random views of our companions. They're thoroughly losing themselves in this achingly spellbinding night. Delano sprints wildly past me, his teeth clashing before he transforms into multiple bird forms, shrieking up at the stars as *maji* glitters down his sleek feathers. Ulf crawls next to a tree nearby, muttering to himself that he can *feel* her, that a *fim* is calling out to him tonight. Erika arches above a group of *solliqas* in the water in one of her many scaled forms. Her fins glow under the moonlight and send dazzling currents of purple, green, and blue light along the water. *Gods*, Ivar is fucking a *solliqa,* and I hope they know what they got themselves into. Athena is giggling as if she's high as the different colored plants flow out of her body, whispering to someone I can't see in the shadows.

They're all losing themselves to the chaos of their *maji*. Powers that could eliminate this entire realm if they're not careful.

I transform into a web of dark clouds, keeping close to the shadow of one of the bigger trees. Any second now, my queen will fall right into my trap.

"Not if you fall into mine first."

Eira flings herself from the base of the tree, the one I was hiding behind, and crashes into me. Her claws latch onto my web, dragging me with her as she darts to a gathering of rocks near the water. I morph into my usual form and stare down at this little fox. I'm utterly breathless and am hoping she transforms back to her humanoid self. I want to bury myself in this feisty *fim*.

"How'd you know where I'd go?" I ask, still huffing down breaths.

She doesn't respond. Instead, she approaches me slowly, brushing against the shadows curling near my feet.

"Our souls are linked. I'll always find where you go."

"Are you afraid of where that'll lead you?"

"I'm not afraid of what consumes you, Nyx. I'll help you find your own light with the light of my own. We'll find all those hard pieces that broke you, and I'll crack them wide open to push all the light back in."

Swallowing, I scratch behind one of her massive ears, enamored by her. "I'll do the same for you, firefly."

Crying out in surprise, I'm pulled upward before landing on my feet again. My shadows funnel around me with a mind of their own. A split second passes where I'm *out-of-my-mind* terrified. This isn't usual. My monstrous demon will take over, but my shadows don't chain me to the ground with their own free will. Before I can wade into the tide of panic coming at me, my humanoid form starts to sprout fur of different colors. I twist and mold into an entirely new creature, at least new to me.

Until my own fox form is staring eye-to-eye with the white and blue vixen in front of me.

"Not quite a panther, but I think this'll do." Eira is practically purring into my mind. She blinks those huge eyes of light and licks the side of my nose before burrowing her head into my neck.

Looking down at myself, I can't be sure of what I even am. I can *feel* that I'm a fox, similar to Eira. But no clear color shines past the wall of shadows and smoke spilling around my body.

Eira cocks her head to the side. *"So interesting. My light can sense patches of white on your fur."* Her eyes move along my whole form. *"And there's bright red and maroon on your ears and tail. Similar to fresh snow dipped in blood. I love it."*

Chuckling, I observe myself grow up, up, up into the shape of a human, leaving that new form behind for now. "I'm still covered in darkness," I murmur. "I have to wonder what that means for our souls."

Eira evaporates into the air as little lightning bugs, swirling in a funnel until she takes her humanoid form.

"Our souls will be just fine. We'll survive this plague because the fire inside of me burns brighter than the flames of Cudhellen surrounding us," she breathes. "And I'll burn bright enough for the both of us if I need to."

My heart stutters, or is that my soul?

"My spirit will always be with you as we burn in our flames together," I murmur.

Eira's eyes flare wide, and her mouth drops open in surprise.

"You've said something similar to me before," she whispers.

My eyebrows furrow while my tongue glides along my teeth. "When?"

She stares at me in wonder and grabs my hand, tracing the outlines of my dark markings. "What I thought was a nightmare. You didn't look the way you do now. You had dark eyes mixed with sapphire and creamy skin. A different kind of prince in a remarkable kingdom far from here. Many, many years ago on Earth. Our lives didn't end favorably in that lifetime, but you were wrong about another thing you said. That fate was never going to be on our side. Because here we are, aren't we?"

I smile so widely it hurts. Of everything that's happened, there's one thing I'm certain of. Fate will *always* be on our side.

A sudden feeling of distress coils deep in my torso. I take a quick glance around the forest, and it occurs to me we might have been out here too long already. And with Eira's comment, I certainly don't want another lifetime to end. Not when she's finally back in Majikaero.

"Eira, sweetheart. Let me take you back closer to the city."

"Why?" She pouts. "I thought we're supposed to unwind tonight."

"That's right," I say. Silently begging any god that will listen to make this easier. "Just that reminder of the plague. Of previous lifetimes not ending in our favor. I don't think we should be this far out here with everything going on. We're *not* like Ulf or the rest of them."

"But it's a *dream* out here, Nyx," Eira whines, throwing her arms around me. "And I have *so* many questions for you. Like what is the realm even made of, do you ever wonder? Where did our *maji* come from? What makes up our souls?" She loses her train of thought for a second, and it occurs to me that she might be drunk on her newly found power. "The possibilities must be endless, right? In a realm pretty free of restrictions. You can even travel in your fancy shadows!"

I chuckle, wondering how I'm going to force her back to the safety of the main road. She has no idea the dangers that exist, even here. "I was wondering when you would bring that up. I can make things appear out of thin air if I reach through space to get to where I want to go. There's a book I have back in my room about time wielders and those who can shape the space around them that I'd love to show you."

She gapes at me, slinking further into the base of another tree. I burst out laughing, her expression hilariously baffled. "I can't wait to see what your abilities are under all that pain."

Smiling, I tug her closer into my arms and brace myself for the oncoming argument. She's rather attached to these trees right now.

But that doesn't matter. Not when I see Jade fly above us—our only warning before all the glowing orbs explode.

FIFTY-FIVE

Eira

What could be worse than death?
Reality.
-King Gainde of Reykashin, Land of Smoke

Explosive sensations trickle down my body, holding me captive. It's hard to concentrate on my surroundings when Nyx looks scrumptious enough to eat, and this *maji* is whooshing through me at exhilarating speeds.

Multiple voices whisper around me, spiraling down, down, down into my well of *maji*. It's like a vision is sinking its talons into my mind, prying my eyes open, making me truly *see*.

Different animals hurtle past me, murmuring words of silk I want to wrap myself in forever. They are creatures I connect to, ones I have yet to become. For I am the light, and the more I embrace who I am, the more I'll discover. They all tell me this, *yes*. That I must learn to walk with fear in the dark. I scream out that I already do that with Nyx. I laugh, thrilled that I can do this. That I can talk with these ancient voices, both a part of me and separate. That I proudly stand next to one of my other soul mates, even with a soul so dark.

A final voice whirls around me. Its lips sweep against my soul and tells me I can do this. That Nyx isn't something to be feared, that he's only misunderstood.

But do I realize who I should actually fear, who I already deem safe? Who will betray me?

I'm jolted from the sensation of exhilarating peace by this confusing question.

No, no, no, no. I tell that raspy, sultry voice. *No, my friends wouldn't betray me!* I scream.

I'm screaming. Nyx is screaming.

"Eira!" He's shaking me so violently, my head is flinging against the ground. "I need you to tell me you're okay!"

A chill skates down my trembling body. I need to tell him. *What* do I need to tell him?

My eyes must snap back into focus because his head falls on top of me in relief. Then I'm scooped up in his arms, holding on for dear life.

"This might be unpleasant for you," he mutters. "But it's the swiftest way for us to get back, and we've *got* to get out of here."

I'm not understanding. But because the gods love for me to be petrified, whether in this realm or the next, I'm quickly brought up to speed. Toxic flames, completely different from my own, rain down from the bursting orbs above us. I'm narrowly safe because of Nyx's shadowy shields, apparently unaffected by the poison trickling out of them.

"Why are the orbs spilling all over us?" I ask him, not quite sure my mouth is forming words. Chaos moves around us at varying speeds. My senses haven't caught up to this new reality, though.

"It's a trap," Nyx huffs, not taking his eyes off me as he sneaks us behind another tree. "A tactic previously used in Wyndera. Glowing orbs float high up in the sky, traveling on the winds, until the *maji* within them explodes in bursts of poisonous smoke and liquids. Our realm has been at peace for so long, it's not something I would have expected. That's a mistake here, firefly. You must *always* be prepared for the unexpected to happen."

A gravelly roar shakes the branches near us, and my soul sputters, close to fainting. A creature far worse than what I saw in the Crystal Trance or back in the library is seething in the distance. Vines coated in thorns curl in thick cords around and through the holes in its face. Large angular eyes swirl in colors of red and silver. Each step the creature takes vibrates from my toes to my chattering teeth, and my vision blurs with how quickly it suddenly lurches forward. Spiked teeth are dripping in an opal liquid I do *not* want to know about and snap viciously at a *solliqa* backed against a tree. I'm preparing myself to watch a soul get eradicated, but the colossal brute snags the poor soul in its claws. And it's *gone*. Dissipates into nothingness as if it melted back into the earth itself. The only sign it was here is the eerie silence left behind.

I clutch onto Nyx like a baby sloth, too intoxicated by the surge in my *maji* to fully function. *Come on, Eira. Get a fucking grip. Pull that fire shield up.* But I *can't*. It's too disorienting, going from a towering high down to watching innocent souls get stolen by a creature five times the size of a *canielor*.

"Gods, what the fuck is that? We're going *now*," Nyx rasps. My gaze wanders up and down the colorful bark Nyx has us backed against. I swear the tree is moving in sharp movements, wielding itself around us in violent motions. Swirling crystal eyes from one of the holes indented in the tree make swift contact with my own, and I yelp into Nyx's shoulder.

He taps my face lightly. "Come on, I need you back with me, firefly. Xylia can only keep us sheltered for so long. I'm taking us right to Eliina, wherever I can sense her. There might be more danger where I'm taking us, and I don't want you at a higher risk of injury than you already are. Plus, your friends might need us."

That gets the gears moving. My life's in danger? *Psh, what-*

ever. My friends need my help? I'm coming, even if I'm leaving a trail of blood on the way.

"Thanks, Xy!" Nyx shouts. "Save the *solliqas* you can find and then get out of here." He flings us into a mass of his shadows. I'm torn in every direction. Voices, scents, locations pull at me, competing for my attention. I'm 99 percent sure I'm going to vomit all over my beloved when we land against a wall, Nyx taking the brunt of the fall for us.

"Are you okay?" He hastily scans my face and down the length of my body.

"I'm fine," I suck in a much-needed breath of air. "But we need to have a talk about all that portaling."

He barks a laugh. "You've only done it a few times!"

"And that might be more than enough. Especially if we're going a longer distance. Now where are we?"

Nyx takes my hand, and I swear he's going to tear it off with how hard he's squeezing it. I don't argue because, honestly, he's a territorial, frightened shadow prince, and I'm barely keeping it together as it is while still coming down from my intoxicated high.

And we're apparently in a fucking dungeon because the night *must* get more exciting.

"Really?" I scoff.

"What?"

"You bring us to a *dungeon*? Are you trying to get us captured or killed? Haven't you seen the movies?"

Nyx slowly blinks at me. "No, I haven't. And we're here because I sensed a number of our companions here and Eliina's scent, which disturbed me. From what I know, Eliina doesn't typically spend her time in Rioa's dungeon. I don't like the heady scent of terror felt from both her and the friends I could sense. I don't know what's happening right now, but this could be another trap laid out for us. Now keep to the shadows as best as you can and get ready to put that shield of yours up."

"You think this is all for *us*?"

Nyx looks over his shoulder at me. "Firefly, there might be a plague of darkness, but that's never stopped this festival before. The one difference is our presence. There's *no way* this isn't intentional."

We sneak along the edges of the hallway, the stones damp and slippery. Nyx's shadows flail out around him like swords. As one would expect, this entire place reeks of mold and stale bread and death. I'm not sure which companions are down here, but my heart lurches when I realize Athena could be one of them. *Gods, no. I'll trade places with her in a heartbeat. And take Nyx with me.*

He throws out a tendril of smoke to stop me. After peering around the corner, his shoulders slump in defeat, and I peer around him, scared out of my fucking mind of who I'll see.

Ivar. Odin. Fraya. Ulf. Hadwin. Daru. Healers. Shifters I've seen around Eliina's quarters. Tryg. Each is chained by a metal as bright as liquid starlight. My eyes bolt from side to side, frantic to find the others. Hoping, yet dreading, that they're also here, so everyone's contained in one place. I've never been more grateful that Athena insisted Zaya stay back in the quarters. At least she should be safe.

I have so many questions. So *many* fucking questions.

My eyes nearly bulge out of my head, and I can tell my soul wants to transform back into the fox. A form it's desperate to take when it feels attacked and on edge. And by the silent clanging in my chest, my soul is *definitely* on edge. A woman is on bloodied knees in the corner, her hands squeezing the dungeon door tightly enough that her hands are shaking. The mixture of wide brown eyes, tangled hair of fire, and eerie smile makes my heart seize up.

"Mayra?!" I rasp. *Why is one of my clients here? How long has it been? Why is she in a dungeon? How the hell did she get here?*

Athena's wail startles me, breaking me out of my spiraling

thoughts. She is as still as a statue, or *was,* because I didn't see a speck of movement, and she is now sobbing against the outside of one of the cells. Hadwin is straining against the chain, his head mere inches from hers. Her hands are trembling, cautiously wiping his bleeding head. My eyes rake down his body, repulsed by the deep gashes and black blood dripping down his torso and legs, pooling all around him.

I realize with a jolt that Ivar, Odin, Fraya, Ulf, Daru, and the others are all in similar states. Ivar and Odin have been tortured and are on the cusp of death. Shards of their bones are poking through shredded flesh, parts of their humanoid forms laying in pieces. Burned feathers lay scattered around them, drenched in the same black blood. Fraya is lying in a heap of stone and silver liquid, wholly unconscious. My heart breaks when I see Daru and Ulf crumpled together in one cell. I know it's Ulf by his wolf form, his fur all mottled and torn off his back, his snout smashed and broken. Daru is in a similar state to Ivar and Odin, except he has bite marks littering his whole chest.

The other healers and shifters are quietly moaning from their own pain, still conscious and somewhat whole. *Thank the gods.*

As much as all this torments me, I'm infinitely more distraught by Tryg. I can't even *believe* what I'm seeing. He looks like my friend, yet there are subtle differences that pull me right back into one of my nightmares. His eyes are darker, with whirls of black dripping out of them. A cruel smile takes over half his face and stretches far too widely to be human. I've seen Tryg with scruff along his jaw when he's worked late nights and has forgotten to shave. This is nothing comparable, not with the way his cheeks are hollowed out and each of his bones push against his flesh in demented shapes, the skin thin and nearly ripping. Jagged cuts lay in filthy layers all over his body, each one oozing a thick, sizzling liquid.

He's a walking, living, barely breathing ghost. And I'm not sure I'll be able to bring his soul back from this.

I hesitantly approach him, waves of light blue fire deciding to finally make their appearance down my arms and legs. Coating me in protection, knowing I'm in need of their aid. Nyx stays right behind me, letting me take the lead with approaching my friend but still ready to cut him down.

"Come closer, darling," Tryg rasps. His voice is strange, throwing me off kilter. It's like cement being poured over my heart. "Come see the truth. It's been an awfully long time since you've been on Earth."

Tears run down the paint Daya so effortlessly drew on my face. I place my hand upon his head, reminding myself to be fearless. *I will walk with my fear in the dark.* I'm yanked into his mind. Completely at mercy to the way his barbed mental shield slices into my soul. And he *pours* everything into me. Until I'm overflowing, the memories bursting into my *solliqa* form, and I'm choking on my tears.

Nyx wrenches my hand away, and we tumble backward to the ground. My body's numb to the icy feel, too caught up in the fear and confusion trampling through me.

Dreadful events are taking place on Earth right now. Dozens of images were shoved into me against my will. Gore and splintered bones and blazing fires and smoke reeking of human flesh. My friends bound together by the hair of corpses, screaming for help in a room of beatless hearts. Astira's hands around a squirming child. Morgan sprinting down a darkened hallway. Shira appears in fragments in an underground tunnel. Scattered explosions from underground. Tears spilling into cracked spaces. Agony and mayhem are everywhere, and the last image Tryg pushes into me has me reeling. It must be him manipulating all of this to hurt me somehow. My friends couldn't be mixed up with a situation so atrocious. Bile rises in a rush up my already raw throat, and I'm gasping for any shred of my withering sanity.

I look at Tryg with round eyes, a window into my conflicting feelings.

"No," I whisper. "No, they *wouldn't* do such a thing."

He *smiles*. It's menacing. A version of him that I don't know.

"I thought you woke up, darling," he laughs, thoroughly unhinged. "You should know we're all just victims of a veiled reality, capable of doing *anything* in Majikaero.

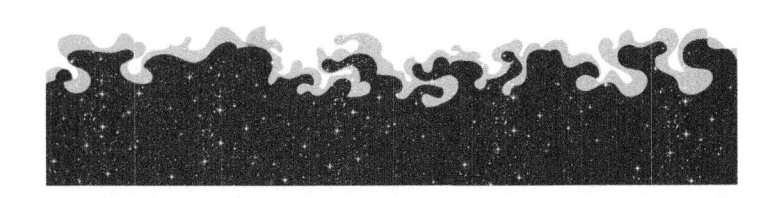

FIFTY-SIX

Nyx

*When you find your almaove, you must do everything in
your power to protect them. You might be the only one who can
when they're at their most vulnerable.*
-Nicola, Goddess of the Soul

Majikaero, this chaotic realm, has shown me love that can dazzle, creatures that might play with your imagination, and nightmares that will devour your entire existence. My soul has come and gone from this world, yet it's stitched into the very fabric of this atmosphere. Not much can surprise me anymore. How could it? When you've survived being ripped from this reality, abandoned by your soul family, even taken advantage of by your friend's monstrous form. You've already looked evil in the eye and lived to tell the tale.

But this shit? What could have prepared me for it? Tryg, who not long ago was a newly created *solliqa,* carrying around a feared past, lunges for Eira with what I sense are invisible hands. He's already drowning in his plagued form. One glance around the dungeon tells me our group is not only split up, but some have been captured by the Council's chains of starlight. I didn't anticipate it ending this way. Not this night, when I was gloriously distracted by Eira's mischief and delicious love.

Ignorant, I know. There's so much that should have been obvious. This shithole reeks of Eliina's scent, the healer who was supposed to protect us. I know better than most how the ones you trust can be the quickest to break you. Ivar and Odin were acting sketchy as fuck before the bells chimed. I've known all along that Tryg would cave to his own personal darkness the moment Eira voiced she was choosing me. On top of all of this, our group already discussed why the Council would bring us to Rioa for this festival, knowing it would be the perfect night to see what we could do. To take advantage of us in all respects. To scoop up all our broken shards, fucking splintered because of the Council themselves. *And we never fucking developed a game plan to deal with this.*

And more than anything, I know deep in my core that it doesn't matter how many times the darkness is chipped away. I want to believe Eira about her shining brightly for the both of us. She's successfully brought souls from two different worlds together and has started both of our healing journeys. Even after exposing some of her deepest, most painful memories to the healers, she's finding the light within. Eira might not have been ready to face the demonic creations in the forest tonight, but she naturally shields herself in fire and is prepared to face her friend who obviously betrayed her.

Arguably, this is even scarier. Eira is fearless and able to approach a terrifying version of who was once her friend. It's a courage not many have, to dance with personal trauma willingly. She's growing and finding herself in such a short time. It's *incredible*.

So, I want to believe what Eira tells me. I do. But let's be fucking honest. Once more trauma wraps its gritty claws around my neck, it won't be long until it chokes the last breath from me.

That's the most fucked up part of this moment. Right here

THE LIGHT WITHIN

in this dungeon, most of my soul is ready to protect Eira at any cost. A piece of it can switch into warrior mode in less than a blink, assessing the room and state of our friends. Another part is calculating possible scenarios and rationales for this mess we're in. But there's *still* a piece of me that connects directly with Tryg. I loathe that part of myself. That I get it—I know why he caved so quickly to the pain. Why he can turn on someone he loves. I know how once the dark pieces of you unknowingly slip out from your control, it can be too heavy of a grief to gather them back up, to clean up a tragic mess that is really your own fault.

It's who I've been and quite possibly who I'll always be, even with Eira's light wrapping itself around me. I'll always be followed by a shadow of self-loathing that will be at the core of my fatal disease.

Proof of this is that I let Eira make her way toward Tryg. I didn't keep my hands clutched tightly in hers or warn her not to touch a *solliqa* that's clearly embraced and welcomed in their demonic self. Seconds tick by before I come to my fucking senses, and I leap forward, ripping her away from Tryg and his cell.

She's covered in blue flames as we clatter to the floor. My entire soul, now full of hate and guilt for letting her go, hopes I get burned in the process of tearing her away. *I deserve it*.

Eira doesn't know or acknowledge any of my internal berating. Her flames still ripple around her as she curls into my chest. White hair drapes around my shoulders, and I nearly crush her with my arms when she starts sobbing. I can tell she doesn't want to with each clench of her fist, each second she forces her breath to calm.

Hiccuping, Eira whispers, "I don't know what to do, Nyx."

I roll us over on the dirty floor, risking mud caking onto her skin if it shields her from the others' devastation and prying eyes. We can focus on them soon, but not yet.

Stroking her head, I mumble, "There's nothing you need to do right now, firefly. Just breathe."

I wish there was more I could tell her right now, another way to smooth her frayed nerves and the sheer anxiety rippling around her. I don't have answers for her yet. The truth is, I'm fucking *terrified* of why my friends are locked up down here. There's no way they betrayed us or were a part of this trap, at least not willingly. I already know it'll be framed as if we're the fucking bad guys, so of course we're the ones who created this disaster, this tragedy of monsters stealing *solliqas*.

But I can't let any of us fall for that. I don't know if I'm worth Eira's healing love, but I have to hold on, convince my friends—the souls who've become my family—to believe in the light and that they can also be fixed. That even if there's a reason to keep them strapped down with the capital's most powerful chains, they didn't do any of this by choice.

Or if they did, then I have to hear them out. Because *no one* ever did that with me.

Eira curls further into me. "I'm just so confused," she mumbles. "What's happened? What *were* those things? Why are only some of us down here? Where is Eliina?" Eira lets out a harsh breath. "And what Tryg showed me? I can't be sure if it's connected to what happened here tonight. But our friends from home are in trouble."

There she goes again. Forming one strong alliance after the other. I don't even know the poor beings still stuck on Earth, and they're now *our* friends. I hope she'll extend that same treatment to my companions when she realizes they might have been involved with what happened tonight.

"Who's the *fim* with the hair of fire?" I whisper against her hair.

"I recognize her as one of my clients," Eira murmurs. "But it doesn't make any sense. Not unless she's part of what Tryg just showed me. I don't know right now."

We lay in silence. Athena's frantic whispers to Hadwin the scarce sounds puncturing the pressured air. I focus on keeping Eira's body as close to mine as possible, willing whatever light she's found in me to transfer into her shivering form. Using bursts of energy can drain any *solliqa* quickly, even one as strong as Eira. I can tell Tryg used his newly found dark *maji* to suck the light right out of her.

Fucker. Maybe I can be saved. I know I wouldn't do that to her.

Or is it more subtle because of our almaove connection?

Snapping me out of my thoughts, Eira clears her throat and sniffles. Feeling her tremble is a stab to my dark heart, but I'm comforted that her blue flames haven't gone down yet. If anything, they're growing larger around us.

"Firefly?"

Eira slowly turns her head to face me, and I forget to breathe. Her eyes are now fully gold, with silver streaks flashing through them. Violently. A haze of dark red seeps around the irises, so similar to Isa when she's deep in her powers and protecting others. Her flames glow brighter until the edges swish aggressively, turning into violet and turquoise crystals.

She wasn't shivering from exhaustion. No. She was shaking with *rage*.

I never knew a creature could be so fucking lethal yet healing at once.

Eira, even lying on the filthy dungeon floor, is the very image of the Queen of Light. Baring her teeth, she growls, "I don't know what's going on here, but we aren't going to lie here and expect others to find out for us. *No one* harms my friends. Not those of light, of dark, of any color in between."

I swallow. "Tell me what you want to do, my queen."

Not breaking eye contact, Eira says almost darkly, "For a moment, we forgot who we are. Pain and agony will do that to a soul. But I'm a healer, and you're a powerful prince. It's time we start acting like it. Beginning with getting our friends out of here."

Tryg cackles, the sound high enough to grate against my ears, and in the blink of an eye, he's gasping around on the dirty floor. One of Eira's crystalized flames jabs into his throat and would have sliced right through him if we weren't in the realm of souls.

"I'm the Queen of Light," Eira murmurs after pushing herself off the ground. "Let's find out what that means."

She shoots me a scorching look and holds out a hand. "Together?"

All the pieces of myself lock together this time. *Our light. Our light will be stronger together.*

Without hesitating or flinching away from her gaze, I curl my fingers around hers and rise to stand next to her. Fragments of her light skitter along my fingertips, up my arm, and around my torso, sheathing my body in a healing armor. The flames encase both of us, blocking my view of our disoriented friends, and lick at my ankles like a simmering pool of fire. They entangle with my smoky shadows—a blistering heat that feels akin to the warmth of home.

Because it is home. *She* is my home. We've faced challenges and adventures and death in plenty of lifetimes together. This is just the next step in our soul journey.

"Together."

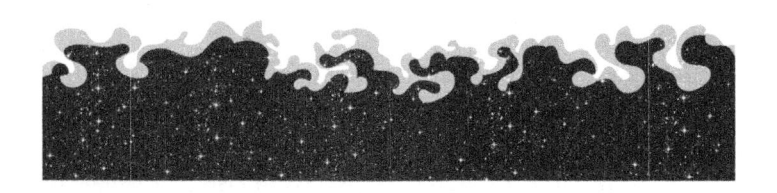

Note from the Author

Dear Reader,

Thank you for taking a chance with my book. This story, along with the rest of the series, is incredibly, deeply personal. Pieces of it were magical for me, while other parts of the story were cathartic. All of my characters represent a different part of my life journey. It was a messy, joyous, unpredictable ride as I threw myself into the world of writing.

I never thought I'd get to call myself a published author. Never in a million years did I think this was a possibility. I was so set on the idea of my "one track". You know, the concept that's hammered into our minds from a young age: Get into college, secure a job, stay there for your entire life and you better be really fucking happy about it. Did I do this? Yeah, a bit. I have no qualms about going to college, except I'm sticking a certain finger up at all those student loans. I discovered so much about myself during my late teens and early twenties. I adore the time I've spent with students, both in the States and in Spain, and I have zero regrets about becoming a licensed clinical social worker. School social workers are absolutely inspiring individuals. Yeah, I said it! All of the school social workers, counselors, teachers, paraprofessionals, and other specialists I've met are hands down, the best.

But I broke out of the mold created for me. I'm still a licensed therapist and likely will forever be one. Walking with people through their trauma and mental health issues is a life-long passion that fuels my soul. This story called to me, though, and ripped me right out of my "reality". I'm so grateful that it did because while I could never imagine calling myself a published author, that's exactly what I am and needed to be.

For whoever is reading this note: Take that chance on yourself. Your ideas are invaluable. Yes, you can write that story. No, it doesn't matter what else you're doing with your life. Creativity cannot be taken away from you. If you're not sure where to start, reach out to me. If you do know where to start but want some encouragement, talk to me. If you just want to feel not so alone in your journey, contact me. I'm here and understand how challenging it is to break out of the life standards dictated to you, how hard it can be to take control of your own life. I know how much it fucking hurts to leave pieces of yourself behind in pursuit of a higher level of your being, especially when your own mental health issues and trauma want to get in the way.

You're not alone.

Love,
Carliann

Acknowledgments

I'm full of so much gratitude for everyone who has come on this journey with me. My heart could truly burst with appreciation and joy. *The Light Within* is my first book—an experience I could never have done without many people in my life! While there are not enough pages to thank every single person, I do want to acknowledge the ones who've played a significant role in *The Light Within* being published.

To my husband, Daniel. You've been my rock this whole time and encouraged me every step of the way. From making me my favorite shaken espresso drink to researching *everything* related to publishing a book to asking editors and agents questions at a reading convention; you're seriously the best partner a girl could ask for. Thank you for being endlessly amazing and never giving up on me, even when the dreaded anxiety and hormonal changes took over. And your proofreading comments were a little too hilarious, haha. You're quite lit, you're quite chill.

To the lovely Rachel. You were the first person to read my book and have become my ultimate hype girl. Your energy has been *everything*. Your sass, your positive feedback, your reactions mid-story. You sharing literally anything related to my story on social media and educating me on the importance of including links with my stories, haha! You being the first person to join my newsletter. I'm beyond grateful to have met you because while you're an amazing alpha reader, you're an even more incredible person and friend.

To my first beta readers, Lyra and Jacqueline. Your feedback gave me insight on what was working and where I could improve before sending my story off for edits. Thank you so much for putting in the time it takes to both build an author up and provide constructive feedback. And Lyra, your comments made me cry happy tears! Thank you for highlighting your favorite quotes and telling me which parts sounded beautiful.

To my editor, Maddi. I remember how terrified I was to send my story to you, but all you've done is provide phenomenal feedback and comments. You didn't just read my book—you saw its potential and handled the edits with love and care. Your developmental edits took my story to an entirely different level. Thank you for *everything* you've done to support me, even though I've got "clogs" in my brain, haha!

To my pets, Berlin, Valencia, Pierogi, and Tatra. You'll never even remotely read or understand this book. That's totally fine. Just being an unhinged orange cat, an endearing black cat, an energetic pup, and a loveable and playful puppy is everything I needed while writing my book. Rest in Peace, darling Pierogi.

To my friends. The ones who encouraged me and matched my excitement levels, if not more so. You know who you are, you beautiful souls! And a special shout-out to Shelby and Sarah. Shelbster, thank you for teaching me the ways of Instagram and truly understanding my love for reading—all the way back to when we met Jodi Picoult! And you're a rockstar for proofreading my book baby. Sarah, you were one of the first people I told about my book. Thank you for your immediate love!

To Nicole. Thank you for seeing the part of me who needed

to write as a creative outlet and then encouraged me when I turned that into an actual story.

To my parents. Thank you for always encouraging me to be creative and to never limit myself. I didn't know that would lead to writing a book, but here I am! You didn't even know I was writing one or what this story was about, and you still immediately asked when you could read it before it came out. I'll never forget the endless amounts of books you bought me and trips to Barnes and Noble. Thank you for planting the idea that books bring infinite joy.

To the indie authors who've helped me along the way. I've been inspired by a number of authors, such as Emily McIntire, Rebecca Yarros, Sarah J. Maas, Philip Pullman, and Leigh Bardugo. But the following indie authors have offered continuous encouragement, love, recommendations, and *so much* more: CJ Primer, Sophie Dyer, Brea Lamb, and Leslie Ballew.

To the artists who have helped my characters come to life. You're all incredibly wonderful and insanely talented. Thank you Emily (Altass Art), Melania (Miss.Pink.Coconut), and Lyssa (Booked Forever Shop). I absolutely cannot wait to continue working with you!

To Jess from Truly Yours PR and anyone who has shared my book on social media. Thank you from the bottom of my heart for believing in my story and helping me to share it with the world.

Special Kickstarter Acknowledgments

There are no words for how incredibly grateful I am to each person who pledged to my Kickstarter campaign. You've supported a new author and helped her achieve her dream. While I'm thankful for each individual who pledged, no matter the amount, there are certain people who pledged to be on a *Special Kickstarter Acknowledgements* page—and for more rewards! Each of you beautiful souls will be listed here for your generosity.

- Ada Vane
- Aleksander Poniatowski
- Amy Taege
- Anna Poulson
- Aunt Nadine & Uncle Dan
- B. MillerBen Prater
- Ben Prater
- Bob & Juana Henderson
- Caja
- Carol Trabold
- Chantelle Raines

- Christina & Gracie Badeaux
- CJ
- Craig Sisson
- Danielle Cass
- Danny & Kit
- Darma Day
- David Pentz
- Dorina Carrillo
- Dr. Niloc
- E. Star
- Emily G.
- Erin V.
- Eugene and Brenda Pentz
- Eva Sabadosa
- Holly Morgan
- Ian & Lynanne Iyengar
- Ian & Tish
- Isaac Samanamud
- Jade May
- Jean Elliston Pentz
- Jenn Acidera
- Jessica
- Jessica Hoyal
- Joella Rosendahl
- Joseph K. Adou
- Josh
- Karen Bulgarelli
- Karen Taboada Buur & Kasper Byberg Buur
- Karli Kehres
- Katherine C
- Katie Angelillo
- K.M. Davidson
- Lisa
- Lorinda Boyer

- Madison
- Mandi Kane
- Megan Rowen
- Michael H.
- Michaelangelo Monty Monterroso
- Morgan G.
- Nicholle Veneklase
- Nikki
- Peter Jansen
- Rene Shirly
- Robyn Mercurio
- Rosa Thill
- Rosangel Leono
- Sabine A McDaniel
- Sam Silveira
- Sandy Smith
- Sarah Fortuin
- Sarah Schroeder
- Shelby & Jose Barboza
- Steve Yasukawa
- Sylwia Dakowicz
- The Ultimate Mother Clucker and CandyLand Queen, Karen Gonzalez
- Yaser Soto
- Zorah Starr

Thank you, again! I'm sending each of you light and love.

PART ONE
A Guide to the Regions on Future Earth & Majikaero

Regions on Future Earth

Previous Earth was a planet once thought to be doomed after nuclear war nearly erupted and destroyed many innocents. While total carnage was avoided, the impact of poverty, trauma, and threats of war wreaked havoc across each country. Violence still bloomed like wild poppies the color of fresh blood. Much of humanity fell to the reprieve drugs and alcohol offered, hugging them in a tight embrace until they were left choking the life out of themselves.

The world fell, no longer flourishing with abundant nature or thriving cultures. Not in the frigid north, nor in the heated south, nor in the beckoning warmth and chilled winds found in between. Citizens were left with a lukewarm version of what was once a land of hope. All of them left to reform what little remained, to construct new country lines, to merge languages and beliefs and colors of people who previously clashed like silver swords in the moonlight.

Another world war is imminent. Grievously unstoppable, and trauma has the world in its clutches once again.

New Africa Territories

Conea Nigoon (Coh-nee-ah Nih-goon)
Previously Nigeria, Cameroon, Equatorial Guinea, Northern part of Republic of the Congo

Guinegalia (Guh-ing-eh-gah-lee-ah)
Previously Senegal, The Gambia, Guinea, Sierra Leone, Liberia

Niya Tunypt (Neye-yah Toon-yi-p-t)
Previously Egypt, Chad, Niger, Libya, Algeria, Tunisia

Sahliocco (Sah-lee-oh-coh)
Previously Morocco, Western Sahara, Algeria, Mauritania, Mali

Sumalpia (Suh-mahl-pee-ah)
Previously Somalia, Ethiopia, Sudan

Tonihana (Toh-nee-hah-nah)
Previously Cote d'ivoire, Ghana, Burkina Faso, Togo, Benin

Ugenya Danican (You-gen-yah Dah-nih-cahn)
Previously Northern part of DRC, Central African Republic, Uganda, Kenya, South Sudan

Zambiana (Zahm-bee-ah-nah)
Previously African countries south of the equator but were obliterated after a nuclear attack

New Antarctica Territories

Antica (Ant-tih-cah)
Large parts managed to survive with little to no habitants.

New Asia Territories

Innmartana (Een-mahr-tah-nah)
Previously countries of Asia east of Pakistan but were obliterated after a nuclear attack

Irtukistan (Irr-tuh-kee-stahn)
Previously Iran, Turkmenistan, Afghanistan, Pakistan

Kopania (Koh-pah-nee-ah)
Previously South Korea, North Korea, Japan, Coast of China, Coast of Russia

Kyazssia (Kee-ah-zee-see-ah)
Previously parts of Russia, Kazakhstan, Uzbekistan, Kyrgyzstan

Yemania Arabia (Yeh-mah-nee-ah Ah-ray-bee-ah)
Previously Saudi Arabia, Yemen, Oman, the United Arab Emirates

New Europe Territories

Belaity (Beh-lah-ih-tee)
Previously France, Belgium, Spain, Italy, Netherlands

Griclin Edinales (Grih-sih-lihn Ed-ih-nah-lays)
Previously Iceland, Greenland, the UK

Hungatia (Huhn-gah-shee-ah)
Previously Croatia, Slovenia, Austria, Slovakia, Hungary, Czech Republic

Kosnia (Kohs-nee-ah)
Previously Bosnia, Serbia, Montenegro, Kosovo, Albania, Macedonia, Bulgaria

Sweazn (Sway-zhn)
Previously Norway, Sweden, Finland, Denmark, Germany, Switzerland

Syreean (See-ree-ahn)
Previously Greece, Turkey, Syria, Lebanon, Israel, Jordan, Iraq but did not survive war attacks

Ukuanova (You-kuu-ah-noh-vah)
Previously Estonia, Lithuania, Belarus, Ukraine, Moldova but did not survive war attacks

New North America Territories

Dakourin (Dah-koh-uu-rihn)
Midwestern United States that survived war attacks

Guaoaera (Gu-wah-oh-air-ah)
Previously parts of Mexico

Idada Calana (Eye-dah-dah Cah-lay-nah)
Western United States that survived war attacks

New Virlina Yorkshine (Nu Virr-lee-nah Yorh-kah-sh-ine)
Previously North and South Eastern United States but was obliterated after a nuclear attack

Riuba Haican (Reye-oo-bee-ah Heye-ih-cahn)
Previously Cuba, Puerto Rico, and other islands but was obliterated after a nuclear attack

Torinarry (Tohr-ih-nair-ee)
Previously southern parts of Canada and Alaska

Zonicoma (Zohn-ih-coh-mah)
Southern United States and parts of Mexico that survived war attacks

New Oceania Territories

New Taszealia (Nu Tah-zee-ah-lee-ah)
Previously New Zealand, Tasmania, parts of Australia

Phindonea (Fihn-doh-nee-ah)
Previously islands surrounding Australia but were obliterated after a nuclear attack

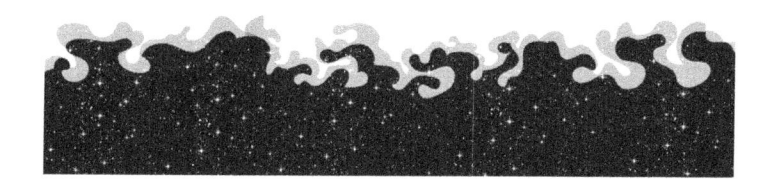

New South America Territories

Bochentuay (Boh-chehn-too-ai)
Previously parts of Argentina, Chile, Uruguay, Paraguay, Bolivia

Guizeuras (Guh-eez-eh-oo-rahs)
Previously Guatemala, Belize, Honduras, El Salvador

Guzuelail (Guhz-uu-ay-lah-eel)
Previously the eastern half of South America but was obliterated after a nuclear attack

Panicaga (Pah-nee-cah-gah)
Previously the southern countries of Central America but was obliterated after a nuclear attack

Zilbia Perador (Zihl-bee-ah Perr-ah-dohr)
Previously Peru, Ecuador, south parts of Colombia, western parts of Brazil

All other countries and locations did not survive.

Regions on Majikaero (Mah-jee-kair-oh)

Drageyra (Drah-gair-ah)
Land of Fire
Bold, Ambitious, Competitive, Direct

Eikenbien (Eye-kehn-bine)
Land of Woods
Relaxed, Calm, Dependable, Receptive

Lagunit (Lah-goon-iht)
Land of Many Waters
Intuitive, Sensitive, Empathetic, Dreamer

Myrellden (Meye-rehl-dehn)
Land of Darkness
Innovative, Progressive, Revolutionary, Builder of Worlds

Reykashin (Ray-kah-shihn)
Land of Smoke
Elusive, Mysterious, Powerful, Ruthless

Rioa (Ree-oh-ah)
Land of Natural Cities, The Capital
Balance, Harmony, Justice, Variability

Sayfters (Saif-tairs)
Land of Clay and Buildings
Patient, Dedicated, Persevering, Motivated by Duty

Shymeira (Sheye-mair-ah)
Land of Tropics
Spontaneous, Erratic, Playful, Comical

Skugvaytir (Skoog-vai-teer)
Land of the Shadows
Logical, Practical, Systematic, Attention to Detail

Sunnadyn (Suhn-ah-dihn)
Land of Sunlight
Passionate, Loyal, Fiery, Loving

Viorfelle (Vee-ohr-fell)
Land of Mountains
Intellectual, Adventurous, Curious, Grounded

Wyndera (Wihn-dair-ah)
Land of Wind
Highly Intuitive, Layered Personality, Moody, Perceptive

PART TWO
Gods & Goddesses

Gods and Goddesses Worshipped

*The following include the most
prominent names found in the
Head Council Library located in Rioa*

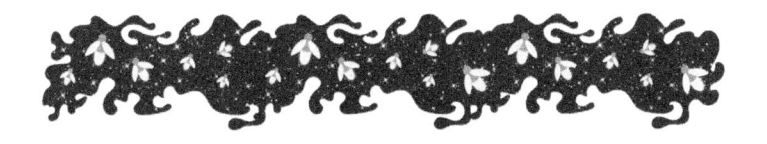

Of Water
Deniz (Deh-neez) and Derya (Dair-yah)

Of Fire
Edan (Eh-dahn) and Valencia (Vah-lehn-cee-ah)

Of Earth
Abarrane (Ah-bar-aine) and Neta (Neh-tah)

Of Air
Aapeli (Ah-peh-lee) and Duncas (Duhn-cahs)

Of Spirit
Cajsa (Cah-shah) and Faramond (Fahr-ah-mohnd)

Of Shapeshifting
Nixie (Nih-ksee) and Perogus (Pair-oh-guhs)

Of Manipulation
Nitika (Niht-ee-kah) and Wrathiala (Ra-thee-ah-lah)

Of Solar
Lahahana (Lah-hah-hah-nah) and Dilay (Dee-lay)

Of Healing
Eliina (Ehl-eye-nah) and Berlind (Berh-lihnd)

Of War
Cairo (Cai-roh) and Dabria (Dah-bree-ah)

Of Intellect
Ove (Oh-vay) and Oaxa (Wah-ha)

Of the Soul
Namid (Nah-meed) and Nicola (Nih-coh-lah)

PART THREE
Character Names & Pronunciations

Main Character Names & Pronunciation Guide

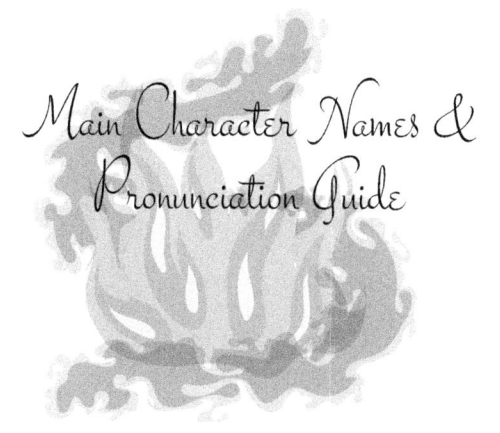

Future Earth

Astira (Ah-stir-ah)

Athena (Ah-thee-nah)

Eira (Air-ah)

Jace (Jays)

Liv (Lihv)

Lyk (Leek)

Morgan (Mohr-gahn)

Ruse (Roose)

Shira (Sheer-ah)

Tryg (Trihg)

Zaya (Zeye-ah)

Main Character Names & Pronunciation Guide

Majikaero

Ambra (Ahm-brah)

Daglo (Dah-gloh)

Daru (Dah-roo)

Daya (Dye-ah)

Delano (Deh-lah-noh)

Eliina (Ehl-eye-nah)

Erika (Air-ih-kah)

Fraya (Fray-ah)

Hadwin (Had-whin)

Hauke (Hawk)

Isa (Ee-sah)

Ivar (Eye-vahr)

Naeva (Nay-vah)

Namid (Nah-meed)

Nyx (Nihks)

Odin (Oh-dihn)

Paloma (Pah-loh-mah)

Rada (Rah-dah)

Stefanie (Steh-fah-nee)

Ulf (oolf)

PART FOUR

Common Majikaero Terms

Common Majikaero Terms & Pronunciation Guide

Alklen (Ahlk-lehn)
Akin to a deer made of shadows, smoke, and other elements of nature

Almaove (Ahl-mohve)
The deepest soul connection and love a solliqa can have

Canielor (Cahn-ee-eh-lor)
After a solliqa has caught the plague of darkness, this is the creature they can turn into before they evolve into a monster specific to their pain and trauma

Dayre (Dai-air)
A small mammal with velvet antlers, hooves, and a long multicolored tail

Drekstri (Drehk-stree)
A dangerous and loyal creature with characteristics of a horse and a dragon

Einral (Eyen-rahl)
A liquid that awakens the mind and body

Fim (Fihm)
Energy that's described as more feminine
A term used to describe souls with feminine energy

Lipva (Leep-vah)
Hydrating water

Maji (Mah-jee)
Magic powers connected to the elements, creatures, and souls

Misn (Mih-sin)
Energy that's described as more masculine
A term used to describe souls with masculine energy

Sairn (Sair-ihn)
A group of solliqas that believe in gods from another world and believe Eira's powers to be bad for Majikaero

Solliqa (Sol-ih-kah)
A soul that exists in Majikaero

Veina (Vai-nah)
A liquid that is similar to a mixture of wine and dark, sweet liquor

About the Author

Carliann Jean has always loved reading, writing, and throwing herself into anything creative. Her path took a turn into the fields of education and social work, where she thrived in the classroom and as a school social worker. She has a passion for helping those impacted by trauma and mental health issues, and in general, she loves to build deep, healing connections. While Carliann adores her current work as a licensed clinical social worker in private practice, she wants to fuse her mental health specialization with one of her favorite things: fiction stories.

She currently writes fantasy romance that focuses on mental

health, trauma, and darker themes. Her goal is multi-purpose. Carliann wants to continue aiding those who have experienced trauma and mental health issues through the art of storytelling. She also wants to bring readers the joy, laughter, tears, and many other feelings experienced from immersing yourself in a character's life.

When Carliann is not writing, she thoroughly enjoys spending time with her husband and pet children, reading more books than she has room for, spending time outdoors, traveling and exploring, stress baking with music, and laughing with her loved ones. She's an Illinois native who felt drawn to the West. If you can't find her cuddled up with her feisty two cats and excitable pup, you'll see her hiking in the mountains or at one of the local shops with a new treat and shaken espresso.

Let's Connect!

I'm all about building connections!
Follow me on Instagram to stay up to date about my books, upcoming events, art and merch, and more. Send me an email or DM if you're interested in working together or have any questions at all.

My website: www.authorcarliannjean.com

- instagram.com/carliannjean
- amazon.com/author/carliannjean
- threads.net/carliannjean
- goodreads.com/carliann_jean

Printed in Great Britain
by Amazon